TEN CROWS
FOR
A TIME OF
JOYOUS BLISS

VERNON OICKLE

Cover design: Rebekah Wetmore
Editor: Andrew Wetmore

ISBN: 978-1-997827-07-8
First edition December, 2025

Moose House Publications
2475 Perotte Road
Annapolis County, NS B0S 1A0
moosehousepress.com
info@moosehousepress.com

Moose House Publications recognizes the support of the Province of Nova Scotia. We are pleased to work in partnership with the Department of Communities, Culture and Heritage to develop and promote our cultural resources for all Nova Scotians.

We live and work in Mi'kma'ki, the ancestral and unceded territory of the Mi'kmaw people. This territory is covered by the "Treaties of Peace and Friendship" which Mi'kmaw and Wolastoqiyik (Maliseet) people first signed with the British Crown in 1725. The treaties did not deal with surrender of lands and resources but in fact recognized Mi'kmaq and Wolastoqiyik (Maliseet) title and established the rules for what was to be an ongoing relationship between nations. We are all Treaty people.

Also by Vernon Oickle

One Crow Sorrow
Two Crows Joy
Three Crows a Letter
Four Crows a Boy
*Five Crows Silver**
*Six Crows Gold**
*Seven Crows a Secret Yet To Be Told**
*Eight Crows for a Wish**
*Nine Crows for a Kiss**
*The View from Here**

Life and Death after Billy
Friends & Neighbours: a collection of stories from the Liverpool Advance
Busted: Nova Scotia's War on Drugs Queens County
Ghost Stories of the Maritimes (volumes 1 and 2)
Dancing with the Dead
Great Canadian Ghost Stories Volume II (co-author)
Disasters of Atlantic Canada: stories of courage and chaos
Canada's Haunted Coast: true ghost stories of the Maritimes
The Editor's Diary: the first 13 years
Angels Here Among Us
Red Sky at Night
South Shore Facts and Folklore
I'm Movin' On: the life and legacy of Hank Snow
Beaches of Lunenburg-Queens

Nova Scotia Outstanding Outhouse Reader
Red Coat Brigade
Ghost Stories of Nova Scotia
Kiss the Cod!
Strange Nova Scotia
Newfoundland and Labrador Outrageous Outhouse Reader
Where Evil Dwells
How to talk Nova Scotian: the Bluenoser's book of slang
The Nova Scotia Book of Lists
My Nova Scotia Home
We Love Nova Scotia: a people's portrait
More Ghost Stories of Nova Scotia
Queens County: a history in pictures
The Second Movement: Nova Scotia's outrageous outhouse reader No. 2
So you think you KNOW Nova Scotia?
Forerunners: Harbingers of Death in Nova Scotia
Through Rain, Sleet or Snow: rural mailboxes of Nova Scotia
Grandma's Home Remedies
Even More Ghose Stories of Nova Scotia
Nova Scotia's BEST Word Search Book, Vol. 1

* available from Moose House Publications
moosehousepress.com

One crow sorrow, two crows joy;
three crows a letter, four crows a boy;
five crows silver, six crows gold;
seven crows a secret yet to be told;
eight crows for a wish;
nine crows for a kiss;
ten crows for a time of joyous bliss.
eleven crows for good health;
twelve crows for improved wealth;
thirteen crows beware for it's the devil himself.

- One version of a common
Nova Scotian folk rhyme

This one is dedicated to Stephen King.
He doesn't know me from Adam, as they say, but this man has inspired
my writing in so many ways.
He is the master of suspense and the macabre.

This is a work of fiction. The author has created the characters, conversations, interactions, and events; and any resemblance of any character to any real person is coincidental.

Ten Crows for a Time of Joyous Bliss

Vernon Oickle

Prologue

It has been ten uneventful years since the New Year's Eve when a mysterious woman terrorized the residents of Liverpool, this seaside town nestled on the banks of the Mersey River, but the crows have remained ever vigilant at their posts, as they have been compelled to do for centuries.

Watching.

Waiting.

Ready to spring into action whenever they must.

They know what the humans don't.

Their hoarse, guttural voices fill the air: grating, cawing, rattling. The ten black sentinels are on edge, feathers ruffled, eyes small but all-seeing.

There is evil afoot. It hangs heavy in the air, clinging to the breeze.

They sense it. They recognize the signs.

Something sinister is coming and it will shake the very foundations of this community. They know this all too well.

The residents have led a calm and peaceful existence since that ill-fated party. Their joyful, blissful lives have continued. Births, deaths, marriages, proud parents at graduations, promotions, gentle summers, and the usual chill of bitter winter storms. But it's been normal day-to-day stuff. No murders. No violence. No crazies on the loose.

Ten crows suddenly sit straighter on their branches, moving their heads slowly. They make a clicking sound, as a human might make by tapping their tongue against the roof of their mouth.

They sound the alarm, warning the others.

Danger. Danger. Danger.

The metallic smell of human blood and steaming-hot organs fills the air, a forerunner of things to come. They shake their wings as a human might shudder. The small feathers on the backs of their necks stick straight up.

Danger. Danger. Danger.

How to apprise the chosen one? He has grown complacent over these past ten years. They've watched over him and rebuffed a few minor challenges without his even knowing of the danger, but this new threat is too big for them. It's the first time in ten years the crows have truly known fear.

They will need his help. He must answer their call, for they are bound to him and he to them, like a ship and its anchor on a tumultuous sea.

He cannot refuse them.

1: The darkness approaches

Friday, April 5

The dark clouds gather, rolling, collecting ominously in the sky, heavy with rain.

"Looks like we're about to get a storm," observes Jimmy Spicer. He releases the engine throttle and watches the birch tree crash to the ground. It hits the dry, baked dirt with a loud crash, sending dust and leaves flying in all directions. "I'd say the rain isn't far off."

The chainsaw goes quiet.

"Hope it holds off until we finish this area at least," he says. "I was hoping we wouldn't have to come back here next week, but if it rains this afternoon, we'll have to call it a day and finish this area on Monday."

He, along with two other foresters, has been working diligently since early this morning, cutting alders, and clearing underbrush on a job site that borders on the Echo Lake Road. They are part of a larger crew working to clear the sprawling woodlot on the outskirts of town to make way for a housing development that's scheduled to start construction later this year. The rocky and rugged terrain has been challenging and slowed their progress, but with this being Friday, the three-man crew wants to finish here so they can start in a new location next week.

"Yuppers," replies Bobby Brighton, another of the crew members. Glancing upwards, he adds, "It's not looking too good right now. Those God-damned clouds are pretty dark. Looks like we could have some thunder, too."

"For fuck's sake," Jimmy curses while scoping out the next tree that will fall to his chainsaw. "I hope not. It hasn't rained for two weeks, and now here it comes just when we don't want it. With any luck, maybe it will hold off for a couple more hours until we finish."

Throwing an armload of branches onto a pile of brush that towers over his six-foot, two-inch frame, Bobby chuckles. "Can't you put in a good word with the big guy and pull out a favour for us?"

"Yeah right." Jimmy wipes the sweat from his forehead with the back of his left hand. He nods to the sky. "If you're talking about the *big guy* up there, I'm afraid I've used up all my favours with him."

Bobby grins. "I know what you mean. He doesn't owe me any favours either."

He leans against a large birch tree and takes a gulp of ice-cold water from his blue, insulated jug. He offers the water to his friend. "You got any big plans for the weekend?"

"Kind of," Jimmy answers. He shakes his head no to the water. "It's Mallory's birthday on Sunday so we were planning on heading to the casino in Halifax tomorrow. You know. Spend the night, have a nice dinner, a few drinks and blow a wad of cash. I've been promising to take her away for a while now, so I figure I better come through soon, or she might replace me."

"If it was me, I would have thrown your sorry ass out of the house a long time ago, but she'll never let you go. You're a catch, or so I've heard. Don't sweat it. You guys have been together way too long for you to worry about Mallory dumping you for someone else."

Jimmy winks. "She knows how good she's got it with me. I remind her every day."

"Yeah! Right!" Bobby smirks. "I bet you do."

"What about you? Got anything planned for the weekend?"

"Me and a couple of the guys were talking about going fishing up at Brier Lake on Saturday, but if it's going to rain, I don't want any part of that. The bugs are bad enough up there on a good day, but I hate fishing in the rain."

"Think you'll melt, princess? You ain't made of sugar."

"I'm as sweet as they come. Just ask all the girls down at The Crows' Nest."

Jimmy rolls his eyes as he notices the crew foreman Mitchell Clarke approaching. The three men were pretty tight friends until Mitchell got promoted a few months ago, a decision that didn't sit too well with the other two, both of whom had seniority over him.

"Better watch ourselves," he whispers to Bobby. "The Big Boss Man is coming."

Bobby exhales. "Better get back to it before that prick blows a fucking fuse."

"Come on, you slack-asses," Mitchell says, joining his co-workers near the pile of bushes they will burn, later when the rain does eventually come.

"I need less talk and more work. If we want to get this area cleared today, then we've got to get a move on."

Jimmy fires back. "We're going as fast as we can in this god-damned heat. We didn't even take a lunch break, so there's no need to ride our asses. We know what we gotta do."

"All's I'm saying, Jim, is that we won't get done if you guys stand around and talk all afternoon."

Mitchell grabs a second chainsaw and primes the motor. "My motto has always been that when there's work to do, the best way to get it done is just to go right after it."

"Yeah, well, I don't give a flying fuck about any of your god-damned mottoes. We're working as hard as we can."

"He ain't wrong, Mitch," Bobby adds. "We've been going at it pretty hard since daylight this morning and it's killing us, especially in this heat. We've got to stop for a breather every now and then."

"So, you've had a breather," Mitchell snaps. "Now back at it."

"Jesus Christ," Jimmy says, pressing the throttle on his chainsaw and revving the sixty-five cubic centimetre motor. "Whatever you say boss. If you want us to work, we'll work."

He suddenly swings the chainsaw directly at his foreman.

"What the fuck?" Mitchell quickly jumps back. "Jesus Christ, Jimmy. Watch it. You almost cut me."

"Sorry," Jimmy says. "That I missed." He swings the chainsaw at the foreman a second time. Mitch barely has time to duck out of the way.

"For fuck's sake, Jimmy," he screams. "What the hell are you doing?"

"I've had it, Mitch. I'm sick and fucking tired of you bossing us around, thinking you're King Shit or something. You ain't no better than us."

Jimmy glares at the other man, his complexion suddenly turning blood red. His eyes become narrow slivers and froth foams at the corners of his mouth. He raises the chainsaw to attack mode and says, "I ain't taking it anymore."

Bobby tries to intervene. "What are you doing, Jim? Put the saw down before you hurt someone. You're hot and you're tired and we don't need this asshole pushing us around. I get that, so just tell Mitch to go fuck himself and let's take a break."

Revving the small engine as he quickly spins around, Jimmy, thrusts the spinning blade deep into his friend's belly, pulls it out and, without blinking an eye, drives it back into the soft flesh.

"I need more than a fucking break," he barks.

Bobby grabs his stomach, his mouth open in a silent scream. He crumples to the ground, the soil under his body quickly turning red.

Mitchell quickly turns and sprints towards the company truck that's parked about two metres down the dirt road.

"Jesus Christ, Jimmy. Why are you doing this?" he screams.

"'Cause I didn't need you riding my ass, that's why." Jimmy revs the chainsaw. "I've had enough of your fucking bullshit."

"I don't know what you're talking about. I'm just doing my job."

"If your job included making us feel like shit, then you're really good at it."

Mitchell reaches the truck and grabs the driver's side door handle. He finds it's locked. "Shit."

"Going somewhere, Mitch?" Jimmy asks, approaching the man he once bailed out of jail in Halifax following a night of drinking and disorderly conduct. "I hope you don't think you're going to use the truck."

He reaches into the front right pocket of his jeans and pulls out the keys. He dangles them in front of his friend's face.

"Come on, Jimmy," Mitchell pleads. "Can't you see that Bobby needs help? He needs a doctor or else he's going to bleed to death."

"Sorry, boss man." Jimmy raises the chainsaw. "But we ain't goin' nowhere."

"Don't do this, Jimmy," Mitchell begs. Backing up against the truck, he raises his hands in a defensive posture. "We can still get Bobby the help he needs."

"Bobby's already dead."

Jimmy swings the chainsaw at his foreman's shoulders. The sharp blade easily saws through the fingers on the man's hands. Burying the screaming blade tightly into the man's neck, he growls, "And so are you."

The blade makes a hideous "sloshing" sound as it slices through the supple flesh. Blood spurts profusely from severed arteries.

Extracting the blade from the man's neck, Jimmy raises the chainsaw high and, without hesitation, swings it down onto Mitchell's head. He watches as the foreman—his onetime friend and boss—spasms several times before his body becomes still.

Stepping over Mitchell's lifeless form, Jimmy throws the chainsaw to the ground. It splashes into a pool of his friend's blood.

Quickly unlocking the truck door, he slides into the cab behind the steering wheel and inserts the key in the ignition. He glances down at his wet clothes, soaked red in the blood of the two men he called friends until just a few minutes ago. Turning the key, he slams the truck into drive and speeds out of the clearing, throwing a stream of dust and rocks in his wake.

Eyes focused on the dirt road in front of him, Jimmy steps on the accelerator, coaxing more speed from the Ford F-150. He races down the road that snakes along the rocky shores of Echo Lake until he sees the flashing warning lights from a forestry harvester up ahead, where another work crew is clearing logs.

He guns the engine, aiming the truck directly at the huge piece of equipment that's swinging a massive log onto a nearby flatbed.

Ignoring the crew members who are madly waving their arms and yelling for him to stop, Jimmy slams the Ford into the rear of the harvester, forcing the large log through the windshield of his truck.

Lightning flashes and thunder cracks as the skies open and the rain begins to fall.

Jimmy's death is instant.

2: The Spirit Crow

Finally, Alex thinks, his Brooks Ghost 15 running shoes keeping pace with his fast-moving brain that's on overdrive. But he feels invigorated today, as if a heavy weight has been lifted. *There's some light at the end of this very long tunnel and I can't say I'm sorry.*

It has taken him almost ten years to earn his medical license and it has been a tough slog at times, but he's glad that he stuck it out. By this June, Alex Goodwin will be able to call himself a full-fledged doctor and he feels good about that.

Besides that, it has been ten years since the crows have called upon him for help or had to intervene in his life. The world has been quiet, and, while Alex has great respect for the crows and what they mean to his family, he hopes he can have a normal life, free of the stress, anxiety, threats, and life-altering events related to them that consumed most of his youthful years.

It really has been ten years of joyous bliss and I seriously needed the respite after everything that happened.

He focuses on the trail that follows the banks of the gently flowing Mersey River and winds through the picturesque Pine Grove Park. This is one of his favourite routes for his daily run. He comes here at least four times a week when he's in town, no matter the season. He never lets rain or snow interfere with his routine, and he never finds it too hot or cold for a run.

Maybe I really am a running fanatic, like everyone says.

But he's okay with that. He's in peak physical condition, he's healthy and he feels good mentally, so he can't complain at people giving him a label.

His eyes dart around his surroundings, always on the lookout for anything unusual. Even though the past ten years have been uneventful, he learned a long time ago to never let his guard down.

As he runs, he admires the bushes, shrubs, and trees lining the trail, all of which are just starting to show early spring growth. He soaks up the natural beauty. He likes the quiet and serenity he finds here as it's the perfect place to think and to put his past, present and future into perspective.

As his expensive sneakers thump on the dusty ground, unusually dry for this time of year, Alex recalls the lessons he's learned.

Ten long years of studying, sacrificing, burning the midnight candle, and working around the clock but I'm just about there. Flashing back over the past twenty-eight years of his life, he's amazed that he's even alive today, considering some of the obstacles that were thrown at him.

Controlling his breathing as he's about to enter the most challenging section of the trail, he grins, bursting with pride as he recalls his mother's advice. "Put in the effort and you shall reap the rewards," she told him many times, pounding the piece of philosophy into his head.

And I sure did that. In spades.

"Thanks mom," he whispers.

Before the medical degree and three years in residency, it was four years in university to get his major in biology.

But it was worth the effort—and the money.

He follows the trail that takes several twists and turns and climbs a series of minor hills that don't pose much of a challenge for him. He's more than equipped to complete this course without breaking into a major sweat, even though the day seems unusually warm. The humidity is especially bad this morning.

He took up running upon the advice of his best friend in university. Jace Woodward told him that running would give him focus and was a great way to relieve stress. Once he started, he didn't stop. Even the heavy storm clouds that are gathering in the mid-afternoon sky, threatening to unleash a torrent of rain, don't intimidate him.

I've run in worse weather than a few showers, he thinks, while silently thanking his friend for introducing him to this healthy habit that has become his obsession.

He's looking forward to seeing Jace this weekend. He and his girlfriend, Luna Edwards, are coming to Liverpool this evening to spend the next three days. He hasn't seen much of Jace this past year since they've both been working on their residencies. While he's been here working under the supervision of his uncle, Dr. Charlie Webster, Jace has spent much of his time at a clinic in Cape Breton.

He met Jace during his first year of university, in one of their biology labs, and they had an instant connection. Kindred spirits drawn to each other: both were introverts and shied away from large crowds, but they hit it off right away. They've been close ever since and he regrets that they've not seen each for several months.

It will be good to see him and to run together again. Time to catch up. We need a blowout before we get into our practices and our careers take over, maybe even settle down and start families.

Now, as his future begins to come into focus, Alex feels he's finally in control of his life. He has a job lined up right here in his hometown, working in his uncle's practice. The plan is for him to take over in the next few years, when Dr. Webster retires.

To top it all off, he plans on asking his long-time girlfriend, Bree Hamilton, to marry him. They've been close since they were sixteen and he knows they are destined to spend their lives together. Now that he's about to complete his studies, and she's working at the largest law firm here in town, on track to become a partner within the next ten to twelve years, it feels to him that they're ready to take the next step.

Finally. After putting everything on hold until after we finished our studies, it's all starting to come into focus, he thinks as he rounds a small turn and then stops abruptly.

A loud, bone-chilling cackling cuts through the humid air. He shivers despite the oppressive heat that's blanketed the region for the past two weeks.

Jesus, he gasps, *Christ.*

It has been a while since he's heard it, but he recognizes the noise right away. He quickly scans his immediate surroundings, his eyes darting from one tree branch to the next. Alex knows he's just heard a crow calling and he's certain the bird was reaching out to him. It sounded urgent, like an alarm.

"Where are you? Show yourself."

The park is quiet today, quieter than it should be for a Friday afternoon in early spring. Usually at this time of year, birds are flitting around, gathering nesting material, singing their songs, and looking for food; but today the birds are missing. In fact, all living creatures seem to be still. He hadn't noticed the weird stillness before now.

This can't be good, he thinks as a movement on a nearby pine tree catches his attention. He's never seen anything like this before.

"What the hell?" His breath catches in his throat.

Based upon the bird's size and the shape of its head and beak and position of its eyes, he's certain it's a crow, but it's not like any other crow he's ever seen.

An albino crow. Now what the hell is this all about?

In all his years of dealing with crows he has never seen an albino, and he finds it both beautiful and alarming. He immediately assumes that the presence of such an unusual bird must be a sign, and a powerful one.

"This can't be good," he whispers.

He watches in awe as the white crow spreads its powerful wings, springs from the tree, immediately catches the gently blowing wind currents and takes flight. Soaring upward, the mysterious bird quickly disappears.

"It isn't."

The deep voice gives Alex a start. He thought he was alone on the trail. He spins around on his heel and comes face to face with a scrawny old man, no more than five feet tall.

"Who are you?" he blurts out. "And where the hell did you come from? I didn't hear you behind me."

With his dirty clothes, unkempt hair, and unshaven face, the old man looks like a hermit, something straight out of one of those news stories he's seen on TV recently about the homeless, a plague that is all too common these days across the country.

"What do you want?" Alex asks.

The stranger appears to be studying him. He feels the old man's eyes running up and down his body, giving him a real good visual inspection.

"Is there something I can help you with?" Alex asks. "I don't carry money on me when I run, so if you're looking for a handout, I can't help you right now. But if you tell me what you need and where to find you, I will get it and bring it to you."

"I don't want your money," the man quickly answers, and for the first time Alex catches a glimpse of the man's teeth which, to him, look to be in pristine condition. It seems odd that someone who portrays the image of hopeless poverty and homelessness would have such impeccable dental hygiene.

"Are you hurt? Sick? I'm a doctor. I can help you if you tell me what's wrong."

"No. I don't need anything like that," the man replies. His speech is clear and articulate and gives the impression of someone who is well educated. "I am here to help you, Alex. To tell you something very important."

"You know who I am?"

"I do. I've been watching you for many years…since you were born."

"What do you mean you've been *watching* me?" Alex is stunned. "I've never seen you before and I think I know most everyone in this town."

"I've been around, Alex, keeping my distance but watching you grow into the fine young man that you've become. You have done well."

"I don't understand."

"I don't expect you to, but you will," the old man says. He turns and starts to walk away.

"Wait. Where are you going? You can't just show up here and drop that kind of information on me without telling me more."

"In time, Alex, but for now I want you to take heed of the white crow's warning. If the Spirit Crow has presented itself to you, it is telling you to be ready."

"Ready? For what?"

"For what is about to happen," the old man says. He looks back over his right shoulder at Alex and motions for him to follow. "Come. Walk with me."

"I am not going anywhere with you until you tell me who you are."

"It's a long story, Alex, but you can trust me. I mean you no harm." The old man smiles. "Come. I want to show you something."

Although he isn't sure if it's a smart move, Alex sprints to catch up with the stranger, who has just turned a bend in the trail. *For someone who appears to be very old, he sure moves quickly.*

"Where are we going?"

"Just a little further down the trail."

"Where did you come from?" Based upon the wrinkles on the man's face and hands, and his diminutive stature, Alex believes the man's age must exceed eighty, at the very least. "I've never seen you around here before."

"And you wouldn't be seeing me today if I didn't want you to see me."

"So why today?"

"Because this is urgent." The old man stops suddenly on the trail and points to a growth of alder bushes where the remains of two raccoons are lying on the ground. Their bloodied bodies are badly mutilated.

"Were they attacked?"

"Yes."

"What happened to them?"

"They were killed."

"I can see that, but who did this?"

"Another raccoon."

"They don't typically kill each other, do they?"

"Not typically, but the animal couldn't control itself."

"What do you mean, *it couldn't control itself?*"

"It has happened before, you know?"

Alex is becoming more confused as the sound of flies buzzing around the dead animals invades his thoughts. "I don't understand."

"That last time was in 1972, but there were several other times in the town's past. It always happens around the solar eclipse."

"What happens?" Alex studies the old man. "You've lost me."

"I remember the last time very well. It was July 10 and the day got very, very dark as the sun disappeared from the sky, and it got very cold. I also remember that, in the days leading up to the solar eclipse, many living creatures just seemed to snap, and turned on each other without being provoked."

Alex shakes his head. "You've lost me."

"It was the eclipse, Alex. And it's happening again. Right now."

"You're telling me that an eclipse drove animals crazy, and they killed each other?"

"Not just animals. People, too. It started three days before the eclipse. They turned on each other, like they were driven by some sort of hidden force or power that compelled them to do things they would never do—like kill each other."

"How could a solar eclipse compel people to kill each other?"

"It's the forces of nature, Alex. The powers of good and evil converging, colliding, like the plates of the earth butting up against each other along a fault line, or like two massive storm fronts meeting each other and releasing a torrent of energy."

Alex remembers hearing on the news that there's going to be a solar eclipse this coming Monday, April 8. He looks at the old man.

"Are you telling me that the raccoons killed each other because of the eclipse that's coming?"

The old man nods. "The Spirit Crow has come to tell you that it's happening again."

"I have never seen anything like this *spirit* crow before."

The old man squints at Alex. "A white crow is a very rare and beautiful sight, and it is usually said to symbolize good luck, power, strength, wisdom, and pure white energy. It doesn't show itself to too many people, but you are special."

"Yeah." Alex grimaces. "I'm special, all right."

"Many people believe that if you see a white crow, it means that something good is about to happen. Some also believe that the white crow is a sign of wisdom and seeing one can be an omen of change or new beginnings, but sometimes it can also be a warning of something darker, an evil on the horizon."

"As in my case?"

"Yes. Our family has—and you in particular have, Alex—a special con-nection to the crows around here, but the Spirit Crow is beyond anything you could imagine. It feels a kinship with you, a bond that runs deep be-cause you are the golden child."

"Because I'm the fiftieth descendent of Alexandria Gorham?"

The old man nods. "That's why the white crow has shown itself to you today as a warning that things around here are about to explode, and you must protect yourself."

"How so?"

"Watch what happens. Pay attention because people, in fact, all living creatures, will snap quickly. There will be no warning. One second, they will seem fine and the next second they will want to kill each other—or you. No one is immune to this power, and no one is safe, but the Spirit Crow will protect you, the chosen one."

"What can I do?"

"Protect your family but, more importantly, protect yourself. You must remain safe."

The old man turns abruptly. "I must leave now."

"Who are you?" Alex calls out as the small-featured man moves quickly along the trail and turns a bend, showing more ability than many people half his age.

Breaking into a quick stride, Alex chases after the stranger, but as he makes the turn, he is shocked to see the old man is gone.

"What the bloody hell?"

3: The Cozy Corner Café

"Hey, ladies. How are my three favourite women doing this afternoon?"

Carly Watkins smiles at the trio gathered around the glass-top table strategically situated in front of a large window that looks out onto the corner of Main and Market streets. It is their favourite spot in the café as it provides the best vantage point for people-watching. They have chosen this location for their weekly coffee gathering—or gabfest, as they call it —ever since The Cozy Corner Café opened for business just over five years ago.

"We're doing great, sweetie." Julie Graham smiles at her daughter. "Why don't you pull up a chair and join us? You look a little frazzled. Have you had a break yet today?"

"Gee, Mom. Thanks for the compliment," Carly replies, rolling her eyes. "I'd like nothing better than to sit and shoot the breeze with you girls, but I don't have that luxury today. Amanda called in sick so I'm doing double duty. It's just Corinna and me today so I won't get a break for a while. As you can see, we're slammed right now. Thank God for Corinna, that's all I can say. She's a peach."

"Are you kidding me? Amanda is always taking time off, which makes it hard on you," Julie says. "What's the good of an employee who sets her own schedule? I know you like her, but I think you need to fire her ass and find someone else who can give you one hundred percent. You need someone more dependable."

"You know I can't do that, Mom. It's true Amanda seems to miss a lot of time, but she's a damned good worker when she's here."

"But she's only here half the time," Julie says. "Meanwhile, you're killing yourself trying to keep up. You can't maintain that pace."

"That's true," Carly agrees. "But she's having a tough time right now and needs the job. I feel I need to cut her some slack."

"Are you looking for someone else to pitch in?" Lisa Hamilton asks, her eyes scanning the lunch menu. "Lauren will be home on summer break in a few weeks. I bet she'd be happy to work here again this year. She loved it here last summer and I don't think she has anything else lined up just yet."

"And everyone loved her," Carly answers. "She's a great worker and she's good with the customers. Why don't you have her drop in to see me when she gets home? Maybe we can work something out."

Lisa nods, then points to the menu. "I'm feeling a little peckish today, so I think I will have your chicken and tzatziki wrap. Your mother tells me it's to die for. And I'll just have water with that, please."

"It is good, but I think Mom's a little partial to everything we serve here." Carly smiles. "What about you, Mom? Are you having lunch today?"

Julie shakes her head. "I think I'll just have a chai latte. Your father and I had a huge breakfast this morning so I'm not feeling especially hungry right now."

"Okay. Got it." Turning to the third member of the trio, she asks, "What about you, Ms. Henderson? Lunch for you today?"

"Yes, please," Samantha Henderson answers. "I'll have the Greek salad and an iced tea. And please hold the green peppers in the salad. I love them, but the damned things give me indigestion."

"Okay. Got it. No green peppers. Give me about ten minutes."

"No rush," Samantha says. "We'll be here a while, as you know."

Carly chuckles. "Right. Time to catch up on all the news around town."

"I think you mean gossip." Samantha grins as Carly turns and heads toward the main counter. Glancing around the table, she adds, "These two are incorrigible."

The three women have become a weekly fixture at The Cozy Corner Café, which Carly opened when she moved back to Liverpool. After their father's death, she wanted her two daughters to be closer to their grandparents. She also felt the need to be closer to her mother, who has been struggling with some health issues in recent years.

"So, girls," Lisa begins. "What's new this week?"

"Actually, not much," Julie replies. "Unless you count the fact that Karen and David Francomb are separated and likely getting a divorce."

"What?" The other women are surprised.

Julie answers with a slight nod. "Rumour has it that she was having an affair."

"No way," Lisa says.

"That's what I heard."

"Who was she having an affair with?" Lisa pries.

"Come on, you two," Samantha says. "That's really none of our business."

"You come on, Sam," Lisa responds. "Aren't you the least bit curious about who she was cheating with?" Turning to Julie, she adds, "What's his name?"

"I don't really know, but apparently, she has been meeting some guy in Bridgewater at least once a week, and I gather it's been going on for quite some time."

"Well, that's a juicy little tidbit." Lisa grins sheepishly. "I feel bad for David, though. He's a nice man. He's also a great teacher. Both my kids liked him, and they did really well in his math class."

"I hear he has taken a leave of absence for the rest of the school year," Julie continues. "For health reasons."

"David and Karen have been together for a lot of years," Samantha joins in. "It's a shame when someone is so unhappy in their marriage that they have to sneak around. It seems so lurid…so dirty."

"It *is* dirty," Julie says. "But people cheat on their spouses for lots of reasons. They may still love their partner, but perhaps there could be something missing in their relationship."

"Maybe ole Davey Boy just couldn't get it up anymore," Lisa says with a laugh. "It happens, you know?"

"Oh my God, Lisa." Julie rolls her eyes at her friend. "You're so bad. Just stop it."

"Yes," Samantha adds. "Why does everything have to be about sex with you?"

Lisa smirks. "I'm just saying what everyone else is thinking."

"Oh no." Julie shakes her head as Carly delivers their drinks to the table. "I'm not thinking anything like that."

"Neither am I," Samantha agrees.

"I can just imagine what you three are talking about," Carly says.

"Actually, sweetheart," Julie says with a smile, "I don't think you can."

"And you don't want to," Samantha adds.

"Okay, ladies. I'll be right back shortly with your food."

"Thanks, Carly," Samantha says. Turning to Julie, she adds, "I just love your daughter. This café has been such a wonderful edition to the downtown. I'm so glad it has all worked out for her. I know she went through a rough spell back then but it's good to see she's found her way again."

"It wasn't easy," Julie answers, a frown showing at the corners of her mouth. "There were a number of years after Leo died that Carly just couldn't seem to find her footing and she struggled. I mean, she really struggled. Cliff and I were very happy when she and the girls moved back here. Relieved, actually. We could help take care of the kids and Carly could take the time she needed to find herself again."

"It was a good move," Samantha says. "And good for you and Cliff to be there for her."

"Always." Julie smiles and takes a sip of her chai latte. "Man, I love this stuff but I'm not sure it's so good for you."

"What are you talking about?" Lisa replies. She studies her friend. "You can afford to consume a few extra calories once a week. Just look at you. You're nothing but skin and bones. Are you sure you're all right?"

"Yes." Julie insists. "I'm fine. Just lost a little weight."

"Lisa is right," Samantha says. "You have lost a significant amount of weight. Have you seen a doctor? Is there something you should tell us?"

"Jesus, will you two please give it up." Julie pulls back from the table. "I've lost some weight. That doesn't mean I'm dying."

Samantha and Lisa exchange glances.

"Okay," Lisa says. "We'll change the subject. For now. Anyone else got any juicy news they want to share?"

"Only that Hunter tells me Ally is getting a promotion at work," Samantha says. "Looks like she's going to be the new principal at the elementary school, starting in September."

"That is so wonderful," Julie replies. "I am so happy for her. She's worked hard and studied hard. Had a baby while still in university but still had the personal drive and determination to get her education degree. And then, to land a good job right here at home. Good for her. She deserves it after the hell her own mother put her through."

"She certainly does." Samantha smiles. "I can't believe how wrong Kate and I were about Hunter and her when this all started, but we're very proud of everything they've accomplished. They both have good jobs, and we have two beautiful grandsons. What more could you ask for?"

"Don't forget Alex," Lisa pipes up. "Look at what he and Bree have accomplished. She's a lawyer and he's going to be a doctor. I am so proud of them."

Samantha nods. "And the good thing is that Alex is going to be taking over Charlie's practice when he retires. We are very excited to have him so close to home. There's such a demand for doctors these days, that he could have gone anywhere he liked."

"Any idea when Charlie is retiring?" Julie asks as Carly arrives at the table with the food.

"Not precisely," Samantha answers. "Thank you, sweetie," she says, watching as Carly places the plate in front of her. "But if I was guessing, I would say it's probably going to be within the next two years."

"Really? That soon?" Lisa asks.

Samantha nods. "Kate says that he's been wanting to get away from medicine ever since Rebecca died."

"That was what?" Lisa replies. "Ten years ago?"

"It was," Samantha says. "Hard to believe it's been that long, but Charlie has never been the same since he lost her, even after all that time. Now that Liam is away at university, it's just him in the house and I think he's having a tough time."

"I just find it hard to believe that he hasn't found another woman after all these years," Lisa observes. "That man is a real catch. Great career, and he's pretty easy on the eyes."

"You never cease to amaze me," Julie says, addressing her friend. "I'm beginning to think you're a sex addict or something. I worry about Warren."

"What?" Lisa laughs. "It's not a bad thing that I can appreciate other men. Warren's been so busy ever since he was promoted to corporal three years ago that he hardly sees me anymore, let alone touches me."

"Marital problems, Lisa?" Samantha probes. "If you and Warren are having issues, don't let it go. My advice is to find someone to talk to before things get so bad that you fall apart."

"We're fine." Lisa casts her eyes down to her food. "We've just had to make adjustments in our lives."

"You don't sound fine," Julie observes. "Want to talk about it? Cliff and I were there once, and it ended in divorce. Thankfully we found each other again, but we lost a lot of good years that we could have had with each other. That is one of the biggest regrets in my life."

"For God's sake." Lisa glares at her friends. "Warren and I are nowhere near a divorce. I'm sorry I said anything about Charlie. Let's talk about something else."

"Well, speaking of Charlie," Samantha says. "I can tell you that he and Oliver are planning a two-month trip to Europe this summer, after Alex graduates and gets settled in. I can see that Charlie is already pulling back from the practice. We'll be lucky if he lasts two more years."

"Whatever will he do after he retires?" Julie asks.

"I have no idea, but I'm glad he and Oliver have each other to lean on," Samantha says, slipping an olive into her mouth. Between chews, she adds, "Oliver is a lot like Charlie. I thought he and Anna would end up getting married and settling down, but that wasn't in the cards for them. Her career was too important to her, and he is such a homebody."

"Does he see much of her?" Lisa asks. "And what about his daughter? Does he see much of Isabel?"

"Not as much as he'd like," Samantha says. "He goes to Halifax as often as he can and Isabel comes here once a month, but it's not what he wants. She'll soon be turning ten and I know Oliver would like to spend more time with her. I think that's one of the reasons he's taking this trip with Charlie. He just needs to get away from all of the stress and put everything into perspective. I think he needs some space so he can clear his head. Both he and Charlie need just need to unwind."

"I get that." Julie nods. "I hope they all find the happiness they deserve."

"What is happ—?" Lisa's words are abruptly interrupted by screaming sirens as three RCMP cruisers fly down Main Street. "What the hell?"

"Must be something major for them to be going that fast through the centre of town on a Friday afternoon," Julie observes.

Samantha nods. "Something is definitely up, and it can't be good."

4: The land of the crows

So much for ten years of joyous bliss, Alex thinks.

He cringes when he recalls when crows infiltrated his life, and he also remembers the past ten years when the world was a quieter place, free of near-death experiences and other mysterious events. He knows the crows are an integral part of his existence and he embraces the legacy of Alexandria Gorham, but he would be lying if he didn't admit that he welcomed the more serene decade.

He liked the idea of feeling like he was normal.

Whatever normal is.

Now, following his unusual encounters at the park this afternoon, he feels compelled to look for answers. It feels like a giant crater has opened up on the earth's surface and he's being pulled into a deep, dark sinkhole, a void with no obvious way to escape.

Clearly, the fun part is over, but the respite was good while it lasted.

After grabbing a quick shower and slipping into a change of clothes following his run, he sits at his desk and opens his laptop. Taking a sip of ice-cold water, he searches "total solar eclipse."

God only knows what's brewing in the land of the crows. But whatever it is, I'm sure it can't be good.

The sudden manifestation of the mysterious albino crow was enough to give his heart palpitations. But it was the appearance of the unkempt old man with his pristine teeth and his ominous message that causes Alex the greatest consternation. The man's words are still bouncing around in his brain like they are playing on an unbroken audio loop.

He's seen enough strange behaviour in his lifetime that he understands he cannot dismiss the man's warning. Add the Spirit Crow into the mix and Alex knows he's already passed the point of no return with this mystery.

He can feel his skin crawl when he thinks about what could be coming for him and everyone else in this town. He knows when events such as these are in motion, they're usually coming at him.

It's usually pure mayhem, like a one-way ticket to hell, he thinks.

He runs his long, slender fingers through his thick white hair, a trait he's developed in recent years when he becomes nervous, like when he's taking an important exam.

Okay, old man. He takes a deep breath. *What did you want? Who are you? Where in hell did you come from?*

He exhales. *You say you know me, but are you a friend or foe?*

"Those are all damned good questions," Alex whispers to his empty bedroom, the same room where he spent most of his youthful years.

He came to live with Samantha Henderson and Kate Webster after his biological family was massacred. He wasn't even three years old at the time of the tragedy, yet he remembers the events as though they occurred just yesterday.

He's glad that Samantha and Kate adopted him because—he shudders at the thought—he has no idea where he would be today if not for those two women who raised and nurtured him. They loved him like he was their own child.

But that's what good parents do. They love you unconditionally.

He's grateful for all they've done for him, supporting him through some very tough times when the world seemed like it was crashing down around him, and celebrating with him during the good times, especially during the past ten years. Alex gives them credit for guiding him through the maze of life. They've moulded him into the man that he has become.

If they were here right now, he'd give them both a hug and thank them for all that they have done for him, but the house was empty when he got back from the park. Since it's Friday afternoon, he knows it's Samantha's routine to meet with friends for their weekly gossip session at The Cozy Corner Café.

He assumes Kate must be at work. She seems to spend an inordinate amount of time at the office these days, but he knows how busy they are because Bree also works at the same law firm. She has also been on a tight schedule, rushing about every day, running from one appointment to the next.

Kate is teaching her well.

He smiles at the thought. But he's happy that Bree is living her dream, even if it means he sees far less of her than he'd like. He almost feels he has to give her three days' notice just to meet her for dinner, which he's doing later today when Jace and Luna arrive for the weekend. He's looking forward to seeing his friends—and her, the young woman he loves.

Leaning back in his black swivel chair and waiting for his search engine to kick out the results of his search, Alex suddenly feels as though something has changed. From the moment he saw the Spirit Crow, the world seems like it has shifted on its axis, and he shudders at the thought.

He focuses on the computer screen.

Something is definitely off kilter, teetering like a wobbly spinning top.

He bristles at the thought of what this means, but his world has always been like that—things changing on a dime. Quiet and peaceful one minute, pure pandemonium the next.

Watching as a list of URL links pops up on the screen, Alex considers what he's doing. He's not really sure he wants to walk down this road with the crows once again, but he knows he has no choice in the matter, because if the crows have come to him, then he understands they must need him.

He also accepts that when the crows beckon, he cannot refuse them. It's his calling—his sacred duty.

My raison d'être.

"I have no choice," he says, clicking on the top link that contains information about the solar eclipse. "I know you need me," he whispers, knowing the crows will hear him, for their bond is unbreakable. "And I will be there for you, just like you've always been there for me."

Now old man, whoever you are, let's see what the hell you were prattling on about.

"A total solar eclipse will take place at the moon's ascending node on Monday, April 8, 2024, between 3:27 and 5:44 pm," he reads aloud. "It will be visible across North America and is dubbed the Great North American Eclipse by some of the media."

He takes another sip of the cold water, hoping the clear liquid will extinguish the fire that's starting to burn in the pit of his stomach.

"Eclipses are powerful celestial events that can energetically cause upheaval and unpredictable events to occur. They can bring unexpected challenges, opportunities and shifts in nature. In many cultures, an eclipse is viewed as a powerful energetic period."

Okay, so that is interesting. Is that what you were talking about, old man?

"Many people around the world still see eclipses as evil omens that bring death, destruction, and disasters. But on the flip side, some cultures believe that an eclipse of the sun can also be an illumination and they see it as a catalyst for change."

Huh. Alex shivers. *Well, that's something. I'm not liking the sound of that. The first bit kind of ties into what the old man was talking about. Maybe he was onto something after all.*

He reads more. "Eclipses are sometimes considered powerful moments for connecting with the divine, the universe, or a higher power. It's a time when the ordinary rules of the world are temporarily suspended, allowing for a sense of unity with a greater spiritual reality."

That sounds better than what the old man was suggesting. He shakes his head. *Nothing sinister sounding about any of that.*

But considering the presence of the Spirit Crow along with the old man, Alex believes that whatever is about to happen in this town will likely emerge from within the realm of darkness.

That's what I've come to expect whenever the crows are involved.

He continues to read. "A popular misconception by many people is that solar eclipses can be a danger to pregnant women and their unborn children. In many cultures, young children and pregnant women are asked to stay indoors throughout the duration of a solar eclipse to avoid the negative energy."

Now that part sounds more like an old superstition than anything more concrete, he decides. *Can't let myself get lost in old wives' tales or they'll swallow me up.*

"So then," he asks, as if an invisible entity were watching over his shoulder while he gently types the next question into the search engine. "When was the last solar eclipse over this part of the world?"

Google quickly spits out the answer. He reads, "The last total solar eclipse to occur over Nova Scotia was July 10, 1972."

Hmmm. Just like the old man said.

He searches the internet for any news reports of unusual activity on that date in Nova Scotia, as the old man suggested. He finds nothing.

"Okay old man," he whispers. "I'm not seeing anything about a crime spree around here in July, 1972. Nothing to support your wild story about people and animals going berserk and killing each other."

Quitting the search program and closing the cover on his laptop, Alex decides that while some of what the old man told him, like facts about the eclipse, may be easy to confirm. Other parts of his story may be nothing more than pure fiction. Since he has no idea who the old man is or if his warning has any credence, he decides he'll have to look elsewhere for answers.

Maybe the library or the museum. He leans back in his chair. *Clearly, I've got to dig deeper. After all, what do I know about this man? He could be living in a warped fantasy world, one filled with delusions and nightmares. Or then again ...*

"I know nothing about him," he blurts out and jumps from the swivel chair.

Quickly moving to the bedroom window that looks out over the back-yard, Alex studies the neighbourhood that's slowly coming back to life with the arrival of spring. This recent stretch of warm weather has lulled the plants out of their hibernation and soon the world will be bursting with fresh, new life.

He likes spring. It's his favourite time of the year, one filled with prom-ises of renewal and rebirth.

Come on, Alex. What are you doing? Ever since ten years ago, when you had your last major encounter with anything related to the crows, you've managed to get away from them, but here you are, getting pulled right back into their world again.

"Do I really want to do this?" he asks.

After pausing as if waiting for someone else to answer, he shrugs. "Do I really have a choice?"

He shakes his head. *No. I do not.*

He knows he is bound to the crows and they to him, because of an an-cient family pact. And while he appreciates that they have looked over him and came to his rescue many times in his earlier life, he was hoping that those events would remain covered in the dust of ancient history.

Apparently not.

He presses his face against the window glass, his eyes scouring the yard for signs of crows. He looks to the horizon. He knows they are close. They always are.

Ever present, they are part of me.

"I know you are out there," he whispers. "I can feel you, sense you. I know you need me, so please come to me. Please show me. What do you need of me?"

He watches in amazement—and slight apprehension—as a murder of crows suddenly ascends from the horizon. They swoop in his direction, their long, powerful wings catching the afternoon air currents, their aerodynamic bodies propelled forward, like arrows, with little resist-ance.

He counts, one by one, as the large, sleek crows land on the barren branches of the maple trees that border the backyard.

"...eight, nine," he counts aloud, "ten crows lined up in a row."

Ten crows for a time of joyous bliss.

Carefully watching the powerful birds, their ember tones muted in the waning afternoon sunlight, he adds, "Ten crows on a mission, but a mis-sion to do what?"

5: Echo Lake Road

Horrific scenes like the one he finds when he arrives at Echo Lake Road cause Corporal Warren Hamilton to wonder why he ever wanted to be a police officer in the first place.

Because it was a calling.

Warren slams the transmission into park and quickly turns off his fully-equipped RCMP Ford Explorer.

A mission. He releases his seat belt, grabs his cap from the passenger seat, checks his holster to make sure his firearm is secure and opens the door of the SUV, all in one fluid motion.

When he joined the RCMP, twenty-plus years ago, Warren wanted to help and protect people. He didn't expect to be pulled into the dark world of depravity and hatred that he sees far too often these days. When he was first posted to a small town in rural Nova Scotia, he thought the crime would mostly consist of break and enters, theft, robbery, the odd assault, and drunk drivers. Maybe the occasional violent crime.

Boy, was I wrong.

Continued exposure to the underbelly of society, where some individuals seem to thrive on hurting others, has worn him down. It's made him cynical and untrusting. He doesn't like how the experiences have made him feel.

But it is what it is, he tells himself just about every day. He's become resigned to the reality that exists in today's world.

And as the person in charge of the local detachment of thirteen officers and two support staff members, he knows he has an important job to do.

These people are counting on me, he thinks, sliding out from behind the steering wheel, placing his cap on his nearly-bald head and surveying the surroundings.

The image of the massive log protruding from the windshield of the black Ford F-150 causes him to pause. An involuntary shiver races up his spine.

"Jesus," he says to Constable Nolan Shaw as the tall, slender African Nova Scotian officer with the pencil-thin black moustache approaches him. He had arrived about fifteen minutes earlier and began the initial investigation. "That looks messy."

"Oh yeah," Nolan says. "Not a pretty sight."

"What've you got?"

"There are two crime scenes." The constable nods toward the truck impaled by a massive log. "This one with a male victim inside the vehicle. It's pretty messy in there." He points down the dusty dirt road and says, "And a second one about two kilometres down there, with two deceased. Both males."

"Shit. Both scenes secured?"

"Yes, sir. Both are locked down tighter than a constipated dog's ass."

Warren just looks at the constable, a trusted officer who has basically become his right hand. After ten years of working beside him, he's become used to the constable's colourful catchphrases and he takes the comment in stride. "Any idea as to what happened here?"

"Not yet."

"Witnesses?"

"About half a dozen." Constable Shaw nods toward a gathering of workers who watched helplessly as Jimmy Spicer rammed his truck into the back of the massive tree harvester. "They all said they tried stopping the truck, but he barrelled right on through. Said the driver died instantly."

"Brutal." Warren studies the Ford truck from a distance. "Any theories as to why someone would do that?"

The constable shakes his head. "But we've just started our investigation, so I hope we can find some answers."

"Anything on the decedent?"

"Only that he was a local fella. Twenty-eight-year-old James Spicer. His friends called him Jimmy. Records show he had a few minor scrapes with the law over the years. Nothing major. Drunk and disorderly in a public place and one serious incident. A DUI."

"Married?"

"Common law."

"Kids?"

"Nothing on the record."

"Prone to violence?"

"Don't have reports of anything."

"Not much to go on." Warren observes. "What about the other scene?"

"We'll have to wait for the coroner to confirm the details of what happened there, but it looks like the two men were attacked with a chainsaw."

"Are you kidding?"

"No, sir." The constable replies. "It was a bloodbath; pretty gruesome."

"Any idea as to why someone would do that?"

"Not a clue."

Warren moves toward the Ford F-150. "Three dead people in one afternoon with no leads to go on." He shivers as cold chills race up his spine. "Feel that?"

"What?"

"The heaviness. It's just hanging in the air. Everything is so still."

"It does feel a little strange around here. Stuffy and hard to breathe. Kind of creepy, if you ask me."

"I did ask you, Nolan." Warren looks at him, raising his right eyebrow.

"Yes." The constable frowns. "I guess you did. And yes, I do feel something. It's—"

"Electric," Warren interrupts.

Approaching the Ford F-150, he adds, "It's causing the little hairs on my arms to stand at attention."

Looking through the driver-side window, Warren feels his stomach churn as he sees the bloodied remains of a young man behind the steering wheel, his head bashed in as the log hit him squarely in the face.

"Jesus," he whispers. "That poor bastard. Didn't know what hit him."

"Actually, Corporal, I think he knew," Constable Shaw observes. "The other workers said it appeared Jimmy targeted the log and, as he approached, gunned the accelerator. It appears it was a suicide."

"There are better ways to kill yourself, Nolan. Easier and less messy."

"I know, but let's just say he snapped."

"No, let's not *just say* anything. We need facts. Let's be sure we follow all protocols on this one, and that means a complete workup of this scene. I want this woodlot scoured, as well as the second scene. We need to talk to everyone who saw anything, doesn't matter how insignificant it seems. I want this done as fast as possible. We need answers and we need them now."

"Understood sir. We're on it."

"Let's go the second scene." Warren turns and heads back to his SUV. "You can ride with me."

The two men remain quiet during the short drive, their eyes focused on the dirt road in front of them.

"You doing okay, Nolan?" Warren asks when they arrive. Turning off the ignition, he adds, "You look a little white around the gills."

The constable nods. "I'm fine, sir. Just thinking about what could have happened here."

"It's a mystery."

Warren opens the vehicle door and slides his left foot out onto the solid ground that's so dry it feels more like concrete. "You okay to look around?"

"Yes, sir." The constable opens the passenger side door. "Right with you."

"What do we know about this victim?" Warren asks as the two officers approach the first body. A blood-soaked chainsaw rests beside the body. "Do we know this guy's name?"

"This is the crew foreman, Mitchell Clarke. He was thirty. Local. Married. Two young kids. Clean record."

As Warren kneels, the sweet coppery smell of coagulating blood fills his nostrils.

"I hate that smell. It's the scent of death. Makes me want to puke," he says. "This poor guy was brutalized. Just look." He points the man's hands. "Some of his fingers were cut off. He tried to protect himself from his attacker."

"It didn't work."

Warren stands and eyes the second body a few metres away. With his eyes glued to the ground, he moves toward the crumpled remains of the final victim in today's massacre and the large red stain surrounding the body. "Who's this guy?"

"This is Bobby Brighton. Not much in the system about him. He was twenty-eight. Another local fella. Not married. No children and no record except a few disorderly conducts, but nothing serious."

"So, these were pretty average guys just out doing their jobs on a Friday afternoon."

Nolan nods. "Just working for the weekend."

"What happened here?" Warren observes piles of alder bushes and felled trees waiting to be hauled away, as well as several pieces of equipment. "It all looks normal."

"Except for the bodies."

"Yes. Except for that." Warren pauses. He listens. Experience has taught him that you can't always depend upon your eyes when you're investigating a crime scene. Sometimes you must let your ears do the work.

"Do you hear that?" he asks the younger officer.

"Sorry, sir, but I don't hear anything."

"Just steady your breathing and listen. Don't say anything."

Nolan does as his superior officer suggested. "What is that?" he asks several seconds later. "It sounds like ... something is growling."

"I don't know what it is." Turning from the body and breaking into a sprint, Warren says to the officer, "But let's not stick around to find out."

Nolan sounds the alarm as he observes the threat emerging from the nearby thick underbrush. "It's coyotes and there's lots of them. It looks like they are stalking us."

Reaching the SUV first, Warren opens the door and reaches for his weapon. He doesn't want to shoot any of the animals, but he will if he must.

Quickly sliding behind the steering wheel, he leans on the horn, hoping the sudden noise will scare away the animals that are getting dangerously close to his friend.

The young officer finally reaches the SUV, flings open the passenger-side door and jumps inside the vehicle. He slams the door just as the pack of coyotes arrive, several jumping on the engine hood and throwing their bodies against the windshield with such force that they leave streaks of blood on the tempered glass.

"This is not normal behaviour," Warren says. "I know they can be aggressive, but not like this."

"How many are there? Seven? Eight?"

"I don't know, but those sonsabitches mean business."

Warren starts the SUV and switches on the sirens, hoping the blaring noise will frighten away the pack of coyotes that seem hell bent on getting inside. "Notify dispatch about what's happening here."

"Yes sir." Nolan quickly grabs the radio from the mic stand on the dash and relays their status. "They want to know if we need back up."

"God, no. Don't send any more officers up here. We don't want to put anyone else in harm's way."

Warren puts the Explorer into drive and quickly moves the SUV forward. He then slams on the brakes, sending the two coyotes flying off the engine hood. He sees them land on the hard ground several metres in front of the vehicle. He sees the impact has left them stunned and confused.

"Now let's get the hell out of here," he says, turning the SUV around and starting back down the dirt road. "Holy fucking hell," he whispers.

The pack of coyotes has formed a line across the road, effectively blocking the officers' only escape route.

"What are they doing?"

"Daring us to cross the line," Warren says.

"What are we going to do? There is no other way out of here."

"I'm going to accept that dare," Warren says, revving the engine. "If they don't move, I'll move their asses."

6: Reggie, Roxy and Rocky

"Hey, little ones," the young woman calls out as she quickly follows the three long-haired, multi-coloured puppies down a side street, one of their favourite routes for their daily walks. She holds tightly to the leashes.

"Please slow down," she pleads. "Remember, you've each got four legs; I've only got two."

She pants as the dogs pull her forward with a brute strength that she doesn't remember them exhibiting in the past. "What's gotten into you guys today? You're killing me. I can't keep up."

Kimmie Rogers had always thought she wanted to be a nurse, but when that didn't work out, she became Nora Blackthorn's personal care worker after the elderly woman's husband, Fred, died of a sudden stroke just over four years ago.

She wasn't looking for anything permanent when she took the job with the wealthy woman. Fresh out of high school, she saw it as something to hold her over until she could figure things out. But the job worked out better than she had hoped, and now she enjoys the opportunity very much as she and the kind-hearted senior have developed what she would describe as more of a close friendship than an employee-employer relationship.

She likes the daily routine of carrying out Mrs. Blackthorn's errands, doing chores around the house, preparing meals, and just spending time with the woman who has accepted Kimmie as an adopted granddaughter. It's a relationship she holds closely to her heart.

In addition to the regular work, Kimmie looks forward to walking Mrs. Blackthorn's "babies," her beloved pet Shih Tzus. The older one, Reggie, and the twins, Roxy and Rocky, enjoy an unparalleled life of luxury in the posh Blackthorn estate, and they return the woman's love enthusiastically.

In exchange, the affectionate dogs expect to be groomed, fed and, most importantly, walked at least three times a day. But that's okay with Kimmie. She appreciates that Mrs. Blackthorn trusts her with the fur babies, and she loves them as if they were her own.

Today, though, when she arrived at the large, sprawling mansion where the Blackthorns have lived for almost fifty years and raised their four children, Kimmie found the elderly woman distraught, fussing and worrying about her puppies.

"I don't know what has gotten into my babies this morning," Mrs. Blackthorn told Kimmie as tears streamed down her wrinkled, apple-doll face. "They were so rambunctious and had so much energy that I just couldn't get them to settle down. Barking and chasing each other around the house. It's been horrible. The little devils just haven't been themselves and Roxy even nipped at me when I was putting her hair up."

Kimmie knows that is unusual, as the dogs normally have a docile temperament. She has always admired the little canines for their friendly disposition and willingness to cooperate, no matter how much Mrs. Blackthorn dotes over them.

"Maybe she isn't feeling well," she suggested, hoping to ease her elderly friend's stress.

While Mrs. Blackthorn didn't seem to think that was the issue, she did agree to have Kimmie call the vet and make an appointment for a checkup.

Even though tomorrow is Saturday, the vet immediately agreed to see Roxy first thing in the morning. Kimmie will drive her to the appointment as Mrs. Blackthorn is finding it increasingly more difficult to get in and out of a car these days.

"Maybe she has a bladder infection," Mrs. Blackthorn conceded. "She usually gets cranky when that's bothering her, but not to the point where she tries to bite me. That's really a worry."

"That's a good reason to get her checked out," Kimmie said. "Better to be safe than sorry."

Mrs. Blackthorn is always willing to ante up for the best treatment for the dogs, no matter the cost. Kimmie hopes Roxy will be all right. She believes if anything happens to one of the dogs, it will probably kill Mrs. Blackthorn.

"Come on guys," she calls while struggling to maintain a tight grip on the leashes that she has wrapped tightly around her wrists and hands. She's pulling so hard that her hands are turning red as the leather straps are cutting off circulation.

"For little dogs, you guys sure do have a lot of strength. What has gotten into you three today?"

She pulls back on the leashes, hoping to keep the dogs under control, but to no avail as she is outmatched by their combined strength.

"Oh no," she cries out as the dogs suddenly jerk forward and get loose, breaking free of her grip. "Please don't run away," she pleads.

Kimmie sprints after the dogs, the three leashes dragging on the ground behind them. This is such unusual behaviour for the little dogs. In the past, whenever she dropped the leashes, the dogs never ran away.

"Reggie. Please stop," she yells, but the older dog ignores her command. Instead, it sprints down the street with its two younger companions in hot pursuit.

She knows if the senior dog stops running the younger twins will also stop.

But the dog clearly has other plans.

"Just don't run out into the traffic," she cries.

The dogs seem determined to get away. But rounding a corner with Kimmie in pursuit, the three Shih Tzus suddenly stop as they meet two much larger dogs that are blocking the sidewalk.

She recognizes the German Shepherds from a neighbour's yard not far from the Blackthorn estate. She's seen them often and she's stopped, talked to them, and given them treats on many occasions. They've always seemed friendly and receptive to her advances.

But she has never seen them out of their yard before, and she doesn't know how they will react to the smaller dogs.

"Oh my God," Kimmie screams. "Reggie. Roxy, Rocky. Come back here at once. Right now."

But it's too late as the larger of the German Shepherds moves quickly and snatches one of the twins from the sidewalk.

Rocky howls in agony as the bigger dog clamps its powerful, vice-like jaws down. It viciously shakes Rocky as if he were a plaything, its white, brown, and grey fur turning red from its wounds. Rocky screams and struggles to break free.

But this is not an even match, and, within seconds, the small dog becomes still.

"Oh my God," Kimmie cries. "You poor, precious baby."

The senior animal, Reggie, positions himself in front of his younger and smaller companion challenging the second German Shepherd.

"No Reggie. Don't do that. Come to me right now. Back away."

Instead, the older Shih Tzu, its white, grey, and black fur bristling, advances toward the larger animal, barking and growling.

As Reggie lunges at the larger dog, Kimmie finally reaches Roxy's leash. Grasping the leather lead, she pulls the small dog toward her as the German Shepherd, its massive teeth visible, meets Reggie's challenge. Grabbing the barking dog in its powerful mouth, the German Shepherd bites down and Reggie immediately howls in pain.

Kimmie knows she cannot help Reggie.

"Come on Roxy." She grabs the small puppy and hugs her tightly. "You and I have to get out of here."

She turns and begins to sprint. She knows her only escape is to get back to the Blackthorn house.

"Run, Kimmie," she tells herself.

Glancing back, she sees the two German Shepherds have broken into a gallop. She knows she will not be able to outrun them.

Despite her size, Roxy is a handful for Kimmie, but the young woman maintains her grip and turns the corner. The Blackthorn house comes into view.

"Lord help me," she cries out at the German Shepherds suddenly grab her from behind, each taking one of her legs and pulling her to the pavement. She lands face-first, the sound of the bone-rattling thud reverberating in her ears.

Instinctively releasing the small dog, she screams, "Run, Roxy. Go home. Go find Mommy."

Kimmie rolls over onto her back and tries with all her might to fend off the attacking dogs. The pain is excruciating as they chomp at her flailing legs and arms.

"Please," she cries out. "Please stop."

The German Shepherds, however, are relentless, biting into any piece of flesh they can find.

As the blood gushes from her open wounds, Kimmie knows she cannot get away from these two powerful dogs.

"Run, Roxy," she cries, the life draining from her body. "Run."

~

For Roxy's tiny legs, the sprint to the mansion takes several minutes, but the little dog finally reaches the expansive yard, the familiar sanctuary she knows so well. Rushing up to the front door, she barks and jumps against the painted wood, scratching against the barrier that blocks her safe passage into the house.

Her only hope is that the human she loves will hear her pleas and reach her in time to rescue her.

"Oh, my gracious," the older woman says as she finally opens the front door. The terrified pup quickly scampers past Mrs. Blackthorn and scurries away to safety inside the house.

"What in Heaven's name is going on out here? Roxy? Where is your brother and where is Reggie? Why aren't you with Kimmie?"

The next few seconds are nothing but a blur as the two German Shepherds bolt through the front yard and pounce on the tiny woman, immediately knocking her off her feet. She lands with a thud on the hardwood floor of the entryway.

As Roxy watches, whimpering, the woman quickly succumbs to the brutal attack.

7: Dinner at the Tethra

It has been a long day, one filled with excitement, anxiety, and a new mystery, but Alex is looking forward to meeting up with his girlfriend, Bree, and his best friend, Jace Woodward, along with Jace's girlfriend, Luna Edwards. They arrived in town about an hour ago.

They agreed to meet for dinner at the Tethra once Jace and Luna were unpacked and settled into the Airbnb that Alex had booked for them. This will be their last time together before their graduation from medical school, and Alex plans a full two days of activities, starting with dinner tonight and including a family gathering that his parents are throwing on Saturday night to celebrate Alex and Jace's graduation.

Sitting at the table for four that's situated near a beautiful stone vintage-style fireplace, Alex surveys the restaurant. The dark paint in hues of greens and reds, combined with the subdued, soft lighting and tasteful antique decorations strategically placed around the expansive room, give him a mellow vibe. The location has become a hot destination on weekends for the locals, and during the tourist season.

He chose it to host his friends because of the comfortable ambience and the great choices on their menu. He knows that no matter what the others are craving, they'll surely find something here that will quench their appetites.

Personally, he likes their seafood fettuccine and he's sure Jace will enjoy the lightly-battered haddock and hand-cut, twice-fried home fries. It's a safe bet, as fish and chips are his friend's usual go-to meal whenever they dine out, something they haven't had a chance to do in quite some time. As for what Bree and Luna will choose, Alex won't even attempt to take a guess at that. *They aren't as predictable.*

He smiles as the tall, good-looking African Nova Scotian man with the athletic build and cocky swagger, accompanied by the very attractive, considerably shorter, brunette with the petite features, enter the restaurant.

Alex waves to make sure they see him.

"Hey, buddy," Jace says. He quickly embraces his friend. "Haven't seen you in so long that I almost forgot what you look like. Still as ugly as ever, I see."

"What's it been? A month?" Alex returns the hug. "And you better watch out who you're calling ugly."

"Not since before Christmas break, my friend."

Turning his attention to Jace's companion, Alex wraps his arms around her in a warm embrace.

"Go on," he says. "Has it really been that long?"

"Yuppers." Jace takes the chair next to his good friend. "Not since before we went home for the holidays. After that, you stayed here to work with your uncle, and I went to Cape Breton. Remember?"

"Jesus." Alex can't believe how he can lose track of time so easily. "I guess it really has been a while." He chuckles. "I hate it when you're right."

"I always am."

"Yeah, right." Alex rolls his eyes.

"So, where's Bree?" Luna asks as she takes the chair directly across the table from Alex. "I hope she's joining us. I'm looking forward to spending some time with her this weekend. We have a lot of catching up to do."

"She'll be here any second," Alex answers. "She got delayed getting away from the office. They're busier than hell over there. I hardly ever see her these days."

Luna smiles. "The busy life a successful young lawyer."

"How are things with you guys?" Alex glances from one friend to the other. "You didn't go and get married without inviting me, did you?"

"We thought about it." Jace smirks. "But Luna wouldn't hear of that. Said she couldn't get married without Bree being there. You, on the other hand"—he chuckles—"we really don't care about so much."

Alex laughs. "Go on, then. Go ahead and make this beautiful woman your wife, and you better do it soon, before someone prettier than you snatches her away."

"Come on. You know there's no one prettier than me," Jace says. "But who are you to give marriage advice? We still haven't received a wedding invitation yet from this neck of the woods."

"Soon." Alex plays the cool card, suddenly becoming coy. "All I'm going to say is that you guys will have to stay tuned."

"Alex, you ole dog. Are you finally going to pop the question?"

Alex quickly changes the subject. "How are things at the Airbnb? Need anything? Just let me know if you do."

"It's all good," Luna speaks up. "Everything is lovely; really comfortable."

"Except for the name," Jace adds. "Hugin and Munin. What the hell kind of name is that for a place with a bed? It's like the name of this restaurant. What is a Tethra?"

"Tethra is not a *what*. It's a who," Alex answers. "Tethra was the wife of the Fomorian sea-god who was said to be a crow goddess who also hovered above battlefields."

"Of course, she was. Why am I not surprised that it would be related to crows?" Jace grins. "So, what is the Hugin and Munin? I suppose they're connected to crows as well."

Alex nods. "It sure is. Both businesses are operated by a nice couple who moved to town about seven years ago. They are retired university professors from Toronto, with an affinity to all things related to crows. They were attracted to our community because of everything they heard about the crows that flock here. We've had more than our fair share of publicity in the past about the unusual crow behaviour in these parts. They heard about it and decided the town was a perfect fit for them."

"What is it with you and crows and this town?" Jace's left eyebrow rises when he asks questions.

"I don't want to get into that right now. We have other things to talk about."

Jace looks sharply at his friend. "Some day, pal, I am going to sit you down and make you tell me the whole story. So, tell me, then: what does the Hugin and Munin mean?"

"In Norse mythology, Odin is the leader of all the Viking gods. He is the god of knowledge, war, and victory. Odin rules from Asgard in a silver tower and he has two ravens that fly all over the world. They are called Hugin and Munin and they sit on Odin's shoulders and tell him all that they saw."

"I might have known." Jace rolls his eyes.

"You might have known what?" Bree interrupts as she suddenly appears beside the table.

Luna quickly rises to give her a hug. "Is Alex boring you with small talk?" Bree whispers in her ear.

"Not at all," Luna answers as she and Bree take their seats. "He's just been telling us some crow trivia."

Bree laughs. "Like I said: small talk." Smiling across the table, she adds, "Hey, Jace. How's life in Cape Breton?"

"All's good." He smiles back. "Great people and wonderful doctors to work with. I learned a lot from them about health care in a rural setting, but I'm happy to see you and Alex though." He winks at her. "Well, I'm happy to see you, at least. It's been way too long."

"It sure has. But once you and Alex graduate and settle into your practices, we'll have to make sure we get together as often as possible before the babies start coming. Let's promise to do that at least once a month."

Luna nods. "If not more often, but let's not get ahead of ourselves with talk of babies."

"We'll see how things go," Alex interrupts as the server arrives at the table. "I know what I'm having."

"How's their fish and chips?" Jace asks.

"I knew it." Alex laughs. "You are so predictable. No worries though. The haddock here is excellent."

After the server leaves with their orders, Bree turns to Alex. "Have you heard from your uncle this afternoon?"

"Uncle Charlie? No. Was I supposed to? I'm not scheduled to work with him anymore until after graduation. He thought I've earned a break, so he gave me some time off."

"I guess you haven't heard the news."

Alex shrugs. "What news?"

"Apparently, all hell broke loose up at Echo Lake this afternoon, where they are clearing land for that new housing development," she answers. "I thought Uncle Charlie might have called you in to help him."

Alex studies his girlfriend, looking for any clues as to what she's talking about. "Okay, Bree, I know you talk in lawyer mode most of the time, but when you say *all hell broke loose*, what exactly do you mean?"

"Sorry. I don't know any of the details, but it's the hot news around town."

"For God's sake, Bree. Just tell me."

"I'm getting to it." She rolls her eyes. "One of the crew members lost it and went on some kind of rampage. From what I heard, there are three dead people. If your Uncle Charlie is on duty, I thought he may have called you to give him a hand. He's probably swamped."

"Didn't hear from him." Alex rises from the table while slipping his cell phone from his pocket. "Excuse me for a few seconds, everyone. I'm going to call my uncle to see what's going on."

Directly addressing his best friend, he says, "And, Jace, don't you dare pick the scallops out of my fettuccine. They're the best part."

Jace acts confused. "I don't know what you're talking about, friend. Go make your call and I'll order a round of drinks for everyone. What will you have?"

"If you're buying, I'll have a whisky sour."

"You got it." Jace smiles.

Returning to the table several minutes later, Alex takes his seat.

"You were right, Bree. Uncle Charlie says police are calling it a murder-suicide."

"That's what I heard." Bree says.

Snatching his drink from the table, Alex takes a large gulp. "There was another incident this afternoon at the Blackthorn house. Apparently, Nora Blackthorn and her personal care worker, Kimmie Rogers, were killed."

"Oh my God. What happened?" Bree says. "I didn't know much about Kimmie, but Mrs. Blackthorn was a real sweetheart. We handle all her legal affairs. Who would want to hurt her? Someone looking for money, maybe?"

"Uncle Charlie said it was some kind of animal attack."

"That's bizarre. What kind of animal attack happens in this town?"

"I don't know. Uncle Charlie didn't get into details, but it sounds awful."

Alex takes another drink of the whisky sour and glances at his friends who appear to be stunned. "I hate to do this, but I think I should go and give Uncle Charlie a hand."

"It's all right, brother," Jace says. "We totally understand. Do what you have to do, and if I don't see you this evening, we'll meet up in the morning for an early run. How about eight?"

"Eight sounds good. I'll swing by and pick you up."

Turning to Bree, he asks, "What do you think, honey?"

"I think you should go. We'll be fine."

Smiling at Jace, Alex says, "I guess you can have my scallops after all."

Outside the restaurant, the early spring air hangs heavy with an evening moisture that's blowing in off the Atlantic. Alex inhales deeply, relishing the salty breeze.

"Ahh, springtime in Nova Scotia," he whispers, making his way to his black Honda Civic. When it came to buying a car two years ago, he went with reliability and performance over the sporty looks. "You gotta love the weather."

Then he shudders at the thoughts of what awaits him at the hospital. He feels guilty about leaving his friends, but he also feels he needs to do whatever he can to help in any emergency.

He's about to grab the door handle when an uneasy feeling washes over him. He knows he's being watched.

By what?

He glances around the parking lot. "There you are," he whispers, spying a murder of crows that have gathered on the branches of a large fir tree. He slowly approaches them. "Are you trying to hide from me?"

He quietly counts the crows. "Ten. ... Of course there are. What's going on, fellas? Do you know anything about today's deaths?"

The crows remain quiet, then suddenly spring from the branches and take flight, soaring off into the grey sky.

"Where are you going? I need answers," he yells after them. "What the hell's happening?"

8: Something in the air

"Hey, you." The extremely thin doctor looks up as Alex walks into the emergency department at the local hospital. "I thought you were having dinner with your friends."

"I was, but I figured you could use my help."

Alex hadn't noticed just how exhausted his uncle looks until he sees him under the fluorescent lights that illuminate the nurses' station where the older doctor is reviewing patient charts. The silver steaks running through his dark-brown hair and the black circles under his eyes accentuate the man's premature old age.

Alex knows the past ten years have been difficult for his uncle. Ever since his Aunt Rebecca died of cancer, Charlie Webster has been struggling with prolonged bouts of sleeplessness and depression. Add to that the burdens of working in a short-handed, underfunded medical system, and Alex knows it's a wonder Charlie is still coping. He's worried about his uncle, but he's relieved his mentor is about to retire and is planning on taking a long vacation with his best friend, Oliver Lewis.

"What the hell happened around here today?"

Charlie shakes his head. "All I know is that we have five deceased individuals from two locations in different parts of the county. Three men and two women. They all died violently, and it all seems like too much of a coincidence to me. The males are already in the morgue, but I've still got to examine the females. Paramedics just brought them in. The police want an initial report before they go to autopsy."

"What do you need me to do?"

"I've got to meet with the RCMP, so I will be tied up for a bit. Would you mind looking after the patients in the waiting room? I don't know what's happened today, but suddenly, the place is packed, and I won't get to them for a while."

"Absolutely, Uncle Charlie."

Alex glances toward the waiting room and immediately feels intimidated by the crowd gathered there. It's practically wall to wall people and he can't recall ever seeing it so packed. "Do what you have to do, and I'll see what I can do about moving some of these people out of here."

Charlie smiles as he turns to walk away. "If you need me for anything serious, have one of the nurses come and get me. I'll be in Exam Room 5."

Watching his uncle stride down the dimly lit corridor, one of the fluorescent lights quickly flickering on and off as he passes, Alex marvels at the man's stamina and drive to keep going through these tough years. He only hopes he has as much dedication and energy if he's ever faced with a similar situation.

Alex draws in a deep breath through clenched teeth, and steels his nerves. He knows this is going to be a long night. "Okay, Dr. Goodwin," he whispers. He's not sure he will ever get used to the sound of that. "Pull your shit together and let's get after it."

Studying a chart, he walks into Exam Room 2, where he greets his first patient, a man who was his grade eleven English teacher.

"Hello, Mr. Harrison. What's going on with you this evening?" Alex asks, assessing the heavy-set, middle-aged man perched uncomfortably on the end of the gurney. The sweat beading on the man's wrinkled forehead and his heavy breathing confirm that he is in distress.

"Hi, Alex." The man wheezes. "I think I'm having a heart attack."

Alex glances at the chart again. "I don't know about that, Mr. Harrison, but based on the vitals they took in triage, your blood pressure is much higher than it should be. It's getting very close to the danger zone, and we may have to keep you overnight. I can't let you go home if it's that high."

"Really?"

"Don't know for sure yet, but we're going to run some tests to try to determine what's going on. High blood pressure hasn't previously shown up in your chart, so this is new. Can you tell me how you feel right now?"

"Crappy," the man answers. He takes a deep breath and adds, "By the way, Alex, it's nice to see you."

"It's nice to see you, too," he says with a smile. He always liked Mr. Harrison.

"I hear wonderful things about you all the time from your mother. Congratulations on becoming a doctor. I am proud of you, Alex."

"Thank you, Mr. Harrison." Alex smiles again. He snugly secures the blood pressure cuff to the man's left arm, just above the elbow.

"I see Samantha every now and again around town. I get all the news from her. She is very proud of you, as she should be."

"Yes. Thank you for that, but please stop talking now so we can get an accurate reading." It's clear to Alex that his former teacher has taken on a few extra pounds since he last saw him. "And please open your shirt for me."

The man quietly complies and Alex places the stethoscope on the man's chest.

"Tell me, Mr. Harrison, are you currently experiencing any dizziness or light-headedness?"

"As a matter of fact, I am, and I've also been feeling some tightness in my chest. I was scared it might be a heart attack."

Alex can see his patient is becoming emotional.

"Is that it? Am I having a heart attack?"

"We can't rule anything out, so we are going to check." Alex listens again. "Now, try to relax. Can you take a deep breath for me and hold it?"

The man breathes in and holds it.

"Exhale. Another one, please."

"It's a heart attack. I knew it. I'm going to die."

"Please calm down, Mr. Harrison. We are just being cautious," Alex says. "I want to get an EKG. Is your wife with you?"

The older man shakes his head.

"How did you get here?"

"I drove."

Alex grimaces. "You know, it may not have been safe for you to drive yourself to the hospital. You could have had an accident if your condition had worsened while you were behind the wheel."

"I didn't want her here. She's trying to kill me."

"What do you mean, she's *trying to kill you*? What makes you think that?"

"Because she put something in my drink?"

"Like what?"

"I don't know but I was feeling fine until she made me a cup of tea, and I haven't been feeling well ever since."

"I see." Alex studies his patient. "Okay, then. We're going to run some blood tests, so if Mrs. Harrison has given you anything she shouldn't have, it will show up. In the meantime, I want you to lie back and get comfortable. We need you to relax."

"That's easier said than done."

"I know, Mr. Harrison, but try not to worry. You may exacerbate the problem if you get worked up. I need to you remain calm so close your eyes and relax."

"Sure, cause that's so easy to do."

Entering Exam Room 1, Alex finds eleven-year-old Sadie Winchester sitting in one of the green plastic chairs, holding her left arm close to her body, tears streaming down her face.

"Well, Sadie." Alex smiles and kneels in front of the chair. "Why don't you tell me what's going on with that arm?"

"It's broken."

"I see. You're sure of that?"

"That's what Mommy said." The girl says between sobs, and Alex can see she's terrified.

He glances to the woman standing over the girl. She is one of the cleaning crew he's seen around the hospital over the past few months. "Hi, Mrs. Winchester." He speaks softly. "Can you tell me what happened to Sadie?"

"I'm not one hundred percent sure," the woman says. "Sadie says that Sean, that's her older brother, pushed her down the stairs to the rec room. But I wasn't there and didn't see anything."

"I'm sure he didn't mean to do it."

"Yes, he did," Sadie cries. "He pushed me."

Alex gingerly touches the girl's arm. She immediately flinches and instinctively pulls back.

"Does that hurt?"

The girl sobs again. "Yes."

"Okay, then." Alex stands to address the mother. "On first glance, there could be a fracture, but we can't say for sure until we get an X-ray."

"Is this going to take long, Doctor?"

He can see the woman is very distraught. "I can't really say. As you can see by the waiting room, we are pretty backed up right now."

"I have a shift at eight and we can't afford for me to lose a night's pay."

Alex glances at his watch. It's almost six-thirty. "We'll be as quick as we can, but we'll have to wait until the radiographer on duty gets here to do the X-ray. I'm sorry, but I have no idea how long that will take. Is there anyone who can come to be with Sadie if we're not done in time for you to go to work?"

"No. Her father's out of town on some kind of fishing trip, or something stupid like that with his friends. They're all useless assholes, all four of them." She rolls her eyes. "And everyone else I know is busy. It is Friday night, you know, and Sadie was going to stay over with a friend because of my shift, but it doesn't look like that's going to work out."

"I can't promise you anything, Mrs. Winchester, but I will see what I can do to move things along quickly."

Smiling at the girl, he adds, "Now, Sadie, I know it hurts, but try to keep your arm as still as possible. Can you do that for me?"

The girl nods.

"Good. We'll get you to X-ray as soon as possible. Depending upon what it shows, we may have to put your arm in a cast."

Sadie starts crying again.

"Don't worry." Alex says. "I promise it won't hurt."

"Thank you, Doctor," her mother says as he leaves the room.

Poor woman, Alex thinks and moves onto Exam Room 3. *What's next?*

His question is answered when he finds a nurse holding a bandage to a young woman's right hand. Blood is seeping through the gauze.

"What's going on here?" he asks, while reviewing the woman's chart. He pulls on a pair of blue, latex gloves.

"Penny." His eyebrows rise as he addresses his patient. "Right?"

The blonde woman nods. He doesn't recognize her from around town, but there are a lot of people moving into the area so he isn't surprised.

"It says here you have a severe laceration to your right hand. May I look?"

When she nods, Alex lifts the bandage and studies the cut. "This looks more like a puncture wound than a cut. How did this happen, Penny?"

"The bitch stabbed me."

Alex glances to the nurse, who nods. "Someone stabbed you? I see here you work in one of the local insurance companies. Would you mind telling me what happened?"

"I asked Sharon to pass me a letter opener, and instead of just passing it to me like any normal person, she walked over to my desk and drove the god-damned thing right into my hand. It hurt like hell. I'm going to kill her when I see her again."

"I don't think you will kill anyone. Did you report this to the police? If that's what happened, it may be considered an assault."

"No, and I don't plan to. I'm going to handle this my way."

"Well, whatever you do, Penny, I would advise you not to engage in a fight with your colleague. That will only make matters worse, and you could get yourself in a whole lot of trouble."

"If I want your advice, Doctor, I will ask for it." The woman pulls back her hand as Alex attempts to examine the wound. "So, what are you going to do about this?"

"For starters, we are going to clean it and then this will need some stitches."

"Jesus Christ. I hate needles. Just wait until I get my hands on Sharon.

I'll break her fucking neck."

To the nurse, Alex says, "Can you please wash the wound? I'll get the lidocaine so we can get it numb."

The nurse nods. "What are you going to use for stitches?"

"I'm going with nylon. Nylon will give her hand more flexibility than anything else."

"How many stitches am I going to need?" the woman asks.

"Just looking at it, I'm going to say at least five, but maybe six or seven. It's a pretty big wound and it needs to be closed so it can heal properly."

"This fucking sucks."

"I'm sure it does." Alex prepares the needle with the lidocaine. "Why do you think your colleague stabbed you? Were you arguing? Is she normally aggressive?"

"I have no god-damned idea," Penny fumes as Alex gingerly injects several doses of lidocaine around the open cut. "Ow." She tries to pull her hand back. "Take it easy. That hurts."

"Just give it a second and you won't feel a thing."

Several minutes later, Alex completes the seventh and last stitch. "There," he says, admiring his handiwork without being too obvious. "All done. I'm going to write you a prescription for paracetamol just in case you need something for pain. It will also help for infection."

"This better not leave a scar," the woman replies, slipping into her jacket.

"Please keep your hand out of water for at least three or four days," Alex says. "I'd recommend keeping it dry for as long as possible. You don't want to reopen the wound."

"Right." The woman snatches the prescription paper from the doctor's hand and leaves the exam room.

"You're welcome," Alex whispers while making notes in the woman's charts.

As he leaves the exam room with his head down, reviewing the chart for the patient who awaits him in Exam Room 4, he nearly collides with his uncle and two RCMP officers who are chatting in the corridor.

"Hey there, Dr. Goodwin," Corporal Warren Hamilton says. "Careful."

Alex glances up from the chart, embarrassed. "Sorry, guys. I didn't see you."

"How's it going, Alex?" Charlie asks.

"Good. But I've noticed something really strange."

Warren's left eyebrow rises. "How so, if I'm allowed to ask."

"You are," Charlie answers.

"I'm not sure if it's anything, really," Alex begins. He glances from his uncle to the police officers, one of whom he hopes will be his father-in-law someday soon. "But I've noticed a pattern emerging in the patients I have already examined, and in just looking at the chart for my next patient—who says a co-worker attacked him with a hammer—everyone is presenting with injuries they sustained in some sort of physical altercation."

Warren asks, "All these people were attacked by someone else?"

Alex nods. "At least, that's what they are claiming. But people seem to be presenting with injuries that appear to be the result of an unusually high level of aggressive behaviour."

Glancing at the over-crowded waiting room, Constable Nolan Shaw asks, "All of these people?"

"I can't say for certain until I examine them," Alex answers. "But that's how it looks. The poor nurses can't keep up. No sooner do they clear a few patients, then several others show up."

"What do you think this means?" Warren asks, glancing from one doctor to the other.

"I don't know." Charlie says. "Most of the time the patients come here for a variety of issues and illnesses. Usually, we only see a few minor injuries in the course of a day. To have this many people show up with injuries inflicted by someone else is extraordinary, in my opinion."

"It's got be something in the air," Constable Shaw quips.

Alex replies, "That may be more accurate than you realize."

9: Saturday morning

April 6

Rolling over in his bed—the same bed he slept in while he was growing up —Alex grabs his phone from the charger on the nightstand.

"Shit." He sighs.

He sees it's still only six-thirty-three. After the night he put in at the hospital—not getting home until almost two-thirty—he had hoped that he might be able to sleep in for a least another hour. He isn't meeting Jace until eight for their run.

But he decides it's no good to lie there hoping he may fall back to sleep, because he knows there's no chance of that happening. His mind will wander, and he'll be jumping to conclusions about the strange things that have been happening since yesterday afternoon, and then he'll start freaking out.

The thing about being a med student and a young doctor is that one's body learns to adjust to less sleep than most people require. He figures he hasn't had a full night's sleep in well over ten years—it ever.

So why would tonight be any different?

Sliding out of bed and moving to the window that looks out over the backyard, he sees the sun is just starting to break over the horizon. He shudders as he wonders what the day will bring.

He decides he must talk to someone and, even though it's very early on a Saturday morning, he sends a quick text to Oliver, his protector, who has been by his side through many of his past run-ins with the dark forces that hang over him and the ones he loves.

While there haven't been any serious threats to him in the past ten years, his instincts are telling Alex that today is somehow different.

Oliver is in Halifax this weekend, visiting his daughter, Isabel, but Alex is confident his friend will want to talk to him. *He always does.*

Hey man. Are you up? Let me know when you can talk.

He presses the send button and glances out the window again. He marvels at the spectacular pink sky that's breaking the darkness of the early spring morning.

How does that old saying go? Red sky at night, a sailor's delight. Red sky in the morning, sailors take warning.

"Shit." He feels the goosebumps rise on his arms. He knows better than to dismiss old wives' tales. He will never dismiss anything just because he doesn't understand it. He knows there are many natural forces in the world that defy logical thinking and simple reasoning.

Sometimes, there are no easy answers, he thinks as he hears his phone buzz.

Oliver's reply is simple.

    I'm awake

Alex chooses Oliver's number and listens as the call rings through.

"Hi, Alex," Oliver answers after the first ring. "What's up?"

Alex moves across the room and takes a seat on the edge of his bed. "I think something's going on that you should know about."

"Are you in danger?"

"Not me specifically. Everyone."

Oliver pauses. "I don't follow. What do you mean, *everyone*?"

"It feels like something in the universe has slipped." Alex pauses to gather his thoughts. "It started yesterday afternoon when I saw the Spirit Crow and then the old man told me it was a sign that something horrible was about to happen. He said it was all connected to the solar eclipse that's going to take place on Monday."

"Slow down, buddy. I have no idea what you're talking about. What's a *Spirit Crow* and what old man?"

"I ran into an old man yesterday at Pine Grove and that was right after I saw an albino crow. It was beautiful, but I think it was the weirdest thing I've ever seen."

"I don't know, Alex. You've seen some pretty weird things."

"Anyway, the old man told me that the white crow was a sign that a terrible tragedy was about to happen. He says it's happened in the past when the forces of the eclipse have compelled living things to turn on each other. Since he told me this, there has been an extraordinary number of violent acts around here. There were five deaths yesterday afternoon alone. God only knows what today will bring."

"Anyone I know?"

"Probably. It's a small town."

"Do you feel you are in any danger, Alex?" Oliver asks. "If I leave right now, I can be back there in less than two hours."

"I don't feel there's any immediate danger to me, but I am worried because apparently this compulsion to hurt people can happen to anyone, without warning. The old man says even the animals can snap."

"I'm coming home."

"No, Oliver. I know this is your weekend with Isabel and I don't want to take you away from her. It's important that you be with your daughter, but I just wanted to talk to you. I always feel safer after we chat."

"It's been so long since anything has happened, Alex. I had hoped that maybe things were finally going to be normal in our world. I've been happy that you can move on with your life."

"Yeah, well, I hoped for that too."

"So, who was this old man you were talking about?"

"He wasn't anyone I recognized."

"Is he dangerous?"

"I don't think so. I mean, I didn't sense that he wanted to hurt me."

"I've taught you to never take anyone for granted because even if they seem kind, they may have ulterior motives. In our world, there are many dangers."

"I haven't forgotten." Alex rises from the bed and goes to the window again. The sky is now clear, and the sun has risen over the horizon. It's truly awe-inspiring. "I just have a feeling I can trust him."

"You need to find out who he is and what he wants. Don't let your guard down around him."

"I'll see what I can find out."

"I don't like this."

Oliver pauses and Alex can feel his friend's anxiety rising. Seconds later, Oliver adds, "And I don't like the idea of leaving you alone and exposed. I feel I should be there."

"I've learned a lot from you over the years, Oliver. I can take care of myself." He glances at the trees in the backyard. "Besides, the crows are here to protect me."

"How many?"

Alex does a quick count. "Ten. I saw them yesterday and they are already out here this morning. They're just watching and waiting."

"The question is, waiting for what?"

"Exactly." Alex pauses. "But I feel safer with them around."

"Call me the minute you feel you're in danger."

"You know I will."

"I don't know any such thing. In fact, if I know you, you'll try to handle this on your own even if it means putting yourself in harm's way."

"No, I won't." Alex says. "You can trust me."

"Can I?"

"Yes, Oliver, but I appreciate your concern. I just wanted to chat and give you a heads up that something could be brewing back here. You know, just in case," Alex says. "Now, I want you to have a great day with Isabel."

"I'll try, but you know I'll be thinking about you and what's happening in town."

Alex chuckles. "How are you and Uncle Charlie ever going to go to Europe for two months? You won't be able to hop on a plane and come back to town if something happens."

"I don't know. Maybe a trip isn't such a good idea at this time. I only agreed to it because it seemed like things had finally calmed down with you, but now—"

"Both you and Uncle Charlie need to get away. I want you to go. And on that note, I have to grab a shower and go meet my friend."

"Jace? How is he?"

"He's fine. We're going for a run at eight, so I've got to get a move on."

"You are the only person I know who has a shower before he goes for a run and then has another shower when he's done." Oliver chuckles.

"I need the first shower to wake me up."

Alex ends the call and studies the ten crows outside his window. The large ebony birds have remained still, hardly moving since he first spotted them.

He grabs his robe and heads to the shower.

Minutes later, he finds his parents in the kitchen, having coffee.

"Well, would you look at that," he says. "Two of my favourite women in the same place at one time. When was the last time that happened?"

"Not recently," Samantha answers. Her eyes sparkle. "Kate's been so busy these days that it feels like I'm sharing the house with the invisible woman."

Kate rolls her eyes and smiles at Alex. "It's been busy at the office."

"Believe me, I know," he says. "You're working Bree so hard that I thought maybe she had relocated to another town and forgot to tell me."

"She wanted to be a lawyer," Kate replies smugly. "That means being busy and sometimes making sacrifices."

"And she really loves the work. Although I'm not sure what that would mean for our family life though. A lawyer and a doctor won't have much time for each other."

"That's the challenge," Samantha says. "If you love each other and you want to be together, then you find a way to make it work."

She reaches across the table and takes her wife's hand. "It's just very important that you find time to be with each other and never stop talking to one another."

"Like you two?"

Kate winks at him. "What are you up to today?"

"I'm meeting Jace for a run, then we're going to have breakfast with Bree and Luna." He grabs a glass from the cupboard and pours himself a drink of cold water from the pitcher in the fridge. "They are going shopping for the day and I'm going to show Jace around the hospital and Uncle Charlie's offices. He wants to see where I'm going to be working."

"Don't forget you're coming back here tonight for a little celebration," Samantha says. "It's not every day that you graduate from medical school, so I'm planning a great dinner. It would be nice if you guys could be back here for six."

"I haven't forgotten." Alex takes a large gulp of water. "What's for dinner?"

"I've already made your favourite lasagne and there will be Caesar salad with garlic toast. And for those who don't like that, I'm making my country chuck roast with mushroom gravy, sour cream and onion mashed potatoes, and rosemary roasted baby carrots. We're having coconut cream cheesecake for dessert." She pauses. "Do you think I need another dessert? Not everyone likes coconut. Maybe something light?"

"No," Alex and Kate answer in unison.

"You know your mother, Alex." Kate laughs. "She can't do anything simple. It's always a major production."

"Who are you expecting?" Alex asks.

"Just a few close family members," Samantha replies. "Hunter, Ally and your nephews, Dominic and Dante. They are so proud of you. Of course, Bree will be here and her parents, as well as Cliff and Julie Graham. They are practically family, so I had to invite them. And your two friends."

Kate adds, "Charlie would be here, but he's working the night shift, so he won't make it."

"It's going to be a full house." Alex pauses and studies the two women. Finally, he says, "So listen. I have a question that I'm sure you're going to find really strange."

"What's that?" Kate asks. "And for the record, Alex, nothing sounds strange anymore."

"There's been a lot of talk about the solar eclipse on Monday. Do either of you remember the last total solar eclipse to pass over the province? According to what I could find on the Internet, it happened in 1972."

Both women shrug in unison, glancing at each other.

"Why?" Samantha says.

"No reason." He chooses not to tell them about the old man's warning. "I was curious about the last time it happened. You know, did anything strange happen around here?"

Samantha shakes her head. "I don't think so but, even though I can remember all the way back to when I was a young child, I don't remember anything about an eclipse ever occurring over this town." She pauses, then adds, "That's very odd, isn't it?"

"Yes," Alex agrees. "Very strange."

"You know what," Kate says. "I can't remember it either. It's kind of like a black hole opened up in my mind and swallowed my memories from that period."

"Right." Samantha agrees. "It's all just one giant blank slate for me."

"You guys are intelligent women. Don't you think you would remember such a thing?" Alex asks. "It's not like an eclipse happens every day."

"You'd think so," Samantha says. "Wonder why we can't remember anything about that."

10: Biters in April

At one time, Warren Hamilton and Cliff Graham were best friends, almost like brothers. But in recent years, as Warren was promoted to corporal and took on more responsibilities with the RCMP, they've grown apart. Not because of any animosity or disagreements between them, but simply because life happened, as it does.

No matter the demands, however, they do make a point of reconnecting every so often, even if it's just to enjoy a beer and to check in on how the other is doing. Neither of them wants to let their friendship slip away entirely.

Warren also knows that if he needs advice on a case, he can always call upon Cliff. After all, even though he has been retired for more than ten years now, Cliff has a wealth of knowledge and experience that he'll readily share whenever he's asked. This is especially true where Warren is concerned, as he's helped Cliff out of many pinches in the past.

Today is one of those times when Warren has asked for help. And even though it's early on a Saturday morning and the offices are technically closed to the public, he's invited Cliff to meet with him at the detachment. He needs to discuss the events from yesterday without being interrupted or without anyone eavesdropping on their conversation.

The last thing he needs right now is unsolicited advice clouding his judgment, so he thinks an unencumbered conversation between two seasoned police officers may give him the clarity he's seeking.

After dispensing with the usual pleasantries and small talk about family, the weather and the Blue Jays' early season woes, the two veteran officers have settled around the wooden table in the detachment's tiny lunchroom, each with a cup of coffee and each waiting for the other to begin.

"Where to start?" Warren takes a large gulp of his black coffee and curls up his mouth. "It's a small town and I know how quickly news travels, especially when it's something *juicy*. I'm sure you've heard all the wild speculation and rumours that have already been making the rounds."

"Funny how so many people know so much about an official police investigation when they have no idea what really happened. Hell, I bet you guys don't even know yet what happened."

Warren frowns. "It's a mystery, that's for sure."

Cliff leans back in the chair that seems too small to handle his bulk. At two hundred and forty pounds and almost six feet, four inches in height, he's a big man by most standards. But there's not much excess fat on his bones. "Sounds like you've got a lot on your hands, my friend."

"You don't know the half of it."

Cliff nods. "Tell me everything you can."

"That's the problem. We don't really know all that much." Warren takes another gulp of coffee, sits the mug on the table and then stares at the dark liquid. "We had five deaths yesterday, all caused by violent acts of aggression. Near as we can determine, the event at Echo Lake was a murder-suicide, although we still don't have any idea what would have caused Jimmy Spicer to go off on a rampage."

"I knew Jimmy," Cliff says. "It was a few years ago now, but he seemed like a nice enough fellow. He lost his way and got into a little trouble when he was younger, but I never saw him as the violent type." He shakes his head. "Never would have pegged him to be a killer."

"That's what I've heard about him, but as you and I know, people can snap without warning. We're hoping the ME can give us a better picture once they complete the autopsy."

Cliff nods. "What about the other case?"

"That's even more bizarre. Both the victims were attacked and killed by dogs. We located the two suspect animals and had them put down right away, so they won't be a danger to anyone else. I didn't want to do that, but we had no choice. The owners were devastated."

"I didn't know it was dogs. Were they known to be vicious?"

Warren shakes his head. "The dogs weren't known to be violent. They were said to be fairly docile animals, but yesterday they even killed two of Mrs. Blackthorn's little pups. It was a mess over there."

"I can imagine."

"But we don't have any idea what caused the dogs to attack like that. These cases do not appear to be connected, and both seem to be random with no compelling evidence to give us anything to go on." Warren takes another gulp of coffee. "And to top it off, lots of people around town seemed to lose control yesterday and became very aggressive towards others. Thankfully, there weren't any other deaths, but Dr. Webster and Alex Goodwin told me there were some brutal attacks reported at the hospital last night."

"Shit happens, Warren," Cliff says. "If there's one thing you can count on, it's that people will always surprise you with how far they can push the limits, especially in this town."

"That may have been true in the past, but it has been a long time since we've seen anything weird like this. I must admit, though, this one has me stumped."

"It only just happened yesterday, so don't be too hard on yourself, Brother. Take a deep breath, look at all the evidence, consider what you know and avoid jumping to conclusions."

"What would you do if you were in charge of this investigation?"

"I'd step back and try to look at it from the outside," Cliff suggests. "Don't make this personal."

"Because you never took any of your cases, personally?" Warren grins at his friend.

"True. I did. So, learn from my example and don't make the same mistakes that I made. I thought I had to personally solve every one of the cases that came my way, and look what happened with me. Remember Maggie Collins?"

Warren nods. "How could I forget? We almost lost you because of her."

"Exactly, so don't let this case do that to you. Step back. Assess the facts and use the officers at your disposal. The constables under your command are well trained to face this type of shit."

Cliff leans forward over the table to get closer to his friend. "I can see how much this is already bothering you but don't get sucked in. You do your job by letting your officers do their jobs. You lead; they follow."

"Easier said than done."

~

Constable Vanessa Bennett has been an RCMP officer for just over seven years. Following in the footsteps of her father and a brother who both worked in law enforcement, she believes police work is a calling and she loves the job, even early shifts on a Saturday morning.

She understands that, while being assigned to secure a crime scene may seem mundane or pedestrian to some people, it is an essential component of the investigation. She knows that keeping the curious looky-loos and scavenging, blood-sucking souvenir seekers and photographers away from the scene at Echo Lake is vital to maintaining the integrity of the case. While some of her colleagues frown upon such assignments, she takes them in stride.

"Someone has to do it," she says, often being the first to volunteer even if that duty means sitting in her cruiser overnight in a secluded wooded area where three people died.

One of the perks of this particular assignment, however, was watching the sun come up over the horizon. With its bright pink hues and brilliant shades of orange mixed with a hint of yellow, it was a sight to behold.

A little slice of Heaven amid pure unadulterated evil, she thinks. *Simply magical.*

When she arrived at Echo Lake last evening, the place was crawling with police officers and forensic investigators, collecting evidence and interviewing witnesses. By ten o'clock, however, the place had cleared out and she was left alone.

She's expecting relief in about fifteen minutes when the investigators are due back, although she thinks they've pretty much collected all the evidence they're going to find at this scene.

This case seems pretty cut and dried to her. *For whatever reason, one man slipped a gear, killed two of his co-workers and then drove his truck into the back of the massive tree harvester,* she thinks, while staring at the large piece of equipment with the smaller truck impaled by a giant log that decapitated the driver. Even though the body has been removed and the vehicle has been covered with several large tarps, the scene still gives her goosebumps.

Why does someone do something like that? She knows there may never be a simple answer to that question as such "sick" acts of violence are never easy to explain. She's been accused of being too cynical over the years, but if there is one thing she has learned, it's that people's depravity knows no boundaries.

She glances at her watch. It's seven-forty-six, meaning relief will soon be arriving.

But last night wasn't so bad, she thinks, suddenly feeling a small pinch on the back of her neck. She swipes at the side of her face as she feels something crawling on her skin.

"Got you, you little bastard," she says, examining the small, black fly squashed between her thumb and finger. "What are you doing here this early into the season?"

Growing up in Nova Scotia and having spent much of her youth in the woods with her parents and two siblings on fishing and camping excursions, Vanessa knows there are no biters in April. The black fly season arrives in these parts promptly in the first week of May.

Yet here you are, you little sucker. She flicks the fly's bloody remains to the floor of her cruiser.

"You're just a little keener than the others, aren't you?" she says. "An over-achiever. But you won't get any more blood from me this morning, you little bastard."

She shrugs off the unseasonable appearance of the tiny fly as a quirk of nature, until buzzing within the car becomes too loud for her to ignore.

"What the hell?" She mumbles, quickly glancing around the vehicle's interior. "Blackflies. This is so strange. You shouldn't here. It's way too early for you."

As more and more blackflies gather, swarming around her head and face, Vanessa quickly checks all the windows and vents to make sure they are closed.

Tight. So how the fuck are you guys getting in?

She grabs the door handle and pushes it open. Frantically swatting at the flies, she slides from behind the wheel and plants her feet on the cold ground.

"Leave me alone, you little fuckers," she screams.

"Vanessa?" It's Constable Nolan Shaw. She had been so preoccupied with the flies that she had not seen him arrive. "What are you doing?"

"Flies." She screams, swatting at the hundreds of insects buzzing around her head. "There's so many fucking flies. Maybe thousands."

"Where did they come from?"

"I don't know." She's frantic. "But they're biting me everywhere and the little fuckers hurt."

Constable Shaw tries to grab his colleague's flailing arms in an effort to calm her down. "Let me help."

"Just get them off me." She swats at her face and hands. Falling to her knees, she cries, "I can't stand it. Don't just stand there, do something. Get them off me."

Nolan quickly grabs his walkie and calls for back up.

"Corporal Hamilton," he says, suppressing the urge to panic. "Are you on mic?"

"Hamilton is a go," the superior officer immediately responds.

"Sir. I am out here at Echo Lake, and something is going on with Constable Bennett. She's being attacked and I need help."

"Attacked by what?"

"Flies. I think there's thousands of them and they're biting her everywhere. What should I do?"

"Jesus. Any other animals in the vicinity?" Corporal Hamilton asks.

Nolan quickly glances around the clearing. "Not that I can see."

"Are the flies coming after you too?"

"No sir. It's like they are targeting Vanessa."

"Try to get her to safety. Look for shelter where the flies can't get her and call for an ambulance. I am on my way."

11: Scrambled eggs and toast

Flora and Teddy Randolph will celebrate their thirty-seventh wedding anniversary later this month and, while they've had a few bumps along the way, they will agree they've had a happy life together. With three children and four grandchildren that they adore, the couple feel blessed in their comfortable—some would point out mundane—existence.

But, as they quickly note, they've had everything they ever needed in their relationship. A comfortable home. Supportive family and friends. A safe environment in which to raise their children. But above all, they had each other and their good health. They are not in want of anything.

Teddy has worked as a welder at the local marine shop for almost forty-one years while Flora stayed at home and raised the children. She loved being a stay-at-home mom, believing that's what she was meant to do as her family was her whole world.

They relished this arrangement and, now that the children are grown with families of their own, the Randolphs are looking forward to his retirement next year. They plan to cash in their savings, sell their home, buy an RV and travel, something they've been yearning to do for a long time.

They've always wanted to experience the world, starting with a long-talked-about road trip across Canada to see the Rockies, and then taking an exciting side adventure down to explore the Grand Canyon and to Yellowstone National Park to witness the eruption of Old Faithful. That's been on their bucket lists almost since the first time they met at one of the weekly Friday night dances down at the local Legion Hall.

But for now, they are content to blissfully go about their regular, mundane lives, happy to enjoy the love they feel for each other and celebrating all the positives they have. *What's another year of work when they're going to have the rest of their lives together?* they figure.

"Morning, honey." Flora smiles while her husband takes his seat at the kitchen table that's strategically located in front of the window looking out over the sprawling backyard where the early spring plants are just starting to come alive. This chair at the kitchen table is where Teddy's been sitting since they moved into this quaint bungalow thirty-five years ago.

They've toiled on this property for over three decades, turning it into their summertime retreat. Teddy proudly points out that the land was nothing more than a pile of rocks when they bought the house. He cleared many of them by hand so that he and Flora could have the backyard oasis they had dreamed of.

"But that's Nova Scotia," he explains the obvious to anyone who will listen, noting the vast amount of fill they've added to the property to create the lush lawn and impressive garden beds. Flora has spent hundreds of hours in the gardens each summer, tending to her plants. She is especially proud of her rose bushes, most notably the Persian yellow variety.

"It's our little slice of heaven," she tells everyone when they rave about the beautiful backyard.

As Teddy settles in to enjoy a cup of tea with his favourite Saturday morning breakfast, Flora continues, "So, I have been thinking."

"I can only imagine." He chuckles and smirks wryly, the way he always does when he's feeling especially playful, as he is this morning.

"Stop it." Flora laughs. "Seriously, Teddy. I was thinking that when you finally do retire next year, the first thing we should do is hold a giant yard sale and unload some of this stuff we've accumulated."

"I think you mean crap. That would be a good idea, but only if you could stand to part with some of these *treasures* that you've collected."

He smiles at his wife as she makes his scrambled eggs and toast just like she's done for almost four decades. It's their usual Saturday morning routine.

"You know, when push comes to shove, Flora, you will never let go of all these things. You're just too sentimental." He pauses and then asks, "Were you pounding something in here a few minutes ago before I came in? I thought I heard someone banging on something."

"I was tenderizing some steak," she replies, not skipping a beat in the breakfast preparation. She's done it so often she thinks she could make his breakfast with her eyes closed. "I'm going to put it in some marinade and then I thought maybe you could barbecue it for dinner tonight. I'll make a potato salad to go with it."

She breaks two eggs into her favourite blue mixing bowl and adds a splash of milk before sliding two slices of wholewheat bread into the toaster, while also thinking about her husband's assessment of her penchant for collecting things. She knows he has a point about what he considers to be clutter.

She clears her throat and says, "It is true that there are some special things around here that I can never part with."

"Like what?"

"Like some of the crafts the kids made for us when they were in school and the cute little gifts they gave us when they were younger, and a couple of family heirlooms. But other than that, I think we really need to downsize if we're going to travel."

He rolls his eyes. "In other words, junk."

"It's not all junk." Flora knows how her husband feels about the many knick-knacks and collectibles she has accumulated and stashed into every little cubbyhole she can find. "But you are right. I'm sure there are a lot of things I could get rid of."

"So why wait until next year? Why not have a big yard sale this summer and get rid of whatever we can," Teddy suggests. "I have been meaning to clean out the garage, so having a yard sale would be a good excuse for me to finally do it. There's so much clutter in the garage, I wouldn't even think about trying to fit the car inside."

"Okay then." Flora pours the egg and milk mixture into the non-stick frying pan she's been using for more years than she can remember. Despite the dents and scrapes, she would never part with the reliable pan as the eggs never stick. "Let's plan on it for some time in mid-June before it gets too hot."

Teddy nods. "That will give us two months to pull some shit together."

"Teddy." When Flora uses her scolding voice, he knows he's crossed the line. "Please don't use that language in the house. You know how much I hate that, and I would think that after all these years you would know better."

"Sorry, dear." He smiles. "And I would think *you* would have learned by now that it's not easy for me to change, but I promise I will try to do better."

"No, you won't."

She retrieves the toast after it pops and spreads a modest amount of non-fat, low-sodium margarine on each slice. His cholesterol was running high at his last checkup and she's worried because he doesn't pay attention to such things. Carrying his toast and scrambled eggs to the table, she places the plate in front of him. She smiles at the only man she's ever truly loved. "I don't expect you'll ever change your ways, but I love you just the same."

She gives him a quick kiss on the top of his balding head before heading back to the stove, where she begins to clean up the mess she's made. "So, what are you up to today?"

"I was thinking I'll start doing a little clean up around the yard." He shakes a good amount of pepper onto his scrambled eggs, something he's always done, even before Flora started making breakfast for him. "It could be fairly nice out there this morning, so I want to get rid of some of those leaves and branches that came down over the winter. I'll haul them out to the municipal chipping yard after lunch. If you'd like to come with me, maybe we can take a little drive after I dump them. We can stop and get an ice cream. Our favourite shop opened yesterday for the season. I know how much you like their sundaes."

"I'd love that." She smiles and watches as her husband puts a large helping of eggs on his fork and stuffs it into his mouth. "How are your eggs, dear?"

He immediately stops chewing.

"Good," he slowly answers. "But did you do something different with them this morning?"

"What do you mean?"

"I don't know. They just taste different."

He glances down at his plate and sees several drops of red liquid mixing with his scrambled eggs. He recognizes it as blood. He spits the eggs back into the plate, puts his hands to his mouth and cries, "Flora. What did you put in the eggs?"

"Just something a little extra to make them special for you this morning."

She slowly moves closer to her husband.

He wipes the blood from his mouth and chin and examines the eggs. "What is that? Jesus Christ." He cries. "Is that glass?"

"Something special just for you."

Before he can react to his wife standing behind him, he feels a knife blade slowly slide from just below his left ear, slice through his throat and exit just below his right ear.

He tries to scream, but the words are muffled by the rush of blood that gurgles from the gash in his throat. His hands turn red as he clamps them over the gaping wound.

"Why?" His word is nothing more than a whisper.

"Just because."

She thrusts the blade directly into the top of his skull. Teddy immediately slumps forward, planting his face in his scrambled eggs and toast.

"Just because," she whispers.

Turning from her husband's spasming body, Flora slowly strolls to the living room and retrieves her cell phone from the charger.

"911." The dispatcher answers on the second ring. "What is the nature of your emergency?"

"Please send someone to 45 Red Spruce Lane. I've just killed my husband."

"Can you please repeat that, madam," the dispatcher requests.

Flora stops talking. She leaves the phone turned on and places it on the coffee table.

In the utility closet off the living room, she finds a strand of yellow rope, quickly ties a noose in one end, goes out of the house through the kitchen door onto the back deck, where she ties the other end around the railing.

Climbing up on the railing, she slips the noose over her head and, without hesitation, leaps.

As the rope goes taut, Flora's neck snaps and she dies instantly.

12: A run in the park

By the time Alex pulls up in front of the Hugin and Munin, Jace is pacing the sidewalk.

Alex shifts his car into park, turns off the engine and puts the window down. He smiles up at his friend. "Sorry, bud. Have you been waiting long? I got pulled into a conversation with my parents and they had so many questions. You know how much they love to chat."

"I may have been out here for maybe about ten minutes, but it's all right. The cool air will do me good."

"Everything okay? You seem a little rattled this morning."

Jace exhales. His warm breath forms a small cloud in front of his face as it leaves his mouth. "I didn't sleep very well last night."

"Why?" Alex glances to the century-old house that the new owners have completely gutted and refurbished. The property had fallen into a complete state of disrepair after the former owner died and the heirs walked away from it because of back taxes and the extensive repairs that needed to be carried out. "Something wrong with this place?"

"Nope. It's very comfortable. Luna slept like a log, but I just couldn't dose off."

"What's going on, Jace?"

"Not sure, brother. Just a little anxiety, I guess. Maybe it's all the excitement of finally wrapping up our studies and planning for the future. It's a lot, you know?"

"Oh yes." Alex smiles. "Remember, I'm in the same boat."

"Not exactly. With you taking over your uncle's practice, your future is pretty much carved in stone. Me, on the other hand, I'm not really sure where I'm going."

"You have a lot of options, Jace. With the doctor shortage across North America and especially here in the province, you could pretty much go wherever you want to go."

"That's just the thing, Alex," Jace admits. "I'm not really sure where I want to go."

"Well, wherever you choose, you better make damned sure that it's some place Luna is going to like."

"Yeah." Jace exhales again. "Right."

Alex studies his friend. "You sure it's not something else that's got your knickers in a knot?"

"Man!" Jace stares at his friend. "You know me so well after all these years. How do you do that?"

"It's just a thing I have."

"Oh yes." Jace looks sharply at his friend. "That *thing*."

"When it comes to the feelings of other people, I just have strong intuitive powers and I'm sensing that there's more to this story than what you're telling me."

Jace glances down at the pavement. "Okay. You're right. It's just so much coming at me all at once. Graduation and deciding where I want to practice medicine. Or even if I'm ready to set up practice. The last few months, I've been thinking that maybe I want to go back to school and choose a specialty."

"In what?"

"I'm thinking neuro medicine or maybe cardiology. I'm honestly not sure which way to go."

"Okay. Well, if that's what you want to do, then do it."

"You know it's more complicated than that."

"Is it?" Alex's right eyebrow rises. "What else is bothering you?"

After a long moment, Jace says, "I promised Luna that once I graduate, I'll be ready to settle down. You know, get married, buy a house, and have kids. She wants to put down roots and I get that. She's waited a long time for me to finish school."

"But you're not ready for that, are you?"

Jace shakes his head.

"Have you talked to Luna about this? You need to tell her what you're feeling."

"I've tried a hundred times, but whenever we start talking about making plans, she always leads the conversation toward a wedding and buying a house. We never seem to talk about what *I* want."

Alex motions toward the passenger side of the car. "Get in. I'm taking us to Pine Grove Park. It's a great place for a run and I think that's what you need right now. It will take your mind off things."

Jace hesitates, then shakes his head. "Nah, I don't think so. I was waiting out here to tell you I'm bailing on our run. I'm just not feeling it today."

"Don't turn your back to the things you like doing. You love running, and it will relieve some of that pent-up stress you're feeling. That's what you've always told me when I've been in a funk."

Jace backs away from the car. "You go, buddy. I'm just going stay right here and try to grab a nap. Bree is supposed to be picking Luna up at nine to go shopping, and once she leaves, I'm going to grab some shut-eye ... I hope. I think a few hours' sleep will do me good."

"I don't want to leave you here alone, not after I bailed on you guys last night."

"Don't worry about any of that, Alex. Duty called. It's what we do. But I need to do this if I'm going to feel like dinner at your parents' place to-night."

"Well, mister, you better feel like it. My mom's cooking up a storm today. Furthermore, you and I are the guests of honour, remember?"

Jace smiles. "Now, go and take your run. I'm going back to bed for a bit."

"Okay, buddy. If you're sure. But I want you to be ready for eleven. I'll be back here to pick you up and then I'm giving you the grand tour of our local medical facilities. And don't forget that we're meeting the girls at one for lunch."

~

Alex parks and gets out of his car. He's disappointed this weekend isn't going exactly how he had planned it.

So much for one last big blow-out, he thinks, sucking in the crisp, damp air and then stretching to touch his toes. It's a bit on the cool side and Alex knows he must warm up first before he starts running or risk pulling a muscle. He feels his muscles flex from the excretion.

Alex has known Jace for several years, and he can't shake the feeling that something seemed off about him this morning. He knows that if he's getting strange vibes about someone, that usually means some sort of negative energy has enveloped that person. That's certainly how he felt about Jace.

He's about to head out on the trail when he senses that he is not alone. A feeling that someone or something is watching him suddenly grips his body. It's an experience he's had many times in the past.

He does a complete visual sweep around the parking area, his eyes roaming over the trees and around the bushes that surround the entrance.

His gaze falls upon a cluster of crows that have gathered in several nearby pine trees.

"So, friends, how many are in your murder this morning?" Alex quickly counts the large black birds that are clearly watching him, their tiny pellet-like eyes roaming over his body, following his every movement. He believes they are examining his very soul.

"Ten." He swallows. The saliva burns as it goes down his parched throat. "Of course, there are," he whispers. "Why am I not surprised?"

Like a chorus of ten tiny nuns, the crows caw, cackle, and bark right on cue.

"Sorry, guys," Alex answers, shaking his head. "But despite all my years of experience with your kin, I still haven't learned your language."

He approaches the trees in which the crows are roosting. They remain steady on their perches like tiny, obedient soldiers awaiting orders.

"These are the times I really miss Augustus," he says, remembering his long-lost best friend, the smartest and brightest crow he's ever encountered.

"He'd know how to connect with me. Why can't one of you have his powers?" Alex asks longingly as his eyes bounce from one of the ten crows to the next. "I know you are trying to tell me something but I'm just not getting it."

Suddenly, as if being spooked by an invisible threat, the ten crows spring from their branches, their powerful wings catching the light breeze, gliding upward and away on the early morning air currents.

"Shit," Alex whispers, quickly glancing around the parking lot. He can sense it, too. He knows he is not alone in this place where he usually finds solitude. He's been coming here for many years to run and relax, but he has never felt the strange energy that has now suddenly enveloped him. It makes the tiny hairs on his arms stand at attention.

He considers jumping back into his car and getting out of here, but he feels compelled to go for his run despite this unseen force that is making him feel as though he is a target.

But a target of what? He wonders as he jogs toward the trail. *This may be one of the stupidest things I've ever done.*

With his eyes moving from tree to tree and peeking around the large boulders that line the winding path, Alex follows the same route that he usually takes when he runs at Pine Grove Park. As an ancient sacred gathering place for the area's Indigenous Peoples, this piece of land holds special meaning to most of the region's inhabitants. He usually feels comfortable here, but today he feels as if he's running on a bed of hot embers.

Alex knows that when his nerves are tingling as they are right now, he must stay on his toes. Through their past run-ins with the dark forces that threaten him, Oliver has taught Alex that he must never dismiss his feelings. His intuition is his best weapon.

With his feet pounding the dried ground, Alex rounds a corner, ascends a minor incline, and rounds another turn before he sees him—the old man he had encountered during his run yesterday.

"Jesus Christ." He immediately comes to a full stop. "Where did you come from?"

"Around." The old man moves to a nearby boulder and takes a seat.

"That's all you're going to tell me?" Alex cautiously moves closer to the old man. Dressed in dirty old clothes that really don't suit him, the man gives the impression of someone in a desperate situation. "Surely, if you've gone to all this trouble to meet me here, then you must want to tell me something."

"Who says I wanted to meet you, Alex?"

The old man looks sharply at him and to Alex it feels like his eyes are looking through him, piercing his body like a sharp needle and going almost to the depths of his very soul.

"But you are right," the old man finally says. "I do have some things to tell you." Patting the rock, he adds, "Come here, Alex. Sit beside me."

"No. I think I'll just stand right here. Now, old man, what do you want?"

"First of all, you don't have to call me *Old Man*. I may be one hundred and four years old, but I do have a name. It's Silas Moores."

"Should that name mean something to me?"

"Probably not, but I will tell you that I am your great uncle."

Alex studies the old man, whom he would describe as a hermit. His eyes roam over the diminutive, frail body that underscores the man's age. His mind races, searching for any memories of such a man from his past. "I don't recall ever having a great uncle."

"I'm not sure you remember your great-grandmother, Clara Underwood."

Alex shakes his head. "She died when I was still a baby, but I have heard the name many times, seen pictures of her and I've read about her in the family history. Seems like she was an interesting woman." He pauses, his eyes focused on the stranger. "But I'm sure I've never heard anything about you, Silas Moores."

"Well, Clara was my sister."

"There is no record of a brother in anything that I've ever seen."

"Not many people knew about me, because that's the way I wanted it. You see, like Clara and all our family, I am akin to the crows and, like you, I have special abilities."

Alex squints his eyes. "Such as?"

"You're skeptical. That's good, Alex. Your skepticism will serve you well throughout your lifetime," the stranger replies. "It will keep you on your toes, and that sense of awareness may save your life."

Alex nods. "So again, I ask, what makes you so special?"

"You are also impatient. You should work on that, Alex." The old man squints at him as if the early morning sunlight is bothering his eyes. "There was a time when it was believed that anyone born on the seventh day of the seventh month was considered to possess special abilities such as the gift of prophecy and the ability to communicate with spirits....That's me."

"So you say."

"So I say. You see Alex, the reason I became a recluse is because I am an empath and am highly intuitive. I can read the energy around me and feel the vibes that emanate from people with incredible accuracy. I'm astute enough to know whether a person or situation is genuine. I expect you know exactly what I'm talking about."

Alex nods but says nothing.

"I can *hear* what isn't spoken, and my sixth sense for reading people is both a blessing and a curse. It means I can't be around people, because their emotions cause me so much pain."

"If that's the case, why are you choosing to show yourself to me today?"

"Because a lot of people are hurting right now and, no matter where I go, I can't escape their feelings. I can't hide from the pain."

"Why is this happening now?"

"Like I told you, it's all tied to the eclipse that's going to happen on Monday. Three days prior to the eclipse something emerges in the universe, a dark force begins to embrace us—a force so powerful that it causes people to lose control. They revert to their basic animal instincts. They fear every living thing and their instinct is to protect themselves. Self-preservation is their priority."

"Even if there is no real threat?"

"Yes. And that's what's been happening. I can't stand how it makes me feel. The pain is electric, like thousands of tiny needles piercing my skin, and I had to come out of hiding to warn you. This threat is real, Alex. You must watch everyone, even the people you love and trust. Be mindful of everyone, because this thing, this power, can affect every living creature—

human, animal, birds and even insects. It can happen in an instant. And without warning."

"What can I do?"

"The Spirit Crow has come to you, which means you are powerful. It will protect you...but it can only protect one person at a time. In the past, during eclipses, it chose to protect me. This time, I am on my own."

"I'm still not sure I understand why the Spirit Crow chose me."

"You are the golden one." The man's words are matter of fact. "You know this. You've already been on an incredible journey with the crows, and they know you are important to them, to this town. They will protect you at all costs because you have more work to do for them."

"This is too incredible to be true."

"You Alex, above everyone else in this town, must believe that nothing is too incredible to be true." The old man pauses, as if considering his next words. "I have watched you grow up, and I know what you can do. Protect those you love, but be mindful, they are not immune to this power and the threat will become more intense the closer we move toward the eclipse."

"When will it end?"

"When the eclipse ends. But be warned. During the eclipse itself, the power will be at its zenith." The old man stares hard at Alex. "No one will be safe. Your challenge is to stay alive and to protect those you can."

"Can it be stopped?"

"It cannot. This cycle has played out for centuries whenever there is a solar eclipse, and the Spirit Crow has protected chosen members of our family for generations. It started with Alexandria Gorham. I'm sure you've read about her in the journal."

Alex nods. "So, if this has happened in the past, why can't people remember anything about it?"

"That's the power of the crows, Alex. The events of these three days are always so horrific that the crows have erased them from the collective memories of everyone."

"But wouldn't the people who survive miss those who died during those three days?"

"They do, but they remember the deaths as being from natural causes or other, easier to accept, events."

"So that's why there are no records of the horrific events you describe?"

"Precisely."

"How can the crows do that?"

"Come on, Alex. You know the crows have their ways."

The old man rises from the rock. "Now, I must be going. Since the Spirit Crow has chosen to protect you during this event, I must get as far away from everyone as I possibly can. I don't want to be around anyone else in case I, or they, lose control."

"Will I see you again?"

"Perhaps." The old man moves further down the trail. "Take care, Alex. Remember, be on your toes and trust no one."

Alex follows but the old man turns a corner and immediately disappears. He's gone as if he was never there.

"Shit," Alex whispers.

I had so many more questions, he thinks, his eyes roaming the woods and bushes around him. *That old man moves quickly for someone claiming to be more than one hundred years old.*

13: Creepy crawlers

Jace Woodward prides himself on being an honest man. His integrity is of the utmost importance to him. That's why he hated lying to Alex and Luna. But he doesn't feel right this morning, not his usual confident, self-assured self. He chose to hide the truth because he doesn't want them to worry about him.

He's been feeling off his game lately, and was chalking it up to his impending graduation from medical school, which means he has some tough decisions to make in the coming weeks.

Now though, as he flops around in the king-sized bed, the handmade patchwork quilt pulled up to his chin for warmth, he really isn't sure what's going on, but something is causing the angst that's boiling and churning in the pit of his stomach. His guts feel like they're in a food pro-cessor.

"Jesus." He rolls onto his back and stares up at the blank, white ceiling.

He doesn't know much about carpentry work except for what he learned from a summer job on a construction site during his first two years in university, but the crack-filling work in this room looks immaculate to him.

He liked doing the hands-on tasks. Back then, it was a time when he could think about things other than human anatomy, skin and bones, and the organs that sustain life. He liked the freedom that such a labour-intensive job provided him.

It was a quiet, simpler time and now, on the eve of becoming a full-fledged doctor, he almost wishes he could live that simple life again, free of all the stress and turmoil that come with such a demanding job. He believes he would embrace the slower pace and relish the schedule of a nine-to-five job that usually also comes with weekends and most statutory holidays off.

But he knows everyone, especially Luna, Alex and his parents, would be profoundly disappointed in him if he decided, after all the time and money he's invested in his education, not to pursue medicine as a career.

Maybe not just yet anyway, he thinks. *Perhaps what I need is a vacation… some time to step away from this stress-filled routine, regain my focus, catch my breath. Surely, I can wait a few months before jumping into something that's going to require me to give my whole body, mind, and soul to the job.*

He only told Alex this morning that he was thinking about returning to school to study a specialty because he didn't want to tell his friend—a man who has become like a brother to him—what is really going on in his brain.

He also lied to Luna this morning because he just didn't feel up to having an in-depth discussion with her right now or, worse still, an argument, as she is laser-focused on what *she* wants, including a house and kids.

Alex and Luna will never understand what I'm going through. They have their futures all figured out and everything seems to be falling into place for them. I, on the other hand, have no idea what I really want.

He knows that when he finally gets the courage to bring it up to his friend, Alex will tell him that he's worrying for no reason.

He'll tell me that I'm more than ready to step up to the next level. He'll also predict that I will be a good doctor. Not sure how he'll know that, but that's what he'll say.

As for Luna, Jace knows she'll become very emotional, thinking that he wants to break things off with her. She'll cry and tell him that he'll be making a huge mistake if he doesn't carry through on his plan to become a doctor.

"No," he whispers, blinking away the tears that are threatening to break through the dam he's built around himself over the years. "I'm not ready to deal with any of that emotion just yet."

When and if I finally do this, I need to know it's what I want, not what she or anyone else wants.

Forcing his eyes closed, Jace grips the quilt tightly, and tries to will his mind to slow down. It's like his thoughts are a hamster running wildly on a small treadmill inside his head. Running and running and going faster and faster yet getting nowhere.

When he gets himself worked up into one of these states, Luna tells him to take a deep breath, switch off his brain and try to relax.

If only it were that easy.

His eyes spring open as he hears the sirens of emergency vehicles screech past the Hugin and Munin, the Airbnb near the middle of town that Alex had booked for him and Luna for the weekend.

"So much commotion for a small town," he whispers. "I wonder what that's all about."

Jumping off the bed, he strides to the window and looks out upon the town's Main Street. The emergency vehicles have already gone out of sight, but he's sure someone's in trouble somewhere nearby as he can still hear the sirens blaring.

Must be serious. Sounded like at least four rescue vehicles responding.

Placing his hands palm down on the windowsill, Jace leans in closer to the window.

"What the hell am I going to do?" he whispers, snapping his eyes shut.

He hopes that when he opens them, he'll see the situation in a different light.

Alex tells me I'm one of the most grounded people he knows. Man, has he ever misjudged me. I'm probably the least grounded person I know.

Opening his eyes a few seconds later, Jace is startled to discover that several large, brown spiders have moved onto the glass and appear to be busily creating their webs. They seem to be oblivious to his presence.

"Fuck." He instinctively pulls back from the glass. He's always hated spiders. But his feelings are deeper than hatred. He actually fears the eight-legged creatures. Luna, on the other hand, is okay with spiders, but she loathes snakes.

"Give me a snake any day over an ugly spider," he told his girlfriend. "Spiders are so god-damned ugly and creepy, and they bite."

"But they are cunning and effective hunters," she countered. "Besides, spiders are clean freaks, wrapping their food in a neat, tidy cocoon-like web. They stash it away to be enjoyed another day. I think that's pretty smart."

"Whatever," he replied, accepting that such a response is a childish retort, less than sophisticated for a man of his level of education and intellect.

She's not wrong, though. They have their place in the ecosystem...just as long as that place is as far away from me as possible.

He shivers as he watches them working in their web.

Arachnophobia is not a joke, as he always points out to Luna whenever she laughs at him. Perhaps it's irrational, but he's suffered from this fear of spiders for as far back he can remember, and he tells her she should stop making fun of him.

"Big baby," she teases in return.

He knows she's only joking but he doesn't like it, and the exchange always ends up with him being pissed at her for a while. The anger doesn't last long, as she usually apologizes for being so insensitive.

Today, his phobia seems to be on heightened alert. Standing in the middle of the room, staring at the window where the initial few spiders seem to have suddenly multiplied in numbers, Jace feels his skin crawl as if the creepy crawlers are moving all over his body.

"Stay the hell away from me. Just keep your fucking distance and we won't have a problem," he says.

Quickly moving back to the bed, he pulls the quilt up to his chin and holds it tight, as if the heavy blanket is a shield that will protect him from the bad thoughts running through his brain....And the spiders.

The god-damned fucking spiders.

With the glass from the window and the quilt offering protection, Jace closes his eyes and tries to steel his nerves.

Come on. Just a little sleep. That's all I need. One hour.

With his mind spinning wildly out of control as if it's caught in the vortex of a screeching tornado and his body feeling like he's trapped on a runaway merry-go-round, he's exhausted. Feeling beat up and kicked around as if he were a soccer ball.

But somehow, despite his inner turmoil, Jace finally drifts off to sleep.

It's a restless sleep, however, one filled with angst, uncertainty, dread, apprehension, fear and...spiders.

"Fuck," he screams, suddenly bolting upright in the bed, sweat dripping from his forehead, his heartbeat drumming in his ears.

He's sure he heard something pounding. Or did he?

Was I dreaming?

He quickly glances around the room.

"What the hell was that?"

Jace pulls his knees up to his chest as if he is a child cowering from a bully. He's sweating profusely.

Come on, Jace. You better get a fucking grip. Pull your shit together and slow the fuck down or someone's going to put your ass in a straitjacket and throw you in a padded room.

A sudden, sharp piercing pain, as if someone stabbed him in the right ankle, races up his leg, following his nervous system to his pain centre.

"Jesus," he cries, flinching his right foot. "What the fucking hell?"

Throwing the quilt off, he freezes in fear as a large, brown spider quickly scurries off his foot and moves up the bed as if it's on a direct path to find another tender spot in which to sink its fangs.

"You mother fucker," he screams and swats at the large spider. "You fucking bit me."

He jumps off the bed and plants his feet on the hardwood floor. Intense pain shoots up his leg. Looking around, he searches for something that he can use to kill the spider.

The arachnid stops on the bed. It remains still. Jace believes it's watching him. Casing him out, looking for a vulnerable spot. He feels like he's its prey.

"Where in hell did you come from?"

Glancing to the window, he can see the cluster of spiders has become so thick there that they are blocking the sunlight from entering the room.

The image leaves him breathless. "You're one of those? But how did you get in here?"

As the pain in his throbbing right ankle courses through his leg, he spies one of Luna's bridal magazines that she had been reading last night before she went to sleep. It's lying on the nightstand.

That will work.

He grabs the magazine, twists it into a makeshift club, and cautiously approaches the bed. The spider is standing its ground, its eight tiny legs ready to recoil if he gets too close.

"I'll teach you to bite me, you little prick." He raises the curled-up magazine above his head and quickly brings it down on top of the spider.

"Die, you little bastard," he snarls. "Die!"

Carefully lifting the magazine, he's relived to see the squashed remains of the arachnid pasted to the bed sheet. He's proud of his accomplishment. It's a big deal to him.

Grabbing a handful of Kleenex from the box that the thoughtful property owners have left on the nightstand, Jace whispers, "You got what you deserve, you creepy brown motherfucker."

He's lost on a sea of turmoil, caught up in the web of fear that the spiders have spun, when a loud pounding at the door snaps him back to attention. The sudden noise almost scares him.

"Jace?" It's Alex. "Are you all right in there? Come on, man. Open the door."

"Alex?" He grabs his jogging pants. "Just give me a second to get my pants on."

"You're suddenly worried about that now, after we shared a room in residence for three years?" Alex laughs. "I've seen your bare ass more times than I care to remember."

"You're early," Jace says seconds later, opening the door.

"Actually, I'm late," Alex replies, as he enters the room. "I was supposed to be here by eleven, but it's almost twenty minutes after and you aren't even ready yet."

"I guess I fell asleep. It won't take me long to throw on some clothes."

Jace grabs a pair of Levi's from the dresser drawer, removes his jogging pants and pulls on the jeans.

"You don't look at all like you rested very well," Alex observes. "And why are you limping?"

"This." Jace raises his right foot and shows his friend the red, puffy spot on his ankle. "Fucking spider bit me."

"When?"

"Just a few minutes ago." Pointing to the window. "Just look at the fuckers gathered over there."

Alex moves to the window and studies the arachnids.

"That is very strange. I've never seen anything quite like that."

"The little bastards pack one hell of a bite. That god-damned mother-fucker took a huge chunk out of me and it hurts like hell."

"Let me have a look at that."

Alex sits on the edge of the bed and motions for his friend to give him his foot. He examines the swollen area, gingerly pushing on the tender red flesh. Jace flinches and pulls back.

Alex nods. "That's quite a nasty bite. We'll stop at the pharmacy to pick up some antihistamines for the itching and something for infection. Maybe some topical ointment and bandages."

"Yes, doctor."

"If it was a brown recluse spider, which is what I'm guessing, then we can't mess around with it. You don't want to get an infection, which could lead to bigger problems. Think you can walk on it or," Alex says with a smile, "or do I have to carry you?"

Jace puts his weight on his right foot. He grimaces.

"I think I can manage." He lies again to his friend. "I'm sure I can get around well enough."

"Okay, then. Let's get going. We don't want to keep the girls waiting."

Jace grabs a pair of socks from the dresser and flops into a padded easy chair "How was your run?"

"Good. I wish you could have come too. It's such a beautiful place. You'd love it there. We'll try to get there before you leave on Monday."

"If I had gone with you, I may not have had this run in with the fucking killer spider."

"Are you sure you're okay? I can tell the girls we can't make lunch, and take to you to the emergency department for a shot for that. You may need something stronger than what we can get over the counter."

"I'm fine." Jace pulls on his sneaker.

"If you say so, but if it gets any worse, I'm hauling your ass to the hos-pital and there will be no ifs, ands or buts about it. Understand?"

"Yes, doctor." Jace repeats. "Anything you say, Ole Wise One."

"Spider bite aside, Jace, what's really bothering you? I could sense this morning that something is weighing on your mind."

"We don't have time to get into all of that right now, but before I go back home, I need your sage advice."

I can tell you're struggling with something. You're having second thoughts about all of this, aren't you?"

Jace nods. "My head's not in a good place right now."

"I'm going to cancel lunch so we can stay here and talk. The girls will understand."

"I don't want you to do that. Let's just go and have a nice lunch. After that, I'm looking forward to you showing me around the hospital. I want to see where you're going to be spending your days and nights."

"If that's what you want," Alex says. "But I'm worried about you."

"Don't be. I'm fine."

Alex slaps him on the back as they leave the room. "You are a really bad liar."

14: Fries and mustard

Momma's Homemade Pizza is the hottest place in town for lunch and dinner. While the name may suggest that the restaurant only serves pizza, in fact the menu boasts a wide assortment of cuisine ranging from healthy homemade meals to a large selection of fast-food choices, including burgers, fries, sandwiches, subs and wraps.

"A joint venture of two sisters, Marsha and Meghan Finch, they started the business about twelve years ago with their mother, Laura," Bree explains to Luna and Jace as they gather in the crowded dining area for lunch. "Laura has since died, but she was well known in these parts for her homemade pizza."

"You'll love the food here," Alex says. "Their hand-cut home fries are great. They do them with the skins on and fry them twice. They are extra crispy and wickedly good. I have them every time I come in here."

"Yes, he does love them," Bree smiles. "Except that he ruins them when he puts mustard on them."

She winks at the man who is the love of her life, the one she plans on spending the rest of her life with. If he ever gets up the nerve to pop the question, she's ready to say yes. "Mustard, of all things. Have you heard of anything so sick and disgusting?"

"Right!" Jace joins in. "That's what I say, too. He's the only person I know of who puts mustard on their fries. Ketchup, yes. Mayo? Okay, maybe." He shakes his head. "But mustard? No, thank you very much. It's gross."

"I don't know what your problem is," Alex says. He dips one of his fries into the healthy puddle of mustard on the side of his plate and takes a bite. He smiles as he chews. "You guys really don't know what you're missing."

"Oh yes I do," Jace fires back with a chuckle. "I remember the time when you talked me into trying it and I thought I was going to lose it. I almost hurled right there in the restaurant."

"I remember." Alex nods "How could I ever forget that face you made? It was priceless. Can I help it that your delicate baby belly couldn't handle a real man's food?"

"Is that what you're calling it?" Bree pipes up. "Man food? I can think of a few better words to describe it."

"Come on you, guys," Luna jumps to Alex's defence. "Let the poor guy eat his so-called 'man food' in peace."

"Yeah. Come on, guys." Alex laughs. "Cut me some slack. It's not my fault that you're not open to trying new things." He takes another bite of a mustard-covered fry. "De-l-i-ci-ous! Now, can we please change the subject, or do I have to discuss some of your disgusting eating habits?"

He turns to Bree. "How was your shopping excursion this morning?"

"Not sure I'd call it much of an excursion." She frowns. "But we had a great time just hanging out together. We found a few tops that we both liked and a couple of little things that we just had to have."

"Things you just *had to have*?" Alex asks playfully. "Such as?"

"I'll show you later." She smirks at him.

"Awesome. I can hardly wait," Alex replies. "What are you guys doing this afternoon?"

"I think we're going to take a quick run into Bridgewater," Bree says. "There's a couple of used clothing stores there that Luna and I are going to check out."

"Don't forget that my parents are expecting us at their place for dinner at six, so everyone will need to have time to get ready. I thought it would be nice if we could get there a little bit earlier, so we don't feel rushed."

"I didn't forget. I'll be back in town no later than four-thirty," Bree assures him. "Or at least that's my plan."

"Tell them about the excitement on Main Street earlier," Luna speaks up. "It was pretty weird."

"Excitement?" Alex's right eyebrow rises. "What happened?"

Bree explains, "I think it was one of the strangest things I've ever seen, and you know I've seen some pretty weird things around this town."

Alex nods.

"As with a lot of strange things that happen around this town, this event involved birds," she says.

"Crows?"

"No," Luna answers, looking at Bree. "I don't think I saw any crows."

Bree shakes her head. "But when we were down on Main Street, we noticed there were a bunch of birds and they were behaving oddly, like flitting around all over the place. They were swooping down and getting really close to the people walking on the sidewalks. It gave everyone quite a scare. There's usually a lot of birds around, but not like this. There were dozens of them, and they were being pretty brazen, more than you would normally see."

Alex asks, "Were they coming after people? Anyone get hurt?"

"No injuries that we could see," Bree says. "But they were getting way too close for comfort, and, to me, they seemed to be agitated and aggressive."

"What kind of birds are we talking about?"

"I don't know," Luna says. "Sparrows. Starlings. Maybe some finches. I'm no bird expert so I can't say for sure."

"And robins," Bree adds. "There were definitely robins in the swarm and people were darting in out of the stores to avoid being attacked. I'm not sure if the birds would have actually gone after anyone, but no one was taking any chances."

"That sounds like pretty weird behaviour," Jace agrees. Chewing a bite of his club sandwich, he adds, "There seems to be lots of weirdness going around today."

"Oh," Bree stares at him. "But it gets even weirder."

"Do tell," Jace says.

"All of a sudden, three very large birds—maybe they were hawks or something like that, but I don't know for sure because they moved too swiftly for me to get a good look—swooped down on the smaller birds and snatched a bunch of them right out of midair. It was kind of creepy how fast and precisely they moved."

"It was the scariest thing I have ever seen," Luna chimes in. "The poor little birds didn't stand a chance. They squealed and cried as the hawks clamped their talons around them and carried them off to do God knows what with them."

"To eat them." Jace laughs.

"I'm glad you find this funny, Jace." Luna glares at him. "It was actually very sad. I felt really bad for the poor little birds. They may have been behaving badly themselves, but they didn't deserve to be whisked away to their deaths like that."

"I know it can be upsetting, Luna, but it's how things work in nature," Alex speaks up, his voice calm and soothing as he tries to defuse an argument between his two dearest friends before it can escalate. He knows how quickly Jace can lose his temper. He's seen it in the past: it doesn't take much to light the man's fuse, sometimes over the most insignificant things.

Staring his best friend directly in his eyes, he adds, "I don't think Jace was trying to be funny. Were you?"

Jace curls up his nose as if the idea of admitting he may have crossed a line is hard for him. He grudgingly whispers, "I guess not."

"Speaking of strange things happening this morning, Jace had his own run-in with a dose of weirdness," Alex says, to change the subject.

"What happened?" Bree asks.

"Tell them, Jace," Alex says.

Jace is slow to respond. "It wasn't anything, really." He stares at the plate of food in front of him.

"Oh, for God's sake, Jace," Alex says. "Why do you look so downtrodden? Get your head out of your ass and just tell them."

"It was spiders," Jace blurts out. "Okay, Alex? Are you happy now?" He glares at his friend. "I had a run-in with spiders."

"Spiders?" Luna reaches under the table and squeezes her boyfriend's hand gently. "Are you all right honey?"

"No, he isn't," Alex says. "One of the spiders actually bit him and I don't like the looks of it. It looks like it's already inflamed, and it's hot to the touch. We're going on a tour of the hospital after lunch and I'm going to ask Uncle Charlie to have a look at it for us."

"Show me," Luna says to Jace. "Let me see what Alex is talking about."

Jace shakes his head. "I don't think it's appropriate for people to look at my swollen foot while they're eating lunch." He rolls his eyes. "Talk about ruining someone's appetite."

"Well, then, you come with me mister." Luna rises from her chair and takes his hand.

"But I'm eating," he protests. "And my food will get cold."

"Your food can wait." She pulls him into a standing position. "Your health cannot. If your food gets cold, we'll get you something else."

"Fine." He tosses his napkin onto the table. "But let's make this quick. That's a damned good sandwich."

Watching as Jace hobbles toward the exit, Luna holding him around the waist, Alex says to Bree, "He's in a lot of pain but he's too god-damned stubborn to admit it. I love Jace like a brother, but, man, he can be pig-headed when he gets fired up."

"Luna can handle him. Is he going to be all right?"

"Spider bites can be nasty, so you have to be careful with them and watch them closely."

"How did this happen?" Bree asks.

"I don't know."

"Wasn't Jace with you on your run?"

Alex shakes his head. "I went to pick him this morning, but he said he didn't feel like going."

"So, this happened at the Airbnb?"

"It seems that way. It was odd, though. Considering how new that place is, there were a lot of spiders around. You don't usually see that around new construction."

"Inside?"

"No, on the outside of the window, but it wasn't like anything I had ever seen before. They were behaving—I don't know—oddly. I will admit these ones also freaked me out, but not as bad as they did Jace. He really does have a deep seeded fear of spiders, but I still got cold chills when I saw them swarming there like...well, like a swarm of birds. There was a lot of them."

"Maybe you should notify the owners. There could be an infestation. I'm sure they'll want to take care of it."

"I was thinking that too." Alex agrees as Jace and Luna return to the table. "Well, Luna," he says. "Looks pretty bad, doesn't it?"

"It does," she says, helping her boyfriend back into his seat. "Alex, if your uncle is going to be at the hospital and can have a look at that, I'd be forever grateful."

"It will be done."

"Now just a second, you two," Jace says. "Are you forgetting that I'm a doctor, too? I don't think it looks too bad. I think I'll be fine."

"Just you hush," Luna tells him, gently placing a finger over his lips. "What harm will it do to let Alex's uncle have a look?"

"Furthermore," Alex says, "haven't you heard that doctors make the worst patients? Seriously, though, buddy, I really think it's worth letting Uncle Charlie have a look."

"Fine." Jace gives in. "If it's going to get you guys off my back, I'll let Uncle Charlie have a look. But," he smirks, "I draw the line at amputation."

15: Up on the roof

Angela Harper has been a member of Merv Morgan's construction crew for four years and she can hold her own against any of her male counterparts. She's seen a handful of men come and go because they couldn't handle the physical demands that come with shingling a roof and many other construction jobs.

But Angela is more than up for the task. She and her co-worker, Chad Winslow, make a good team. This Saturday morning, they are working on a massive, three-story, multi-level roof as the spring construction season has quickly swung into high gear, with the list of impending jobs growing like a spring wildfire.

They understand Merv, who is one of the kindest and hardest-working men Angela has ever known, will not turn down any jobs because, as he says, "You have to make hay while the sun shines."

It's the same with shingling jobs, he tells her. If there's a way to work in a new client, she expects Merv will add the job to the quickly growing list.

Known as roofing specialists, Merv's company is in high demand throughout the southwest region of the province. They already have enough jobs lined up to take them into the middle of August and it's only early April, but she's sure they'll still be shingling roofs well into November, unless the weather turns too nasty, as it did last year.

"I thought Merv was going to be here to help us this morning," Angela observes.

She grabs a bundle of asphalt shingles from Chad and hauls it up to the peak of the thirty-four-foot roof. They'll start here at the top and work their way down. At the pace they're going, they expect to complete this part of the roof by suppertime. They'll pick up the job on Monday morning, as Merv has a strict no-work-on-Sunday policy.

"Did you forget that it's the first Saturday?" Chad grunts from the exertion. "Merv helps out at the firemen's breakfast on the first Saturday of the month."

"You're right. I totally forgot about that."

Angela rips open the bundle and starts placing a row of shingles across the peak as Chad grabs his air nail gun and joins her there. "Don't know what's up with the ole memory these days. I'm only thirty-two. Surely," she says with a laugh, "I can't be getting dementia just yet."

"Oh, I don't know about that," Chad says as he begins to nail the shingles into place. "I always thought you were a little senile." He laughs. "You know, a few shingles short of a bundle."

"Speaking of senile, did you hear that piece on the news last night about how they say the eclipse can cause some people to lose their minds and go crazy? They say it can cause people to snap without warning and make them do all kinds of crazy things, even attack other people, maybe even kill them."

"Didn't see that," Chad answers. "But I'm not much of a news watcher. There's too much doom and gloom. I can't handle it and those politicians that are always on television talking about all the good things they're doing *for the people* when the truth is, they're really just full of shit. All they think about is lining their own pockets and that usually means screwing the little people, like you and me."

"I guess there is some truth to that," Angela says. "Anyway, you do remember there is an eclipse coming this Monday, don't you? Are you worried about that?"

"Nope. Not in the least." He pauses and looks at his work partner. "Should I be?"

"After I saw that item on the news, it got me wondering if that might have had anything to do with what happened at Echo Lake. They say Jimmy Spicer killed those other men before he killed himself."

"I heard that. Sounded brutal." He takes a deep breath. "I knew Jimmy."

"Didn't know that. But I'm not surprised. You seem to know everyone in town."

"It was before your time, but he worked on Merv's crew for about a year. Seemed like a nice enough fellow. He was very quiet and kept to himself, but he was a hard worker, I'll give him that much. And I never knew him to get mad at anyone. Damn near floored me when I heard about what happened yesterday."

"I guess it's true that you never know what people will do." Angela looks at her friend and shakes her head.

"I think you would have liked Jimmy." Chad continues to secure the shingles in place. "We're almost out of shingles again. Want to go down and send up a few more bundles?"

"I can do that."

Angela carefully moves down the roof, making sure not to lose her footing on the steep slope. She's wearing a safety harness this morning, unlike her partner, but it would still be painful if she lost her balance and fell. It's not a good feeling when those ropes snap tight as the sudden jolt rattles your bones. "How many do you want?"

Chad surveys the peak. "I'd say at least six bundles. That should give us enough for the saddle and the peak."

"Why don't I bring up eight, or maybe a dozen? We're going to need them anyway."

"Right on."

Casting his eyes about the neighbourhood, Chad can see most of the town from where he's standing. "Did you check out the view from up here? Our little town looks amazing, especially in this morning light."

He drinks in the beautiful vista with his eyes, the mid-morning sunshine creating a natural glow over the entire town as the Atlantic Ocean stretches beyond the horizon and disappears into infinity. He likes working in the outdoors, especially at this time of year.

"It sure does," she says. "I was thinking earlier that I don't know why anyone wouldn't be happy living here. This place is pretty spectacular. If only everyone could see what we see from way up here. I'm sure I wouldn't want to live anywhere else."

"Karen and I have often discussed moving to the city, where the money is better on construction sites, but we like the quality of life here. We want the kids to grow up in the same small town where we were raised, and finish school here. If I'm honest, I don't ever want to move."

"I'm with you." Angela glances upward as the sky suddenly darkens. "Say, Chad. Did you notice all those seagulls flying around overhead? I've never seen so many of them in one place over land like that. What do you suppose they see?"

Chad looks around the yard below and then casts his gaze skyward. "They are scavengers, so it's likely they've spied something to eat. Don't know what it would be, though, as I don't see anything that would attract so many of them at one time."

He moves to the next section of the roof. "Peculiar behaviour for them. They usually stick to the wharves."

"I never liked seagulls." She reaches the ladder.

"Why?"

"Not really sure. They kind of creep me out."

"They can be pretty brazen. One time I saw one of them snatch a tuna sandwich right out of a man's hand on a job site, but I have never seen them hurt anyone."

"Don't care," Angela says. "I just don't like them."

"Whatever." Chad turns his attention back to the shingles. "Time to get back to work. If we want to finish this section before lunch, we better get after it."

As Angela moves to the first rung of the ladder, her eyes are pulled upward again. "Hey, Chad," she calls out. "You may want to duck. That flock of seagulls is heading towards you."

"What?" He stands and sees the flock of large, white and grey birds streaming in his direction as if they are zeroed in on him. "What the fucking hell are they doing?"

Dropping the air nailer, he quickly throws up his hands to protect his face.

"Get out of the way, Chad," Angela screams.

She watches, horrified, as her co-worker, her friend, swats at the seagulls. The unusual behaviour sends goosebumps racing up her arms. The scavenger birds seem intent on causing him harm.

"Fuck," she hears him scream as the seagulls nip and snap as his face and the exposed skin on his arms. "Leave me alone, you fuckers."

"Come on Chad," she yells while moving down a couple of rungs on the ladder. "We've got to get off the roof."

The seagulls make contact, plucking large chunks of skin from his bones.

Angela watches in horror as Chad, attempting to back away from the attacking birds, struggles to maintain his balance.

"Be careful," she calls. "You're going to fall."

"I'm not going to fall," he yells, while furiously waving his arms about his head. His blood-covered fists connect with several of the powerful birds, sending them squawking as they fly away. "Get out of here. I will be right behind you."

She steps down a few more rungs, her chest tightening from the panic. "Can I help you?"

"No. Get down to the ground."

She scurries down the ladder, her steel-toed boots making a loud thud when they finally hit the ground.

She calls, "Come on, Chad."

Backing away from the ladder, she watches in horror as her co-worker and friend suddenly plummets to the ground, landing squarely on his back. He hits with such a loud thud that she's sure he must have shattered every bone in his body.

She falls to her knees beside her friend. "Chad?" She gently touches his body. "Are you all right? We've got to get out of here."

His limbs and neck are twisted and bent like pretzels. The blood streaming from his nose, ears and the corners of his mouth confirms that her friend is dead.

She sobs. "I told you to use the harness." She shakes him again. "Why didn't you listen to me?"

With the seagulls flocking above her, Angela decides she cannot stay here out in the open. She determines Chad's truck is the only sanctuary available to her. The house is locked while the owners are away for the day.

Angela sprints toward the truck, the seagulls immediately swooping down toward her. She only has a few seconds before they reach her.

"God damn it to hell." She suddenly remembers that Chad was driving this morning. He probably has the keys in his jeans' pocket. She just hopes the truck doors aren't locked because if they are, she'll be screwed.

With the seagulls in pursuit, Angela reaches the truck and pulls on the handle of the passenger-side door. She's relieved when it opens.

"Thank you, Jesus." She slides into the truck cab and slams the door shut behind her.

And none too soon. She screams and flinches as several large seagulls smash head-first into the door window. The unholy thud reverberates throughout the truck cab, causing her to shudder.

"What the fuck is this all about?"

She sees there is no key in the ignition.

"Shit." She is trapped in the truck.

She considers the odds of her rushing to his body to retrieve the keys and then getting back safely to the truck before the gulls make mincemeat out of her.

And what if the keys aren't on you, Chad? Then what? I'll be screwed, that's what.

As the seagulls continue their assault on the truck cab, smashing into the front windshield and side windows, leaving bloody streaks and cracks in their wake, Angela reaches for her cellphone.

When she thrusts her hand into the empty pocket of her navy hoodie, she remembers that she had put her cellphone down on a nearby pile of lumber before she went up on the roof because she didn't want it to slip out of her pocket and break.

Now what?

She knows it's no use to lay on the horn, hoping someone will hear the noise and come to her rescue, because the house is in a secluded area and there are no neighbours for several kilometres in any direction.

As the killer birds continue their assault on the truck cab, she tries to gather her thoughts.

She figures she has three choices, none of which would be easy nor safe. She can wait here in the truck until the gulls smash their way inside the cab and tear her to shreds. She can make a mad dash to Chad's body to get the keys, which may not even be on him, or she can run to the pile of lumber to grab her phone. None of the options seem viable to her.

"What if I trip? What if I'm too slow? What if the seagulls are too fast?" *What if I can't find Chad's keys?*

She suddenly realizes there is a fourth option.

"Merv," she whispers, quickly glancing at her watch and realizing that it's almost time for the firemen's breakfast to wrap up. When it's over, her boss will eventually show up to see how she and Chad are doing.

"He always does," she says to no one. "The question is, can I wait until he shows up?"

What if this is the day he decides not to show up?

She shakes her head. "No. I know Merv. He is reliable."

"That's it," she whispers. "I am going to wait for Merv."

~

As Merv Morgan pulls his truck into the driveway, he expects to see his two best workers up on the roof, laying shingles.

"What the hell?" he whispers.

He parks the truck, opens his door and slides his feet out onto the gravel driveway. The cool afternoon breeze blowing in from the Atlantic Ocean licks his face.

He doesn't see either Chad or Angela. But he knows they're here somewhere, because Chad's red pickup is still in the yard.

He approaches the other truck as he scans the yard, hoping to see his crew is simply taking a break. Something doesn't feel right about this place.

"Chad? Angela?" he calls out. "Where are you guys?"

When no one answers, his internal alarm goes off. He knows that such a disappearing act isn't normal behaviour for either of these workers. They hardly ever take a break, and he gives them extra shifts because he knows he can count on them.

"Je-s-us." The breath catches in his throat when he sees the streaks of blood and cracked windows on Chad's truck. "What happened here?"

As he sprints toward the vehicle, his eyes focus on the truck's interior. His heart pounds as he fears the worst for the woman who is not just his employee but also his friend.

"Holy hell," he whispers, seeing Angela slumped over in the truck cab.

"Angela?" he calls out, quickly running up to the driver's side door and pulling on the handle. "Shit. God-damn it."

It's locked.

"Angela, can you hear me? He pounds on the window, hoping to rouse her. "Are you hurt?"

"Merv? Is that you?" She mutters and slowly opens her eyes.

"Unlock the door, Angela."

He sees her move and the door locks pop open. "What time is it?" she whispers as he opens the door.

"Ten after two," Merv answers, leaning into the truck. "Is this your blood?"

She shakes her head, still dazed. "It's not my blood."

"Who beat up the truck?"

"Seagulls."

"Seagulls?" Merv quickly glances around at the house and yard. "I don't see any seagulls."

"There were hundreds of them. They were everywhere."

"Well, they aren't here now. Are you sure you aren't hurt?"

"I think I'm okay, just scared. It was terrible. They just kept coming and coming."

"Where's Chad?"

"He's over there." She points toward the ladder. "He's dead."

"Dead?"

"The seagulls killed him….Pushed him off the roof."

"Why didn't you call for help if something was wrong?"

"I didn't have my phone." She starts to sob. "I didn't have my phone and now Chad is dead. Why did the seagulls kill him?"

Fishing into his jacket pocket, Merv pulls out his phone and dials 9-1-1. He then hands his phone to her. "Tell them where we are and ask them to send help right away."

She grasps the phone in her shaky left hand and asks, "Where are you going?"

"To check on Chad."

"No," she cries. "The gulls will get you, too."

"I need to help him." Merv turns from the truck and closes the door. "You stay here until help arrives. Lock the doors again."

~

"Please, Merv," she pleads watching her boss sprint toward her lifeless co-worker. "Please stay here."

She watches in horror as flocks of seagulls suddenly descend from the sky, quickly overpowering Merv and knocking him to the ground. Within seconds, there are hundreds of them covering his body and she cries as they rip and tear his flesh from his bones.

"Merv," she sobs. "Why didn't you listen to me?"

16: Doctor's orders

Leading his best friend into the emergency department following his tour of the hospital where he will be working, Alex shows Jace into an exam room and directs him to hop up onto a gurney.

"You just sit your ass right there, mister, and I don't want you to move a muscle," he says. "Understand?"

"Yes, sir. Whatever you say, sir."

Alex slips into a pair of blue rubber gloves, his patience wearing thin. "Enough screwing around for one day. By how badly you're limping, I can tell your foot is swollen and you're in pain. It's time that you start to take this more seriously."

"Come on, Alex. Don't be such a tight ass."

Jace assumes his usual cocky, self-assured persona that Alex knows is just a façade his friend puts on to mask his true identity, that of a vulnerable, compassionate and deep-thinking young man who will make a great doctor someday, if he just gets out of his own head.

"You're always wound so tight it's a wonder you don't implode." Jace laughs at his weak attempt at humour that Alex knows is designed to deflect attention from himself.

"That's because I know when there's a time to kid around and when there's a time to be serious." Alex motions for his friend to remove his shoe and give him his foot. "This, my friend, is one of those times to get serious."

Following Alex's instructions, Jace removes his shoe and presents his bare foot to his friend. "How does it look, doc? Are you going to have to amputate?"

Alex examines the red, puffy area where the spider sank its fangs into the skin. "It is swollen and it looks like the wound is getting worse, but I don't see any ulcerating lesions yet, so that's a good thing."

"See? I told you that you worry too much."

"And you don't worry enough." Alex rolls the gloves from his hands and tosses them in the trash receptacle. "You sit your ass right here. I'm going to find Uncle Charlie. I want him to have a look at this before we leave. It's pretty inflamed so I'm sure you need something for infection."

"Fine." Jace lies back on the gurney, rests his head on the paper-thin pillow and closes his eyes. "I'll just wait right here for you, Dr. Alex." He raises his two thumbs. "Hey, man. That's got a pretty nice ring to it. I think you've finally arrived at your destination."

"What a dick." Alex laughs. "Now," he adds, as if he were addressing an impetuous young child, "don't you go anywhere."

It takes him about half an hour to make his way back to the exam room. His uncle, Dr. Charlie Webster, is with him.

"So, Mr. Woodward," Charlie says as he follows his nephew into the room. "Alex tells me you've got a nasty spider bite on your foot that he wants me to examine. Is that okay with you?"

When Jace doesn't answer, Alex gives him a gentle shake. "Jace? Are you sleeping?"

"Huh?" Jace slowly opens his eyes. "What? Alex? What's going on?"

"Are you all right? You didn't answer when Uncle Charlie asked you if it was okay for him to examine your foot."

"Sorry. I guess I must have fallen asleep and didn't hear you come in."

Alex feels his friend's forehead with the back of his hand, just as his mother used to do him when he was a child. "You feel warm. I think you may have a slight fever."

"Here." Charlie passes a digital thermometer to his nephew. "You better check it to be sure. A rising temperature can be a sign of infection."

"Could the infection really be spreading that quickly?" Alex places the thermometer on his friend's forehead and presses a small green button. "He was only bitten a few hours ago."

"Could be. I've seen a few bad spider bites in my time and some of them can get pretty messy."

Charlie pulls Jace's foot closer so that he can get a better look at the inflamed ankle. "Venom from some spiders can be pretty potent, especially brown recluse spiders. They're nasty little buggers." Turning to Jace, Charlie asks, "Do you know if you're allergic to any spiders?"

Jace appears dazed but slowly shakes his head. "I don't think so, but I don't know for sure. I've never been tested that I know of."

The thermometer beeps, indicating it's done.

"His temp is 37.9. Almost 38," Alex says. "He definitely has a low-grade fever."

"Check his blood pressure," Charlie says.

"Already thought of that."

Alex applies the blood pressure cuff to the upper portion of his friend's left arm. He turns on the machine and watches as the numbers flash on the small display screen. "Be still," he tells Jace. "No talking."

Seconds later he says to Charlie, "It's 140 over 70. Pretty high for a person of his age."

"Hmmm." Charlie lists symptoms as they are presenting. "Slightly high fever. Elevated blood pressure. Redness and tenderness around the bite area but no visible blisters yet. Swelling of the foot."

Directing a question to Jace, Charlie asks, "Do you feel sick to your stomach? Any dizziness?"

"No." Jace answers, his voice nothing more than a whisper. "But I'm really dry. My mouth feels like a desert."

"That's the spiking fever," Alex says. "I'll get you some ice water in just a second."

"So, Jace, my friend," Charlie says. "It looks to me like you are having an allergic reaction to the spider bite."

"So, what are we going to do, Uncle Charlie?" Alex asks. "Antibiotics? Do you have to admit him?"

"I don't believe we need to make him stay in the hospital overnight," Charlie says. "But I would like for him to stay here for a bit so I can watch him. I just want to make sure the symptoms don't get any worse."

"Is that really necessary?" Jace asks as he tries to sit up.

"Yes." Alex gently pushes his friend back down on the gurney. "It is necessary if Uncle Charlie says it's necessary."

"Just for an hour, maybe two," Charlie adds. "I'm going to give you a shot of epinephrine right now to counter the spider's venom. I'm also giving you a prescription for Cephalexin." Looking at the two young doctors, he asks, "You guys both know what that is, right?"

"It's for infection," Alex answers, proud that he knew the answer to his uncle's pop quiz.

Jace remains quiet.

Charlie nods. "I'd also like to see you get a topical antibiotic ointment to apply directly to the bite. I would suggest Bacitracin. It's pretty strong and should do the trick. Apply it at least four times a day for a couple of days. It will help relieve the itching. You should be back to your normal self in a day or two."

"Thank you, Uncle Charlie," Alex says. "We'll get that and the prescription at the pharmacy when we leave here."

"Yes, thank you, Dr. Webster," Jace adds, his throat almost too hoarse to speak.

"No problem, guys," Charlie smiles as he jots his notes on a chart. "What did you think of our fine little hospital, Jace? It's pretty well equipped for a rural facility, don't you think?"

"It's impressive," Jace replies even though it's painful for him to talk.

"No need to say anything, Jace. You just rest and Alex will get you some water," Charlie says. "It is impressive and you know, we could always use more doctors around here. Ever think of coming to our beautiful community and setting up your practice? You might enjoy working beside your friend here. You guys would make a great team. Just what this town needs. Young blood full of energy and new ideas. You could make a really nice life here."

Jace merely shrugs.

"Well, it's something for you to think about." Charlie hands him the slip for the prescription. "If you ever want to talk about it, you can call me any time"

"Maybe not," Jace whispers, a sheepish grin plastered on his face. "Your spiders are too fucking nasty for me."

Charlie chuckles. "Yes, it would appear that they are, and they don't seem to like you too much."

He nods to Alex. "Walk with me for a minute."

"Everything okay with Jace?" Alex asks as they walk down the corridor.

"I'm sure he'll recover from the spider bite, but is there something else going on with him?"

"I don't know what you mean."

"I can't quite put my finger on it, but something seems off with him. You should watch him closely. He's definitely keeping something bottled up."

Alex says, "I've noticed that, too, and I'm starting to worry about him."

"Do you know if he's stressed out about anything? You guys should be flying high these days. After all, you're both about to graduate and start your new lives."

"I think he's really stressing out over what's going to happen after he graduates."

"Has he talked to you about it?"

"Not yet," Alex admits. "He's a hard nut to crack. He'll only talk when he's good and ready to talk. The more you try to force him to open up, the more he pulls back."

Charlie looks into his nephew's eyes. "I don't know what it is, Alex, but I think you need to find a way to reach him. I sense he's got lots of pent-up issues and could be on the verge of a breakdown. I've seen that before and, trust me, you don't want him to crash. If he does, he's going to fall hard."

"Should I be worried?"

"I know you have special abilities, Alex. I've seen you use them over the years, and I suggest that you use them now with your friend. You need to find out what's bothering him and help him to work through it."

Alex considers his uncle's warning. "Okay, Uncle Charlie. I'll talk to him."

Charlie flips to the next chart. "Now, I've got to see the next patient. This place has been a like a zoo all day. So many people with so many serious problems."

"Why didn't you call? I would have come in to help you."

"You've got other things that you need to do, but thanks." Charlie smiles. "I am sorry I can't make your celebration dinner tonight, but you know I'm really proud of you for everything you've accomplished."

"I know," Alex says. "I appreciate all your support over the years. I couldn't have done it without you."

"Now, go and check on your friend. Give it an hour or so, and if there's no major change for the worse, then you can take him home."

By the time Alex has returned to the exam room, Jace is on his phone, reading a text.

"Luna says they're leaving Bridgewater now and heading home," he says as Alex sits on the black stool that's beside the gurney. "She wants to know if we need anything."

Alex shakes his head. "I'm all good."

"I'm going to ask her to stop at the liquor store and get me a bottle of vodka. You sure you don't want anything?"

"Again, no."

"Fine. I was just asking."

"Sorry about that. I didn't mean to snap at you."

"No problem, brother." Jace smiles, his fingers quickly typing out a text to his girlfriend. "Can we leave now? I'm ready to get out of this place."

"Uncle Charlie wants us to wait here for at least an hour to make sure the epinephrine is working."

"Do we really have to?"

Alex squints at his friend. "What is going on with you? You know this is standard procedure for someone who is presenting with an allergic reac-tion."

"Jesus, Alex," Jace snaps. "Calm down, bud. I was just asking."

"I know, but that's just the thing. You shouldn't have to ask. You've studied this material as much as I have, and you've treated patients. You know this is how it works. Don't be such a shithead."

Jace becomes quiet. Seconds later, he adds, "Sorry, man. I don't mean to be a pain in your ass. Maybe I should just go back to Halifax right now."

"You're not a pain in my ass and you aren't going anywhere." Alex smiles. "Our friendship means a great deal to me, and I'm worried about you."

"You don't have to worry about me." Jace flexes his bare foot. "See? The shot's working and the bite already feels better."

"I'm not talking about the spider bite. I'm talking about your emotional state."

Jace hesitates and then replies, "I don't know what you mean."

"Okay then. Let's do it your way." Alex says. "What's with the vodka? I've hardly seen you take a drink of alcohol before. Why do you want a drink today?"

Jace squints. "We're celebrating, aren't we? Isn't it a tradition to have alcohol when you're celebrating?" He pauses. "Although I will admit, it doesn't feel like much of a party right now."

"I know you're holding something back," Alex says. "And whatever it is, it's eating you up on the inside. We're friends and you can confide in me. Whatever you tell me will stay between us."

Jace turns his face toward the ceiling and becomes quiet. Alex sees tears trickle from his friend's eyes.

Several minutes pass with neither of the young men speaking.

Finally, Jace whispers, "I'm struggling, Alex."

"I know. Can you tell me what you're struggling with?"

Jace slowly turns to look Alex in the eyes. "Life," he whispers. "I'm struggling with life."

Alex takes his friend's hand and squeezes it. "We all have struggles, but I'm here for you. Any time. Anywhere."

"Can we just go?"

Alex glances toward his friend's foot and says, "Okay. If you really want to go, we'll go. But, be warned, if I see anything I don't like, I'm bringing your ass right back here."

"Yes, doctor." Jace smiles. "Whatever you say, doctor."

"I say put your god-damned shoe on and let's get going."

Alex knows this conversation has only just begun.

17: A deer in the headlights

With the local courthouse being phased out several years ago in favour of a larger and more modern regional justice facility, Bree Hamilton has driven from Liverpool to Bridgewater and back again so many times, she's sure she could make the thirty-minute trip with her eyes closed.

But she is a cautious driver and remains laser focused on the road ahead. She is always aware of her surroundings. Her father, a long-serving RCMP officer, taught his children to pay attention and keep their eyes on the road whenever they are behind the wheel of a motor vehicle.

"Because the life you save, may be your own," he told Bree and her sister, Lauren, many times when they were learning to drive.

Warren Hamilton preached these "safety-first" lessons to his daughters so often that Bree believes there is no way she could ever forget them. The hazards of having a police officer for a father, she often jokes, chiding her "over-protective" father, every chance she gets.

Despite the good-natured ribbing, Bree takes his advice to heart, not only about safe driving but in just about every other aspect of her life. The one thing she never listens to him about, however, is her clothing. When it comes to modern fashion sense, she tells him he has none.

She knows he would definitely roll his eyes and not approve of the slightly-revealing dress she just purchased in Bridgewater, and, in a way, that makes her feel good about her choice.

He's had far too much influence over me, she thinks while navigating the busy highway, her eyes scanning the route ahead for any possible threat, darting from shoulder to shoulder. She knows the bushes could be hiding possible dangers. Her eyes then bounce back to the yellow centre line.

The man's made me such a paranoid driver. She smiles, thinking back on all his lectures. *I love him with all my heart, but sometimes he's just too much to handle. The life of a cop's daughter, I guess.*

"What do you think Alex will say about that sexy dress you bought for his graduation ceremony?" Luna asks from the passenger seat.

It's still daylight, but the sun is starting go down and Bree hates driving at dusk, as the rays are just starting to sink below the horizon, creating dark shadows that sometimes make it difficult to see approaching vehicles. It can be a harrowing experience when a car suddenly seems to appear out of nowhere.

She finds driving at dusk so challenging that whenever she and Alex are together in a car, she's always in the passenger seat because she likes the freedom of not having to worry about—as her father puts it—"The other idiots on the road."

But this afternoon the responsibility is all hers and she takes that duty very seriously. However, Luna, with her constant chatter and incessant questions, can be a distraction. Bree would never say anything to her, though, because they're friends. Bree takes her friend's lighthearted nattering in stride. She usually finds Luna's wicked and sometimes warped sense of humour very endearing.

"I'm sure he'll love it," Luna says.

Bree enjoys spending time with Luna, who grew up in the Yarmouth area. They've become very close friends since they first met in university, even though they don't see each other these days as often as they would like. Especially not since their boyfriends, the soon-to-be Dr. Alex Goodwin and soon-to-be Dr. Jace Woodward, took up their residencies in different parts of the province as a requirement of their training.

Bree worries that her best friend wouldn't be able to handle a prolonged separation from her boyfriend and, based upon what she has observed while spending several hours with her, she thinks she was right to be concerned.

It was good for Bree that Alex came to Liverpool, as she was already working in her hometown at the law firm run by Alex's mother, Kate Webster. But Luna stayed in Halifax, where she was working at a large PR firm while Jace spent several months in Cape Breton without her.

"I don't know if he'll like the dress," Bree answers Luna's question. "Maybe it's a little too risqué for such a sophisticated event."

"Don't be silly. I bet Alex will love it. He'll see you in that sexy little number and get an instant hard-on."

"Oh my God, Luna." Bree laughs while maintaining a tight grip on the steering wheel. "You're going to make this girl blush."

"All's I'm saying is that you're going to be one sexy little babe in that red-hot number. That dress fits your skinny-ass form like a God-damned glove. I'm really jealous of how fine you looked in it when you tried it on. It was made for you." She laughs. "He'll want to ravish you right there in the graduation hall."

She laughs again. "I can see it now. He'll give it to you real good and make you scream with delight."

"You're incorrigible." Quickly glancing at her petite friend, Bree smiles and then turns her attention back to the road. "I did look pretty hot in it, didn't I?"

"Are you kidding me? If I was a guy, I would have done you right there in the that dress shop. Those old gals would've wet their panties if they could have seen what I would have done to you."

"Jesus, Luna, you're a bad little bitch. How does Jace put up with your filthy mind?"

Bree feels the mood instantly change. Silence fills the car. The two young women look straight ahead at the road in front of them, the yellow line hypnotizing them into a more subdued mood.

When she can no longer handle the silence, Bree whispers, "I'm sorry, Luna. Are you all right?"

"I'm fine."

Bree can tell she's lying.

"Did I say something to upset you?"

Luna shakes her head.

"Want to talk about it?"

"There's nothing to talk about," Luna says, her teeth clenched tightly.

Her voice has become soft. Her words are distant. Gone is the sense of joy and laughter that only seconds earlier had filled the car.

Bree glances at her friend. "I've had the feeling ever since dinner last night that something was bothering you. I hope you know that you can talk to me if something is wrong. I'm here for you...always."

"I know." Luna sighs. "You're such a good friend."

"Well, if I'm such a good friend, why don't you tell me what's got you feeling so down?"

An awkward silence fills the car again. Bree concentrates on the road ahead.

"I'm not sure where Jace and I stand right now," Luna finally says.

Bree switches off the air blower, so she can better hear her friend. "Don't you love him?"

"I do. With all my heart."

"Then don't you think he loves you?"

Luna hesitates and then says, "I do. I'm sure he loves me very much."

Bree shakes her head. "If you love each other, then what's the problem? Alex and I actually thought you guys have been planning a secret wedding behind our backs. And I must tell you, my friend, if I find out you're planning a wedding without including me, I will never forgive you."

"Trust me, Bree, you would be the first to know about it." Luna glances out the side window. "You do know that whenever I eventually get married—to Jace or someone else—you are going to be my maid of honour, don't you?"

"I never assumed anything, but I had always hoped I would be, and I want you to stand with me when I marry Alex."

"He still hasn't popped the question?"

"Not yet, the bugger. And he knows the suspense is killing me."

"He's just waiting for the right moment. But he'll ask. You don't have to worry about that. It's very clear to everyone that Alex is madly in love with you," Luna says. "As for Jace and me, I'm not so sure."

"You don't think he wants to marry you?"

"I really don't know what he's thinking...or feeling. Whenever I try to talk to him about what's next for us once he graduates, he clams up tighter than a virgin in a monastery and I'm left trying to figure out what in hell we're doing."

Bree can sense her friend is almost in tears. "I had no idea you were going through that. Why am I just hearing about this now?"

"I didn't really know what to tell you. Ever since Jace was in Cape Breton, he's become withdrawn and aloof. He is definitely not himself, but I can't figure out what's going on with him."

"Is he okay, physically, I mean? He's not sick, is he?"

Luna shakes her head. "I don't think so. But I'm not sure he would even tell me if he was."

Bree considers her next question, then asks, "Is he, you know, sexual? I mean, is he still interested in you, physically?"

"God, yes. If there's one thing his pissy attitude hasn't affected, it's his sex drive. I think that man's dick has a mind of its own. I've seen it rise on demand."

"Most of them do." Bree laughs, but she notices her friend doesn't join in.

"I'm not sure that his wanting to have sex with me isn't just his way of relieving stress," Luna says. "Sometimes there's not any love in our love making. It has become very mechanical." She looks directly at Bree and asks, "Know what I mean?"

Bree's heart breaks for her friend. "The guys have been under a great deal of pressure this year. Maybe it has something to do with that," she says. "Between residencies and making sure they have all their necessary credits to graduate, they've had a lot on their plates. I've noticed a big change in Alex, too. Maybe all that stress is finally getting to Jace. Maybe once he graduates and settles down into a regular routine, he'll be more like his old self again."

"I really don't think that's it. Jace usually can handle as much pressure as you can throw at him. I think there's something else going on."

"Would it do any good if I asked Alex to talk to him?"

"Hell, no." Luna's answer is swift. "If Jace finds out that I've even talked to *you* about this, he'll be pissed. He would be so embarrassed if he knew you guys had any idea that we were having trouble in our relationship."

"Of course," Bree assures her friend. "I won't tell Alex anything, if that's what you want."

Bree can feel her friend glaring at her.

"Promise me, Bree," Luna pleads. "You won't tell Alex."

Bree nods. "I promise I won't say anything to Alex."

"Okay. Okay. Let's change the subject before you make me cry."

Bree stares at the road ahead. Finally, she asks, "Have you noticed the amount of roadkill we've gone past today?"

"Now that you mention it, I have noticed a lot of dead animal bodies along the road, but I just thought it was normal for this area."

"You grew up in this part of the province, Luna, and you know this isn't normal. I mean, you typically see the odd raccoon or porcupine or sometimes even a skunk—which usually stinks to high heaven—but you don't typically see anything like this...bodies on top of bodies."

"Why do you suppose that is?"

"I have no idea, but I find it very creepy."

Bree's eyes dart from side to side. She suddenly feels overwhelmed, as if a heavy weight has been placed on her shoulders. "I really don't like this. Something doesn't feel right.".

"Holy shit, Bree," Luna suddenly screams. "There's deer in the road!"

Bree instinctively hits the brakes.

18: What is your emergency?

Molly Knight has been a 9-1-1 operator for three and a half years. She loves the job because she likes being able to help people. Never one to become easily flummoxed, she's always felt she was made for this job. Often under immense pressure, she's able to remain calm and rational, keeps her cool and remains focused on the task at hand.

And she never takes the calls personally because she knows that will accomplish nothing and it certainly won't help those who are in distress and making the call.

Molly has answered a wide range of calls during her time with emergency services, from murders and attempted suicides to premature births and industrial accidents, to major house fires and natural disasters. She feels she can handle just about anything, but the number of strange calls she's taken over the past twelve hours have pushed her, and all the other operators, to the breaking point.

"9-1-1," Molly answers when her call board lights up. "What is your emergency?"

"Please help me," the woman cries, almost as if she is out of breath. "Send an ambulance."

"Ma'am. Are you hurt? Can you tell me what happened?"

"Yes." The woman sobs. "I'm hurt....Bleeding."

"Okay, ma'am." Molly remains calm, speaking in a soothing voice. "Can you tell me your name?"

"It's Bonnie," the woman cries again. "Bonnie Bookman. Help me. It hurts so much."

"We are sending help. Is it Mrs. Bookman?"

"No. I'm not married."

"Very well. Ms. Bookman, can you tell me your address?"

"565 Evergreen Drive. Please hurry."

"The police and ambulance are on their way, Ms. Bookman. Can you tell me what happened?"

The woman struggles to speak. "They attacked me."

"Has someone hurt you, Ms. Bookman? Are they still in your home?"

Several seconds pass before the woman answers. "It wasn't anyone. It was my babies." She sobs. "My babies attacked me and there's blood everywhere. I don't know what's wrong with them. Why did they attack me? They have never hurt me before."

"I'm sorry, Ms. Bookman, but what did you mean when you said your *babies* attacked you?"

"My cats. It was my cats."

Molly is surprised. "How many cats are we talking about? One? Two? More?"

"Seven."

"You have seven cats?"

"I love cats. They are my babies."

"Why did they attack you?"

"I don't know," the woman cries. "They are usually kind and gentle and I love them so much. But I was in the bedroom putting laundry away, and they turned on me without warning." She sobs. "Please send someone. I'm bleeding very badly."

"The ambulance is close," Molly answers. "Do you know where the cats are now?"

"I don't know. But don't let anyone hurt my babies."

"We'll try not harm them, Ms. Bookman. Are they with you?"

"No. I'm locked in the bathroom. I don't know where they are."

"Okay, the ambulance is very close. You should be able to hear it in a few minutes."

"They didn't mean to hurt me."

"I'm sure they didn't, but do you have any idea why they would turn on you?"

"No." The woman sobs. "They were good one minute and then, all of a sudden, they just came at me. I didn't know what to do. Their claws really hurt."

"I'm sure it did," Molly says, her voice mellow and soothing. "You should be able to hear the ambulance. They are pulling into your driveway right now."

"Thank you dear. I will go and meet them."

"No, Ms. Bookman," Molly replies. "Please just stay where you are. The first responders will come to you."

"It's okay, dear."

Molly hears the woman open the bathroom door.

"Oh my God," the woman cries. "They are here. Ohhh. It hurts. I can't get them off."

Molly listens. She hears a thud as she assumes the phone lands on the floor.

"Ms. Bookman?" she asks. "Are you there?"

There is no answer.

"Ms. Bookman…?"

~

It has been almost forty-five minutes since Molly took the call from Bonnie Bookman and she's still shaken by the woman's pleas for help.

She's dealt with many emotional calls from people in distress but, as she is a cat lover herself, with two of her own "babies" at home, this one has left an impression.

Come on, Molly. She shakes her head, as her switchboard lights up again. She knows someone else is in trouble and needs her help. She hits the answer button.

"9-1-1. What is your emergency?"

"Foxes. They jumped me." The man's voice blurts into her receiver. "God-damned things got all my chickens."

"Please tell me what happened," Molly replies, using the calmest voice she can muster. "Are you hurt?"

"Yes." The man answers. "God-damned things bit me."

"Okay, sir. Please tell me your name and address."

"Wade Murray. I live at the end of Maple Ridge Road. Send the police."

"We are dispatching an ambulance and the police. They will be there shortly."

"I don't need an ambulance," the man tells her. "I need the police and tell them to bring guns. They need to shoot the bastards."

"It's standard procedure for the paramedics to answer 9-1-1 calls if there is an injury. They will have to check you out, Mr. Murray," Molly tells him. "Can you tell me what happened?"

She hears the man take a deep breath. He then says, "I was in the house eating my supper and watching the news when I heard a commotion in the backyard. When I got up to check it out, something was chasing my chickens around the yard. It was a god-damned fox."

"Have foxes ever come after your chickens before?"

"No." His answer is quick and sharp. "Never. And I've had a lot of chickens around here over the years. Never seen no foxes, though.

Damned thing killed two of my best laying hens."

"Okay, Mr. Murray. What happened next?"

"I got my rifle and went out in the backyard. I would have killed the bastard if I could have got my sights on him, but I didn't know there were more of them out there. I only saw the one from my window, but there was a whole pack, and when I got in the yard, they jumped me and knocked me to the ground."

"Do you know how many there were, Mr. Murray?"

"Maybe five or six, and the bastards have a wicked bite on them. I need the police to shoot them."

"Are the foxes still around your yard?"

"They were there when I checked a few minutes ago. I could see them running around. They killed all my chickens."

"Are you in the house now?"

"Yes. I managed to beat the bastards off with my rifle, but I think I'm hurt pretty bad. I see lots of blood."

"Is your house secure?"

"Yes. The door is locked but—"

"Mr. Murray? Mr. Murray? Can you hear me?"

Molly hears the sound of shattering glass and a muffled cry for help.

"Mr. Murray?" she whispers.

~

It has been one hell of a night but now, as Molly nears the end of her twelve-hour shift, she's looking forward to getting home and taking a nice long bath. She's hoping the hot water will soak away the memories of the day's horrific calls.

She will tell anyone who will listen that she has never experienced another shift quite like this.

And I'm sure the other operators will agree, Molly thinks as she takes a sip of her ice-cold water. It's been one bizarre call after another and, for whatever reason, many of them involved animal attacks.

Never heard anything like it before.

Now with only thirteen minutes to go before she can sign off for the day, Molly steels her nerves as her switchboard lights up.

Now what?

"9-1-1," she calmly says into the mic. "What is your emergency?"

"Please send an ambulance." The woman's plea sounds urgent. "I'm hurt."

Molly's instincts kick in. She pushes her own personal thoughts aside. "What is the nature of your injuries?" she asks the caller.

"Animal bites," the woman cries. "I've been bitten by a raccoon. It attacked me."

"I see. What is your name and address please?"

"Joanie Holdright. I'm at 63 Park Street."

"Okay. It's Mrs. Holdright, right?"

"Yes." Her voice is so soft, Molly can hardly hear her.

"Paramedics will be there in about ten minutes. Police will be there shortly."

"Please ask them to hurry. It hurts a lot."

"They are coming as quickly as they can. Can you tell me what happened, Mrs. Holdright?"

"After supper, I did the dishes and was taking my compost out to the green bin, and when I opened the lid, there was a big raccoon in there, staring up at me. It was huge and it nearly scared me to death. Before I could close the lid, it jumped out and attacked me."

"Did it bite you?"

"Yes, it bit me many times, and it hurts so much."

"Where is the raccoon now?"

"I don't know. I managed to get it off me, and I ran to the house. I thought it was going to going to kill me. It followed me but luckily, I keep an old broom on the back doorstep. I grabbed it and kept hitting the beast until it turned and ran away. I don't know how many times I hit it. I was so scared."

"Was it just the one raccoon, Mrs. Holdright?"

"That's all I saw. But it was big bugger. Tore big chunks of skin from my arms and chest and it even got me in the face a couple of times. There's a lot of blood. I was a nurse before I retired and I'm sure some of the wounds will require stitches."

"Okay, Mrs. Holdright. I'm sorry you had to go through such an ordeal this evening. The paramedics will see to your injuries when they get there. I'm sorry for the delay, but it should not be much longer."

"I have lived here all my life, and I have never seen an animal behave like that. Never. What could have gotten into it? Was it sick or something? I really wasn't going to hurt it. I just wanted to get away."

"I don't know." Molly shakes her head. "But there seems to be a lot of that going around here today."

~

With five minutes to go until the end of her shift, Molly takes a deep breath. She's relieved that it's almost time to go home, but she also knows that sometimes those last few minutes of any shift can be among the longest an operator may have to endure, especially on a crazy day like this one.

"Come on. Come on," she whispers to the clock.

Then she feels her heart sink as the light on her console blinks on.

"I knew it," she whispers, quickly answering the call.

Tamping down her rising anxiety, she says into the mic, "9-1-1. What is your emergency?"

"We've had an accident," the woman cries. "Our car hit a herd of deer on Highway 103. Please help us."

19: A death among them

Death has come again, and Alex's emotions run amok. His head spins. His heart is heavy.

He sits in his black Honda Civic, staring at the murder of crows that is congregating in the trees surrounding the modest bungalow where he spent his formative years.

He recalls the events of the past two days. He shudders as chills rush up his spine. And now, the appearance of these crows has left him struggling to put the events into perspective and to regain his equilibrium.

He feels as if the world is closing in on him, choking off his air supply, and he's gasping for his last breath.

"Something," he whispers, "is seriously wrong around here."

Alex recalls the warnings from his great-uncle Silas Moores earlier today. The old man told him about people and animals behaving oddly—even with deadly results—in the three days leading up to a solar eclipse, like the one that's coming on Monday afternoon. He is certain that what he is witnessing is the manifestation of that phenomena.

What the hell can I do about it?

"Nothing." His great-uncle's words reverberate in his ears. "There is nothing you can do about it except to protect yourself and the ones you hold dear. Keep them close."

How do I do that?

His mind is flooded by images of the patients he's treated since last evening. His heart aches when he thinks about the violent ways in which the people have been maimed or killed.

Then there are the animals. They have gone berserk.

"God-damn it," he whispers, wishing that Oliver was here with him right now. He's certain his life-long friend—his protector, anointed by the crows—would know what to do.

But in Oliver's absence, Alex is left to his own devices.

"Protect them all," he whispers, turning off the car's engine and leaning forward to rest his forehead on the steering wheel. "Like that's going to be easy."

He believes the warning from Silas is not to be taken lightly.

I've got to get everyone together in one place on Monday afternoon, but first we've got to get through the next forty-eight hours and Christ only knows what will happen in that time.

A commotion snaps him out of his thoughts. Alex glances around the yard and what he sees there leaves him shaken. Hundreds of crows have now come to roost. It's as if the trees in the backyard have been painted black by an invisible artist.

"Oh my God," he whispers, watching as ten crows emerge from the flock and land on the grass not far from where he's parked. They form a tight circle. The other crows remain on their perches, watching.

Alex carefully opens his car door and steps slowly into the late April afternoon air, the cool breeze tossing his thick white hair around his head. An unholy and unnatural quietness fills the air.

Amid the murder, he spots the carcass of a large crow resting at the centre of the circle. He has only ever seen this phenomenon once before, but he knows exactly what's happening.

This, he knows, is a crow funeral, a rare event not often witnessed by a human.

As if revering the dead crow, the ten black sentinels have issued an alert, harsh and urgent.

Caw! Caw! Caw!

Their cry is distinct, their pain palpable. They call to their brethren, near and far.

Within moments, more crows arrive, settling onto whatever aerial perch allows good viewing of the corpse and the birds around it. There could be as many as a thousand crows of various sizes and shades of black.

The crows ignore the human in their midst for they know he means them no harm.

Alex advances to edge of the circle. His gaze comes to rest on the remains of the dead crow, its black feathers hideously stained by the red of its blood. He fights the urge to vomit.

Something or someone killed this crow. Alex knows there will be hell to pay when the flock finds out who or what is responsible for this desecration. And they will find out, of that he is sure. He also knows the crows will want retribution.

He understands the crows. Now though, he can see that it is their time to mourn.

For a few minutes the crows remain quiet and still, only to break into a chorus of shrill calls. Back and forth, silence and then aggravated calls of sorrow continue for perhaps fifteen minutes until, nearly all at once, the birds launch from their perches and disperse into the cool air, leaving branches to quiver in their wake.

But the ten remain, their tight circle unbroken.

Alex holds his ground, taking slow shallow breaths. He is honoured to have borne witness to this phenomenon that so few people have ever seen, and he does not want to spook the crows. Their twenty pellet-like eyes remain fixed on the dead crow's remains.

He shivers at the sight. It is as though they are in communion with the dead.

Finally Alex slowly steps out of the circle, removing himself from this union. In unison, the ten crows turn their heads, locking their gaze upon him.

Alex shivers. It feels as though the stares are cutting through him, reaching to his very soul. He is certain these crows will not harm him, but he knows they want something from him.

"I understand," he whispers, eyes wide, never blinking. "What would you have me do?"

Like a choir in a large cathedral, the chorus of ten crows emit a mournful, low-pitched cackle, followed by a series of sharp caws, cries and screeches.

"Of course, I will help you," Alex answers. "Whatever you need."

As Alex returns to his car and opens the trunk, the ten crows spring from the ground and move to over-hanging tree branches. From their perches, they quietly watch his movements as if supervising his actions.

Retrieving a vinyl shopping bag that he uses for groceries—the only suitable receptacle he can find in the trunk of his car—Alex returns to the body of the dead crow and kneels beside it in the wet grass. He remains silent as words are not necessary nor do they seem appropriate.

He glances at the ten crows on the branches. Their twenty eyes glare at him. Unblinking, they convey their message.

"Right," Alex whispers, bowing his head to the dead crow.

With the aid of a stick, he scoops the feathered remains into the bag and then stands straight. The bird's blood leaves a pool on the cold ground.

"There," Alex says.

The ten crows prance and manoeuvre across the branches. Heads bobbing. Eyes blinking. Beaks opening and closing, silently signalling their approval.

"I will take good care of your kin," he tells the ten. His heart is heavy with sorrow for the crows. He knows that when one in the murder dies, the entire flock feels the loss.

"I will bury your mate someplace safe."

Satisfied that this human—the golden one—will do what is necessary, the ten crows spring from their perches and take flight. They soar up and out of sight. Alex watches them disappear into the late afternoon sky and wonders what they will do next.

He returns to his car and places the bag in the trunk.

Wave after wave of sorrow wash over him. He feels their loss deeply, and knows he must help the crows because, when the time comes, they will be there for him.

They always are.

20: The aftermath

"Hey, honey," Samantha calls from the kitchen as Alex enters the house and makes his way toward her. "Did you have a good day?"

"It was fine," he lies to his mother.

His encounter with the crows has left him shaken and emotionally drained, but he chooses not to tell her about that. The kitchen is filled with the unmistakable sights, sounds and smells of someone cooking an elaborate feast.

"Just fine?" she asks.

"Yup. Just fine."

He sits on one of the stools next to the kitchen peninsula and watches his mother. She is busily putting the finishing touches to the menu she's planned for the dinner party she and Kate are hosting to honour Alex and Jace on their impending graduation from medical school.

"It doesn't sound like you had an especially good day," she observes. She looks at him through a cloud of steam that's rising from the stove. "I thought you and Jace were spending the day together."

"That was the plan." Alex frowns. "But nothing went quite exactly as we had hoped."

"Really?" She stops stirring whatever is in the large cookpot. "Anything serious going on?"

Alex considers the question. "I guess you could say that. Jace was bitten by a large spider this morning and he's hurting pretty badly. Uncle Charlie prescribed some antibiotics and medicinal cream for any infection, but Jace is in a lot of pain. It's very difficult for him to walk. I feel really bad for him."

"Why didn't you bring him back here with you so we could keep an eye on him? He could have rested in Hunter's old room."

"Jace insisted on going back to the Airbnb. Said he wanted to take a nap before dinner. Bree and Luna should soon be back from Bridgewater, so Luna will be there with him."

"That sounds awful," Samantha says. "Of all the unusual things to happen while you're on a weekend getaway. Spider bites are pretty rare, aren't they?"

"They happen more than you think."

"Poor Jace. Well, let's hope he's feeling better for dinner this evening."

She motions toward the stove and cupboards that are filled to overflowing with dishes, pots, and pans. "Because someone has to eat all of this food."

Alex laughs. "I did warn you not to go overboard. But, in typical Samantha Henderson fashion, you didn't listen to anything I said. But you never listen to anyone else, so why am I not surprised?"

"Stop it." She winks at her son. "You sound just like Kate."

"It smells amazing in here, though. I'm starving."

"It's going to be a while until dinner. Want me to fix you a little snack to hold you over?"

"No, but thanks anyway. I don't want to spoil dinner. Speaking of Kate, where is she? I thought she was going to help you."

"That was the plan," Samantha says. "But she was called into the office for some emergency meeting."

"On a Saturday? What's up with that?"

"I have no idea. All she told me was that it had something to do with a big case they are working on, and that it couldn't wait, but she promised she would be home in time to help with final preparations. We'll see how that goes."

"Wonder if Kate tried to call in Bree," Alex says. "I'm sure she would have dropped everything and gone to the office if she had been called. Kate is training her well. Those two are so much alike it's really uncanny and, I admit, it scares me a little how driven she has become."

"Kate knows how important this weekend is to you guys, so I'm sure she wouldn't bother Bree while your friends are here."

"Watch out for Monday, though."

Samantha nods. "Monday could be a hell of a day."

"Speaking of Monday, because this weekend has gotten off to such a crappy start, Jace and Luna are now planning to stay in town for an extra day or two. Would you mind having everyone come over for a late lunch before they go back to the city? I thought it would be nice to have a little send-off for them."

Samantha stops stirring again and stares at her son. "I guess we could do that, Alex, but you do know Monday is not a holiday, don't you? People will be working and it may be difficult for them to get away."

"But Monday is also the solar eclipse, isn't it? I was thinking it would be fun to have a little viewing party for everyone. I'll see if I can scrounge up some of those special glasses that you need to look at it. It's supposed to be a big deal."

"I guess it would be fun to have a viewing party. They say it won't be visible in this part of the world for another twenty years, so let's do it. We'll be able to clean up the leftovers and I'll make a few sandwiches. You know, just something light."

"Now, when you say *light,* you're not talking about a seven-course meal, are you?" Alex laughs.

"Don't be a smart ass, mister." Samantha joins in the laughter. "You know I like to cook for people. So, sue me."

"Careful, Mom. Your wife and daughter-in-law are both lawyers. You never know who they'll sue or for what reason."

"My daughter-in-law?" Samantha looks at him, squinting through the cloud of steam. "Something you want to share with me, young man?"

"No," Alex replies sheepishly. He's aware that everyone has been waiting for him to pop the question. "I just meant that Bree may as well be your daughter-in-law, that's all."

"You're sure that's all?"

"Yes, Mom. I'm very sure."

"I wish you and Bree would get married," Samantha observes. "It's long overdue. Now that you're done with your studies, is that going to happen soon?"

"No pressure, right Mom?"

"What? I think you guys are perfectly suited for each other and I would like to see you get married. What's wrong with that?"

"Absolutely nothing but maybe tamp down your enthusiasm just a little bit." Alex answers as he feels his phone vibrate in his pants pocket.

Quickly glancing at the Smart Watch on his wrist that's synced with the phone, he adds, "I better get this call. It might be Bree or Jace. Or maybe Uncle Charlie. He seemed pretty slammed when I was there earlier today."

Seeing the number flash across the small screen, he shakes his head. "Nope. Not any of those guys. It's Warren. I wonder what he wants."

~

Responding to Warren's call, Samantha and Alex speed to the hospital, stopping at the Hugin and Munin along the way to pick up Jace. Samantha also called Kate and she will meet them there.

According to Warren, Bree and Luna were in a serious car accident. He doesn't know how either of the girls are doing, but he did confirm there were no fatalities.

At the hospital, Alex, Samantha and Jace gather in the waiting room with Bree's parents, all hoping Dr. Charlie Webster will soon appear and fill them in on the girls' condition. Neither Warren nor Samantha will allow Alex to go into the examination room as they have no idea what horrors could await him there.

Warren tells everyone that the accident occurred on Highway 103, just before the Brooklyn exit. "It appears Bree swerved to avoid hitting some deer."

"Deer?" Alex asks.

"Yes. It looks like the car flipped a couple of times before coming to rest on its roof in the ditch. Fire fighters had to use the Jaws of Life to get them out of the wreck. Constable Shaw said they were wedged in there pretty tight."

"Oh my God," Alex cries. Samantha hugs him close to her. "Please let them be all right. I don't know what I will do if anything happens to Bree. There's so much we have to do….So much I need to tell her."

"Come over here and sit beside your friend." Samantha takes Alex by the arm and leads him to an empty chair next to Jace, who has been sitting quietly, his head buried in his hands.

"How are you doing, Jace?" she asks, kneeling in front of him and taking his right hand. "How is your foot?"

"It hurts like hell, Ms. Henderson, but I could care less about myself." He brushes tears from his eyes with the back of his left hand. "I just want Luna to be all right."

"I know you do, sweetie," she whispers, gently squeezing his hand. "We all want that."

She stands and looks at the distraught young men. "Please listen to me. I know it's hard because you are both doctors and I'm sure you think you know what's best, but we can't jump to any conclusions. Let's just wait until we hear from Charlie. We need facts, not conjecture."

"Right, Mom," Alex agrees. "But that's easier said than done."

"I've been through this before and jumping to conclusions does not help anything."

Alex springs to his feet. "I should be in there, helping Uncle Charlie. He's got a lot to deal with right now and I could give him a hand."

"Or," Samantha says, gently pushing him back down in the chair again, "you could sit right here and wait. Your uncle will come to see us just as soon as he has anything to tell us."

The minutes slow to a crawl and Alex feels like he's going to jump out of his skin. Every nerve ending is tingling as if someone is sticking hot needles into him.

"What's happened?" Kate asks, rushing into the waiting room. "Is there any news?"

"Nothing yet," Alex greets his second mother. "We're just waiting for Uncle Charlie to come out and talk to us. He's examining Bree and Luna right now."

"How long have they been in there?" Kate asks. She grabs Alex and hugs him tightly. "Do we know what happened?"

"Roughly forty-five minutes. All I know is that they had an accident and it involved deer," Alex answers, glancing toward the set of large wooden doors that lead from the waiting area to the examination rooms. He grits his teeth, bracing for what he's about to hear. "Here comes Uncle Charlie now."

"Okay, folks," Charlie says, motioning for Bree's parents to come and join the others. "I figure it'll be easier to tell you all at once rather than individually. Is that all right with you all?"

"Yes," Warren says. "Please, Charlie, just tell us how they are."

"Considering what I've heard about the accident, it could have been a lot worse," Charlie begins.

"Are they all right, Uncle Charlie?" Alex interrupts as Samantha puts her arm around his shoulders. He pulls away.

"Both girls are going to recover, but they will both require some time to get back on their feet, as they did sustain some serious injuries."

"Bree?" Warren asks. "How is she doing?"

"Bree has a fractured right knee and a broken left wrist," Charlie says. "She also has several lacerations and broken ribs from where the seatbelt snapped tight across her chest." He remains stoic but firm. "She also sustained a concussion, most likely when the airbag deployed."

"What about Luna?" Jace asks. His quivering voice is hardly a whisper.

"Yes." Charlie looks at Alex's friend. "She has a lot of cuts, and some required stitches. She's also got a lot of major bruising, but, luckily for her, there are no broken bones. Like Bree, Luna has a concussion, but it looks like the seatbelt did its job. However, she is going be extremely sore for a while."

"That's it?" Jace asks. "What aren't you telling me?"

"There is some internal bleeding, but it doesn't appear to be life-threatening," Charlie says. "She suffered several broken ribs and one of them punctured her left lung. She's in distress as breathing is very painful for her, so we've sedated her and have her on oxygen."

"Does she need surgery?" Jace asks.

"Charlie shakes his head. "But we need to keep her here for at least twenty-four hours to make sure the lung can heal without intervention. If we do decide we have to operate, then we will transfer her to Bridgewater or possibly even Halifax, where they are better equipped for the procedure. All in all, though, I think both girls were lucky to escape major injuries."

"Doesn't feel like they were lucky," Alex replies.

"I know," Charlie agrees. "But try to look at the bright side, Alex. They will both recover from their injuries. They just need time to heal."

"When can we take Bree home?" Lisa asks.

"It will be a few more hours. She needs to have a cast put on her wrist, so that will take a while. You were a trauma room nurse, Lisa, so you know what to look for as far as the concussion goes?"

Lisa nods, tears streaming down her cheeks.

Alex wraps his arm around his friend's shoulder to offer support. "Jace and I would like to see them now."

Charlie nods. "You two come with me. Parents," he adds, "you will have to wait right here for a while longer."

~

"I'm sorry you had to go through this," Alex whispers, softly squeezing Bree's right hand. "I feel so bad that you're in so much pain."

"It's not your fault." She forces a slight smile. "As for the pain, I honestly don't feel too much. I think your uncle was pretty generous with the meds."

"That's a good thing."

"You need a haircut." She reaches up and brushes a few loose strands of hair from his eyes. "Did you ask him for special treatment for me?"

Alex shakes his head. "Whatever Uncle Charlie did, he did it on his own."

Nodding toward her left wrist, she asks, "Is this going to have any long-term effect on my ability to write? You do remember that I'm left-handed."

"I don't think there should be any long-term impact. You may require some physio to restore full movement once the cast comes off, but I think you'll be fine."

"I hope so."

Alex can see tears forming in her eyes.

"It was so horrible," she whispers. "I was so afraid that we were going to die, and I wouldn't see you again."

"I was afraid for you, too." He stifles his tears, refusing to let her see him cry.

She takes a deep breath and flinches. He can see she's suffering from her injuries. She says, "Please tell me that Luna is going to be all right."

"She's going to be fine." He speaks softly. "Jace is with her right now and she's resting comfortably. They have her sedated. Do you remember what happened?"

"I remember everything. I was almost to the Brooklyn exit when a herd of deer appeared right out of the blue. Must have been six or eight of them in the middle of the road. It happened so fast. I swerved to avoid hitting them, but then I got into the loose gravel on the shoulder and lost control of the car."

After a moment she continues, "We just kept flipping over and over and then, when we stopped, the car was resting on the driver side, and I couldn't get out. It hurt a lot. I blacked out for a few minutes and, when I came to, I couldn't move my legs and I had a massive headache. I was so worried about Luna. She was crying and screaming for help." Bree sobs. "But I couldn't help her...I couldn't reach her."

"It's all good now. You are both going to fully recover. Everything is going to be fine."

Bree's voice is nothing but a whisper. "I remember one more thing that I didn't tell the police about."

"What's that?"

"I remember crows being there. They were in the trees around the car. I saw them. I felt them. They stayed with me the whole time while I was waiting to be rescued. I felt safe with them there."

"Do you know how many there were?"

"No. It was too dark to count them, and my head was pounding, but I knew they were there for me. I knew, Alex, and I felt better knowing they were there."

"Do you think there could have been ten?"

Bree pauses, thinking about Alex's question. "I can't say for sure," she whispers. "But, yes, that sounds about right."

21: Momma's Homemade Pizza

Most people in town would agree that Russell "Rusty" Davidson is a strong pillar of the community. Trustworthy. Intelligent. Reliable. Hardworking. He's seen as a true leader in every sense.

A father of three, a soon-to-be grandfather, and a two-term member of the town council, Rusty is the kind of volunteer who steps up to give freely of his time whenever asked because, as his wife, Monica, jokingly tells him, the word "no" is not in his vocabulary.

Rusty is also the kind of guy you want in your corner and this evening, after working for the past eight hours at a day-long flea market sponsored by the hospital auxiliary to raise money to purchase equipment for the local health care facility, he's exhausted.

"But it was for a good cause," he tells his wife through his hands-free connection as he drives down Main Street. He's heading to Momma's Homemade Pizza, his go-to place whenever he craves takeout.

He's ordered his usual large pizza with the works, including pineapple, for supper because, as he told Monica, he didn't feel like coming home and cooking after putting in such a long day. Saturday evenings are tradition-ally Rusty's night to prepare dinner.

"How did the flea market go?" his wife of thirty-six years asks. "Were there many people around? I wanted to come by, but I knew it would be crowded and I couldn't handle that today."

"Good call, because the place was packed. In fact, it was so tight when the doors first opened that people couldn't get up to the tables to see what we were selling. But we raised a lot of money for the hospital," Rusty says, stopping at a crosswalk to allow several pedestrians to safely pass. He's a conscientious and cautious driver. He knows how quickly accidents can happen if you're not paying strict attention to the road, to the other drivers and to pedestrians.

"But the responsibility is always yours," he told his three children when he taught them each to drive. It was a duty he relished.

He enjoyed spending such quality time with his children and he misses all three now that they've grown up and moved out of the house. But he's thankful he and Monica will soon have a grandchild to spoil. It will be their first and they're very excited about the addition to their family.

"But first things first," he whispers while stepping on the gas pedal once the pedestrians have passed the front of his car. "My pizza awaits."

~

Sisters Marsha and Meghan Finch, the co-owners of Momma's Homemade Pizza, love Saturday nights. Not only is it the most lucrative evening of the week for their business, but it's also an opportunity to become reacquainted with old friends and catch up with neighbours they may not have seen in a while.

Sometimes the place is like Grand Central Station, but they are grateful their establishment is one of the town's weekend hot spots. Oftentimes they see regulars like Rusty Davidson, who called his order in a few minutes ago, and sometimes it's old friends the sisters have not seen in a very long time, people who have moved away from town but have come back for various reasons.

This evening, the place is packed with people meeting to celebrate birthdays, to have dinner with friends before going to a movie, to gather for a relaxing meal after a busy workday, to rekindle a floundering romance or to enjoy a first date.

Tom and Cathie Turner have brought their three children—Marcus, Bryson, and Elizabeth—to the restaurant to celebrate their daughter's sixth birthday. Momma's has become their regular destination for family functions, as each of the children can find their favourite items on the menu.

For Marcus, it's a cheese and pepperoni pizza, while Bryson always orders a small lasagne with garlic bread. Elizabeth, the birthday girl, has ordered her usual—a mini-meatball sub. Tom loves their donairs while Cathie sticks to her usual, an Italian-style panzerotti with extra Italian sausage.

"They are such a lovely family," Marsha says to her sister as she places the order with the kitchen and prepares their beverages. "I enjoy seeing them. The kids are always so well behaved."

"Yes," Meghan agrees. "They are good kids, but I've always found Cathie to be a little snooty and kind of standoffish."

"Really?"

"Maybe it's because I went to high school with her," Meghan elaborates. "But to me, she's always been stuck up. I've always felt inferior around her."

"Humph. I've never experienced any of that that with her. Maybe it's because I'm a few years older than you two and didn't really know her all that well in school but, whatever the case, she's always very nice to me."

"That could be it." Meghan agrees. "It used to bother me, but I don't really care anymore."

"Doesn't sound like it," Marsha replies, her voice laced with a healthy dose of sarcasm. "You shouldn't care what anyone else thinks. Look at you. You've got a wonderful husband and two great kids. You're a co-owner of a very successful business that we and Mom grew from the ground up, and, besides all of that, you have the best sister in the whole wide world. What more do you need?"

"Yeah, right." Meghan chuckles. "But seriously. I'm over it."

Nodding toward the table where four of the local teenagers—Bentley MacLeod, Heidi Elliot, Sheldon Baker, and Amy Richards—have been awaiting their orders, Marsha says, "Speaking of people we really like, those four kids have been coming in here for a while now. I've grown to really appreciate them."

"Yeah, me too. They never give us any problems," Meghan agrees. "Seem like great kids. They told me they were going to a movie, and I don't want them to be late. No one wants to walk into a theatre once the movie has started. Kind of ruins the whole experience."

Her sister nods. "One of us may have to go back there and help clean up the backlog. The kitchen is getting slammed pretty hard right now."

"I'll go," Meghan says. "I notice Wanda, Cheryl and Dawn have just come in. Why don't you go over and take their orders?"

"I'll do that. I want to see how they made out with the flea market and find out who got the gift certificates we donated for the gift basket."

"By the way," Meghan adds, "did you see Ted and Kelly Walker hiding over there in the corner? I think they're trying to lay low. Wonder what's up with them?"

"They might be trying to find a quiet place to talk," Marsha says. Grabbing an order pad, she adds, "I hear they're having marriage troubles."

"What? No way. I thought they had the perfect marriage."

"Appearances can be deceiving, sis." Marsha pauses, considering her own comment. "What's it been for them? Must be fifteen years at least. I know it's around that because they got married pretty close to when Peter and I got married and we're pushing sixteen years in June."

"To see them putting on airs around town, you'd never think they were having relationship issues. I like them both and I hope they can work out whatever's going on."

"I should go over there and get Wanda's order before she jumps down our throats."

"She's not like that, is she?"

"Are you kidding me?" Marsha stares at her sister, her eyes squinting. "She can be a bitch with a capital B if you cross her."

"Well," Meghan says. "Let's not cross her then."

"Oh, don't you worry, sister. I'll be the friendliest, most cordial, most accommodating server Wanda has ever seen." Marsha laughs. "She wouldn't dare to lose her temper with me."

"Seriously, don't over sell it."

Marsha glances around the packed restaurant. "Say," she whispers. "Isn't that Jack?"

"My Jack?" Meghan cranes her neck to get a clear view of where her sister is pointing. She nods. "That's my Jack. Any idea who he's with? I don't recognize him."

"It's Christopher Tate. I've seen him around town a lot. Seems like a nice boy. Is Jack dating him?"

"I've never met him, and Jack doesn't tell me too much about who he dates. Do you know anything about him?"

"Not really, but the Tate family seems nice. Are he and Jack in the same school?"

"Like I said, Marsha, I don't know anything about him."

"If Jack was my son and was dating someone that I hadn't met, I'd march right over there and introduce myself. You are his mother, after all, and he must want you to meet Christopher or they wouldn't have come in here. He had to know you were going to see him."

"I can't do that." Meghan pulls back at her sister's suggestion. "If Jack wants me to meet a boy he's dating, he'll bring him over and introduce us. Imagine how embarrassed he'd be if his mother just showed up at the side of the table."

"Okay. I'm just saying that if I was his mother, I'd want to know as much information about the boy as I could get."

"Oh, believe me, sister. I want to know everything about him that there is to know, but I choose to wait and do things the right way."

"So, you're saying I do things the wrong way?"

"Sometimes." Meghan shrugs. "Now that's enough chitchat. I've got orders to check on in the kitchen and you've got to get your ass over there to Wanda's table before she blows a fuse."

Marsha nods. "And while I'm at it, I'll just swing by Jack's table and meet Christopher."

"Don't you dare."

"I'm just kidding." Marsha laughs as she slides out from behind the counter. "Or am I?"

~

As the sign for Momma's Homemade Pizza comes into view, Rusty Davidson turns off his phone, takes a deep breath, and, with his eyes narrowed to tiny slits, slams his foot to the accelerator and aims his car at the front entrance.

Once those inside realize what's about to happen, they have no time to react.

22: Black and white

Sunday, April 7

It is 6:13 in the morning by the time Alex walks out of the hospital. He shivers. It's an unseasonably cool morning but it is still only early April, which means any type of weather is possible. He wonders if winter is ever going to loosen its grip on the region.

The sun has just risen, revealing a world painted white with heavy frost. The ten ink-black crows that perch in the trees not far from the building's rear exit create a stark contrast that isn't lost on Alex.

The staff parking area behind the hospital is empty. The silence, seeming to reverberate off the frost-covered cars that have been there since last evening, is so loud that it's deafening. It's a stark reminder that the universe is off kilter.

Alex shivers again. He feels alone, isolated from the rest of the world. He knows that feeling is the result of what he's just witnessed and what is happening around him, as the people of this town are caught up in forces they could never understand.

That was a rough one, he thinks, happy to put that night behind him.

He inhales deeply and then exhales, his warm breath forming a dense white cloud that hangs in front of his mouth. His chest hurts, both from the minuscule ice crystals in the frost-laden morning air and from the emotions he's feeling. His head is also reeling from the impacts of what he just experienced. He shakes in the cold as he prefers warmer temperatures.

"What are you doing here?" he says to the crows.

The crows quickly bob their heads and strut about on the tree branches, their twenty beady-like eyes blinking in unison as if they are sending a message in Morse code. He doesn't understand it, not yet, anyway.

He marvels at their precision, their unity, and their energy at this time of day. While the rest of the world is just starting to stir, the crows appear to be fully charged and raring to go.

I sure could have used some of that energy a few hours ago.

Alex wasn't supposed to work last night. But, in fact, nothing about last night went as it was planned. No gathering with friends and family. No dinner. No celebration.

After the accident, he was hoping to spend the night with Bree as she was understandably upset, but when his uncle Charlie called him for help as patients from a mass casualty incident started arriving, he couldn't say no. There were thirteen victims of the crash, but fortunately—or unfortunately, depending upon one's perspective—there was only one immediate death.

There were many serious injuries among the victims, with the lives of three people still hanging by very thin threads. Once those patients were stabilized, they were transported by air ambulances to the province's regional facility in Halifax that's better able to handle the serious injuries.

Alex thinks he'd like to do a tour of duty on the medical helicopter someday. But he knows that can't happen any time soon. Right now, he's exhausted, and when he takes over his uncle's practice, he'll have plenty on his plate, so any diversionary side jobs—even brief ones—will have to wait until he's better established.

This morning, he's looking forward to getting home and grabbing some sleep. Once rested, he plans to spend the entire day with Bree, Jace and Luna, who, he hopes, will be discharged from the hospital this afternoon.

Charlie was concerned about her lung following the accident, but the last time Alex checked on her, she seemed to be doing well and was resting comfortably. He was relieved that she wasn't more seriously hurt.

Man, he thinks, blinking in the morning sunlight. *This entire weekend has been a write-off. Jace and Luna will never want to come back to this town. Can't say I'd blame them.*

He yawns and wonders if he should even be driving. He's so tired that he's not sure he can see properly, let alone focus on the road. He longs to close his eyes, even though he's not sure he will be able to sleep as the images of the bloodied victims from the incident at the pizzeria are seared into his brain.

Do doctors ever become immune to the fallout of such a tragedy? He shakes his head. *Not likely.*

Walking toward his car in the staff parking lot, he can't stop thinking about the parade of patients that kept arriving. The crows follow him and find perches on fir trees not far from his car.

Bloodied cuts. Broken bones. Fractured limbs. Internal injuries. Tears of agony. Cries of anger and disbelief. For a while, it seemed like a never-ending flow of broken and bloodied bodies.

He's not sure how he, Charlie and the third doctor on call, Finn Doyle, got through it all, but, somehow, they managed, dealing with the more serious injuries first and then working their way down the list to the least injured.

And each patient had one question—why did Rusty Davidson drive his car into the pizzeria and hurt so many people?

Did he have a heart attack? Or maybe a stroke? Did he swerve to avoid an animal that darted in front of his car? Or maybe it was a pedestrian? Was there something wrong with his car? It must have been a mechanical malfunction, many victims concluded, because Rusty would never intentionally do anything like this.

Alex shakes his head. No one can say for sure what happened, as Constable Nolan Shaw pointed out to the doctors when he arrived at the hospital to talk to some of the victims. Trying to piece together the events that surround such a tragedy can't be easy, Alex concludes.

Impossible, he thinks. *Kind of like putting a shattered femur back together or stitching up a massive laceration that needs twenty-three su*tures, *or telling a loved one that a family member may not make it.*

The patients were of little help to the RCMP officer. They had few answers. The crash happened so quickly.

In fact, Alex knows there may never be an acceptable explanation, as Rusty didn't survive his injuries. He can't tell them what he was doing, or thinking, or experiencing at the time of the incident. He was killed when his car was crushed under a pile of debris.

There will be an autopsy, probably as early as today, as authorities and victims want quick answers. And his family, of course. They want answers, too.

No, Alex shakes his head. *They 'need' answers because, despite all the good things Rusty did for this town, his legacy will now be one of death, destruction, shattered futures, and broken dreams. That's all everyone will remember him for, if they remember anything at all.*

Alex believes he knows what compelled the middle-aged man to turn his car into a deadly projectile and aim it at a restaurant full of people out with their families and friends, enjoying a meal and laughter, making memories, and living their best lives.

Growing up in this town, he knows most of the victims from personal experience.

Marsha and Meghan Finch, the owners of the pizzeria, have been a big part of this town for years and this incident will surely devastate them, personally and perhaps financially. More importantly, though, he's worried about the younger sister, Meghan. She was one of the three people sent to Halifax as she was seriously injured when the front of Rusty's car pinned her against the restaurant's main counter, causing major internal injuries. Alex isn't sure she'll make it. Charlie and Dr. Doyle determined that her spleen and liver were likely compressed by the force, causing serious bleeding inside the organs. It appears the impact tore the lining of the organs, causing blood to spill into the peritoneum, the space in the abdominal cavity that contains the intestines, liver, and spleen.

It's a serious injury and Alex is praying for Meghan to pull through, but he knows it's touch and go. Sending her to Halifax, where specialists in internal medicine can treat the injuries, was Meghan's best chance at survival.

Alex is also worried about Tom Turner, the second victim airlifted to Halifax. The man in his early forties suffered serious back and spinal cord injuries after he threw his body over his six-year-old daughter to protect her from falling debris. He saved his daughter; unfortunately, it's not clear if Tom will ever walk again because of his crushing injuries.

The good thing, Alex thinks—if there's anything good to come from this —is that the little girl, Elizabeth, wasn't injured. *Not even a scrape.* He knows enough about fate not to question such things, but he wonders, *how can that be?*

He also knows the third victim taken to Halifax. He dealt with Bentley MacLeod about a week ago when he was seeing some of Uncle Charlie's patients. Bentley came in because he needed a physical and medical forms filled out as part of an application process for a summer job. A strong, strapping young man, Bentley is facing the fight of his life, dealing with major head injuries he sustained when he was thrown against the restaurant's stone fireplace.

Right now, he's on life support with major brain bleeding, but Alex would not be surprised if he hears soon that he's been declared brain dead.

Gritting his teeth, Alex sucks in a large mouthful of the cool morning air. He knows the MacLeod family very well. He went to school with Bentley's oldest sister, Debbie. They are a close-knit bunch, and if Bentley doesn't pull through, they will be devastated. The kid was known locally to be a genius with a free ride waiting for him at a long list of prestigious universities throughout North America.

Alex leans back against the side of his car, fighting the urge to cry. All of

Bentley's dreams. His hopes and wishes. His aspirations…his future, could be lost and for what?

"Why?" he says to the crows. "Why is this happening?"

Recalling the warning he received from Silas Moores about the effects of solar eclipses, Alex knows the crows can't help him except to provide moral and spiritual support, and he needs more than that.

He wishes he could do something to help people—his family, friends and neighbours—because he knows that if what Silas said comes to pass, the situation is going to worsen as the solar eclipse draws near. Even the people he loves could be in danger.

"Jesus." He shakes his head and closes his eyes. "What else can happen?"

The crows caw and coo softly as if they are trying to comfort him, perhaps cautioning him about tempting fate.

He opens his eyes and stares at the ebony sentinels, their black feathers glowing against the frosty white backdrop. "I know there's nothing you guys can do, but I want to help people. How can I just stand by and wait for the next vicious attack or killing? People are getting hurt and dying. I need to help them. At the very least, I must warn them."

The crows squawk in unison. He knows they feel his pain for they are connected by a thread that spans several centuries.

"I know you would help if you could, but if I tell people what is happening, they'll think I'm crazy."

He becomes quiet and stares at the crows, focused on his feathered friends. "I'm not crazy," he whispers. "Or am I?"

The crows, too, become quiet, then slowly pull back, forming a semicircle on the branches not far from Alex.

He feels his heartbeat quicken, and his stomach does a somersault. It's like his mind is about to explode. "What the bloody hell?"

He's stunned to see, amid the circle of black crows, the white crow. Its pale, frosted feathers stand in stark contrast to the purplish-black, iridescent feathers of its brethren.

"You?" Alex whispers as he slowly approaches the tree in which the ivory-coloured bird—the Spirit Crow—is perched.

He's close enough to see that, while the eyes of the other crows are black like the darkest night, the eyes of the albino crow are a light red.

"Can you help me?"

The Spirit Crow remains quiet and still, as if frozen in time. It stares at Alex, its eyes occasionally blinking.

The air is charged with electricity. Goosebumps rise on Alex's arms, and chills chase up and down his spine.

The ten black crows stand at attention, as though they are the honour guard...the sentinels.

The circle is complete, the bond is tight. The young man and Spirit Crow have become one. Their eyes are locked. He hears the majestic crow's message as if it were speaking to him.

"I am no ordinary crow. I am a mystery born of light and shadow! With the silent pride of white feathers, I write my story across the sky. Some call me a miracle, others a blessing. We are brothers—the blood of my blood, the breath of my breath. You are the chosen one. You are the defender against evil."

The Spirit Crow blinks several times. It then flaps it wings and the bond is broken.

Alex gasps for air, struggling to breath. He stumbles backwards. He fights to maintain his balance. "Jesus," he whispers.

He watches as the Spirit Crow and its ten companions take flight. He understands his role. He knows what he must do.

His path is clear.

23: Waffles or French toast?

Samantha and Kate are chatting in the living room over coffee when Alex walks through the front door.

"Hey, honey," Samantha greets him. She offers him a smile. "Rough shift?"

"Oh my God." His words are full of anguish. "You have no idea. I think it has been the worst shift I've ever put in. I hope it wasn't a sign of what's to come."

"You must be exhausted," Samantha observes. "Can I get you a coffee, or maybe you would prefer a chamomile tea? That will take the edge off and maybe help you relax. I find tea works better for me when I'm feeling overwhelmed."

"No, thanks."

Alex hangs his coat in the hallway closet and goes into the living room to join his parents. He takes a seat on the sofa next to Samantha, closes his eyes and rests his head against the beige-coloured textured upholstery.

The world goes quiet, and he suddenly feels like he's falling, spinning out or control, losing his grip on reality.

His eyes snap open and he stares at the ceiling. Regaining his grip on reality, he murmurs, "What are you guys doing up so early on a Sunday morning? You should still be sleeping."

"Are you kidding?" Kate replies. She's sitting in the matching armchair across from the sofa. With her legs folded up under her slender body like a teenage girl, she looks tiny, but Alex knows that she can be a formidable opponent in the courtroom—and in life. Many adversaries have misjudged her over the years because of her size.

She grimaces at him. "We haven't even been to bed yet so give us an hour and I'm sure our asses will be dragging."

"Who could sleep after a night like that?" Samantha adds. "That was such a horrible thing down at the restaurant." She looks directly at Alex. "How is everyone doing?"

Alex returns her gaze bleakly. "You know I can't tell you too much about any of the victims, but a couple of them aren't out of the woods yet. However, it could have been much worse."

"Those poor people," Samantha says. Tears trickle down her cheeks and she quickly rubs them away. "So much death."

"There seems to be a lot of that going on," Alex says.

"Your mother and I took a little drive last night and went past the restaurant. We couldn't get close, obviously, because the police have the area cordoned off, but the place is a mess," Kate observes. "What would make Rusty do that? He was such a generous man. I worked with him on a couple of projects in recent years, and I liked him a lot."

Alex shakes his head. "We'll just have to wait to see if the police can provide any answers."

Samantha speaks up, "So many people hurt. So many lives destroyed. This town will never be the same."

Alex nods. "It's a real tragedy."

"Are you hungry?" Samantha asks. She touches his arm as if the gesture will sooth his emotions. "How about waffles or maybe French toast with cinnamon? That used to be your favourite when you were a little boy. It always made you feel better whenever something was bothering you."

Alex is not surprised at her question. He knows his mother thinks food will solve everything. He shakes his head. "I couldn't eat anything right now. I just want to have a quick shower and then get a couple hours' sleep before I go over to see Bree. She's at her mom and dad's place because they didn't want her to be alone at the apartment."

"I don't blame them. Any word on how she's doing?" Kate asks.

"Not yet and I didn't want to bother them at this time of day. I know Warren has been out most of the night because I was speaking with him not too long ago, but I hope Bree and her mom are sleeping," Alex says. His voice sounds ragged.

"I told her not to worry about coming into the office at all this week, and to take as much time as she needs to recover," Kate says. "But you know Bree. She resisted my whole argument. I forgot just how good she is at arguing."

"Now you know what I deal with every day." Alex smiles. "You've taught her well."

"Yes, well." Kate rolls her eyes. "Maybe she'll listen to you."

"That would be a first."

"I appreciate her enthusiasm, but her health has to come first. Tell her if she shows up before next Monday, I'll send her home."

"I will pass along the message and we'll see how it plays out." Alex pauses and then adds, "So, guys, I really want to apologize for your dinner being ruined last night."

Samantha replies, "It's not like any of it was your fault."

"I know but it's really a shame that no one had the chance to enjoy it, and it all smelled so good. What are you going to do with all that food?"

"Not sure yet. I can freeze some of it, but a lot of it will have to be eaten within the next day or two, or it will spoil. I'll probably just end up tossing some of it."

Alex smiles. "Remember how I was talking about having a gathering on Monday to observe the eclipse?"

Samantha nods. "I liked the idea."

"Now we even have more reason to bring everyone together. Will the food keep until tomorrow?"

Samantha considers for a moment. "It will be fine. I may have to make fresh gravy and salad as the one I've already prepared will be too wilted to eat, but that's no big deal. But like I told you, tomorrow is Monday, and everyone will have to work."

"Not everyone and"—he winks at Kate—"I'm sure people can sneak away from the office to have lunch with family."

Kate nods slowly. "But I can only get away for an hour or two at the most as we'll already be short-handed without Bree."

"I'm not sure Hunter and Ally can get here on a Monday," Samantha says. "She'll be teaching, and he'll be at the store."

"I'll talk to Hunter," Alex says. "He's the store manager so surely, he can pull himself away for a few hours. And since the eclipse doesn't happen until after school hours, there's no reason why Ally can't get here with the boys. I will also talk to Bree's parents and make sure they can come over. Maybe Warren can get away from the detachment for a little bit."

"You seem to really want this lunch to happen," Kate observes. "I didn't realize you were into all that eclipse hoopla."

"It's just that it's a unique event," he says. "Besides, mom made all this great-smelling food, and we can't let it go to waste." He grins. "Furthermore, you guys owe me and Jace a celebration."

"That we do," Samantha agrees. "And since you brought up Jace, Kate and I have decided that we would like you to bring Luna here when she gets out of the hospital. Do you think she's getting out today?"

"I don't know yet. I will have to talk to Uncle Charlie about her status, but do you really want to bring her here? They've got the Airbnb booked for two more nights."

Samantha shakes her head. "If Luna isn't going home to Yarmouth to be with her parents, then she needs to be someplace comfortable where there's someone to take care of her. Besides, didn't you tell me Jace is also injured? From the spider bite?"

Alex nods. "But I'm hoping he's feeling better now that the antibiotics are in his system. He stayed at the hospital to be with Luna. I checked on them this morning. She was resting comfortably, and he was asleep in a chair."

"It's settled then," Samantha says. "Luna and Jace can stay in Hunter's old room until they are ready to go home. They can come by whenever she's discharged."

"Yes, Mom." Alex knows the decision is final. And he thinks it's a good idea to have his friends where he can watch over them both. "I will help Jace check out of the Hugin and Munin this afternoon."

She smiles. "I feel better knowing they'll be here, especially since they are both injured."

"And thank you both for agreeing to do all of this. Jace and Luna are very important to me and Bree, and I'm worried about them. I'll feel better with them here and you looking out for them."

"It's no problem," Kate says. "Besides, you know your mother loves to have someone to take care of. This is right in her wheelhouse."

"So, I'm a nurturer," Samantha says. "And I like taking care of people. You knew who I was when you married me."

Kate chuckles. "I sure did."

Alex watches as the two women who adopted him many years ago smile at each other, their mutual love still obvious.

"So," he says, "now that that's all settled, I'm going up stairs to have a shower and take that nap. I'll set my phone alarm, but if I'm not up in three hours, would one of you please call me?"

"Sure," Kate answers. "But, Alex, is there anything else bothering you?"

"I'm not sure what you mean."

"It seems like you're suddenly carrying a heavy burden around with you," Kate replies. "I noticed the change in you yesterday."

Alex glances from one woman to the next. "You two never cease to amaze me. You always seem to know when something is bothering me."

"Call it motherly intuition," Samantha says. "Or it could have something to do with all the previous experiences we've had with you, but what's going on? It has been many years since the crows have come around, but are they bothering you again?"

"They never *bother* me, Mom, and they've always been around. It's just that, for the past ten years, they've been keeping a low profile because there were no serious threats." He grimaces. "You know." He uses air quotes to emphasize his point. "Ten years of joyous bliss."

"I take it that's changed," Kate says.

"Yes, but not how you think."

"Don't be so cryptic, Alex." Kate says. "Just tell us what's going on."

"Okay. Okay."

He quickly relays the story of meeting his great uncle in the park, and how the old man warned him about the effects of the eclipse. He also tells them about the Spirit Crow and how it will protect him, but that everyone else in this town could lose control, reverting to their basic, violent instincts.

"And this only happens during the solar eclipse?" Kate asks.

Alex nods. "It starts three days leading up to the eclipse and keeps escalating until it's over."

"So, you're telling us that all of these acts of violence that have suddenly been occurring are because of that?" Samantha asks.

"I know you probably don't believe me, but that's what's going on."

"Why wouldn't we believe you, Alex?" Kate replies.

"Oh, I don't know. Probably because it sounds insane."

"The crows can't do anything to protect the people from this mysterious force?" Samantha asks.

"Whatever it is, it's too powerful and they can only protect the chosen one."

"And that's you?"

"Yes." Alex feels somewhat sheepish that he could be protected while all the people he loves could be facing an unknown fate. "I wish there was something more I could do to help everyone else in this town."

"That's why you want to bring the family here during the eclipse?" Kate asks.

He nods. "So I can watch over them."

"Protect us, right?"

"Exactly, but I don't know what I can do. Supposedly, this force, or whatever it is, can touch anyone, anywhere at any time and without warning, so everyone is vulnerable. I figure if we're all together we can at least keep an eye on each other."

"Well then, let's make that happen." Samantha nods. "We'll be here, and we'll make sure the others are here as well."

"Thanks. You guys are always so understanding."

"Is there anything else we can do?" Kate asks.

"I don't know what that would be. I wish I knew someone I could talk to about the eclipse, but I don't know any astrophysicists."

"Neither do I." Kate says. "But I do know an astronomist who works at St. Mary's University. "I've known Dr. Louise Beanlands ever since we did our undergraduate studies together at Dalhousie. She's one of the leading astronomists in the country. I can try to put you in touch with her if you thought that would help."

"Really? That would be awesome. When?"

"Well, not right now." She smiles at him. "I think it's a bit too early on a Sunday morning for that. I'll text her later this morning."

"I'd like to talk to her today if possible."

"I haven't spoken with Louise in quite some time, so I'm not sure how she'll respond," Kate says. "But I'll see if I can arrange a time for you to call her today."

"Thank you so much, Kate." He rises from the sofa.

"No problem. I'm happy to help."

24: A dog and a rifle

Valerie Freeman hates having to get up early on Sunday morning to take Mitzie, her gentle golden retriever, for a walk. She loves the dog with all her heart, but Sunday is the one day of the week Valerie has to sleep in, since her job at the local hardware store requires her to work morning shift the other six days.

And she needs the sleep after a busy week of a full-time job, taking care of household chores and making sure the children get to all their commitments. It's exhausting and it hardly seems fair to her that everyone else in the house gets to sleep while she's up at the crack of dawn.

The thing is, now that she's outside in the cool air, she would never be able to go back to bed. Now that she's up, she's up for the day.

It's still early. The sun hasn't been up very long, but Mitzie seemed especially restless this morning, almost agitated. So here they are, walking in a desolate part of town that, with the early morning mist rising from the nearby river and the sun still hiding behind the low-hanging clouds, almost has an eerie quality to it.

The neighbourhood is quiet and she's fuming mad as she walks the dog along Edgewater Street, where she's lived for the last ten years since she and her husband, Jeffrey, bought their modest, three-bedroom house.

Valerie doesn't blame Mitzie for getting her out of bed, as she's only doing what her body needs her to do. Instead, she's pissed at her husband. She blames his lazy ass for not even having the decency to offer to walk the dog so she could sleep.

But why would today be any different than any other day? she wonders.

She's not surprised by his lack of caring for her or his lack of commitment to the marriage. He checked out of their relationship many years ago. He just hasn't bothered to move out of the house.

This was supposed to be Jeffery's job. When she agreed to get the dog *for the kids*, the deal was that he would look after her, including taking her for morning walks. That commitment lasted maybe two weeks before the responsibility fell to Valerie. Now he is still home in a warm bed while she's bundled up with her winter coat wrapped tightly around her night dress while her slippers aren't doing much to keep her feet warm.

Next time, she tells herself, *I should make sure to dress more properly for this time of year.*

Since she never goes anywhere without her phone, Valerie quickly texts her sister, Janet, who lives in Newfoundland. It may be early, but she knows Janet will already be up. She never seems to sleep.

"Can you believe it?" she types on the small letters of the phone's keypad. "J is still in bed while I'm freezing my ass off walking the dog. Effing asshole."

"Always been an asshole," Janet quickly replies. "You knew that when you married him."

"I thought he'd change."

"He will never."

"I see that now."

"Mom and I tried to warn U," Janet answers her sister. "You wouldn't listen."

"Yes." Valerie nods as she types. "You did try."

"We went to school with him. You knew he was going to be trouble."

The past twelve years have been tough on Valerie. While both she and Jeffrey go to work every day, they can't get ahead financially. With the mortgage, payments on two vehicles, the costs to keep their kids in their favourite activities, utility costs, groceries and day to day living expenses, they can't seem to dig themselves out of the deep hole in which they find themselves.

The strain is wearing on Valerie, and she's not sure her husband shares the burden. Jeffery has always had a carefree personality, but she wishes he would step up to the plate more and take some of the stress off her shoulders.

She longs for him to be more invested in their relationship, and interact with the kids more. She's not sure he even likes the kids, she's sad to admit.

"What are you going to do?" Janet asks.

"I don't know."

"Have you talked to him?"

"He always blocks me out whenever I bring up money or anything else."

She pauses to allow Mitzie to sniff around the roadside, as she always does before she does her business.

"You're just going to let him get away with it?"

"I really should talk to him." Valerie can imagine her sister nodding her head with her I-told-you-so posture on full display.

"I don't know how you can put up with all that shit," Janet writes.

The wind catches Valerie's long, black hair and tosses it around her head while Mitzie chooses a spot to pee. She blows into her hands to warm up her fingers so she can reply to her sister. Even though it's April and supposed to be spring, she wishes she had brought her mittens.

She types, "I feel trapped here."

"Leave the prick."

"I can't do that."

"Why not?" her sister answers.

"I can't leave the kids with him. God knows what he would do."

"Take them with you."

"To where?" Valerie replies.

"Come to St. John's. Stay with us for a while. Rudy won't mind."

"I can't move the kids. Their school is here. Their friends are here. Mom is still here."

"We have schools in Newfoundland, you know."

"Smart ass."

"And the kids are only young. They will make new friends and Mom will be just fine."

Valerie stares down the street. Her sister makes perfectly good sense, but how can she even consider such an idea?

"It would cost a lot to move there."

"You don't need a lot."

"I need to think about it."

"If you want things to change, you will have to change them."

"U R right."

Valerie is so lost in her phone that she fails to notice the navy-blue Jeep Wrangler speeding down Edgewater Street in her direction. By the time she hears the vehicle behind her, it's too late to react.

The Jeep rams her, sending her sprawling face-first to the ground. Valerie drops her phone and the dog's leash.

She hears Mitzie yelp and sees the dog sprint away with the leash trailing behind her.

Slowly rolling onto her back, Valerie feels the pain radiating everywhere. She can hardly move. She knows she's badly hurt.

She recognizes the Jeep. It's their car.

"Jeffrey?" she whispers, shaking the haze from her eyes.

She hears her husband get out of the car. She hears his heavy footsteps on the loose gravel.

"Help me, Jeffrey," she pleads, her voice nothing more than a whisper. "I'm hurt. I think you broke my back."

Her husband says nothing. After kicking at her legs as if to make sure she can't get up, he returns to the Jeep.

"Where are you going?" she cries.

She hears him put the Jeep in reverse. He backs up a few metres. Then he guns the engine.

"Jeffrey," she screams. "What are you doing?"

The last thing Valerie Freeman feels is the Jeep's front tires crushing her mid-section, her ribs breaking, the broken bones spearing her internal organs.

As Jeffrey speeds off, Mitzie slowly approaches Valerie's body. She nudges Valerie and sniffs. Then she lies beside her and rests her head on Valerie's chest, whimpering.

The phone dings several times.

"Valerie?" her sister's text reads. "Are you there?"

The dog blinks. She whimpers.

"Answer me, Valerie."

~

Returning home, Jeffrey parks and turns off his Jeep.

He goes into the house and heads directly to the den. He unlocks the gun cabinet and lifts out the 30-06 Springfield that he uses for hunting. He removes the lock that secures the trigger, then loads five shells into the chamber.

With the rifle in hand, he walks down the hallway to the bedrooms where his seven-year-old-daughter and nine-year-old son are sleeping. He stops at the first door, takes a deep breath, and then pauses.

He listens for any movement for several seconds. He then turns, walks back down the hallway, leaves the house and he makes a beeline to the Jeep.

Sliding behind the steering wheel, he positions the butt of the riffle on the floor, props it up between his knees, puts the end of the muzzle into his mouth and, without batting an eye, pulls the trigger

25: Brainwashed

Alex is relived to discover that, by the time he arrives at the home of Bree's parents, Lisa and Warren Hamilton, she's awake and resting comfortably in the living room, where her mother can closely monitor her. Warren has been called away to the scene of an apparent murder-suicide on Edgewater Street.

Word of the incident has spread quickly around town on this Sunday morning, as it has with all the previous cases in recent days. Alex is worried for Warren, as this mounting death count has put everyone on edge.

"So, you're telling me that all of these accidents, animal attacks and acts of violence are somehow connected to tomorrow's solar eclipse?" she says quietly.

Bree, who is lying on the sofa, looks at her boyfriend, the young man she hopes to marry if he ever gets up the nerve to ask her. Her eyebrows raised and her face twisted in a state of confusion, she stares at Alex.

Her reaction doesn't really surprise him. He understands that she will need to know facts before accepting what he told her. But, out of everyone in this town, he believes Bree will require the least amount of persuading. After all, she's been through a lot with him and the crows over the years.

He takes her hand and squeezes it gently. "I know it's a lot to accept, but I believe that this force my Great Uncle Silas was talking about is not only affecting people but, in fact, is influencing every living creature around here, and it's causing them to resort to their basic violent instincts, which are to hunt and kill."

"And you don't think it could all be a huge coincidence?"

Alex shakes his head. "You know I don't jump to conclusions about such things. And I don't believe in coincidences."

"Do you think that would explain why the deer stood in the middle of the road yesterday? That their instinct to run was overpowered by their instinct to attack? Come to think of it, they did seem really aggressive."

"I believe that is probably what happened."

"Wow. That's a lot to digest."

Alex can tell Bree's thinking, trying to come to grips what she's heard.

Seconds later, she asks, "So if this has happened in the past with previous eclipses, like the old man told you it has, why haven't we heard anything about it? I'm sure this would be something people would remember and talk about, especially with another eclipse coming tomorrow."

"Silas said the crows are not powerful enough to protect everyone from the effects of this mysterious force, but they can somehow eradicate our memories. It's very bizarre, but, while people know their family members and friends have died, they remember them as dying from natural causes or accidents and not as the result of violent acts."

Bree shakes her head but remains quiet. He knows she is digesting the information.

Alex continues, "I've looked up some death records from the date of the last eclipse in 1972, and all it says is that death was by natural causes. There were eleven deaths around that time. Now, if you're talking about coincidences, there's a major one right there, as the chances of that many deaths by natural causes in a short period in a small town like this, are rather remote."

"How and why would the crows do that?"

"The how part, I understand," Alex says. "I believe the crows are powerful enough to influence our minds and thoughts. They've done it before. Just ask Oliver." He squints as he adds, "It's the *why* part that I don't understand. If people have done these horrific things, then why not allow us to remember them?"

"To protect us, maybe," Bree suggests. "Our minds are fragile instruments, Alex. They can be broken under enough pressure, so it could be that the crows believe this is the best way to protect everyone."

"I understand that."

"Haven't you always said the crows' top priority, other than to protect you and other members of your bloodline, is to protect the inhabitants of this town?"

Alex nods.

Bree continues, "Imagine how everyone would feel, having to live with the knowledge of such horrific events having occurred in this town. Maybe everyone would abandon the place because of some *curse* they've heard about. People flee what they can't understand. That is another human instinct."

Alex studies the face of the petite young woman he's loved since they were sixteen. Her explanation is right in line with what he is also thinking.

"It makes sense," he says.

"Are the crows powerful enough to do all of that?"

Alex nods. "Without question."

"Is there any way to know who this force is going to affect next?"

"According to Silas, there's nothing we can do to protect anyone against this force and there's no way of knowing who is going to be affected next. He said no one is immune, but as we get closer to the eclipse happening, we can expect the incidents of violence to keep escalating."

Bree shivers. Her voice almost a whisper, she asks, "What are we going to do, Alex?"

"We have to keep our loved ones close and watch over them," he tells her. "And if we see any change in anyone, we have to try to prevent them from carrying out any acts of violence."

"How the hell do we do that?"

"We stay close to them."

"That's easy to do with mom as she's here waiting on me hand and foot, but dad's out working," Bree says. "I was worried about him before you told me all of this, now I'm just plain scared for him."

"I'm scared for him, too, but we both know there's no way he's not going to do his job. And I think it's going to get worse."

"Jesus," she cries. "I have to warn him."

"How do you think he will react?"

"Well, Dad always keeps an open mind. He believes he must always be willing to accept things he doesn't understand. But asking him to accept this story that seems so, I don't know, so far-fetched, could be a stretch. But maybe he'll listen to me," Bree says. "He knows there's something special about you and the crows, but he doesn't know the whole story."

"Can you call him and ask him to come home so you can talk to him?"

"I will, but first can you tell me more about this Spirit Crow?"

"Of course." Alex smiles. "According to Silas, it's the special protector who appears to the chosen one in the days leading up to an eclipse. It is the only time the white crow ever appears around here."

"And that means you are immune to the effects of this mysterious force?"

"Yes, thanks to the Spirit Crow. I guess it's a special perk of being the chosen one."

"What if I turn on you, Alex? What if I do something to hurt you?"

"You would never do anything to hurt me, my love." Alex squeezes her hand. "And I will be right by your side to keep you safe. I will not let anything happen to you."

"What about everyone else?"

"Samantha and Kate are aware of what's happening. Since we didn't have our special dinner, they've agreed to have a lunch party tomorrow afternoon," he says. "We must make sure we get everyone there. Do you think you can make sure your father comes?"

"That could be a tall order, depending upon what's happening. If it's going to be that wild around here, then I suspect Dad's going to be very busy."

"You have to try, Bree. If we can get everyone together, then we can keep an eye on each other and prevent them from hurting each other." He pauses and then adds, "Tell him it's important to you."

Bree nods. "I will try my best, but *Duty first* is his motto." She adds, "What are we going to do until then? Isn't it dangerous out there?"

"You should stay here with your mother, but watch her closely. I know she would never do anything to hurt you but until this thing passes, we cannot trust anyone."

"And you?"

"I am going to the hospital to pick up Jace and Luna. Mom and Kate have offered to let them stay there for a couple of days until they go home. They are worried about Luna and want to have her close so Mom can take care of her. You know what Mom is like, doting over everyone."

Bree chuckles. "That's one of the reasons I love her so much. She's a very special person."

"Yeah." Alex laughs. "I'm happy that Jace and Luna will be staying with us. And what about you? How are you feeling?"

"You mean other than having a massive headache—which, by the way, has gotten whole lot worse since you told me all of this—and the throbbing in my wrist and knee, I'm feeling pretty good."

"Are you taking the Ibuprofen every four hours like Uncle Charlie told you to do?"

"Yes, and Mom would never let me forget." Bree smiles. "Thank God for drugs."

Alex nods. "Thank God for drugs…and our mothers."

"I know I got lucky yesterday. The injuries could have been much worse or"—tears form in her eyes—"Luna and I could have been killed."

"But you weren't. I believe the ten crows were watching over you."

"Why would they do that?"

"Because they know how important you are to me." Alex squeezes her hand again.

26: There, but for the Grace of God

When her husband divorced her almost two years ago, Charlotte Lake thought it was the end of the world.

But it wasn't.

In fact, it was just the beginning of a new chapter in her life.

Gordon left her for another man, and Charlotte was devastated. She was convinced she was responsible for the dissolution of their marriage, that she had failed him somehow. She blamed herself for being a heartless, cold woman who brought little love into their relationship, and for a long time, she couldn't see that she and Gordon had simply drifted apart.

The church had always played an important role in her life and ultimately, with the help of her pastor, Charlotte realized that the love had drained from their marriage many years earlier. She came to understand that they no longer had anything in common, except for their two children, who, they agreed, were the best thing to come from their relationship.

It took Charlotte a long time to stop blaming herself for driving Gordon into the bed of someone else—another man, nonetheless—but eventually she found solace and comfort in the church. Now, she never misses a Tuesday or Thursday night Bible study, or a Sunday morning service. She's even studying to become a lay minister, something she had never thought she would want to do until her pastor suggested she'd be good at preaching.

Larken, her ten-year-old daughter, and Blake, her thirteen-year-old son, would agree their mother likes to "preach." They've grown weary of her holier-than-thou attitude and, no matter how often Charlotte tells them it's their choice, she insists they accompany her to each Sunday service.

They reject their mother's judgmental condemnation of their friends and many others who inhabit this town. They hate it that, for some reason, she feels superior to others, and they especially don't like it when she points to someone else and says, "There but for the Grace of God…"

For Larken and Blake, however, it's easier to comply with their mother's demands, rather than arguing that they don't like going to church. This Sunday, though, Larken has decided that, no matter how much her mother insists, she is not going.

"Larken, baby," Charlotte calls from the kitchen. "Your breakfast is ready. Please tell your brother to come to the kitchen right now before it gets cold. I need you to have your breakfast so that we can do the dishes and get ready for church."

Charlotte insists that she and her children have breakfast together each Sunday morning before church. It's always pancakes, but only pancakes, as bacon, ham or sausage is not permitted in their house because, according to Charlotte, meat from pigs isn't clean for them to eat.

When Larken and Blake ask why they can't have such meat with their pancakes like "normal" people do, Charlotte tells her children the Bible teaches them it is unclean for God's people to eat pork.

When they continue to argue, pointing out that they have bacon, ham and sausage whenever they eat at a friend's house, Charlotte becomes incensed and quotes Leviticus 11:7: "...and the swine, though it divides the hoof, having cloven hooves, yet does not chew the cud, is unclean to you." She also threatens to forbid them from seeing their friends.

The children have learned not to question their mother's beliefs or risk being on the receiving end of one of her lengthy religious sermons or, worse, suffer at the end of her "beating" stick. Instead, they accept her directives when at home and secretly enjoy bacon on their hamburgers when they eat out with their friends. It's just easier that way.

But this morning, for some reason, Larken has a craving for bacon. She cannot explain it, but it's the only thing she can think of. She likes it crispy, almost burned, and she decides that this morning she's going to tell her mother she wants bacon.

She's had enough of her mother's "crazy" ways. In fact, this bacon ban is just one of the many rules that she's grown tired of. She's also fed up with being told what to wear, which friends to hang with, where she can go, what television shows to watch, what books to read and what music to listen to.

None of her friends have to put up with such nonsense from their parents, and she hates it that her mother controls every aspect of her life.

It's not normal and it has to stop, Larken thinks as she wearily slides from her bed and slowly makes her way down the dimly-lit hallway to the tiny bathroom that she shares with her brother and mother. It's a small thing, but she wishes she had her own bathroom like her best friend, Jasmine. *She's so lucky she lives in such a nice house.*

"Larken?" her mother calls from the kitchen. "Did you hear me? It's time to get up and get ready for church."

"Yes, Mother," she calls back. "I heard you the first time. I'm up and just going to use the bathroom."

She stares blankly at herself in the mirror over the bathroom vanity, wondering if there is any way out of this situation. This has never been a happy household, but the past two years have become unbearable for her and Blake.

That woman has definitely gone over the deep end, Larken thinks, blinking the sleep from her eyes. *She is stark raving crazy, and I'm not putting up with it any longer. I want some bacon, God-damn it.*

She and Blake have seen a considerable shift in their mother's personality, and they wish Gordon would have taken them with him when he moved out. But their father chose his new boyfriend over his children, telling them that Derick doesn't want children around their house.

She can't understand why her father would abandon her and Blake. *It's not like we're small kids or anything. He wouldn't have to look after us. All we need is a place to go so we can get away from this crazy woman.*

While she and her brother haven't talked about this, she's sure Blake feels the same way.

I'd leave here in a second, she thinks as she brushes her teeth, dreading going downstairs. She spits in the sink, watching the toothpaste swirl down the drain with the water.

If I only had some place to go. Maybe I should ask Jasmine if I can come to live with her. They have lots of room in that big ole house.

She stops by her brother's bedroom on her way downstairs. She taps lightly on the door, then opens it just a crack and whispers, "Blake? Are you awake?"

When her brother doesn't respond she says, "Okay, mister. I called you. If you don't get up and come down for breakfast, that's your decision, but you'll have to deal with the nut case."

Taking a deep breath, Larken goes down the stairs, walks into the kitchen and sits at the table.

"Good morning, sweetheart," Charlotte says, placing a plate with two pancakes in front of her daughter. "Are you ready for church?"

"Not really," Larken answers. "Do I really have to go to church today?"

"Are you sick?"

She shakes her head.

"Then yes," Charlotte snaps. "You must go to church, and I don't want to hear another single word about it. And I don't want to be late, so eat up. I want to get there early enough to get good seats. You know how much I hate having to sit behind other people. I like to see the preacher when he delivers his sermon. He's so good."

Stabbing her fork into her pancakes, Larken sighs. "Yes, Mother."

"Now," Charlotte says, "where is your brother?"

"I called him, like you told me to, but he didn't answer me, so I came right down to the kitchen. I didn't want you to be pissed off at me."

"Larken Lake! Watch your language." Her mother glares at her. "This is the Lord's Day. It's not a time for any of your foolishness. You know cursing is not allowed in my house."

"Yes, Mother. Sorry. I forgot."

"You forgot?" Charlotte is seething. "Well, young lady, if I ever hear that kind of language coming from your mouth again, you will feel the stick. Have I made myself clear?"

"Yes, Mother. Perfectly clear." She stares blankly at her mother. "Can I have some syrup, please?"

"*May* I have some syrup, please?" Charlotte corrects her daughter. "And yes, you may."

"Thanks."

Placing the bottle in front of her daughter, Charlotte says, "You eat your breakfast and I'll go up upstairs to see what's keeping your brother."

"He's probably still asleep. He was up pretty late. I could hear him pounding around in his room. I think he was playing a video game or something."

"He knows I don't want him playing those things, not in my house…not anywhere. They're evil."

Larken shrugs. "I'm not sure what he was doing, but it was loud, whatever it was."

"We'll just see about that." Charlotte starts out of the kitchen but turns to add, "And what have I told you about tattling on your brother?"

"To mind my own business."

Her mother disappears from the kitchen and clumps up the stairs. Seconds later, Larken hears her shouting and she knows her brother will regret not getting up when she tried to wake him.

Larken watches the syrup drip from the mouth of the bottle, pool on top of the pancakes and then run down the sides onto the plate. She knows her mother will be angry when she sees how much syrup she's taken, but she has decided she doesn't care about that. *Whatever.*

"Where is your brother?" Charlotte asks as she returns to the kitchen.

"I thought you told me Blake was upstairs in his room?"

Finding the kitchen empty, she calls, "Larken? Where are you? Didn't I tell you to eat your breakfast?"

Silence fills the kitchen.

"Larken?" She screams, her voice sharp with anger. "You better show yourself right this minute, young lady, or else!"

"Or what, Mother?"

Spinning around, Charlotte comes face to face with her daughter. "Where were you?"

"On the front porch, Mother."

"What for?"

"I had to get something."

"Show me what you're hiding behind your back."

"Okay, Mother," Larken says, slowly bringing her brother's baseball bat out from behind her back. "If you really want to see it."

"Is that blood on Blake's bat?"

"Maybe you should take a closer look," she says, quickly swinging the bat toward her mother's head.

Charlotte falls back and throws her arms up to protect herself. "What are you doing?"

"This, Mother," Larken says, delivering blow after blow to her mother's head until the woman stops screaming.

"Something I should have done a long time ago."

She throws the bat to the kitchen floor. It lands on her mother's clean tiles with a sickening thud. Her mother's body spasms a few times and then goes still.

Larken returns to the table to finish her pancakes. She has to step over one of her mother's shoes. *It must have come off when Mother tried to run away.*

"And tomorrow morning," she says to the bloodied remains, "I want bacon with my pancakes."

27: Death by natural causes

Faced with a list of questions about what is happening in his hometown, Alex hopes Dr. Louise Beanlands, one of Canada's most renowned astronomers can provide him with some answers. She is based at St. Mary's University in Halifax and he is pleased that Kate was able to line up a phone conversation for him with her old friend.

Dr. Beanlands is considered a leading expert in the study of the origin and structure of the universe, including its planets, stars, galaxies, and black holes. Recalling the warnings that he received from his Great Uncle Silas Moores just two days ago, Alex hopes the scientist will be able to help.

What could cause someone to lose control of themselves to the point that they would attack and maybe kill someone else, even someone they love? he wonders as he dials the doctor's phone number on his cell while sitting in his car outside the hospital. He's here to pick up Luna and Jace, as soon as Uncle Charlie gives her the okay to leave.

"Hello," the woman answers on the second ring and Alex thinks she sounds nice enough. Her voice is very pleasant. "Louise Beanlands here."

"Hi Dr. Beanlands," he replies. "I'm Alex Goodwin. Kate Webster's son. I think you were expecting my call."

"Hello yourself, Alex. You are a prompt young man, aren't you? When I told Kate to have you call me at noon, you really pay attention."

"Yes." Alex chuckles. "My mother has taught me well."

"How is Kate? It has been many years since I spoke to her, but I was just thinking about her the other day and wondering how she was doing and then, right out of the blue, I received her text"

"She's doing very well although she's working way too much these days."

"My family accuses me of the same thing, but I'm glad to hear Kate is doing well. I've always liked your mother very much and wish we had kept in closer contact. I'll have to text her and suggest we meet up for lunch the next time she's in Halifax."

Alex likes this woman very much but *she's a talker.*

"So, young man," she continues, "if I understand what your mother said, you need some help understanding how, or even *if,* a solar eclipse can affect people to the point where it makes them more aggressive."

"Yes. I need to know if an eclipse can change people's personalities to the point that it could make them to do things they wouldn't normally do."

"Things such as?"

Alex pauses, choosing his next words carefully. "Such as, cause a person to become aggressive and maybe even want to hurt others."

"Are you suggesting maybe even kill them?"

"Yes," he says after a brief pause. "In extreme cases, even kill people."

There is an awkward silence. Alex wonders if she thinks he's a nut case.

"Well, not that I'm aware of," Dr. Beanlands finally answers. "Past research suggests that the behaviour of some livings things, especially birds and nocturnal animals, can be influenced by the effects of an eclipse, but I can't say I've ever heard of any cases where someone may have been killed because of it."

"I believe the last solar eclipse in this part of the world was in 1972."

"It was." She agrees and Alex hears her hesitate before she asks, "Why? Is that important?"

"Here is something that could be counter-intuitive to what you know," Alex says. "During the three days leading up to that eclipse, this town experienced eleven deaths. That's an abnormally high number of deaths for a community our size in such a short time span."

"It sure is, but are you suggesting that was the result of the eclipse?"

"I don't believe in coincidences and I'm not sure I believe all the deaths were by natural causes."

"What does it say on their death certificates?"

"Death was recorded as natural causes," Alex says. "But that's a large cluster of deaths to occur in three days. That doesn't seem right to me."

He gives Dr. Beanlands time to think about this information, then asks, "Does that sound right to you?"

"Well," she replies, and he knows she's hesitating, perhaps reluctant to embrace what he's suggesting, that something more nefarious was at play in 1972.

She continues, "I will admit that what you're saying does seem highly unusual. But if the deaths weren't the result of natural causes, what else would it be. And why wouldn't the death certificates record the correct information?"

"That's another story." Alex does not want to get into discussing what the crows can do with Dr. Beanlands. "But what I really need to know is if the eclipse could have caused something to happen to these people… maybe cause them to become violent to themselves or others?"

"Not likely. Not on its own, but I have long believed an eclipse can impact other natural elements which in turn may affect human behaviour."

"I don't follow."

"What if the eclipse did something to the ozone layer? Could that then influence what people do?"

"Do you think that could happen?"

"Yes," Dr. Beanlands replies without hesitation. It's clear to Alex that she has been thinking about this issue for some time.

She continues, "In fact, I've been studying that phenomenon for the past two decades, ever since I stumbled across a study conducted by Dr. Eldon MacMartin, a professor at this university who died several years ago. That study pointed to a distinct pattern where the ozone gets extremely thin over some parts of the world leading up to and during an eclipse. Maybe it's just a strange confluence of events but the last time the ozone was this thin around this part of North America was … can you guess?"

"Are you saying 1972?"

"That's what I'm saying."

"Would a thinning ozone layer have such a serious impact on living things that it could lead to extreme behavioural changes?"

"Let me help you try to get a handle on this," Dr. Beanlands says. "Nova Scotians, like all humans, benefit from a protective layer of ozone located in the Earth's upper atmosphere. I assume you understand that, Alex? It's basic science."

"I understand about the ozone layer and how it works."

"Very good. It blocks harmful ultraviolet or UV rays from the sun, acting like a natural sunscreen for planet Earth."

"Pretty basic but important to our survival."

"It is," Dr. Beanlands says. "Now, over the past century, certain chemicals created and released by humans have greatly damaged the ozone layer, which has then reduced the amount of protection from harmful UV that it provides to us. The ozone layer has been thinned most at the earth's poles, especially over Antarctica. But Nova Scotia is also negatively affected by a thinner ozone layer and increased UV radiation."

"And you're saying this thinning is more prevalent around the time of a solar eclipse, like in 1972?"

"That is correct. And it's happening again, right now."

"Should this concern us?"

"It should concern everyone, Alex. The increase in UV radiation that results from a damaged ozone layer has harmful effects on human health and the environment. For example, higher UV causes more cases of skin cancer and eye cataracts in people. It weakens people's immune systems. It also damages crops and other plants, and causes serious harm to the organisms at the base of food chains in lakes and oceans. It causes damage to synthetic building materials, like plastics, causing them to release harmful components into the environment."

"But could it lead to extreme changes in human behaviour?"

"There is no hard data to back that up. However, it seems to me that it could, indeed," Dr. Beanlands replies. "Unfortunately, many of the impacts of increased UV radiation will only be fully understood in the future...once it's too late to do anything about it. This is because of complex interactions with other changes in the environment by human-generated activities such as smog, climate change, and acid rain are bringing about."

Alex mulls over this information. He then says, "Let me ask you, Doctor, is it possible to pinpoint if the ozone is thinner over one geographical area than in others?"

"That is possible. Why?"

"I'm just trying to wrap my head around what all of this means."

"It's a problem that is almost one hundred percent created by humans. The more we abuse the environment, the worse we can expect these things are going to become."

"Is there anything we can do about all of this?"

"Yes! We can stop destroying our planet."

"Amen to that," Alex says.

"Even if humans stopped everything right now, today, it would take years—maybe decades—to reverse the effects of what we've already done to our planet. The damage is that severe."

"We're screwed, aren't we?"

"Let's just say that humans have a lot of work to do to undo the damage we've caused."

"Okay, Dr. Beanlands," Alex says, reflecting on what he has just heard. "You have been very helpful. I appreciate you taking the time to speak with me, especially on a Sunday."

"It was my pleasure, Alex, but have I given you anything useful?"

"More than you could ever know."

"I'm glad I could help."

"Jesus Christ," Alex says after he ends the call. *Have we really caused all of this?*

28: She shoots, she scores

As in hundreds of towns and cities across the country, street hockey is a favourite pastime for the young people on Liverpool's Chestnut Street, a quiet, dead-end road that borders on a large grove of chestnut trees that early settlers planted hundreds of years ago.

In the late 1700s, during and after the upheaval of the American Revolution, British citizens loyal to the monarchy relocated from the fledgling United States into parts of Eastern Canada, and, it is said, many of them carried a chestnut in their pocket. It is also said they planted the chestnut wherever they settled in Nova Scotia and many of those trees, such as the ones that surround the historic homes on Chestnut Street, have remained for centuries.

It's a great neighbourhood in which to raise a family, safe and removed from the hustle and bustle of the busy downtown area. Those who live on Chestnut Street hardly ever lock their doors and many generations of parents have allowed their children to play and roam freely throughout the neighbourhood with very little fear for their safety. It's the perfect location for a game of street hockey, especially on a Sunday.

Jake Murray, Tommy Green, and Rudy Marshal have been playing pickup hockey together ever since they were in elementary school for more than a decade. Joanne (Jo) Hudson joined the game three years ago when her family moved to town from Ontario. Rugged and a physical player, Jo fits right in with the boys. She also has wild skills, which impressed the trio of wannabe NHLers.

With four players, the games often become competitive affairs as Jake and Tommy usually team up to take on Rudy and Jo. They're well-balanced contests with Jake and Rudy in net for their respective teams while Tommy and Jo handle the offensive charge, pretending they are their favourite major league players helping their team to win the Stanley Cup. They all have big dreams to play professional hockey someday, the kind of aspirations only young people can have.

But they work at their game. Most weekday afternoons after school and weekends find the foursome out on Chestnut Street, playing their version of Canada's favourite pastime, and this Sunday is no different. With their families busy doing whatever it is they have to do to get ready to face another work week, the four are pounding the pavement, intent on sharpening their skills.

"Come on, Jo. I'm ready," Jake screams as Jo steals the ball from Tommy and quickly breaks toward the opposing team's net.

Jo has incredible speed. She's much faster than any of the boys, but Jake prepares for the wind up. Crouching in the net, emulating his favourite NHL goalie, poised to stop her shot, he taunts his opponent.

"You better watch out, Jake," she says. "You're about to meet your maker."

"Take your best shot," he tells her while trying to make his body large enough to block any shot she takes.

Jo makes a beeline toward the net, eyeing the top lefthand corner, which is Jake's vulnerable spot. With her sneakers pounding on the pavement, Jo speeds forward, winds up and then slaps the ball with all the force she can muster.

Like a shot from a rifle, the ball soars over Jake's shoulder into the net.

"She shoots, she scores," Rudy screams. "That makes it four to two," He loves rubbing salt into wounds. He knows Jake would do the same if the shoe was on the other foot.

"She got lucky," Jake fires back, slapping the ball to Tommy. He's pissed that she got the better of him. "The game ain't over yet."

"Luck has nothing to do with," Jo smirks. "It's all skill, my friend. All skill."

"Skill, my ass." Jake's anger is starting to boil over. Of the four players, he's the one who most hates to lose and he's known to have a short fuse. "You ain't that good, Jo. You just think you are."

"And you're just pissed that a girl is better at this game than you." She knows how to push his buttons. "Someday, when I'm playing in the NHL, I'll wave at you from centre ice." She laughs.

"In your fucking dreams," Jake replies sharply, "Ain't no way that they're ever gonna let girls play in the NHL—ever."

"They will so," she says, chasing after Tommy. He is attempting to corral the ball and head toward Rudy, who is now crouched in his net, waiting to block the shot. "You just wait and see."

"Get real, you stupid bitch."

"Hey," she screams. "That's not called for. If you don't like losing, then you shouldn't be playing."

"Bitch," he fires back.

Jake's word cuts like a knife, bringing the game to a screeching halt. Even though the four players have always played fast and loose with the rules of the game, they have always had one hard-fast edict—insulting the other players is strictly prohibited. Jake has crossed the line.

"Come on, Jake," Rudy yells. "That's not good for the game."

"I wasn't talking to you. Mind your own god-damned business."

Tommy stops mid-chase. The ball trickles away from him as he turns to his teammate. "What are you doing, Jake? Just let it go."

"Jo snatches the ball and heads back toward Jake's net. "He's a sore loser, that's what's wrong."

"Yay, Jo," Rudy cheers. "Show Jake how it's done."

"Come on, Jo," Jake snarls as he crouches in the standard save position, determined to beat his nemesis.

Quickly stopping, Jo brings back her stick, slaps the ball and sends it soaring once again over Jake's shoulder. "You never learn," she says, raising her arms over her head in victory. "Make that five to two."

"You fucking cunt," Jake screams.

Rushing from the net, he hits the teenage girl squarely in her chest with such force that he knocks her off her feet. She lands hard on the pavement, her butt and elbows taking the brunt of the fall.

"Jesus, Jake," Rudy screams, rushing to assist his teammate. "What the hell are you doing? If you keep this up, I'm not going to play anymore."

"Wimp," Jake taunts as Rudy reaches for Jo and tries to help her up off the pavement.

She brushes his hands away. "I don't need anyone's help."

Rudy quickly backs away. "Are you hurt?"

"Nope." She jumps to her feet. "That weaselly little prick ain't strong enough to hurt me."

Tommy joins Rudy. "Just let it go. Jake didn't mean anything."

She bends to retrieve her hockey stick. "He's pissed that a girl can kick his ass."

Jake's eyes are narrowed to tiny slots and spit froths at the corners of his mouth. "Like that's even possible."

She moves toward him. "I'm a better player than you and I can prove it."

You'll never be better than me in a million fucking years."

"My grandmother is a better player than you and she's almost a hundred years old." She laughs. "Anyone with a good wrist shot can get past your left shoulder."

"I just let you score on me."

"I can score on your ass every time I want to if I go for the shoulder. It's your weak spot. You just can't get to that corner fast enough. You haven't got the speed or the skills to stop that shot."

"Stop it you two," Tommy says. "Let's just get back to the game before someone says something they're going to regret."

"I don't regret nothing," Jake sneers. "She thinks she's better than all of us."

"I'm certainly better than you, you little ass clown. You'll never be a real hockey player."

Jake pulls up his stick and swings it toward her.

Jo quickly ducks to avoid the attack.

She raises her own stick and swings it toward Jake.

He also tries to duck but he isn't quick enough. The stick catches him on the right side of the face.

"Fuck," he screams and drops to his knees.

"See," Jo sneers. "You're just not fast enough to avoid my slap shot."

"Come on, Jo." Rudy says. "Let's get out of here before someone gets hurt."

"Jo hit him," Tommy argues. "She's the one looking for a fight."

"Jake swung at her first." Rudy throws his stick over his shoulder in disgust. "This game is over. I'm going home."

"Seriously?" Jo says. "You're quitting while we're ahead?"

"I'm not interested in fighting," Rudy tells her. "And I don't care if we win or not. It doesn't really mean anything."

"Well, I care," she says. "You can go home if you want to. I can take them all on my own."

Tommy shakes his head. "I think I'm done, too. You guys win."

"Fucking babies," Jo fires back. "All of you."

"Go to hell, Jo," Tommy fires back. "I've got a shitload of homework to do before tomorrow, so I'm done."

He turns and sprints to catch up with Rudy, who has gone to move his net out of the way for traffic.

Jo shouts after him, "Excuses! You'll all see when I'm playing in the NHL and you guys are driving the Zamboni."

"I'll stay and play some more," Jake says.

"I don't think so," she answers while walking away. "I'd only make you cry again."

"Bitch."

"What did you say?" She stops, turns, and glares at him.

"I said, you are a bitch."

"I'd advise you not to say that again, you prick." She inches toward him. "Or I will drive my stick so far up your ass they'll have to remove it by pulling it out through your mouth."

"You don't like that?" Jake takes a step back. "Too fucking bad because that's what you are. A bitch. A—"

Jo brings her stick down on Jake's head. He stumbles backward and falls into the net, hitting his head on the pavement.

"For fuck's sake," he stutters, grabbing his head. "You cut me, you fucking bitch. I'm bleeding."

"You got what you des—" Jo stops suddenly and backs away from the net as Jake stumbles to his feet. "Come on, Jake. Get up. Come with me."

"You better run." He's seething with anger. "I'm going to kick your fucking ass."

"No, Jake." She backs further away. "Run as fast as you can. There's danger."

"What the fuck are you talking about?"

"Run, Jake!" she screams. "There's a bear behind you!"

"There aren't any bears around here."

"It's coming right for you." Jo keeps backing away.

"Bears," he scoffs. "What a bunch of bullshit."

"Run, Jake. Run!"

29: The ants go marching

After helping his friends settle into Hunter's former bedroom on the second floor, Alex finds his mother in the kitchen, frantically cleaning.

"Hey, mom." He stands in the doorway and watches the middle-aged blonde woman sprint around the kitchen, wiping and scrubbing any and all surfaces she comes across. "What cha doin' in here?"

"Ants," Samantha replies, swatting at a row of black carpenter ants that are marching single file across the cupboard. They appear to be on a mission. "All of a sudden, this place is crawling with ants. There must be hundreds of them. I don't understand it. We've never had any problem with ants around here before."

"That is very weird." His mother appears to be flipping out. "When did you first notice them?"

"Just little while ago. Suddenly, there were ants everywhere. It's like they're invading."

He glances around the room. "Where's Kate?"

"I sent her to the supermarket to get me some bug spray. I can't have ants crawling around everything, especially not with guests staying with us." She wipes her forehead with the back of her left hand. "How are Jace and Luna doing?"

"I think they're doing all right," Alex answers. "Jace helped Luna get into bed. She's very tired and wanted to have a nap. It's probably the pain meds that are making her drowsy. Jace is checking some emails and will be down in a few minutes."

"I've put more clean towels in the closet next to the bathroom and there are spare blankets in the bedroom closet if they find it cold. There's all kinds of food here and if they want anything special, all they have to do is ask. If we don't have it, we can get it."

Alex grins. "Just calm down. Jace and Luna are perfectly fine. I've already told them where everything is, and Jace won't be afraid to ask if he can't find something. There's nothing timid about him."

"I just want them to be comfortable."

Alex gives his mother a gentle hug. "I know you do, but they don't expect special treatment, so I just need you to relax."

"Not likely with all these damned ants crawling all over the place." She pulls back from him and points to a row of black ants that stretches from the baseboard near the sink all the way up the cupboard and toward the stove. "I mean. Have you ever seen anything like this before?"

Alex shakes his head. "I can't say that I have. You've never complained about there being an ant problem in the house."

"There's not an ant problem in my house." She glares at him. "I keep a clean house, mister, and you know it. There are no bugs in my house."

"Sorry, Mom. That's not what I meant. What I meant to say is that we don't normally see ants in the house."

Samantha nods. "And I really don't like it. What are your friends going to think?"

"Trust me, Mom. After what they've gone through over the past couple of days, I don't think they will see anything weird about them."

"Anything weird about what?" Jace asks as he enters the kitchen. "Sorry if I'm interrupting something."

"Nothing to worry about, bud," Alex replies. He motions to a stool where Jace can sit to take the pressure off his injured foot. "That was quick. Did you check all your emails that fast?"

"Decided not to bother with them right now." Jace perches on one of the stools. "Luna fell right to sleep as soon as she hit the bed, and I didn't want to make any noise to bother her."

"Can't you check them on your phone?" Alex asks.

"I left my phone in the car." Jace wiggles his right foot. "And this bloody thing is still bothering me, so I didn't feel like going out to get it."

"Those antibiotics should be working by now. I'll look at it in a few minutes for you but try to stay off it as much as you can."

"Yes, doctor." Jace grins.

"I'll get your phone for you," Alex offers. "Where are your keys?"

"Shit. Upstairs in my jacket pocket," Jace says. "Oh, well. You don't have to worry about the phone right now."

Noticing Samantha frantically swatting at her cupboard doors, he asks, "You got an ant problem, Ms. Henderson?"

Samantha nods. "And I have no idea where they're coming from. I've never been bothered with them before today."

Jace turns to Alex. "It's like the spiders at the Airbnb. They appeared out of nowhere and they kept coming and coming."

"Yes." Alex has a pretty good idea what's causing the odd ant behaviour, but he chooses not to share his thoughts.

"You know, Ms. Henderson," Jace says, "watching you swatting at those ants reminds me of my grandmother."

"How so?" Samantha asks.

"I remember visiting my Grammy in Digby when I was a little kid. Whenever she had a bug problem, she would mix equal parts of white vinegar with water and then take an old squirt bottle and spray the little creeps with the mixture."

"Did it work?"

Jace nods. "It did. She was full of information like that and it's a lot safer than some of that crap you buy in the stores with all their chemicals. Do you have any vinegar?"

"I do." Samantha reaches into a cabinet next to the stove.

"How about a squirt bottle?"

"Right here under the sink."

Opening the cabinet door under the sink, she screams and jumps back. "Oh my God, Alex. Look at them under there. There must be thousands of ants."

"Step back, Mom." Alex peers into the cabinet. "Jesus."

"I don't know, but it's weirding me out."

"Well." He carefully reaches into the cupboard and retrieves the squirt bottle. "Until Kate gets back with the bug spray, why don't we try Jace's grandmother's solution?"

"I guess it's worth a shot."

Samantha fills the squirt bottle about half full with vinegar, then fills it the rest of the way with water. She gives it a shake. "Let's see if this works."

"Let me do it, please." Alex takes the bottle and sprays the vinegar and water mixture on the army of ants in the cabinet.

"Be careful, Alex," Samantha warns. "We don't know if those ants will bite."

When the mixture lands on the ants, they quickly disperse. Soon there are no more than a couple dozen scurrying around the counter and on the floor. "Did this stuff really just scare away all those ants that quickly?"

"See." Jace comments from his perch. "Leave it to my old Grammy. She had a solution for everything."

Samantha shakes her head. "I'm not so sure it was the vinegar and water that did this. I've seen ants before and I've never seen so many gather in such large numbers and then disperse so quickly. And they seemed so aggressive. It just isn't normal."

She turns to Alex and asks, "Why is this happening?"

He shakes his head. "I have no idea."

"Something as weird as this would be right up your alley."

He hates lying to his mother, but says, "I don't have any idea. I am not an expert in ant behaviour."

Samantha stares at him. "Something very weird is going on around this town, and if there's one thing I've learned it's that if there's something weird happening, you're usually right in the middle of it."

"My God, Mom. What do you think I am? The devil or something?"

"The only thing that would make this even weirder is if a murder of crows suddenly showed up on our front yard."

Alex stares at her but says nothing.

"Hey, Sam. I'm home," Kate announces as she comes through the front door. "And I've got your bug spray. Where do you want it?"

"We're in the kitchen," Samantha answers. "Thanks for getting it, but I'm not sure I need it anymore. Sorry to send you on a fool's errand."

"It's all right," Kate says, entering the room. "Hey, Alex. Jace. Are you helping your mother get rid of the ants, Alex?"

"Already done," Samantha answers. "Sorry buddy," she says and quickly stomps on the last ant that's scurrying across the tiled floor. "You snooze, you lose, mister."

"Wow," Kate says. "That was pretty aggressive, honey. Ants got you a little on edge?"

"I'm fine." Samantha bends and wipes up the remains of the ant with a paper towel. "This little bastard won't be ruining anyone's picnic anytime soon."

"Come on, Mom," Alex says. "I think you're losing it."

"Speaking of losing it," Kate says. "Guess what I heard at the super-market."

"I hate to ask," Alex says.

"A bunch of kids were playing street hockey over on Chestnut Street and a bear attacked them."

Samantha says, "There are no bears around here."

Jace speaks up. "Based upon everything that's happened over the past few days, do you think it's all that strange that a bear would show up?"

"Good point," Samantha says. "How are the kids, Kate?"

Kate shakes her heard. "I heard no one was killed, but one of the kids was mauled pretty badly and is in the hospital. Poor Charlie. He's certainly had his hands full the past few days."

"He sure has," Alex says. "I wouldn't mind going in and helping him for a few hours if he needs me."

"I could go in, too," Jace speaks up. "Providing your uncle will agree to supervise me. I mean, we're not officially full-fledged doctors until we graduate, right?"

"I'm sure he wouldn't mind, but are you sure you would be up for that?" Alex asks. "You just said your foot was too sore to walk on."

"I'd manage," Jace replies.

A sudden, loud thud on the living room window causes the foursome to jump.

"What was that?" Jace asks.

Samantha rushes to the living room and discovers a crack in the largest window. "Holy hell. I wonder what did that."

"Let's check it out." Alex quickly goes to the front door and steps outside. He stops on the front steps and calls back, "Mom. Remember what you said a few minutes ago about a murder of crows in the front yard?"

"Please don't tell me it was crows."

Alex shakes his head as he retreats into the house. "No crows. Just lots of other birds."

Kate and Samantha join him in the doorway.

"Birds," Samantha says. "Hundreds of birds."

Alex scans the front yard. "Robins. Blue jays. Pigeons. Cardinals. Sparrows. You name a bird and I bet it's out here."

"So, what do we do now?" Jace asks.

"I don't know." Alex closes the front door. "But we aren't going anywhere for a while."

30: The view from up here

When Gary Rollins' twin sons, Ely and Ty, said they wanted to take a sight-seeing flight over the town and surrounding region to celebrate their eighteenth birthday, he knew exactly who to call.

Gary has known Stu Hiscock since their high school years and, even though he wouldn't consider him to be a close friend, they have remained cordial in the more than thirty years since graduation. To fulfill his sons' birthday wish, Gary called Stu and planned this Sunday afternoon flight adventure.

Based upon the excitement in the cozy cockpit of the Cessna 172 Sky-hawk, the gift appears to be a big hit with the boys. Gary is relieved because, as the twins get older, he is finding it more difficult to please them.

Gone are the days when a small party for friends at the local bowling alley with hot dogs and cake would make them happy. Now the boys' requests are more elaborate and more expensive, but he tries to give them what they want—within reason and when financially possible.

Ever since he and Rita divorced, Gary has had an obsession to be the favourite parent. He knows it's not fair to upstage his former wife, but he doesn't care what she thinks or feels as it was her decision to leave him for another man.

Even though it has been almost five years since the divorce, he's still very bitter about how their marriage ended. Rita tells him they just grew apart, but he blames it on her cheating ways. He's not sure why he ever trusted her in the first place.

So, when Ely and Ty said they wanted to see the town from the sky, Gary just knew he had to make it happen. Stu has been a fixture on the local flying scene for as long as he can remember. He was one of the driving forces behind the effort twenty years ago to establish the local airport—a small, paved landing strip on the outskirts of town with a fuelling station, a small office building that doubles as the communications centre and a storage shed.

But, as Stu points out to Gary, it serves the purpose for him and other flying enthusiasts in the area, and that's all that matters.

Gary has no idea why one of his sons is interested in learning to fly, but when Ely began to express a desire to obtain his pilot's license, Gary did some research. He was surprised to learn that there's more local interest in flying than he would have thought, and he's impressed to learn that there are several people in the area who have their pilot's license.

Gary hopes today's two-hour sight-seeing excursion will serve as Ely's introduction to flying, as he's asked Stu not only to show the boys the spectacular sights from up there, but also to explain to them what it takes to become a pilot.

Now, as they circle over town in Stu's four-seater, the experienced pilot points out local landmarks, including their house, their grandparents' house, the hospital, the RCMP detachment, the post office, the bank where Gary works, and the high school where Ely and Ty are completing grade twelve.

When they graduate in June, the boys will go off to university, so Gary is happy to have this quality time with them. Ely is heading to Acadia University in Wolfville, where he is enrolled in environmental studies, while Ty will be attending the Culinary Institute of Canada at Holland College on Prince Edward Island. Afraid that he won't see them in the future as often as he'd like, Gary is trying to make the most of it while he can.

"So, boys," Gary says to his nearly-six-foot-tall sons who are squeezed tightly into the compact back seats as Stu brings the plane down and does a low fly over of their school. "What do you think of the view from up here?"

"Oh my God, Dad," Ely replies. His eyes are as wide as saucers.

For Gary, Ely's unbridled emotions bring back happy memories of past Christmas mornings when his sons were young kids and found that Santa had fulfilled their wishes. He smiles.

"It's awesome, Dad," Ely enthuses. "Thank you for doing this for me."

"For us," Ty speaks up, afraid that he may be overshadowed by his older brother, as is often the case. "I like it, too, although it's not exactly what I would have picked for my dream birthday gift."

"What would have you picked?" Stu asks. He glances back. "You're Ty, right? Sorry. It's just that I find it hard to tell you two apart."

"I am and no worries. We get that a lot." Ty glances at his father in the front passenger seat. "The truth is, I wanted to go to Toronto to see a Blue Jays' game, but dad says that was too expensive. Maybe someday, he says, but I'm not holding my breath. When it comes to what I want to do, it never happens. It's always *someday*."

"Come on, Ty," Gary responds sharply. "Do you have any idea what it would cost to take the three of us to Toronto for an entire weekend of baseball? Tickets to the games. Hotel. Food. Flights. Even if we didn't buy souvenirs—which you know we'd end up doing—it would have cost me a small fortune. I would love to take you if I could, and you know it."

"Yeah. Sure, Dad. I know it." Ty frowns. "You always make sure Ely gets what he wants but I always have to wait."

"For Christ's sake, Ty," Ely snaps. "Why do you always have to make Dad feel bad when he's doing something nice for us? You are never satisfied. You're nothing but a spoiled brat."

~

Ty turns his head and looks out the tiny window just as a flock of birds fly past. He shudders as one of the birds turns and looks him directly in the eyes. He can't shake the feeling that the bird—maybe a duck of some sort —was looking directly through him.

Although he's upset, Ty does not respond to Ely's comment as he knows his brother is just trying to bait him into an argument. There was a time when he would jump headfirst into a heated discussion with his twin regardless of the time or place, but he's learned that arguing with his brother gets him nowhere.

As identical or monozygotic twins—conceived from one egg and one sperm—Ely and Ty are almost the mirror image of each other; but their personalities are as different as day and night.

"Tell me, Ely," Stu asks, "do you think you would ever like to get your own pilot's license?"

"Yeah, I'd like to. Is it hard to get?"

Stu shakes his head. "It's easier than you might think."

"Really?" Gary joins the conversation. "Just how easy?"

"According to Transport Canada standards, you only need a minimum of forty-five hours' flying time to get your license, but most aviation experts and experienced pilots will tell you that you should bank about ninety flight hours to meet the required practical standard," Stu explains. "When you think about it, though, that's not really a lot of time."

"Not really." Gary agrees. He smiles at his older son, who is listening intently to Stu's every word.

Stu continues, "Of course, flight times vary depending upon factors such as weather, availability of a plane and your commitment to the program, but"—quickly glancing at Gary beside him—"if you're really serious about learning, Ely, I'd be willing to give you a few lessons to get you started."

"Really? That would be awesome. Can I, Dad?"

"I don't know, Ely," Gary answers. "Depends on the cost."

"It wouldn't be that much," Stu says. He smiles at Gary. "I'll give you the reduced rate for family and friends."

"Come on, Dad." Ely reaches to the front and squeezes his father's shoulder. "Can I?"

Gary says, "We'll see, Ely, and of course I would have to talk to your mother before we make any plans. She'd be pissed if I agreed to let you do something like this before I talked to her."

"Of course," Ty speaks up. "What else is new? Anything big brother wants, big brother gets."

"Come on, Ty," Gary says. "Please don't do this right now. Can't you see how excited Ely is?"

Ty rolls his eyes. "Whatever excites Ely. That's all that's important, right? Far be it for me to ruin his day."

Gary's response is sharp. "We'll talk about this later."

Ty turns to look out the side window again. He marvels at the landscape below.

"What about this plane, Mr. Hiscock?" Ely asks. "Did you pay a lot for it?"

"For God's sake, Ely." Gary shoots his son a sharp look. "That's not the kind of question you ask anyone, especially not someone you just met."

"It's all right," Stu says. "I really don't mind." Glancing over his shoulder at Ely he adds, "Let's just say it cost me enough."

Gary says, "You'll have to excuse the boys. They are just excited to be up here."

"Not a problem." Stu says. Nodding to Ely, he continues. "It's a good sign that he asks questions. This, my young friend, is a Cessna 172 Skyhawk. It's one of the most popular personal aircraft among beginner pilots. It is a reliable and versatile training airplane, with excellent handling. It would be perfect for you to learn in."

"Cool." Ely glances around the interior of the small plane. "I could see myself flying one of these babies."

"Of course, you could," Ty whispers. "You always get what you want."

Gary turns and stares at his younger son. His narrowed eyes convey his disappointment that Ty seems intent on aggravating his brother.

"I own three planes, but I like this little Skyhawk the best," Stu says, "because it has a good cruising speed. You can get where you're going efficiently while enjoying the view from up here. Another thing I like about this plane, is it's a great aircraft for beginner pilots looking to gain experience and explore the world from the skies."

"Three?" Ely is thoroughly impressed. "Wow, Mr. Hiscock. You must be rich."

"Come on, Ely." Gary says. "Don't be so nosy. I raised you better than that."

Stu shakes his head and laughs. "Nope. Not rich. Some people like cars and trucks or other toys. I like planes."

"I could see myself owning three planes someday," Ely says.

"Yeah," Ty replies. "In your dreams, maybe."

"Screw you," Ely fires back. "You're just mad because Dad won't take you to see your precious Blue Jays."

"I'm mad because I never get to do the things I really want to do."

"Okay, Ty," Gary snaps. "That will be enough. Mr. Hiscock does not want to hear you guys argue."

"Sure, Dad," Ty answers. "Let's just make sure Ely's happy and content."

"Let it go for today, Ty, and enjoy the view. It's spectacular from up here." Gary points down. "See? There's your school and there's the soccer field over..."

He quickly turns to look at Stu. The pilot has suddenly grown quiet, staring straight ahead with a blank face as if he's in some sort of daze or trance.

"Stu?" Gary says. "Stu? Hey, man. What's happening? You don't look so good."

It's as if Stu can't hear the words.

Gary asks, "Are you sick? Did the boys' arguing upset you?"

Stu simply leans forward, oblivious to his passengers.

"Dad," Ty screams. "Were getting too close to the ground!"

"Stu?" Gary says. "Shouldn't you pull up?"

Stu, ignoring his passengers, pushes the stick forward and the plane goes into a steep descent.

"Stu." Gary screams. "Do something. You need to pull up before—"

31: Crash and burn

News that a small plane has crashed into the high school's soccer field has quickly spread through the town. By the time Corporal Warren Hamilton arrives, he can hardly manoeuvre his RCMP Ford Explorer through the burgeoning crowd to find a parking place near the scene.

"To hell with it," he mutters. Stopping quickly, he slams the SUV into park, and switches off the ignition.

Under normal circumstances, Warren would never block a road, but as his SUV sits right now, he's cutting off any exit for at least three other vehicles. But at this point, he really doesn't give a damn.

"You park near the scene of an emergency so you can be nosy while preventing emergency personnel from getting to the accident, then you pay the price," he says to his windshield.

He grabs his uniform hat from the passenger seat and slips it onto his balding head, throws open the SUV door and steps out into the crowd, which has grown to hundreds. He hates it when the suffering of other people becomes a spectator's sport. *Humanity is broken*, he thinks.

"For Christ's sake, people," he mutters, roughly pushing his way through the crowd of curiosity seekers. "Let me through, please. Get out of the fucking way."

The deeper he gets into the crowd, the more frustrated he grows.

"Get the hell out of my way," he says to a group of large men and women who are blocking his access to the soccer field. *Unless they are with emergency services, then they've got no business being here.*

"Well, excuse us," one of the larger men replies. He steps up to Warren, a foolhardy move that evokes a light chuckle from his companions.

"You think this is funny, asshole?" Warren snaps.

Coming toe to toe with the large man, he says, "Move your god-damned ass right now, or I will move it for you and you'll be spending the night in a jail cell. You want to test me?"

The man glares at him for several seconds and finally nods. "I understand."

As the man slowly shuffles to the left, Warren advances through the crowd. He emerges onto the soccer field that's still soggy from the spring thaw. He sees fire crews are using some sort of foam on the flames that are shooting from the wreckage of the plane.

He waves to Constables Nolan Shaw and Vanessa Bennett who are on the opposite side of the field, keeping onlookers back from the wreckage. They were the first officers to arrive at the scene.

They cross the field to join him.

"This doesn't look good. Please tell me what we have here."

Constable Shaw nods toward the wreckage. "What we have here is what's left of a Cessna 172 Skyhawk. According to eyewitnesses it seemed to be flying over the school and then it went nose first into the field and burst into flames. We believe there were four occupants."

Warren is almost afraid to ask, but he has to know. "Causalities?"

"Afraid so, sir," Constable Bennett says.

"Locals?"

Constable Shaw nods. "The plane was owned by a Mr. Stuart Hiscock. It seems he was operating the aircraft with three passengers."

"Is he—?"

Constable Shaw says, "It appears he died upon impact. We have to wait until the fire department gives us the all-clear before we can remove the remains to the morgue."

"After everything that's been happening around here over the past few days, the morgue must be nearly overflowing," Warren observes. "I feel bad for Stu. He was friendly and always had time to chat when I ran into him on the street or at the post office. He loved to talk about flying."

"Sorry for your loss, sir."

"What about the others in the plane?" Warren asks.

"The second casualty is another adult male," Constable Shaw reports. "He was still alive when we arrived, but succumbed before the paramedics could get him out. All he was worried about were his boys."

"There were kids on the plane?" Warren asks.

"Two teenage boys," Constable Bennett says.

"And what's their status?"

"They are both alive and on their way to the hospital," she says. "But they are badly banged up. Two firefighters were injured while getting them out, as they were wedged tightly in the back seats. Luckily, they got the boys out before the wreckage became fully engulfed."

Warren looks at the constables. "Who are we talking about here, guys?"

Constable Shaw answers. "The second decedent is a middle-aged male, Gary Rollins, and the injured passengers are his sons."

"Ely and Ty," Warren adds.

"You know them?" Constable Shaw asks.

"I know the family fairly well." Warren glances toward the smoking wreckage, his heart breaking. "Gary was the manager at one of the local banks, and his boys are all-star athletes at this school. They are two really great kids. I'm glad to hear they are going to be all right, but I feel badly for Gary. He was a nice guy, and those boys were his whole life."

He then asks, "How are the firefighters who were injured?"

"I hear they will be fine," Constable Bennett says. "Superficial burns and some minor cuts."

"That's something positive, at least." Warren scans the smouldering remains of the aircraft. "Anyone have any idea how this happened?"

Constable Bennett shakes her head. "Hopefully the black box will tell us something, if they find it."

"It doesn't appear to be a weather problem," Constable Shaw says. "What do you want us to do once the fire is extinguished?"

"The Transportation Safety Board will want to do their own investigation," Warren says. "We'll need to lock this place down, tight, and post some officers until the investigators arrive. The last thing we want is to have souvenir seekers trying to pick up keepsakes to sell on the internet."

"Understood, sir." Constable Shaw nods. "Four officers should do it."

"Now," Warren says. "I see the mayor has arrived and is talking to the fire chief. I better get over there and talk to them before Mayor MacAvee does something stupid like hold a press conference in the middle of the soccer field."

"He wouldn't do that, would he, sir?" Constable Bennett asks.

"Politicians are always politicians, and the mayor is always looking for an excuse to get in front of the television cameras," Warren says.

32: Nocturnal creatures

Monday, April 8

The events of the past three days have shaken the residents of this quaint, seaside town to their very core, but Alex knows that, somehow, the crows will work their magic, and when it's over, no one will remember the truth behind the events that have left people dead, injured and broken.

But Alex will know the truth. At times like this he wishes he was like everyone else. However, he accepted a long time ago that he's different. Special. With extraordinary abilities that only a few people in his close circle of family and friends know about.

And it is those abilities that will protect him from harm today, thanks to his bond with the Spirit Crow, but it also means he won't be able to forget any of the pain and suffering that he's witnessed.

He hasn't figured out how it all works, but he knows everyone around him is in danger.

And I can't stop it, Alex thinks as he lies in his bed and stares at the nondescript ceiling. His inability to sleep has been a plague he's endured for many years, and he's grown accustomed to this scene that represents the vast void of nothingness.

It's now almost two o'clock on Monday morning and his attempts to put all these events into perspective have failed miserably. He knows he won't sleep tonight. The mysteries surrounding the crows have conspired once again to wreak havoc on his mental stability. They've forced him to wonder if he's lost grip on his own sanity.

Why do these things happen only during a solar eclipse, and how do the crows wipe the memories of everyone in this town everyone except me and those who were the chosen ones in earlier generations, like Great Uncle Silas?

Alex blinks and rubs his eyes. He tries to stifle the panic building in the pit of his gut. His breathing is laboured and sporadic. The fear he feels is as real as the blood pumping through his veins.

Hot and cold at the same time, he shivers under the blankets while beads of sweat pool on his forehead. His mind kicks into overdrive.

The Chosen One. What does that even mean? That I'm special? That I deserve to be saved while everyone else in this town is dispensable? Who decides who can live and who can die?

He turns onto his right side to face the window over his desk, the same piece of cheap, press-board furniture at which he studied for years before he left for university. The same desk where he hides Alexandrea's journal, an historic document that tells his family's amazing, disquieting story.

With his head resting on the hard foam pillow, he can see the full moon. It hangs in the sky in all its brightly glowing glory, turning the nighttime a murky grey colour.

Mocking him. Taunting him. Warning him of the things yet to come. And reminding him of events that he could not control. It's a heavy burden for one person to carry.

Why me? I didn't ask for any of this and, even though I love the crows, at times I wish this curse had fallen to someone else.

He inhales, deeply. His lungs hurt, like someone has reached into his chest and is squeezing them.

But it hasn't happened to anyone else. I'm the cursed one or, I suppose, the blessed one, depending upon how you look at it.

He exhales forcefully. He feels his heartbeat quicken like it's about to explode through his rib cage.

He knows he's lucky in one sense because, no matter what happens between now and the eclipse this afternoon, the Spirit Crow and its brethren will protect him from bodily harm. His mental acumen, however, may be another story as the moon slowly overpowers the sun and, for a short time, takes control of humanity on this part of the planet.

My challenge, as Silas Moores explained, is to protect everyone else— the people I care for. The people I love. Bree. My parents. Her parents. Hunter and his family. Uncle Charlie. Oliver. Jace and Luna. I don't know what I would do if I lost any of them. I only wish I could protect everyone else in this town.

He shivers at the thought of others being injured or killed, but he will do whatever he can to protect those close to him.

Bringing his loved ones all together this afternoon makes sense to him. It was the only way he could think of to have everyone near him at the same time, close enough to where he can protect them during the eclipse.

Throwing the covers off his lean body that's now dripping in sweat, he swings his muscular legs around and plants his feet on the cold hardwood floor. He sits on the edge of the bed, trembling, staring out the window at the full moon. So beautiful, but also so deadly.

No one else knows what's really going on. Except for Uncle Silas and the few people that I've confided in and the crows, of course. Can't forget about the crows. Those feathered warriors know everything that happens around here.

He thinks about calling Oliver in Halifax, but he decides it's way too early to bother his friend and protector.

He carefully moves to the window, choosing not to turn on any lights. With his parents' room just down the hallway and Jace and Luna resting in the bedroom next to his, Alex remains quiet. The last thing he wants to do is to wake anyone else.

Surely, there would be lots of questions, but he knows no one else would understand what's going on with him and with this universe.

Hell, I don't even understand what's going on even though the crows and Uncle Silas have tried to warn me.

What would he tell them? That the eclipse could affect them in such a way that it may make them hurt or even kill a loved one?

They'd think I was insane.

Placing his forehead on the cool windowpane he glances around the backyard. Shadows fill in all the nooks and crannies, turning the outside world into an ominous place.

Hell, maybe I am crazy. But what is sanity? What we accept as normal or what we perceive to be normal? There is a difference, isn't there?

He swallows, his throat so dry that the saliva hurts as it feels like hundreds of minuscule knives are slicing their way through the tender tissue. He resists the urge to gag.

"Nope," he whispers. His warm breath fogs up the glass. "Not nuts." *Just living a nightmare … a dark, terrifying dream that's far too real.*

His gaze is drawn to a sudden movement above the treetops. *Crows. At this hour?*

Alex knows that would be strange behaviour as they are usually roosting at this time of night, their murder hidden from predators that sometimes challenge the crows for supremacy over their domain.

Glancing at a small, digital clock that's been on his desk since he was a youngster, he sees that it's nine minutes after two.

What in hell are crows doing out at this hour?

Staring at the flock as it moves quickly toward his window, Alex suddenly realizes that these are not crows at all, or any other species of birds, for that matter.

He shuffles backward. "Bats," he mutters. "What the hell?"

He shudders at the image of their wings flapping wildly in the bright moonlight. *You never see flocks of bats in these parts.* Or at least that's what he thinks he remembers.

And why are they heading in this direction?

He feels fear taking control of his body, the alarm bells ringing in his head.

Are they coming for me?

All of sudden, there is a cauldron of dozens of bats outside his bedroom window. Targeting him, he believes.

Shit. The breath catches in his throat. *What do I do?*

Several of the bats violently slam their tiny, brown bodies into the glass, the thuds so loud that they sicken him. He wonders if the commotion is loud enough to disturb the others.

Even though he's sure the bats can't get into his room, his first instinct is to run away, but he doesn't want to disturb his parents or his friends. *I don't need anyone losing their shit because bats are trying to get into the house.*

He plants his feet on the hardwood floor and watches as one bat after the other slams its tiny body into the window, some hitting so hard that they leave a red streak on the glass before plummeting to the ground.

"Jesus," he whispers, afraid that the bats may actually break through the glass. *Then what?*

Alex begins to do what he always does in such situations—ask the crows for help. Closing his eyes, he silently calls out to his majestic black guardians.

Several tense minutes pass as the bats continue to smack against the glass with a crunch that it causes Alex to wince. Then the crows come, answering his call, and he watches as they descend from the grey sky. With beaks open and talons poised to strike, the crows zero in on the bats.

The crows pluck the bats from the moonlit sky, ripping the much smaller creatures to bits and ending the threat they pose to the chosen one.

"Jesus." Alex watches in horror, amazement and, if he's being perfectly honest, gratitude, as the crows do what he knew they would do—protect him.

Then a light tapping at his bedroom door gives him a start, his breath catching in his throat. He spins around and stares at the door, hoping that whoever is out there doesn't just decide to walk in.

Slowly, he opens the door a crack and is surprised to find Luna standing in the dimly-lit hallway.

"What are you doing up at this hour? Did I wake you?"

"God, no," she whispers. "I haven't been sleeping. I think the bright moonlight made me restless, but I heard some sort of banging noise in your room and wondered if something was wrong. Are you okay?"

He nods. "I am fine. Sorry for disturbing you, Luna."

"What is that banging?" She cranes her neck as if hoping to catch a glimpse inside of his room.

"Everything is all good in here," he lies. "Maybe it's just a branch hitting the side of the house."

She shakes her head. "It didn't sound like a branch to me."

Alex quickly tries to change the subject. "How are you feeling? Your pain meds should help you sleep. Did you take them?"

"I did. Jace made sure of that."

"Okay, then you should go back to bed. Rest is important to your recovery. Can you make it back to the room on your own or do you need my help?"

She looks intently at him, and Alex suddenly feels uneasy. It's as if she is studying him. Icy fingers run up his spine.

"You okay, Luna?" It feels like the temperature has suddenly dropped ten degrees in just a matter of seconds.

"Yes, Alex." She turns and begins to walk away. Glancing over her shoulder, her eyes narrow, she adds, "I think it's the moon. The bright light is keeping me awake."

Alex watches her slip through the next bedroom door, closing it behind herself.

Now that was just plain weird. What has gotten into her all of sudden? Maybe it's residual trauma from the accident or maybe it's something worse.

"Jesus," Alex whispers. "I hope it's the effects of the accident."

Stepping back into his room, he closes the door and moves to the window, where the life and death dance between crows and bats is over. The crows have disappeared, but he knows they have not gone far.

"And you," he says to the remains of a bat that is stuck to the outside of the window. "You have learned the hard way that I am off limits."

33: Wild things

It's still early and Alex hasn't slept much—if at all—but he braces for the events of this fateful day that promises to be more challenging than even he can imagine...and he can imagine a lot of things.

He pulls his jeans up over his muscular running legs and slips a light blue sweatshirt down over his head of thick, white hair. He glances out the blood-smeared window, searching for any straggling bats that might be lurking, and wonders how he will explain that mess to his mother.

The crows' aerial skirmish reminds him of another battle years ago, a fight between crows and their mortal enemies, owls. He cringes at the memory, thankful he hasn't seen any owls around these parts in recent years.

As if there's not enough problems. The last thing I need to think about right now, would be owls.

As he makes his way downstairs and into the kitchen, he notices the sun is just starting its leisurely ascent in the morning sky where it will await its rendezvous with the moon later this afternoon.

It's a celestial dance that has occurred for eons but one that he hadn't paid particular attention to until now. The moon may be the smaller, less powerful celestial body, but today it will have the upper hand over the sun.

In the kitchen, Kate and Samantha are enjoying their morning coffee and conversation before Kate heads to the office and Samantha begins preparations for this afternoon's gathering.

"Good morning, guys," Alex says. Despite being drop-ass tired from lack of sleep and worrying about whatever the eclipse will bring with it today, he tries to sound chipper and upbeat. It's a rare occasion that he would reveal his real emotions to his parents. "You're both up early today."

Kate answers, "I always go in early on Monday morning to get things rolling for the week and, with Bree being off today, there's more prep work to do."

"Geez, Mom." Alex pours himself a cup of black coffee. "It's a good thing Bree isn't here to hear that comment. You do remember she was hurt in a car accident just a day ago, don't you?"

"Yes, Alex." Kate replies sharply. "Of course, I do and I'm glad that she's going to be all right, but I'm just saying that Bree being off for the week makes more work for me and everyone else at the office. It wasn't meant as any form of disparagement. It's a fact."

"Well, please don't say anything like that around Bree this afternoon at the party. It would hurt her feelings to think she's caused any problems for you and she already feels bad enough about missing time at work."

Alex brings his coffee and joins his mothers at the table. He continues, "But I know what you mean. You take one person out of an already-over-taxed situation, and you create turmoil. I work in the health care system, remember? Now *there's* pandemonium."

Kate studies his face. "Didn't sleep well again? You should really ask Charlie to give you something to help you with that."

"I never sleep well, but I refuse to take medication."

Samantha joins the conversation. "It's going to be a busy day. Are you guys ready to experience this wondrous event this afternoon?"

Kate shakes her head. "I really don't get what all the fuss is about. So, it's a solar eclipse. They happen every couple of years, don't they?"

Sensing that Kate could be thinking about bailing on this afternoon's event, Alex says, "I happen to think it is a very big deal."

"How so?" Kate asks.

Samantha winks at her wife. "For God's sake, my love, let the man have his coffee before you start grilling him on celestial mysteries. Why does everything have to be such an inquisition with you?"

Kate chuckles. "Let me try this again. Why do you think it's such a big deal?"

Alex stares into the steaming coffee in the blue ceramic mug, one of a set of four he bought as a birthday gift for Samantha when he was six or seven. They are different colours—red, green, yellow and, of course, blue. And she still uses them.

"It's an example of how vast and mysterious the universe is and how tiny and inconsequential we humans are in the overall scheme of things." He pinches his pointer finger together with his thumb to emphasize the point. "And because it's so rare to see a solar eclipse in this part of the world, I think it's something we should celebrate."

"I agree." Samantha frowns at Kate, a silent message to her wife to stop being such an old frump. "And on that note, let's review what's happening this afternoon so that we're all on the same page."

Alex nods. "You've got the food handled, right?"

"I do," Samantha assures him. "Just some last-minute refreshing to the leftovers from your dinner that never happened and we're good to go."

"The only other thing is making sure everyone gets here," Alex says. He turns to Kate. "You are going to make it, aren't you?

"I'll try my best."

"No, that won't do. I need you here."

Kate looks at him. "You *need* me here?"

"Okay, Kate." Samantha jumps in. "We get it. You're busy, but please be here if you can. For Alex's sake."

Kate nods and takes a sip of coffee. "We'll see how the morning goes."

"Good," Alex says. "And as far as I know, everyone else is going to be here. Even Uncle Charlie said he'd come if he can get away from the hospital."

"He said he would block off a couple of hours this afternoon, but you know what the emergency department is like," Samantha says.

Alex nods. "You don't know from one moment to the next if you're going to be able to pull away even to use the bathroom, sometimes." He chuckles, "You have to learn to take a pee when you have the chance, because you never know when you'll catch another break."

"You sound just like my brother." Kate laughs. "He says he's learned to pee on demand. Maybe you've been around him too long."

"I don't think so. Uncle Charlie has been a great mentor."

"That's my brother, the teacher. He loves to tell people what to do." Kate glances at her phone and rises from the table. "Well guys, it's time for me to get ready for work. I've got a lot to do this morning if I'm going to get back here in time for the party."

~

"Good morning, everyone," Jace says as he limps into the kitchen. Luna follows closely behind.

"Hey you two." Samantha says. "Can I get either of you anything? Coffee? Breakfast?"

"You're the perfect host, Ms. Henderson," Jace replies, taking a seat at the table. "I'll just have coffee please if it's no bother."

"I'll get it, Mom," Alex offers, rising from the table. "I know how he likes it." Glancing at Luna he asks, "Can I get you something, Luna?"

"I wouldn't mind a cup of tea."

"We can do that," Samantha says. "What would you like? We have the regular Red Rose tea because that's the only brand I like, and we have green, peppermint, or chamomile."

"I'll take a green tea, please," Luna quickly answers. "If it's no trouble."

"No trouble whatsoever, dear. I find green tea to be a little strong. How about some honey or lemon just to take the edge off?"

"Lemon would be wonderful, thank you."

A few minutes later, as everyone enjoys their beverages, Samantha addresses her guests. "You both had a rough day yesterday so we're really glad you decided to stay with us for a while."

"Thank you for having us," Jace answers. "We're probably going to head back to the city tomorrow."

"There's no need to rush," Samantha says. "We have the room so you can stay as long as you'd like."

Luna replies, "We'll see how things go." She throws a sharp glance at Alex and adds, "Who knows what today will bring?"

Samantha smiles and sips her coffee. "Sleep well last night?"

"Like a freaking log," Jace quips. "I think I must have passed out as soon as my head hit the pillow."

Alex says, "That was most likely the medication taking effect. How does your foot feel today?"

"It's a little better, I think," Jace answers, flexing his right foot. "But it still hurts to walk. I didn't realize a spider could pack such a powerful punch."

"Some spider bites cause problems, especially if they become infected," Alex says. "Why don't I take a look at that for you later?"

"If you wish, doctor." Jace grins and takes a sip of coffee. "Ahhhh. Just the way I like it."

Luna speaks up, "With two sugars in it. It's a wonder you don't have diabetes."

Jace chuckles. "I like it black and sweet, just like me."

Samantha asks, "How did you sleep, Luna?"

"The bed was very comfortable," Luna says, "I slept like a log, too."

Alex wonders why she isn't being truthful with his mother, but he chooses not to press the issue because he doesn't want to discuss what happened with the bats.

Luna adds, "I didn't hear a thing after we went to bed last night until I heard the birds chirping outside the window. What a nice way to wake up."

"Not so nice if you're trying to sleep in late," Samantha suggests. "But yes, most mornings I enjoy waking up to the birds chirping in the spring. There seems to be lots of nests around the yard this year."

"There seems to be a lot of wildlife around this town, period," Jace observes. "Is it always like this?"

"You do realize you're in a rural part of the province, don't you?" Alex answers with a smile. "This isn't a concrete jungle."

"Yes, but there seems to an overabundance in this town. And they seem to be really aggressive toward humans." Jace shakes his head. "Like they're out to get us."

"You're just being paranoid, honey," Luna quickly answers. "Must be the drugs you're on."

"I don't think so. These drugs wouldn't make me feel this way."

Samantha speaks up, "I agree with you, Jace. There seem to be more wild things around these days than normal. Just yesterday, for instance, I had to do battle with ants, and I never have an ant problem in my house. Ever!"

"See." Jace stares at his girlfriend. "Even Ms. Henderson has noticed that something is slightly off."

"I think you jump to conclusions far too quickly," Luna replies. "You're always looking to find something wrong. Nothing is ever good enough for you."

"Wow." Jace pulls back from the table. "Where did that come from?"

"Hey guys," Alex speaks up. "Maybe you should let this one go. Yes, there are lots of wild things around here, but you're in the country and that's all there is to it. There's nothing nefarious or sinister about it."

"Forget it, Alex." Luna pushes herself away from the table. "You can't reason with him. He's always right."

Jace replies, "What's your problem this morning?"

"I don't have a problem," she snaps. Turning to Samantha, she asks, "Is it okay if I have a shower now, Ms. Henderson?"

"Absolutely, my dear. I'll show you where everything is."

"Jesus," Jace says after Luna and Samantha have gone upstairs. "What just happened?"

Alex shakes his head. "I have no idea."

34: An aerial attack

While all her friends were off elsewhere in the world, pursuing their lofty educations and high-octane careers, Brittany Whitelaw remained in Liverpool, where she married her high school sweetheart, Emmet Fitzpatrick, with plans of immediately starting a family.

She's not sure why, but Brittany always wanted five children. It just seemed like a manageable number to her. However, by the time she turned thirty-seven, she had all but given up hope that her dreams of becoming a mother would happen for even one baby, let alone five.

But then, after trying most of the fertility treatments available to her in Canada and following numerous miscarriages, a miracle happened, and Dolly was born just after Brittany's thirty-eighth birthday. She and Emmet were elated. They had endured the trials that had been laid on them and they were subsequently rewarded, not once but twice as their son, Elijah, was born three years later.

Now she is in her early forties, and her doctors have recommended that she not have any more children out of concern for her health. They suggested that Emmet should have a vasectomy, which he refused. Her doctor then recommended that Brittany have a hysterectomy to prevent another pregnancy. It was for her own health and wellbeing, they cautioned her.

But Brittany also refused medical intervention, choosing instead to let their fate be determined by a higher power. Even though she is not overly religious, she reasoned, if she was meant to have another child then so be it.

Now, with Dolly in her first year of elementary school and Elijah just turning two, Brittany prays to have another baby and she is determined not to let anyone talk her out of it. Not her doctor, not her mother, not her two sisters, and not even her best friend, Natalie, can convince Brittany that it's time to put her health first.

"Think of Dolly and Elijah," Natalie told her. "What would become of those precious little babies if something happened to their mommy?"

"It's out of my hands," she responded, as she does to any who offer similar advice. "I'm ready for whatever is meant to be."

Today, as she walks her daughter to school as she does every sunny morning, Brittany is finding it hard to contain her excitement because she believes she may finally be pregnant for the third time.

She's yet to tell Emmet, as she doesn't want to get his hopes up too soon. She plans to swing by the pharmacy on her way home to pick up a pregnancy test. If the results are positive, then she and her husband will celebrate this evening.

If not, she won't even bother to tell him she took the test.

"Mommy," Dolly says. The little girl clings to the handle of the stroller in which her young brother is sleeping. "Can we go visit Aunt Dawn and Uncle Trevor after school?"

"I'm not sure about today, sweetie," Brittany answers. "It depends on what Daddy has planned for after work."

"Okay, Mommy."

"I don't think it's Aunt Dawn or Uncle Trevor that you really want to visit with, is it sweetie? It's more like that you want play with Barkly, isn't it?"

"I love Barkly. He's so big and fluffy." The little girl is bubbling with excitement, her blond curls bouncing as she walks. "I wish he lived with us."

"If we have time, I'll take you over to Aunt Dawn's so you can see Barkly."

Barkly is a seven-year-old Bernese Mountain Dog who, despite his massive body, is very gentle with Dolly.

As Dawn says, "Barkly would not hurt a flea. He's just a big, fluffy teddy bear."

As they turn the corner onto School Street, Brittany notes again three large birds that have been circling overhead ever since she and the children left their home. She is beginning to think the birds are following them.

Observing the birds swooping and gliding above the houses and tree-tops gives her goosebumps and she suddenly feels vulnerable. The birds seem to be stalking them.

"Hey, Dolly, do you think you can walk any faster?"

"Maybe."

Brittany quickens her pace. "Hang onto Elijah's stroller and try to keep up with me."

"Okay."

The three birds seem to be flying even lower now. Brittany has no idea what type of birds they are, but they look threatening.

She continues to walk at a brisk pace.

"Mommy. I'm tired and my feet hurt. Can we slow down, please?"

Brittany takes her daughter's hand and tries to remain calm. "It's just a little further to your school."

"Mommy," Dolly suddenly says. "Big birds are coming."

Brittany scoops Dolly into her arms. "Come on, honey. We've got to go faster."

She breaks into a steady trot.

"Mommy," Dolly cries. "I'm scared."

In the rush, Brittany fails to notice a large rock in the middle of the sidewalk. She stumbles over it, twists her left ankle, and tumbles to her knees. She hits the pavement with an impact that jolts Dolly from her arms.

"Dolly!" Brittany screams as her daughter lands on the ground in front of her. "Are you okay, sweetheart?"

"No," the young child sobs, grabbing her right arm. "It hurts, Mommy."

Brittany quickly pulls herself to her feet and rushes to her daughter. "I'm sorry I dropped you, honey."

"Mommy," Dolly screams. "The birds are coming."

Snatching her daughter into her arms again, Brittany grabs the stroller and begins to run. Seconds later, the first bird connects, striking her on her right shoulder.

"Oh my, God," Brittany screams. The attack is so powerful that it almost causes her to drop her daughter again. Instinctively, she pulls Dolly tighter to her body. "Just hang on."

She can see the school, but she isn't sure she has the strength to reach it. Her knees ache from the fall and her shoulder and ankle hurt like hell, but she is determined to get her babies to safety.

Brittany reaches down for an inner reserve of strength and commands her legs to move forward, even though it feels like her kneecaps are going to fall off.

"Mommy," Dolly screams. "They're coming again."

Seconds later, she feels powerful talons sink into the back of her scalp, removing a large clump of hair. The searing pain is instant and intense.

"Somebody help us," she yells. "They're after my babies."

She wonders why no one is coming to her rescue. *They must hear the commotion.*

Suddenly, as if her plea has been answered, she hears tires screeching and brakes squealing. A moment later someone grabs her from behind.

"Ma'am," a male voice says, "come with me before the birds come back."

Spinning around, she sees an RCMP officer. His cruiser is stopped in the middle of the street, its red and blue roof lights flashing.

"Take my baby." She thrusts the stroller at the officer.

"I've got him," the officer says. He reaches into the stroller and removes the baby boy. "You and your daughter go to my car."

Brittany cries as she darts toward the police cruiser. "I thought we were goners."

"I saw the birds attack you," the officer says. Holding the baby snugly against his bullet-proof vest, he opens the passenger side door.

"Get in, quickly," he tells her, glancing skyward.

When Brittany is in the passenger seat with her daughter, the officer hands her the baby and slams the door. He sprints to the other side of the cruiser.

He's just about to safety when two of the birds strike his shoulders. He staggers as if someone hit him with a baseball bat.

He jumps into the cruiser and pulls the door shut. The third bird, its beak snapping, lunges through the open window, grabs a chunk of flesh from his arm.

"Shit," he screams and swats at the powerful bird.

It pulls back and, like a seasoned hunter, thrusts its beak at the officer again, this time opening a gash on his cheek.

"God-damn it," the officer yelps.

With one arm he swats at the bird while with his other hand he unsnaps his holster and draws his pistol. He aims out the window and fires one shot into the air.

Startled, the birds beat a hasty retreat.

The officer grabs the mic from its stand on the dash. "Dispatch. 22D3. Shots fired. Officer needs assistance. Send immediate back up."

"10-4. Location?"

"Corner of Church and School Streets."

"10-4. Back up is rolling."

He places the mic back on the dash and turns to Brittany and her children. "Sorry for the loud bang. Are you and the children all right?"

"I think so." She hugs them tight. "Thank you for saving us. Who are you?"

"I'm Constable Shaw." His smile is made hideous by the blood dripping from his face onto his uniform.

"Nolan Shaw," he adds. "Are you sure you aren't injured? I saw you take a couple of direct hits."

"I'm okay but you're bleeding. Are you going to be all right."

She pulls a tissue from her pocket and hands it to him.

"Nothing serious." He wipes the blood from his chin. "Help will be here in a minute."

"What were those birds?"

"My father was an experienced bird watcher and, when I was younger, I sometimes accompanied him," Constable Shaw says. "It's been many years since I've seen them, but I believe those were sharp-shinned hawks."

"I had no idea there were hawks around here."

"They are very rare in these parts, but you can find them," he answers. "They are very powerful and agile flyers and hunt prey like songbirds and small rodents."

"And humans," Brittany says. "Do they usually attack people?"

"Not usually," the constable says. He glances out the windshield. "I think they've gone away."

Brittany says, "That shot did the trick. It scared me half to death, though."

"I didn't know what else to do."

"Will you get in trouble for firing your gun?"

"Once I report what happened, I should be okay. But I'll need you to fill out a report, when you feel up to it."

She nods. "Whatever you need. You saved our lives."

35: A meeting of the minds

"Sorry I'm late," Corporal Warren Hamilton tells the three men seated around a table in the mayor's office. The mayor has convened the early morning meeting with those in charge of the town's emergency services to review the events that have rocked this town during recent days.

Mayor Mac MacAvee—who hasn't been in the office for a full year yet—glares at Warren but says nothing. He's known for being a stickler for details, including punctuality.

"I had an emergency to attend to this morning," Warren explains unapologetically while taking a seat at the table. For him, it's always duty ahead of everything else and he hates the bureaucracy that comes with the responsibility of overseeing the detachment.

"I hope everyone is all right," Fire Chief Jon Sutherland replies. He offers his friend a knowing smile. He and Warren have a mutual respect.

"Yes." Warren returns the smile. "I won't get into details, except to say it was one of the oddest things I've heard of."

"Seems to be a lot of *odd things* happening around here these days," the mayor says.

Warren nods.

"Okay then, since everyone is here now, maybe we can get started," suggests Dr. Charlie Webster. He is chief of staff at the local hospital and his perspective is vital to the town's overall health and wellbeing. "I've got a lot of patients already waiting for me."

"Agreed." Glancing around the table, the mayor says, "I believe you all know Carolyn Freeland, the town manager. She will keep notes. Now, let's get down to business."

The middle-aged man shivers as he asks, "Can anyone tell me what is going on in my town?"

"Well, sir," Warren says, "since last Friday afternoon we've been called out to one violent crime scene after another. We've never seen anything quite like it."

"And do you have any idea why this is happening?" Mayor MacAvee asks.

"Not a clue." Warren glances at the fire chief for agreement. "All we know is that these acts of violence appear to be random."

Chief Sutherland says, "It's a bloody mess, that's what it is."

Charlie speaks up, "The most pressing question for us right now is how to stop all of this craziness. We've been going full tilt at the hospital for the past three days and the medical staff is basically running on coffee fumes. I don't think they can handle much more."

He shakes his head and adds, "The injuries range from minor injuries to life-threatening wounds. Most have been inflicted by someone else."

"Is it possible to ask for help from any of the nearby hospitals?" the mayor asks. "Let's call for help if we have to."

Charlie answers. "We have already reached out to Bridgewater hospital. We're still waiting to hear from them, but we'll press them again if we become swamped today. They're short-staffed, too—like all hospitals these days—but let's hope they can spare a few people to help us."

The mayor adds, "Let me know if you need me to call them. We've always done our part when they need help and now, they owe us."

Jon observes, "Here's hoping that it won't be so crazy today. We're all reaching our limits."

"Jesus," Warren responds. "Are you trying to tempt fate, Jon?"

The fire chief nods. "My guys are exhausted after last night's plane crash. If we're talking about weird things, that must be at the top of the list. Everyone who saw the crash said it was like the pilot just decided to ditch it."

"Are you saying it was deliberate?" the mayor asks.

Jon shakes his head. "We won't know for sure until the transportation safety board completes its investigation."

"Why would anyone do something like that?" Charlie asks.

Warren answers, "That's the question: why are people doing what they're doing? Most of these people are fine, law-abiding citizens who just seem to lose control and lash out at whoever is in front of them. Maybe the pilot was hit by whatever is affecting everyone else."

"It's a theory." The fire chief nods. "But what on Earth could cause people to become so violent?"

"Have the investigators arrived yet?" the mayor asks.

"They have." Jon answers. "We've turned everything over to them."

"I've got six officers up there to provide assistance with security, so we are spread pretty thin," Warren reports. "If we get too many calls today, we'll also have to reach out for reinforcements. We're all exhausted."

The mayor asks, "Will they come?"

"They will if I ask them," Warren replies. "But let's hope it doesn't come to that."

"So, I have a question," Jon says. "Has anyone ever seen anything like this before? This is usually such a quiet place."

"I don't know," Warren answers, glancing at Charlie since he's lived here longer than anyone else in the room.

Charlie shakes his head. "Never seen anything like it, but by sister's wife, Samantha Henderson, would be the person to ask. She's kind of the local expert on weird things. If there have been other cases like this in the past, she would likely know about it."

"We'll be seeing her later today," Warren says.

"Meanwhile," the mayor says, "that doesn't help us with what's happening right now." Glancing around the table, he adds, "Why this town? Has anyone heard of this happening anywhere else in the province, because I certainly have not."

"No, sir," Jon quickly answers as the others shake their heads.

Warren adds, "Strange things have been known to happen in this town. That doesn't mean we shouldn't be worried. Something extraordinary is at play here."

"I wish my nephew was here," Charlie says. "I'm sure he has a theory."

"Really?" the mayor asks. "Why your nephew?"

"Alex Goodwin is my daughter's boyfriend, and I agree with Dr. Webster," Warren says. "He's very much in tune with the natural order of things, perhaps more so than most of us. He'll probably have some ideas on what's happening."

"I know young Doctor Goodwin," Mayor MacAvee says. "He treated my wife not too long ago. Nice young man, and really knows his stuff. Maybe I should have a conversation with him"

"Kate and Samantha are having a little get together this afternoon," Charlie says. "You should stop by their house, Mr. Mayor, and talk to Alex. He's going to be there."

"You don't think anyone would mind if I just showed up uninvited?" the mayor asks.

"Absolutely not," Charlie replies.

"None of that will help us if we get slammed today," Jon says. "I'm more concerned about how we're going to cope if this continues."

"I share your concern," Warren says. "But at this point all we can do is to react to whatever occurs."

"I'm very worried about how all of this is playing out," the mayor says. "What if people begin to panic?"

"I'm not so sure that it's panic we have to worry as much as it is over-reaction," Charlie says.

"Isn't that the same thing?"

Charlie shakes his head. "Panic is one thing. We should be worried about people jumping the gun and reacting to something they perceive to be a threat when, in fact, there may be no threat there."

"That will happen," Warren says. "There is no way to prevent that. It's human nature."

"What I'm hearing, then," the mayor says, "is that there's no way to predict what's going to happen next and no way to prevent violent acts from happening and, in turn, our emergency services are being run ragged. Does that sum it up?"

The others nod.

The mayor sighs and rises from his chair. "Gentlemen, I was looking for more definitive answers this morning and all I got is more questions. I don't think we've accomplished anything here, so I will let you go get after your duties, but I will ask you to keep me posted if anything happens."

"Sir," Carolyn speaks up. She has remained quiet throughout the discussion. "May I say something?"

"Absolutely." The mayor sits back in his chair. "You have the floor, Ms. Freeland."

"I'm wondering if anyone else has noticed that, in the middle of all these tragic events, the one thing that has been missing has been crows? They're usually everywhere, watching and doing whatever it is they do. But I haven't been seeing them in recent days. Anyone else find that weird?"

"Please, continue," the mayor says.

"It seems to me that the crows have just disappeared. When I come to work every morning, it's normal to see crows hanging around the town hall, but have you seen any today?"

The mayor glances out the window and then shakes his head. "Come to think of it, I have not."

"Don't you find that strange?" Carolyn asks. "It's like something has frightened them away."

"Maybe they aren't hiding," Charlie says. "Maybe they are regrouping."

"Maybe they are afraid of something," Carolyn suggests.

"Maybe they know something we don't know," Jon says.

"The crows are mysterious creatures," Warren says. "I'll be the first to admit that I know nothing about crows, but I know someone who does."

Charlie glances at him. "Alex," he says.

Warren nods. "If there is one person who can maybe answer our questions about crows, it will be Alex."

"Well, that settles it, then," the mayor says. "We need to talk Dr. Goodwin."

36: Nobody's buddy

R & S Convenience Store has been a fixture on the town's east side for more than two decades. Owned and operated by Randy Jenkins and Scottie Fullerton, the over-crowded store, with its burgeoning shelves crammed full of grocery and snack products, boasts that it has "everything everyone needs for whatever occasion."

Randy and Scottie have known each other for almost thirty years. Their partnership dates to when they worked at one of the large grocery store outlets in nearby Bridgewater.

After working together in the grocery industry for several years, Randy got the opportunity to purchase a small convenience store in his hometown. When he pitched the idea, Scottie, who grew up in Bridgewater, jumped at the suggestion of going into business with his friend and colleague.

While the business has been very successful, the two men have not always seen eye to eye. With both Randy and Scottie having equal ownership in the business, decision-making is sometimes difficult. This is especially true when it comes to investing in new products or doing an addition to the building so they could expand their small sandwich counter into a full-fledged deli offering a wide selection of cold cuts, made-to-order party trays, subs, sandwiches, and ready-for-the oven pizzas.

The idea has proven to have been a wise investment as the very popular deli shop has repaid the men's investment tenfold.

Randy will concede that Scottie seems to have a knack for coming up with ways to move the store in new directions that usually prove successful and lucrative.

"I'll admit that Scottie's intuition is usually spot on," Randy says. "I should learn to listen to him more often, but then again, my wife says the same thing about me when it comes to our relationship. They both tell me that I'm pigheaded and always need to be right, but, as it turns out, I'm usually wrong."

However, while their professional relationship has sometimes been bent out of shape, their friendship and respect for each other has always remained intact, leading them to find acceptable solutions to their stan-doffs.

Randy is a family man with three children still in school, including a daughter, Sandi, in grade eleven. She works at the store evenings and weekends.

Scottie, on the other hand, says he will never settle down. He likes the freedom that comes with being single, but he does have a steady boyfriend whom he has been dating exclusively for almost two years. He insists that while he and Daniel have discussed the idea of moving in together some-time, he will never get married.

"If Daniel is looking for a more permanent commitment, he better look elsewhere," he tells anyone who asks him if they'll make the relationship legal.

Today, though, despite any past professional or personal turmoil, it's business as usual for Randy and Scottie. Monday is traditionally shipment day, when the bulk of their orders arrive. That requires their full attention as deliveries must be received, checked, entered into inventory, unpacked priced and put in their designated places, on the shelves in the store or in the stockroom.

It usually takes them a full day to complete the task while their three employees run the store and deal with customers, but it's a setup that has worked well for them over the years.

This morning, as the clerks go about their business in the front of the store, Randy and Scottie are busy reorganizing and clearing the stockroom while they await the first shipment of the day.

"How in the world did we manage to accumulate so much stuff over the years?" Scottie asks as Randy stacks several large boxes in the far left-hand corner of the stockroom. "We've either got to extend the building or stop ordering so much stuff. All our profits are tied up in inventory."

"Sorry, buddy. That's on you," Randy replies, puffing as he tugs on the boxes. As he gets older, this physical labour is becoming much more chal-lenging than it was when he first started in the business.

"What do you mean, that's on me?" Scottie asks. He brings his hands to rest on the broom handle and leans his chin on them. He's been sweeping for the last half hour, and he needs to take a breather. "None of this stuff is mine."

"Are you kidding?" Randy nods at a collection of boxes stacked in a corner. "All of that stuff is yours. You said you were only going to store them here temporarily while you moved from your apartment to your house. That was over three years ago. So much for being *temporary*."

"First of all," Scottie snaps, "none of it is 'crap'. And secondly, it's not all my stuff. Some of those boxes contain the Christmas decorations and other stuff we use in the store throughout the year, so don't try to put to all of this on me."

"Well," Randy huffs, "aren't you the one who handles all the decorations and promotions?"

"Only because you won't help me."

"That's because I'm no good at it."

"That's a cop-out. It's just one more thing you expect me to do." Scottie glances at the boxes in the corner again. "If you want me to get rid of that stuff, I can throw it out, but then we'll have to buy all new decorations when Christmas comes. Do you have any idea how much that will cost us?"

"Don't be ridiculous," Randy fires back. "I didn't say that you had to throw any of it out. I just said it's taking up a lot of room that we can't spare. You know how tight it gets in here on shipment day."

Scottie stares at his business partner, his eyes narrowing, his nostrils flaring.

Randy continues. "I just think it's time that we find a different place to store these things, that's all I'm saying, so don't get defensive. But while we're on the subject of doing things differently, I want to talk to you about a few changes—"

"Changes?" Scottie hates it when Randy comes up with what he thinks are *good ideas*. "What kind of changes?"

"Like hiring another person to help us in the stock room."

"A warehouse manager?"

"Exactly. Someone who could take charge of this place so we can concentrate on other things."

Scottie scowls. "I'll have to think on that."

"What's to think about, Scottie?" Randy glares at his partner as both men assume their stand-off postures. "I'm getting too old to do this heavy lifting. And another person to help us with freight and inventory would take the pressure off us. It would also give you more time to work in the deli. You've been saying you'd like to get back in there again and deal with the customers. You love doing that, don't you?"

"Yes, I do. I love it, but we can't afford to hire anyone else right now, not in this economic climate," Scottie answers. "We've already got three full-time employees who work the front for us and two part-timers. If we're talking about hiring another employee for the warehouse, then we have got to cut costs somewhere else."

"Are you saying that you want to fire someone from the front store?"

Scottie nods. "I don't see any other way. Maybe we can cut the part-timers and use their salary to hire another full-timer back here."

"Are you kidding me? This business is doing well enough that we can afford to hire another employee without cutting anyone. Besides," Randy says, "one of those part-timers is Sandi, and there's no way I'm telling my daughter that she can't work with me anymore. And you know as well as I do that we need all those employees out front. There's no way two people can handle it seven days a week."

Scottie says, "If I'm not in favour of adding more staff and you're not willing to cut anyone to make room for a warehouse guy, then I guess it's just going to be you and me back here on stock day."

"If that's the case, then you better start pulling your own weight, because I can't do this on my own anymore."

Scottie can feel his blood boiling. "I'm out here every Monday busting my ass just as much as you are."

"Yeah. Right."

"What does that mean?"

Randy picks up another heavy box of canned fruit and places it on the stack. More deliveries are due any time now. "It means that I do all the heavy lifting while you do the easier stuff like sweeping and counting. You spend half of the day talking to the delivery guys."

"What a load of crap," Scottie snaps. "Are you really saying I don't carry my weight?"

"That's precisely what I'm saying. Socializing is your greatest skill."

Scottie rushes toward his friend. Coming toe to toe with his business partner, eyes bulging with anger and nostrils flaring, he spits out, "You're so full of shit. I do just as much around this place as you do and you fucking well know it."

"In your fucking dreams."

"You always do this, Randy," Scottie says, the spit frothing at the corners of his mouth. "When you can't get what you want, you throw a hissy fit and take your anger out on me."

"That's because you think you run this place." Randy gives his friend a shove. "But don't forget, buddy boy, we're equal partners around here. Sometimes I think you forget that."

"I don't forget anything." Scottie steps back up to his partner. "But I think you forget how much overhead and debt we're carrying, especially with the cost of everything going through the god-damned roof. We can't just keep spending money like we have an endless supply. And don't call me 'buddy.' You know how much I hate that. I'm nobody's buddy."

"Too bad, buddy." Randy shoves him again.

Scottie raises the broom he's been holding and smacks the wooden handle down on Randy's head, breaking it in two pieces. "I told you not to call me buddy."

"What the hell are you doing?"

Grabbing his head, Randy shuffles backwards. He stumbles over a box and falls backwards. His head hits the concrete floor with a sickening thud that reverberates off the cinder block walls.

Scottie jumps on Randy, grabs his friend by the ears, and slams the back of his head against the floor.

"I told you not to call me, buddy." His eyes are narrowed to tiny slots and his mouth is twisted. Spittle flies in all directions. "But you just don't listen to me."

The back of Randy's skull is no match for the concrete floor.

Blood pools around his head and grey matter leaks from the crack in the back of his skull.

"You should always listen to me," Scotty tells the lifeless form under him. "You know I'm always right."

37: There will be hell to pay

By the time Alex arrives at Pine Grove Park, Oliver Lewis is already waiting for him in the parking area. Alex gets out of his car and approaches the tall middle-aged man with the finely chiseled physique, tousled brown hair and neatly trimmed beard. The man who emerged as Alex's protector years earlier is a litany of contrasts between sexiness and brooding.

"Hey, Oliver," Alex says. "Have you been waiting long?"

Oliver smiles as he leans against the red half-ton truck that he uses in his general contracting business. "Maybe ten, fifteen minutes, but that's okay. It gave me time to think."

"About what?" Alex gives his friend a tight hug as only a good friend would. The fact is, he thinks of Oliver more like a brother than his actual brother, Hunter. "How are Anna and Isabel?"

"They're both doing fine but that's not important right now." Oliver steps out of the hug. "What's more important is what's going on with you. You sounded more than a little stressed when we talked. I can sense something is wrong, so I knew I had to come back right away."

"You know how I met my Great Uncle Silas Moores and the Spirit Crow on Friday, but there's much more," Alex answers. "Let's take a walk and I'll fill you in on everything."

Choosing his words carefully, Oliver says, "If the owls have come back after all these years, just tell me. I know what those bastards are capable of doing and if I have to face off with those sons-a-bitches again, I'll do it."

"God, no. It's nothing like that, thank Jesus. Things are bad enough around here right now that the last thing I need to deal with would be those bloody owls."

"That bad?" Oliver's right eyebrow rises.

"Worse than you can even imagine."

Alex heads toward the trail that leads around a small lake at the centre of the park, the tall centuries- old pine trees creating a natural canopy that blocks out much of the late morning sun and casts oddly shaped shadows across the carpet of pine needles that cover the ground. "Come on."

Oliver jogs to catch up. "If it's not owls, what is it?"

"It's literally all living creatures—humans, animals, birds and even the bugs."

Oliver glances at his young friend. "What the hell are you talking about?"

"It's all connected to today's solar eclipse," Alex says. "And for reasons that I don't understand, it's reacting with the thinning ozone layer and causing living things to resort to their basic instinct—kill or be killed."

Alex maintains a fast pace as the trail meanders through many bends, skirts the lake, and climbs the small hills, and as they walk, he pours out the story: the Spirit Crow, Uncle Silas, the eclipse making people mad, so many deaths and acts of violence, and why nobody remembers this happening before.

As the trail flattens, he stops to catch his breath. Oliver, beside him, says, "And you are the Chosen One which means you are protected?"

"Yes, and before me, it was Great Uncle Silas."

"And this *magical crow* is only powerful enough to protect one person?"

"Yes. But it's spiritual, not magical."

"Can I meet this Great Uncle Silas or see the Spirit Crow? I'd like to talk to him."

"That's why I asked you to meet me here," Alex explains. "I'm taking you to the place where I first met them."

"Okay then. Let's do this," Oliver says. "I'm anxious to learn more."

"There are no guarantees. Silas says the Spirit Crow usually only appears to the one it has chosen to protect."

"But I am your protector, so maybe it will be different for me."

"That's what I'm hoping," Alex says.

He leads his friend to the exact spot where he first encountered the old man and the albino crow. "This is where I first met my great uncle."

"And you didn't know about him before Friday?"

"Never heard of him. He isn't mentioned in any of the family documents or books that I've seen. I didn't even know that my great-grandmother Clara Underwood had a brother."

"I guess we shouldn't be surprised by anything we hear about your family, Alex," Oliver observes. "There are many skeletons stashed away in those family closets."

Alex stammers as he feels a sudden wave of electricity rush through his body. The shock waves tingle to the point that they hurt. "Did you feel that?"

Oliver studies his younger friend. "Are you okay, Alex? You look really flushed."

Alex gasps for air. "I'm not all right. I suddenly feel very light-headed and dizzy."

"Come with me."

Oliver takes the younger man by the arm and leads him to a large boulder a few feet off the trail. "Sit here until it passes."

"Thanks."

"What happened, Alex?"

Alex struggles to speak. "I have the feeling something is very wrong."

"More wrong than the strangeness you've already told me about?"

"Yes," Alex focuses on several small black clumps resting in the early spring grass. "More wrong than that." He points. "See them?"

Oliver moves to where his friend is pointing. "Jesus," he says. "It's—"

"Crows." Alex interrupts, his heart falling into his stomach. "And they're all dead. Please count them."

"There are nine."

Alex rises from the boulder, struggles to maintain his footing, and glances around the trail.

"Where are you, number ten?" He calls out, his voice cracking with emotion.

"Here, Alex," Oliver calls to him. "It's over here."

Alex joins his friend. "Is it dead?"

Oliver shakes his head. "I don't think so, but it's not looking too good."

Alex kneels beside the dying crow, its ebony feathers covered in bright red blood. He whispers, "What happened to you and the others?"

The crow, its wings barely fluttering, slowly opens its eyes and connects with Alex.

"You brought me here, didn't you?" Alex says. "You wanted me to see this, didn't you?"

The crow blinks several times but remains quiet as it struggles to hang onto what life it has left.

Alex brushes away his tears. "Who did this?"

Oliver kneels beside his friend. "It looks like they were all shot."

"Who would dare to shoot my crows?"

"I don't know. Can it give us any clues about what happened here?"

Alex gently scoops the limp crow into his hands, the blood dripping through his slender fingers and forming small, red pools on the ground. He speaks softly. "Let's see what you can tell me."

The crow stares at its human friend. Bird and man make eye contact.

"I see the crows," Alex says seconds later. "They are the ten. They have come here to commune with the Spirit Crow. It is close."

Oliver stands and glances around the wooded areas that border the trail.

"There were three of them—young men," Alex says, tears streaking down his face. They have guns, and they begin shooting the crows, picking them off one at a time. The crows try to escape but the boys are too fast."

His voice quivers. "One at a time the crows fall from the trees and from the sky. Their blood-soaked bodies hit the ground. They are all dead."

Alex shakes his head as the bloodied crow closes its eyes for the last time. "This one is gone, too."

He places the body of the crow on the grass, stands, and backs away, wiping his bloodied hands on his pants.

Oliver asks, "Do we bury them?"

Alex shakes his head. "We leave them where they rest. The other crows in the murder will take care of their own. They have a ritual they must follow."

"Where does that leave you now?"

"The crows will send ten more to watch over me. But that's not the worst of it. The crows will seek vengeance and they will go after those three men. There will be hell to pay."

"Can you save the men?"

Alex shakes his head. "I cannot. The crows won't stop until they've dealt with all three. No one can help them now."

He scans the trees. "We have company."

"Company? Who?"

"The Spirit Crow." Alex nods toward a nearby pine tree. "It has come. Can you see it?"

"Yes." Oliver stares at the albino crow with its stark white feathers and glistening pink eyes. He has seen a lot of strange and unusual things over the years since he started serving the crows, but even he has not seen anything quite like this. "It is beautiful."

Alex moves toward the rare white crow. It remains still and quiet.

"What does it want?" Oliver asks.

"It wants me to know that it will protect me. And it wants to tell me that the time is now."

"What time is now?"

"It's time for hell on earth." Alex says.

38: Hell on earth

Excitement mounts as the clock ticks toward the eclipse time. People across North America anticipate the arrival of the solar eclipse, anxious to observe the celestial phenomenon that comes shrouded in mystery, myth, and legend. It hasn't been seen in this part of the world in decades and its impending arrival has sent a ripple of anxious curiosity and nervous anticipation throughout the population.

That's especially true for Liverpool residents, as this region of Nova Scotia hasn't experienced a solar eclipse since 1972. The eclipse should be visible locally from about 3:27 to 5:44 this afternoon.

Meanwhile, people in town are going about their lives, doing their daily chores, carrying out their work duties, gathering with family, and just doing whatever they have to do to fulfill their responsibilities. Except for the impending standoff where the moon reigns supreme in the sky for a brief period, all seems normal.

~

Todd Beacham has been a truck driver since he graduated from high school. It's all he ever wanted to do and it's all he knows.

He loves his job but now, at age of sixty-three, he believes he's ready to retire from the road. Thinking about the thousands of kilometres he's put under him since he got behind the wheel of his first big rig at the age of twenty-one, he figures it's time to step aside, especially now that he and his wife, Debbie, are expecting the arrival of their first grandchild.

Regretting all the time he lost with his own two children while he was on the road, he sees this grandchild as being his second chance to get it right. He knows his son and wife will raise their child with love, but he wants to be a good grandfather, and that means sticking closer to home.

While he's all but made up his mind to retire from his life-long profession, the thought of leaving the road causes his stomach to churn. He's not sure what he'll do with his time. He's not used to being home every day and he's not sure Debbie is looking forward to having him around so much.

"I don't need you under foot all the time," she tells him, while suggesting that he should consider looking for a part-time job, one that will keep him busy but also keep him close to home.

She's got a point, he thinks while steering his truck along Highway 103 past the Brooklyn exit, en route to the Liverpool turn-off where he'll drop off this load and pick up another to take back to Halifax tomorrow morning. He will be on the road by five o'clock.

I'll probably go nuts if I'm stuck in the house all day.

Finding a part-time job then, seems like a good solution, and he knows where he's going to look. He's heard the local school board is looking for bus drivers. With his pristine driving record and many years of experience handling large trucks, Todd is convinced he would be a good bus driver.

The only question is, can I handle the kids?

He's discussed this idea with Debbie, and she insists he would be perfect for the job. "Of course, you could handle it," she tells him. "The kids will love you."

But he's not so sure Debbie isn't just telling him what he wants to hear just to get him out of the house.

He's decided that when he gets back to the depot after dropping off this load, he's going to give the foreman his three-week's notice. Then he'll apply for a bus driving job.

He's relieved by his decision. For the first time since he's contemplated retirement, he feels content that he's made the right call.

He sits up straight behind the wheel of his truck as he sees a red Toyota Prius approaching on the opposite side of the highway, heading towards Bridgewater. Gently touching the brakes as he's about to descend a small hill, he thinks the compact car will make the hill and zoom right on by with no issues.

By the time he realizes he's wrong, it's too late.

His heart leaps into his throat as the Prius crosses the yellow line and takes aim at his truck. It's like the driver has intentionally veered into his path.

"Jesus Christ," he screams.

Jamming on the air brakes, he struggles to keep the truck from jackknifing, which would likely cause the trailer to flip over.

Seconds later, the Prius slams into the rig's front bumper.

"Please, God," he prays, "let me live to see my grandbaby."

~

Nick Parker believes beagles are the best breed of dog on the planet. He loves them and he's had beagles for as a long as he can remember.

"What's not to love?" he replies whenever someone asks him why he's so enamoured with beagles. "They have a great disposition. They're loyal friends. They're kind and gentle, especially around children. And they return your love unconditionally."

He got his first beagle puppy from his mom and dad on his twelfth birthday and doesn't remember a time when he hasn't had at least one beagle in his home. His girlfriend, Paige, tells him he's obsessed with the dogs, and he agrees. However, he points out, it's a healthy obsession.

Right now, he has three beagles—Skipper, the oldest; Lulu, the only female; and Ringo, named after his favourite Beatle. Ringo is also the youngest of the trio.

Nick walks the beagles at least three times a day, regardless of the weather. Today, as the noon hour traffic is just starting to pick up, he leads the dogs down Main Street or, to be more precise, he chuckles to himself, they are leading him down the sidewalk.

The dogs seem to be more enthusiastic today than normal; more rambunctious, pulling on their leashes with such force that he's afraid they will break free of his grasp.

"Come on, guys. Slow down." He walks quickly to keep up with the dogs, pulling back on the leashes. "Take it easy, Skipper. What's gotten into you guys today?"

The beagles ignore their human and continue to make their way down Main Street, pulling and tugging the slender, tattooed man behind them. They are intent on pursuing whatever mission they appear to be on today.

The dogs are usually very friendly around people. Accommodating and affectionate, they'll stop to enjoy the attention heaped upon them, allowing people to pet them and enjoying the treats that strangers sometimes give them. However, Nick has noticed that the one thing these they don't like is bicycles.

He doesn't remember them ever having a problem with cyclists, but their attitudes clearly change whenever anyone on a bike approaches them. Such is the case today as a stranger on a bike heads in their direction.

Nick doesn't recognize the man, but he's worried that the driver appears to be coming directly at him and the dogs.

"Stop," he yells. "Can't you see my dogs?

Skipper, Lulu and Ringo see the man on the bike and go berserk, barking and pulling on their leashes.

The stranger, without hesitating, plows his bike into the dogs. They snap and nip at the man, and pull him off his bike. He lands with a thud on the paved sidewalk. The dogs are all over him, biting and chomping at any area of exposed flesh.

"Good," Nick sneers. He kicks the man's legs for good measure. "I told you to stop. Now you're getting what you deserve."

~

If there is one thing Alice Barnes hates more than anything else on the planet, it has to be rats and mice. The mere thought of the rodents getting anywhere close to her sends her into a tailspin.

The fear goes back to when she was just six years old, visiting her grandparents in nearby Caledonia. One day, when she was helping her grandfather clean the horse barn, a mouse ran across her bare feet. It scared her half to death, causing her to have nightmares and panic attacks.

Thirty years later, Alice still harbours a deep-seeded fear that someday, the rodents will invade her house and come after her.

Her husband, Ivan, calls the fear irrational, but he doesn't understand what that experience did to her. At the time, she was a timid little girl whose self-esteem was so fragile that she was practically afraid of her own shadow. The fear is still real, and the mere mention of rats or mice drives her into a tizzy.

It's natural, then, that she's worried by reports that over the past few days, people have seen increased numbers of rodents around town.

"You're just being paranoid," Ivan tells her. "We don't have rats or mice in our house. You are perfectly safe here."

But today, Alice isn't so sure. Ever since Ivan left for work and the children went to school, she's been hearing strange noises in the walls and ceilings. She's terrified that her worst fears are coming true. She's simply too afraid to do any of the chores, not even the laundry.

She's locked herself in the bathroom and has called her mother, Mona, for help.

"Now honey," Mona says, "we've talked about this before. You're just letting your imagination get the best of you. You have to get a grip."

Alice crouches, shaking, in the bathtub as the sounds of the scratching and nibbling intensifies. "I can hear them, Mom. They're all around me in the walls and in the ceiling. They're trying to get me."

"No, they aren't. We've talked about this. You can't let this fear control you, Alice. I know you always do laundry on Mondays so why don't you get off the phone and get that started?"

"I can't, Mom. They're everywhere in the house and they're coming to get me," Alice cries. "Ask Dad if he'll come over and have a look around."

"He's already out in the workshop and he won't like the idea of dropping whatever he's doing to come over there for no reason."

"Do it for me, Mom."

"Okay, Alice. I'll ask, but it will probably be an hour before he gets there. You know how he drags his feet whenever I ask him to do something."

The call over, Alice scans the walls and ceilings. She glances at the floor. She's sure she sees the tiles move. She shivers as the thundering of hundreds of tiny feet in the ceiling gets louder. Her worst nightmares are coming true.

~

The crew has been on the scene since six-thirty this morning when reports of a break in the water main on Hemlock Street started coming.

Veteran employee Roy Talbert, newcomer Grant Turner, and foreman Will Wilson were immediately dispatched to locate the leak. Additional workers joined them after eight o'clock to carry out repairs.

Now, at lunchtime, they have a large section of the road dug up and the water shut off to a major section of town. They anticipate that it will be cut off for most the day.

"Let's get this broken section out of here as fast as we can," Will says. "The homeowners are pretty pissed that they don't have any water. I'd be unhappy, too."

"Not sure what they expect," Roy replies. "We can't work miracles. This rotten old pipe must have been put here over a hundred years ago."

Will says, "No matter how old it is, we've got to get it fixed today or the residents will have our heads."

"When will the new pipe be here?" Grant asks.

"Supposed to be on site by three this afternoon," Will tells him. Addressing the other members of the crew, he adds, "Okay fellas. Let's get this done."

"We're doing the best we can," Roy answers. "The way I see it, it will get done when…" His voice peters out.

"Roy?" Will turns to his co-worker, a man he's known for more years than he can remember. "What were you saying?"

"I don't know what's wrong." Roy stutters. He grabs his left arm.

"Are you having a heart attack?"

"I don't know." Roy sinks to his knees. "It just hurts like hell."

"Jesus." Will says. "Is that blood?"

Grant scrambles out of the pit and grabs the older man. "I think he's been shot. Call an ambulance."

~

Cleaning the debris of winter from the gutters is one of Joe Turnbull's least favourite springtime chores, but it's a job that's got to be done. He likes to get at it early in April and he decides this Monday morning seems like a good time.

With his air buds stuck in his ears, Joe can block out the rest of the world and go about his business while listening to George Strait, his favourite country artist. If he has to do this hateful job, at least he may as well try to enjoy himself.

After snapping the plastic collection bag to the belt around his waist and slipping on his rubber work gloves, Joe grabs the tiny trowel that fits perfectly into the gutter pipes and climbs the ladder.

I suppose it could always be worse, he thinks, soaking up the early spring sunshine. *It could be raining, and this would have to wait for another day.*

And as anyone who knows Joe will attest, he hates waiting.

Reaching the eve of the house, Joe begins to dig into the gutter with his trowel, scooping out the wet leaves and other gunk that has accumulated there over the winter and depositing it in the plastic collection bag. He's about five minutes into the task when he suddenly feels a piercing pain on the back of his neck.

He reaches around to see if he can figure out what's bothering him, being careful not to lose his balance. As he does so, a large hornet appears and buzzes around his face.

"What the hell are you doing here? Isn't it a little too early for hornets?"

Joe quickly removes his blue baseball cap and swats at the hornet. "Shoo. Leave me the hell alone, you little bastard."

Within seconds, a swarm of aggressive hornets descends upon him, driving their stingers into his skin.

"Jesus. Jesus. Jesus," he screams, ducking and swaying. He takes one step down the ladder, loses his balance, and plummets to the ground.

He lands flat on his back, the air buds popping out of his ears just as George Strait launches into the chorus of *Check Yes or No*, one of his favourite songs. He throws up his hands to protect his face as the hornets keep coming.

He tries to get up, but he can't. Intense pain shoots down his legs and arms.

"Help," he cries out, hoping his wife will hear him.

~

Norma Fleming, a trained personal care nurse, has been working for the eighty-nine-year-old Abraham Pearce for just over two years. His family hired her to take care of him after he suffered a stroke and became immobile.

Totally paralyzed on the left side, the old man barely speaks. Restricted to his bed and the wheelchair, Mr. Pearce is confined to this centuries' old house where he and his long-deceased wife once operated a general store.

The Pearce business closed decades ago, but Mr. Pearce believes he must get up every day and go to work. Norma is convinced that the old man believes he is still living in the sixties.

"It's a nice day, Mr. Pearce," she says as she positions him in his wheelchair. "Why don't I wheel you out to the veranda for some fresh air while I clean up in here?"

She knows he can't speak, but she watches for any facial expressions or head movement to indicate whether the old man likes her suggestion. Seeing no indication, she begins to push the wheelchair to the stairlift that will take them to the main floor.

"It will do you good to get outside into the sunshine," she says.

She's about to push the chair onto the lift when she abruptly changes direction and makes a beeline to the stairs. Reaching the lip of the first step, Norma unfastens the belt that keeps him in place, gives the chair a gentle shove and releases the handles.

The wheelchair tumbles over the edge of the top stair and begins its quick descent down the twisting flight of twenty stairs. The chair bounces and crashes onto the black and white tiled floor at the bottom. The old man is ejected upon impact, his head smashing on the floor.

"There you go, you old bastard," Norma mutters, smiling proudly as blood pours from the gaping wound at the top of his head. "I hope you enjoyed the trip, but you gotta watch that first step. It's a doozy."

~

For the murder of crows observing the activity from their perches throughout town, it appears that this place has truly become hell on earth.

39: The truth hurts

Luna and Jace had planned on a happy future together. She understood that their buying a house, getting married and starting a family had to wait until after he graduated from medical school and established his practice. She told him that no matter where he went for work, she'd happily come with him.

It's what they both wanted, or so she thought, but now she isn't so sure. In recent months, Jace has become withdrawn, pulling back whenever she tries to talk about their plans, telling her that he needs to put his full attention into his studies.

She accepted that pushback at first, but she has come to believe that he was using his studies as an excuse to avoid the topic. Now that he's completed his training and is about to embark on his career full time, she wonders if he'll find another excuse to keep putting her off.

It will tear her heart apart if he's no longer committed to the plan but, even though it will be tough, she's sure she'll get over it. If he's no longer invested in spending his future with her, then she needs to know what he wants to do.

She's quite capable of taking care of herself, and she's tired of putting her life on hold while waiting for him to decide if he's ready for the next step. She's starting to think that she's already given him far too many years of her life.

Luna knew from the first time she met Jace that she loved him, and she knows in her heart that he still loves her. However, she also knows that there's something that he's not telling her—something that's created a wall between them. Now though, she's decided she wants answers, and with him graduating from medical school, the present seems like the right time for them.

She's ready for the whole shebang—marriage, a house, children. She wants at least three. But if Jace isn't into it, then maybe it's best that they go their separate ways. She's tired of living in limbo, somewhere between the mysterious void of uncertainty that surrounds their relationship and her ultimate happiness.

I deserve better.

The thought of breaking up with the man she loves is causing her great angst, but it has become painfully clear that if she wants answers, she will have to take control of her own life.

She's been trying to rest upstairs in Hunter's former bedroom, but the thoughts running through her brain prevent her from relaxing. If Jace ever decides to come up to check on her, she plans to finally ask him what's going on.

Lying on her side, the multi-coloured comforter pulled snugly up to her chin, Luna stares out the window. Her eyes are pulled to a flock of birds. She has no idea what kind they are, but she finds them almost hypnotizing as they swoop and glide over the tops of the pine trees in the backyard.

She's mesmerized by their beauty, grace, and agility, but mostly by their power. She wishes they could carry her away to some place safe and cozy, a place where everything is just as she imagines it should be.

But she believes the sharp pain that's gnawing in the pit of her stomach and the incessant pounding in her head are signs that something is terribly wrong in her world. She is certain that the *something* involves Jace.

It feels like a freight train is barrelling straight for her and she can't get out of the way. It's as if she's tied to the tracks like the helpless damsel in one of those old silent movies she used to watch with her grandmother. She feels like the victim of the story's dastardly villain who controls the narrative.

She flops on the bed and stares up at the ceiling. It's a total void, much like her future. She takes a deep breath and then exhales. She decides, however, she will be nobody's victim.

"Luna?" Jace's soft voice snaps her out of her stupor.

He slowly opens the bedroom door and sticks his head into the room. "Are you awake? Alex's mom has made lunch, and she wants to know if you feel up to eating with the rest of us. It smells really good. Perhaps you might feel better if you ate something."

A sudden wave of emotions washes over her body, gripping her like an angry parent would shake an impertinent child. She trembles like a solitary leaf of a branch desperately clinging for its life in the middle of a windstorm.

Come on Luna. Get a grip, she tells herself.

She swallows and almost chokes on her own saliva. She stifles the urge to vomit.

"Just come in here please," she says quietly. "I want to talk to you for a minute."

"Sure." Jace limps slowly into the room and stands at the foot of the bed. "What's up?"

She sits up, pulling her knees to her chest and pats the bed beside her. "Sit here, please."

"Okay." He sounds hesitant to her. She can see his eyes examining her as if he's expecting her to spring forward and attack him.

"For God's sake, Jace." She pats the bed again. "I'm not going to bite you."

"No." He chuckles nervously, and he sits beside her. His robotic movements convey his reluctance to be near her.

"I just want to talk."

"About what?" His voice is almost a whisper.

"Us. Our future."

"This isn't the time or place."

When he tries to stand, she grabs him by the arm. "I need to know what's going on with you."

"I don't want to do this right now, Luna."

"Well, I do. I'm worried about us. It's giving me a massive headache and you know I never get headaches."

"It's probably the effects of the concussion." He slips into his doctor mode. "You did suffer a major blow to your head not even two days ago."

"I don't think it's from the accident." She's trying hard not to cry. "I'm sure it has something to do with us."

Jace says nothing.

She continues, "I've felt for a while that you are pulling back from me. Are you getting tired of us, Jace?"

"There are other people in the house so let's wait until we get home tomorrow to talk about this. We'll have more privacy there."

"I'm tired of waiting. I want to discuss it now and I need you to be honest with me." Her face twists into a mask of anguish. "What is going on with you, Jace?"

"Fine." He throws his hands up. "If that's what you want, then here it is." He pulls back from her. "I still love you very deeply, but I don't know what I want. I've spent all these years and a ton of money studying to be doctor, but I'm not sure that's what I really want to do. Until I figure that out, I don't think I can make a commitment to you."

"You're just figuring this out now?" Her voice is hardly a whisper. "After all these years?"

He swallows and says, "I think I knew it a while ago but didn't want to accept it."

"Do you want to break up with me?"

He shakes his head. "I'm not saying that. But right now, getting married and trying to settle down while I'm in this state of confusion wouldn't be fair to you or to me. I think what I really need is a break."

She wipes her eyes. "From me?"

"From everything."

"For how long?"

"I don't know. For as long as it takes."

"Does that include time away from me?"

He sucks in a mouthful of air and then answers. "Yes." His voice is hardly a whisper.

His words are like a dagger to her heart. "You're saying you need to get away from me because what? I'm too demanding? Too overbearing?"

"This doesn't have to be a big deal."

She stares at him. "Of course, it's a big deal, Jace. When the man you love, the man you thought you were planning a future with, tells you he wants a break from you, it's a big fucking deal."

He rises from the bed. "This is why I didn't want to tell you. I knew you would be upset."

"Just get out," she explodes. "I can't even look at you."

"I'm not trying to hurt you. I just need to find out who I am. I think getting away for a while will give me the time and space I need to think and to put things into perspective."

"You shouldn't have to put *me* into perspective at this point in our relationship." Her eyes narrow into slivers. "Now just leave me the fuck alone."

At the door, he turns to look at her. She can see he's on the verge of tears. "I'm sorry, Luna. I really want to work through this with you."

"Just get out."

"Okay, but what about lunch? What do I tell Alex's mother?"

"Tell her whatever the hell you want."

40: Whatever normal is

Warren hits the tiny red button with his long, bony index finger and tosses his cellphone onto the passenger seat of his police SUV. He takes a deep breath, leans his head back and exhales.

"Jesus," he whispers, shaken by the news that more acts of violence have been reported this morning throughout the region. He's struggling with how to handle the landslide of complaints.

What is going on around here, he wonders, staring through the dirty windshield at the crumpled remains of the red Toyota Prius. The car is wedged tightly under the front bumper of the transport truck Todd Beacham was driving.

He knows Todd is a good citizen and a conscientious and careful driver. He's relieved the trucker escaped the collision unscathed—physically, at least. Emotionally, however, could be another story as Warren knows that serious accidents can have lasting psychological impacts on those involved.

As for the driver of the car, that's a different scenario. While Warren is relieved that the young woman didn't die in the crash, he is dismayed that she was seriously injured. She will likely be facing several surgeries and months of rehab to get back to normal.

Whatever the hell normal is these days. He sighs. *But it could have been much worse.*

Warren glances at the small screen as his cellphone begins to ring again. It's his wife, Lisa. For a second, he thinks about letting the call go to voice mail, but then he grabs the iPhone and presses the green button.

It might be something involving one of the girls.

"Hi, Lisa." He tries to remain cordial, but the adrenaline is pulsating through his veins, as it does whenever he's at the scene of a serious MVA. "This is not a good time, so, unless this is urgent, can I call you back?"

"It's not really urgent, I suppose."

She sounds like she's out of breath, but he believes she might be a little miffed by his curt attitude. But he is on duty, and Lisa knows that unless it's an emergency, she shouldn't be calling him.

"Sorry," she continues. "I hadn't heard about any accident. I was just checking if you are going to make it to Samantha's get-together this afternoon. She'd like everyone to be there by two."

Warren rolls his eyes.

"I don't know." He tries not to snap at her for bothering him with this. "I'm pretty busy. All hell has broken loose and we're stretched pretty thin. As much as I love Bree and Alex, I just can't drop everything to go to a luncheon."

"But you promised Bree you would be there to help celebrate Alex's graduation. She's counting on you."

"I know, but I can't make any promises and I've really got to go. I see the fire chief and I have to talk to him."

"I'll just meet you there, then." Her tone is insistent.

"Yes. If I can make it. Now I really must go."

"Okay. I'll see you this afternoon."

Warren turns off the phone without saying goodbye, but he knows she's used to that.

He opens his SUV door and swings his long legs out of the police vehicle, his large force-issued boots hitting the pavement with a thud.

No time for pleasantries today.

He stands beside the Explorer and studies the crumpled wreckage of the Toyota, still amazed that no one died in this crash. The one saving grace for the drivers is that the car didn't catch fire upon impact.

There but for the Grace of God.

He strides toward Chief Jon Sutherland, the stocky but good-looking man wearing the red helmet who has stationed himself beside the fire department's rescue rig to supervise his crew.

"How are you doing, Chief?" Warren extends his right hand to the man he greatly respects.

"About as well as can be expected, Corporal." The fire chief grasps Warren's hand and squeezes.

He grimaces and Warren wonders if his friend is injured.

"I just don't know how much more my crew can take," Jon continues. "They've been run pretty ragged the last few days."

"Haven't we all?"

"We've been dispatched to so many emergencies since Friday afternoon that they're all starting to become one large blur."

"It's the same for my officers. If things don't soon slow down, someone is going to snap,"

Jon nods. "And that someone could be me. I have never seen anything like this. Have you?"

Warren shakes his head. "It just doesn't seem logical that all of these events have happened back-to-back-to-back like this. This isn't normal, not even for this town where strange things are known to happen."

"Got any theories?"

"Nothing that would sound sane." He nods at the fire chief, his eyebrows raised as if he's pondering a life-or-death question. "Know what I mean?"

"Sadly," Jon replies. "I do."

"So, what happened here, Jon?" Warren studies the wreckage that will have Highway 103 closed down for hours while authorities conduct their investigation and then do cleanup.

"Beats me," the fire chief answers, keeping a close eye on three members of his crew who are working to extricate the female driver from the mess of twisted metal that was once a Toyota Prius. It's a painstakingly slow process as the firefighters must be careful not to cause additional injuries to the woman during the rescue.

"We'll bring in an accident recreation analyst to have a look," Warren says. "There's one right in Lunenburg so it won't take him long to get here."

"Getting any clues from the truck driver?"

"One of my officers is taking his statement right now, but I understand he's shaken up pretty badly. It's going to take a while to get an accurate picture."

"I just don't get it," Jon observes. "Other than this little hill, the visibility on this stretch of highway is pretty good, and it wasn't storming."

"Sometimes it can be the smallest thing," Warren suggests. "Maybe the driver got a phone call, or something ran in front of her car, and she swerved to avoid it."

"A deer, maybe?"

Warren shrugs. "Whatever happened, we're lucky we don't have a fatality, for now, at least." He nods toward the crushed car. "How long until your guys get her out of there?"

"It's going to take them a while as she's wedged in their petty tight. But the paramedics have given her something to keep her calm. They suspect she may have a punctured lung."

"Shit. I know what that's like. It's pretty painful."

"More than that, though, she may have a spinal cord injury as she said she can't feel anything below her waist, or move her legs."

"Damn. That's not good."

"So they've got her immobilized as best they can, but we have to move as quickly as we can to free her because the sooner that she receives medical treatment the better. It's no easy job, though."

"I see that," Warren says, as his attention is suddenly drawn to the RCMP cruiser that's parked on the opposite side of the road. Constable Vanessa Bennett is waving for him to come over.

Warren crosses the road and sees the truck driver is sitting in the back seat of the cruiser. "What's up, Constable Bennet?"

"I've just finished taking Mr. Beacham's statement."

"And what does he say happened?"

"Mr. Beacham says the Prius swerved into the path of his truck, and they collided head-on. He says he couldn't avoid the car."

"Did he say how it happened?"

"Well, that's just the thing," Constable Bennet says. "Mr. Beacham says the driver deliberately swerved into his path."

"He means, *it looked like* she swerved into his lane, right?"

The constable shakes her head. "We went over this point several times and he's pretty insistent that this was a deliberate act."

Warren pauses and considers the constable's report. "An attempted suicide then? It happens more often than we think."

"Mr. Beacham is pretty upset so it's possible he's confused," the constable says. "I guess we'll have to wait until we can talk to the driver of the Toyota."

"She's going to be incapacitated for a while, from what I hear. It could be days before we can speak with her."

"For now then, I'll just leave the cause of the accident as unknown in my report?"

"Yes, stating that it was a deliberate act would have serious implications for the woman, so we must be one hundred percent sure that's what happened."

"What about Mr. Beacham? I'm done with him for now."

"He needs to go the hospital and get checked out," Warren says. "Tell the paramedics to take him whenever they are ready."

"Yes, sir. Where do you want me next?"

"You stay here and keep control of this scene. The highway is going to be closed for several hours because they can't move the car until they get the driver out."

His cellphone rings just as he tells the constable, "You're in charge of this scene. The fire department will handle traffic control. Make sure they don't let anyone into the crash site."

"Understood."

Glancing at the phone screen as he steps away from the cruiser, Warren is surprised to see that it's Julie Graham calling. She's the wife of his best friend, Cliff. She never calls him, so something may be wrong.

"Julie? Everything all right?"

"Yes, we're all fine, but thank God you answered." She sounds frazzled.

"What can I do for you?"

"I'm over at The Cozy Corner Café and we've got a problem."

"What kind of problem?"

"I'm sure you know the Nash boys, don't you?"

"Oh yes, Jeremy, Jacob and Jason Nash. What are the entitled little pricks up to now?"

"They had lunch but now they are refusing to pay the bill and they're becoming rowdy and obnoxious, disturbing the other customers," Julie says. "I'm not worried about the money. I just want them out of here before something serious happens."

"Are they getting physical with anyone?"

"Not yet. But you know those boys. I could call Cliff to come over, but I'm afraid of what he'd do to them."

Warren heads back to his SUV. "He'd kick their asses to hell and back again. I'm on my way."

He slips the phone back into his jacket pocket. *As if I don't have enough on my hands already, now I've got to deal with those pricks who think the world owes them something.*

He's suddenly taken aback by a murder of crows walking and hopping on the highway near his vehicle.

"Ten," he whispers.

Isn't it supposed to be ten crows for a time of joyous bliss? So much for that!

He slowly approaches the crows, speaking softly. "You guys have any idea about what's going on around here? If this is your idea of joyous bliss, I'm really not feeling it. I think something may have gone off the tracks here."

The crows stop prancing, becoming very still, like ten tiny black statues in the middle of the road. Their twenty beady eyes stare at Warren. He shivers.

He now knows what it means when someone says their blood runs like ice water through their veins.

41: Twenty minutes after one

Arriving at The Cozy Corner Café, Warren glances at the digital clock in the dash of the Ford Explorer. It's almost twenty minutes after one. He knows Lisa expects him to be at Samantha's by two, but he may not make it on time.

She'll get over it, he thinks. *Or maybe she won't.*

He always tries to put his family first, but sometimes the job gets in the way.

Besides, Warren knows that if he doesn't answer Julie's call for help, she'll turn to Cliff, and if his friend shows up here, there will be hell to pay. Cliff is very protective of his family, and messing with his daughter is one sure-fire way to get his attention.

He makes a beeline to the door of the small café that Carly opened after she moved back to town a few years ago. He's pissed that the Nash boys would choose today to go on one of their stupid trouble-making sprees, as he hasn't got time to mess around with these idiots.

Still, he knows these guys are a handful and can be trouble as he's had many past run-ins with them. With them, it only takes a second for a situation to escalate from minor to major.

And you can never let that happen, Warren reminds himself. He opens the door and enters the busy café. *Never turn your back on them.*

Jeremy, Jacob and Jason, the children of Sebastian Nash, one of the wealthiest and most powerful men in town, believe that their father's influence and money give them free rein to do whatever they desire even when it breaks the law.

But not on my watch, Warren thinks.

He spots the three young men, who range in age from sixteen to twenty-one, hovering at the front counter, laughing and making rude and inappropriate comments.

"Hey, boys." Warren strides up to the trio of cocky troublemakers, quickly scanning them for any sign of a weapon. He'll have to work extra hard to restrain his desire to kick their asses.

They turn and glare at him.

He stands toe to toe with the trio. "You come in here this afternoon looking for trouble?"

"Constable," Jeremy, the oldest brother, replies with a sly grin that Warren would love to slap off his face. "We're just hanging around, having a little fun. Nothing serious."

"It's corporal, and don't you have some other place to be?" Addressing the youngest brother, Jason, he asks, "Shouldn't you be in school?"

"Didn't feel much like going today. I'm sick."

"You don't look sick."

"I've got a cold." He fakes a cough with his face aimed directly at Warren.

"You really are an ass."

Jeremy pushes his brother aside. "Did you just call my brother an ass?"

"I did." Warren knows that these guys are looking for a fight. "You're all being jerks."

Glancing at Julie and Carly behind the counter, he adds, "I suggest you pay the nice ladies whatever you owe them and then haul your asses out of here before I throw you all in a cell for the night. And trust me, boys, you don't want that."

"We're not paying anything for that slop," Jacob, the middle brother, speaks up. "I wouldn't give it to my dog."

"Yet I heard that you ate it all." Warren feels his temper starting to flare up. Nodding to Carly, he asks, "What's the bill?"

"The total, including taxes, is $63.83," Carly answers, her voice trembling.

"You are going to pay the bill, and then you are going to leave here quietly and without a fuss," he tells them. "You got that?"

He holds his ground against the trio. He'd never admit it to anyone, but he suddenly feels intimidated by them as together, they create an imposing threat. But Warren refuses to back down. He must show them that he is the authority in this situation, or he knows if they see any signs of weakness, they will control him.

"What if we don't?" Jeremy asks.

"It's simple. I'll put you in jail and then I'll call your daddy. Do you really want your father involved in this?"

Jeremy says, "He'll be pissed if you bother him. Dad's not a fan of the police."

Warren nods. "I'm sure he isn't, but I'm also sure that he's not a fan of getting calls to take care of trouble his idiot offspring create. So, why don't we avoid all of the unpleasantness? Just pay up and leave, and that will be that. You can be on your way and these nice ladies can go back to work."

"I don't think so." Jeremy moves closer to Warren. "The food wasn't worth six cents, let alone sixty dollars."

Warren is struggling not to lose his temper.

"Come one step closer, Jeremy, and I'll put you in handcuffs in front of all these nice people who came here for a quiet lunch. Now, just back up."

"You and what fucking army?" Jeremy huffs.

He shuffles even closer to Warren. His breath brushes Warren's face, sending shock waves through the officer's body.

He reacts on reflex, grabbing the young man's arms and spinning him around. He pins Jeremy's arms against his back and applies pressure, preventing him from striking back. The more Jeremy struggles, the tighter Warren's grip becomes. "I have given you several warnings so now it's off to a cell for you."

As Jacob and Jason move toward the officer, Warren stares at them. "Back off, you two, or you'll be joining your brother in a cell."

The brothers come to a standstill.

Warren says. "I am taking Jeremy out to my car. Jason. You are going to leave first, and I will follow you. Jacob, you are going to stay here and pay the bill then come out to my car. If you run, I'll track you down and things will be even harder for you."

Turning back to Jeremy, who is struggling, Warren tightens his grip and pushes him toward the door.

He asks the others, "Do you boys understand what I just said, or do you need me to repeat myself?"

"Yes." Jason steps in front of his oldest brother. "I understand."

"Jacob, I want you to pay the bill."

"I'm doing it." The middle brother retrieves his wallet and fumbles through his credit cards.

In the parking lot, Warren opens the back door of the police SUV, keeping an eye on Jason, who he feels has the most potential of the lot.

"Just stay where you are," he says to the teenager, who is leaning on the engine hood. "And don't make any sudden moves. Do you understand?"

Jason nods.

He turns his attention back to Jeremy. "Get in and watch your head."

"You'll be sorry you harassed us, asshole." Jeremy is seething, his complexion blood red. "This is police harassment."

Warren slams the car door and turns to the younger brother. "What are you doing, Jason? Why are you letting your brothers lead you down this road? Nothing good ever comes from this type of attitude. You need to pull yourself together and fly straight before they make you do something stupid that you'll regret."

He turns to Jacob, who has now joined them.

"There. I paid the fucking bill," Jacob says. He throws the receipt at Warren's feet. "Now what?"

Jeremy pounds on the reinforced glass of the SUV's backseat window. Warren's plan is to let the young man stew for a few more minutes, hoping that will give him time to settle down.

"Are you taking us to jail?" Jason asks. The tremble in his young voice conveys his worry over such a possibility.

Warren shakes his head. "Not this time. I am going to let you go, but I never want any of you to ever show your god-damned face in this café ever again." He pauses to emphasis the point. "Do you understand me?"

"Yes." Jason nods.

Warren glares at Jacob. "And what about you?"

"I wouldn't want to go back in there anyway," the middle brother fires back.

Warren grabs the handle of the back door. "Now, let's see if we can get your idiot brother to calm down."

"Good luck," Jason whispers.

Warren opens the steel-reinforced door designed to restrain even the most violent offenders. "If I let you out of here, are you going to behave yourself?"

"I don't have to answer to you," Jeremy fires back.

"I'd be quiet if I were you, because I do have the power to take you to jail or to let you go." He squints at the young man in the back seat. "Which do you prefer?"

"Well," Jeremy slowly answers. "I don't want to go to jail."

Warren knows he has no remorse for the trouble he's caused. He's just worried about what his father would say about all of this, but that's fine because, at this point, Warren just wants to finish this farce.

He motions for him to get out of the car. "Get your sorry ass out here. Why do you have to be such a shit? You've got so many opportunities in front of you, yet you just can't seem to stay out of trouble. Why is that?"

Warren has made a fatal mistake. Despite his years of training and experience, he has turned his back on the younger brothers.

Jason, the youngest, grabs the officer's SIG Sauer P226 and pulls it from its holster before Warren can react.

As the shot rings out, ten crows immediately spring from the perches where they have been observing the activity. Their mournful cackling reverberates off the trees and buildings. It sends shock waves throughout the universe.

Soaring overhead, the ten crows watch as Warren slumps to the ground.

42: Eclipse sickness

Kate takes a deep breath to steel her nerves and enters the kitchen through the back door. Judging by the mix of fragrant aromas that greet her, she knows Samantha has been cooking for a while now.

That means Sam will likely be upset with her for not getting home at the appointed time, but she hopes her wife will understand and forgive her.

"Man," she says, taking on a cheerful persona and hugging her wife, who is standing over the stove. The slender blond woman is shrouded in a cloud of steam that's rising from the bubbling pots on the four burners. "It smells fantastic in here."

"Glad you could make it." Samantha glances at the clock. "I asked you to be here by no later than one-thirty to help me with last-minute prep. It's almost two and people are starting to arrive."

"Sorry, my love, but you know it is a workday for me." Kate gives her wife a quick peck on the cheek. "I'm lucky I got here at all. I was in a meeting with an important client and had to excuse myself. I don't think the client was too impressed that I had to leave."

"Yeah, well, it's a workday for me, too, but you know how important this day is to our son. You could have at least tried to be here on time." Samantha fusses with a sauce that's bubbling on the righthand front burner. "It's not like I ask you to do this all the time."

"Now that I'm here, what can I do to help?"

Samantha frowns. "I've got everything handled in here, so why don't you go into the living room and see how everyone is doing?"

"Everyone else here already?"

"Not yet," Samantha replies. "Alex and Bree are in the living room with Oliver and Lisa. She came alone and Warren is going to pop by when he can. He's pretty busy. Jace and Luna are still upstairs. I think they've had a rough day. They will come down when they're ready."

"What's going on with them?"

"Alex told me they are having relationship troubles so I suggested that he should give them some space. The last thing anyone wants is someone else offering advice, even if they mean well."

"That's easier said than done, sometimes."

Samantha stirs the sauce. "Oh, and before I forget, Charlie called to give his apologies. All hell has broken lose at the hospital. He says he's been rushed off his feet all morning."

"Seems like all hell has broken lose everywhere."

Samantha stops stirring and stares at her wife. "What do you mean?"

"When I left the office, there were a bunch of emergency vehicles in front of The Cozy Corner Café," Kate says. "I couldn't see anything though, so I have no idea what that means."

"Wow, that can't be good."

Kate shakes her head. "That's one of the reasons I'm late. The police have that place locked down, so I had to take the long way around town."

"Shit." Samantha lifts the lid to another pot, releasing a puff of steam. "I hope Julie and Carly are okay. Do you think I should call them?"

"I wouldn't bother them right now. I'm sure Warren will fill us in when he gets here." Kate retrieves a pitcher from the refrigerator and pours herself a glass of cold water. "Has there been any word from Hunter?"

"He's just waiting for school to get out at two-thirty, then he's going to swing by and pick up Ally and the boys. I'm looking forward to seeing Dominic and Dante. They're growing up way too fast."

"It's convenient that they are all at the same elementary school," Kate observes. "Can you believe it that Dante is almost through his first year of school?"

"Right? And Dominic's going to be done grade two in June." Samantha shudders. "I suddenly feel so old."

Kate chuckles. "You and me both." She takes a sip of water "What time were you planning on eating?"

"The eclipse is supposed to start around three-thirty so I was hoping we could start to eat around two-thirty. I told people not to eat lunch before they came, so I would imagine they're all getting pretty hungry at this point. I'd like to get things squared way with the food so we can all enjoy the spectacle."

Kate suggests, "Everyone who is here by two-thirty can start to eat, and anyone who comes late can join us when they arrive. You don't really have to stress out over this."

"Yeah. I do." Samantha wipes the sweat from her forehead. "I wanted this weekend to be extra special for Alex and his friend, but nothing has gone according to plan. He's been in and out all weekend helping at the hospital and then Bree had the accident."

"These things happen, honey." Kate reaches out to give her another hug.

"Just don't." Samantha pulls away. "I need to concentrate on what I'm doing so I don't break this sauce. The best thing you can do for me right now, is just leave me alone so I can make sure everything is ready on time."

"Okay. Okay. I get it," Kate retreats. "No need to be so testy."

"I'm not being testy. I'm just busy."

~

In the living room, Kate sees Alex is chatting with Bree, Lisa, and Oliver.

"Can I get anything for anyone?" she asks. "Since Samantha is preparing enough food to feed an army—not that anyone should be surprised to hear that—I'll be your host, for now."

"We're all good. I'm happy that you could get away from the office." Alex answers. He pats the sofa beside him. "Come and join us. I was just telling Bree and her mom about the crows that Oliver and I discovered at Pine Grove this morning."

"Oh?" Kate takes a seat next to her son. She gives his knee a gentle squeeze in the process. "What are those black-feathered creatures up to now?"

"They were all dead, Mom."

"What? How?"

"Someone shot them," he says. She can see that Alex is trying hard not to show his emotions, but she knows what the crows mean to her son, so she's sure his heart is breaking. "There was so much blood, the poor things. Someone used them for target practice."

Oliver says, "It was a terrible thing for someone to do."

"Any idea who would do something like that?" Kate asks.

"We have an idea," Oliver says. "Alex picked up a few clues."

"He's very astute when it comes to crows." Kate watches her son for any indication as to how he's handling this situation. "So, what do you do now?"

"*We* don't do anything," Alex says. "The crows will take care of this themselves."

"Take care of this how?"

"The crows will hand out whatever form of justice they deem necessary, so if I were the ones responsible, I'd be watching my back," Alex explains.

Lisa interrupts. "When you say *hand out justice*, what exactly are you saying, Alex?"

"I mean it will be harsh." Alex's voice is void of any emotion. "They must pay for what they've done."

Lisa leans back. "You make it sound like the crows will target whoever was responsible. Would they hurt someone?"

Alex meets her gaze. "The crows will do what they must. And whatever they do, they'll be justified."

"They wouldn't kill someone, would they?" Lisa asks.

Alex and Oliver exchange glances.

Silence grips the room until Kate picks up the conversation. "So, what about this eclipse? Anyone know anything about this so-called miracle of the universe that we're all here to experience? It's kind of crazy when you think about all the hoopla it's caused. No matter where you go, it's all everyone is talking about."

Bree says, "I've been doing some research on the subject."

"Of course, you have." Kate smiles at the young woman who has managed to make herself into a valuable asset at the law firm. "What do you know?"

Bree glances at the others. "I'm sure everyone knows that a solar eclipse happens when the moon passes between the sun and earth, blocking most of the sun's light. It's kind of eerie when it happens."

Everyone nods.

Bree continues, "Did you know that the last eclipse of the sun over Nova Scotia happened on July 10, 1972?"

"I actually knew that." Alex smiles at the young woman he hopes to marry someday soon.

"Yes," she chuckles. "You would know that, Mr. Know It All."

He winks at her, a gesture that doesn't go unnoticed by Kate. She can see how much these two love each other and her heart fills with happiness for them.

"But," Bree continues, "did you know that, during an eclipse, the temperature can plummet by as much as ten degrees?"

Kate shakes her head. "I didn't know that." Turning to Lisa, she asks, "Did you know that?"

"I didn't," Lisa whispers. She glances at her cellphone. "It's almost quarter after two. Where is he?"

"Warren?" Kate asks.

"He promised he would be here by two."

"Something has probably come up." Kate decides not to tell her friend about the police activity she spotted down at The Cozy Corner Café.

"Excuse me," Lisa says. "I'm going to go give him a quick call to see where he is. I'll be right back."

"I'm sure everything is all right with Daddy," Bree says as Lisa slips out of the room.

"Just let her go." Alex smiles at his girlfriend. "She's worried."

"What else you got, Bree?" Oliver speaks up. "I'm curious to learn more about the eclipse."

"They're saying this eclipse will begin at 3:27 end sometime around 5:44."

"A lot of bad shit can happen in all that time," Oliver observes.

"What an unusual thing to say," Kate says.

"It's just that I've heard stories of people losing their minds and doing crazy things because of an eclipse."

"That's all just legends and myths," Kate says.

"Are they?"

Alex glances at Oliver and then to his mother. "Here's something you probably don't know. Studies have confirmed some people have reported feeling physically sick ahead of a solar eclipse. Scientists call it *eclipse sickness*."

"Come on, Alex," Kate answers. "Is that even a real thing? Sounds like mass hysteria to me."

"Yes, it's a real thing. It's blamed for causing weird feelings, head-aches, and insomnia, according to what I read. Sometimes it makes people do things they wouldn't normally do."

"Violent things?"

Alex nods. "I read somewhere that NASA had previously denied that eclipses have an impact on human health, but new research may suggest otherwise."

"Huh." Kate takes his hand. "Who knew?"

"Damn it," Lisa says, returning to the living room. "Warren didn't an-swer. I tried twice and it went to voice mail both times. That's really un-usual for him."

"He's probably, just busy," Bree suggests. "Come sit down, Mom. He'll get here when he can."

Lisa's phone rings and she glances at the screen. "It's Julie. Sorry, everyone, but I'm going to take this."

Kate watches as her friend slips back into the dining room. She's sud-denly getting a bad feeling. A sudden knock at the front door grabs her attention.

"There." She jumps to her feet and strides to the main entrance. "Here's Warren now."

Swinging the door open, Kate feels her heart skip a beat when she sees Constables Nolan Shaw and Vanessa Bennett on the doorstep.

"Constables." Her breath catches in her throat. "What's going on?"

"On my God." The heart-wrenching cry comes from Lisa in the dining room. "Warren has been shot."

43: When the sky darkens

The darkness advances, quietly, purposefully.

It moves stealth-like across the land as a cunning and skilled hunter prepares to pounce upon its unsuspecting prey.

It creeps like the evening shadows, reaching out its slender fingers in the waning light as the moon slips ominously in front of its much larger celestial parent, blocking the sun's rays and draping a dark shroud over the small coastal town nestled peacefully on the rugged Atlantic shore. The moon and sun have done this dance for eons.

It's dark like the evening, in the mid-afternoon on an early spring day, and the forces of nature are spinning out of control, conspiring to wreak havoc on those who reside here. Churning and turning. Boiling like a simmering pressure cooker about to blow its lid.

Nothing is as it should be.

As the sky darkens and the streetlights blink on as if it were dusk, the crows rustle about in their murder. The black birds are restless, riled up. There are hundreds of them. Big and small. Young and old. Healthy and sick. Leaders and followers.

And there are warriors. Scores of warriors with killer instincts, set to defend and protect their brethren.

There is discontent and chaos within the flock. The anxious cackling sends ripples of fear and anger throughout the roost, ruffling thousands of black feathers. Their anger is palpable.

Death has landed at their threshold and there will be hell to pay.

In turn, the crows will demand that those who are responsible pay dearly. There can be no escape, for they will show no mercy.

The first ten had been chosen for their mission because of their connection to the Golden One. They were slaughtered, shot down by three delinquents on the hunt for trouble.

They have found it, for the crows will come for them. The black-feathered guardians of this town will have their revenge.

In the world of the crows, justice is swift, and it is harsh. An eye for an eye, a life for a life.

With the sun and the moon moving into alignment, the light gives way to the darkness and the air temperature plummets. The crows gathered in this murder, their senses heightened, know it is time.

With ten new crows now leading the way, the flock takes flight. Justice will be served this day.

~

A total solar eclipse is the most spectacular celestial phenomenon that earth-bound humans can behold. Most will agree, it is truly a miracle of nature.

Even though the sun is much larger than the moon, it is far away enough compared to the other that they both subtend almost exactly the same size in the sky. This is how the sun and moon appear on this day.

Standing in the window of Hunter's former bedroom, Luna watches as the last of the sun disappears behind the moon, an ominous darkness growing in the west. It is the moon's shadow racing toward the town, bringing a peculiar night to the late afternoon.

The colour of the sky changes from grey as brushes of scarlet and golden hues of sunset tint the horizon in all directions. It is a masterpiece. Mother Nature has outdone herself.

Mesmerized by the awesome sight, Luna leans forward and rests her forehead on the cool glass. Bolts of electricity charge through her body, coursing along her nervous system and travelling from her brain to the very tips of her fingers and toes.

She feels energized.

"Alex has left," Jace says as he enters the room.

Luna is nonresponsive. She continues to stare, trancelike, out the window.

"Did you hear me, Luna?" He speaks softly as he approaches his girl-friend. "Alex took Bree and her mother to the hospital so they can see how her father is doing."

Luna says nothing, her gaze held captive by the quickly-approaching darkness.

He wants to pull her to him and hug her tight to comfort her, but he hesitates. He isn't sure if she is still mad at him because of what he told her earlier. He decides it's probably better if he doesn't push her.

"His parents are still here though," he says. "If you're hungry, there's lots of food. I don't know about you, honey, but I could eat."

She remains still and quiet.

"Everyone's pretty upset over what's happened to Bree's dad," Jace continues. "It doesn't sound good for him. Poor Bree was so distraught. I wish there was something I could do for her."

She doesn't acknowledge that she hears him.

"I feel bad for Warren," he continues. "He seems like a really nice guy. Alex told me he was shot in the head."

He steps back, unsure of what Luna might do.

"I know you're angry with me, but can't you at least talk to me?"

He stares at the back of her head. She might as well be on that ominous moon above them.

"Okay," he says finally. "I want you to know that I still love you very deeply and I want to plan a future with you."

He pauses to gather his thoughts, waiting for her response.

"It's just that I need to have a little space right now, so that I can re-group. It has been a long, tough slog for me to get through these last few years and I'm exhausted. But that doesn't mean I don't love you or that I don't want you in my life."

He rubs his eyes.

"This is hard for me, Luna, because I never want to hurt you."

He waits for her to respond, but she doesn't.

He moves to the door. "I hope that you can forgive me."

He stops in the doorway.

"I am going to leave you alone," he says. "I'll be downstairs. Come down and find me when you're ready to discuss things, or just to eat. I'll wait for you."

~

Samantha and Kate work quietly in the kitchen. For the second time in three days, they are cleaning up the remnants of a meal that hasn't happened.

"Jesus." Samantha breaks the silence. She snuffs back her tears as she scrapes the Caesar salad into a plastic container and snaps the cover closed. That will keep it fresh until someone feels like eating it. "I can't believe that someone would shoot Warren."

"Me neither," her wife answers. "You never think it will happen to someone you know."

"Who the hell would do such a thing?"

Kate pours the tomato sauce from the pot into a glass bowl where it will cool before it goes into the refrigerator. "Warren knows he takes his life into his own hands every time he puts on that uniform, but you never really expect to hear about something like this happening in our town."

"I can't stop thinking about Bree and Lisa." Samantha wipes way the tears that are flowing down her cheeks. "And poor Lauren. What are they ever going to do if Warren doesn't make it?"

Kate places the pot in the sink and fills it with warm water. "I'm sure it's going to be touch and go for a while, but Warren is strong and has a lot to live for. We have to remain positive that he's going to pull through this."

"It's not easy for me to just pray for a miracle but I'm glad Oliver has gone with them. He'll look out for them."

Leaning against the counter, Kate says, "And Charlie's there, too. Alex said he'd call us once he knows more about Warren's condition, but he's sure they'll have to operate."

"It sounds very dangerous. I mean, we are talking about them cutting into the man's brain," Samantha says. "Wonder how long it will be before we know something concrete?"

"It probably all depends upon where the bullet has ended up."

"Maybe when Jace comes down, we can ask him what that kind of sur-gery would entail."

"Maybe," Kate says.

Samantha wipes away her tears again. "Talking about one of our friends being shot seems so surreal. But there have been a lot of strange things happening around here."

Kate nods. "We were just talking about that in the living room before the police showed up. If you believe in the legends, it's very possible. But I don't buy any of that."

Samantha shivers. "Well, I do, because there are lots of stories about this sort of thing happening in the past."

Kate bites her lip. She knows better than to engage in a conversation with Samantha on such a topic.

Glancing out the window, Samantha adds, "It looks like the eclipse is starting. Do you want to go outside and watch it? Alex found us some of those special glasses that can we use."

Kate thinks for a second and then shakes her head. "Not really. Do you?"

"Alex was the one who seemed to be the most excited by all of this, but I'm not really in the mood anymore. Let's just get everything cleaned up and then maybe drop over to the hospital and be with everyone, unless you must go back to the office."

"Not today," Kate says.

There is a sudden loud thud. Samantha drops the bowl of salad and dashes toward the living room. Kate follows closely behind.

In the living room, they find Jace sprawled on the floor at the bottom of the stairs. He isn't moving.

Glancing up, the two women see Luna standing at the top of the staircase, looking down at the crumpled heap of her boyfriend. Her eyes are glazed and unblinking.

"He slipped," she murmurs.

To Samantha and Kate, her voice seems mechanical, void of any emotion.

~

Outside, the murder of crows, led by the ten, soar over the house.

As the sun disappears behind the moon, the black birds head into the darkness. They are on a mission.

The time for justice has arrived.

44: The fury of the crows

Jeremy, Jacob and Jason Nash were precocious and mischievous kids practically from birth. While other children their ages were out playing with their friends, the Nash boys were looking for ways to aggravate their parents or to antagonize their neighbours.

As they got older, their schemes grew increasingly wilder and more extreme until today they are the bane of their father's existence. And, as the police would agree, a curse on the community at large.

But most people in town know you dare not retaliate against the Nash brothers lest you rile up their daddy. To cross Sebastian Nash is to bring great risk upon yourself for, despite their misdeeds, he will ruthlessly defend his sons at all costs. If the boys feel entitled, their father is pure evil, encouraging his sons' behaviour by defending them regardless of their infractions.

When the brothers set out this morning from their family's sprawling estate on the south-eastern edge of town—the sixteen-room mansion with the massive, in-ground, Olympic-size pool covered by a glass dome that is a testament to Sebastian's place at the top of Liverpool's power hierarchy and, some believe, the criminal underground—they may or may not have gone looking for trouble.

But trouble is exactly what the siblings find this afternoon. Subjects of a province-wide manhunt, the Nash brothers have chosen to hide in the one place they think no one would think to look for them—Pine Grove Park. They believe hiding in their own backyard is their smartest move.

It's where today's bloody rampage began, when they brought their rifles into the naturally-secluded sanctuary where wildlife and birds roam freely. Here the trio thought they could do some target practice without fear of being interrupted or caught by authorities. Their father had taken the boys to the shooting range when they were young so, in a way, they reason, he sanctioned their actions.

As the ten crows fell victim to the young men's idiocy, the Nash boys had no idea of the fury they were about to unleash.

The crows want retribution against those who slaughtered their brethren. According to the natural order of the universe, there will be no forgiveness. It is an eye for an eye, tit for tat—a life for a life.

Now, as the mid-afternoon sun disappears behind the moon and the ominous shadows move in like a creeping monster about to pounce, the Nash brothers cower within the bowels of the park. They hide under the thick canopy of pine trees and plan their best escape route.

But there can be no escaping their fates.

When Jason, the youngest brother, pulled the gun from Warren Hamilton's holster, he just thought the move would impress his older brothers. It was Jacob, the middle brother, who grabbed the gun from his hands, causing it to discharge.

They don't know if the officer is dead or alive. They didn't stop to find out. The idea of helping him never crossed their minds.

"I was just going to scare him," Jason cries. "That's all. It's Jacob's fault that the gun fired."

"Fuck off," Jacob screams. "If you hadn't taken the gun in the first place, none of this would have happened."

"Both of you, shut the fuck up," Jeremy commands. "It doesn't matter who pulled the god-damned trigger. If that cop is dead, they're going to blame all of us."

"But it just went off. It was an accident."

"Those police issued guns don't just *go off*," Jeremy snaps. "They are built not to misfire so one of you must have pulled the trigger. But we're all in deep shit because of what you idiots did."

"Yeah, well you aren't mister innocent in all of this," Jacob points out. "You're the one who wanted to eat at that diner. You're the one who refused to pay when the bill came. That's why they called the police, so this is all your fault."

Jeremy grabs his younger brother by the throat and squeezes. "Shut up, or I'll knock your god-damned teeth down your throat."

"Jacob is right," Jason says. "If we hadn't gone into that café, none of this would have happened."

Jeremy pushes Jacob away. "Both of you just shut. I need time to think how we're going to get out of this."

Jason throws his hands up, "Just be quiet for a minute. Listen. What is that noise?"

The older Nash siblings stop squabbling.

"Do you hear that?" Jason whispers. He glances around the heavily-wooded area.

Jacob nods slowly. "What the hell is that?"

He turns to their oldest brother. "Do you know what that is, Jeremy?"

The oldest brother shakes his head and looks up at the sky. "Whatever it is, I don't like it."

Suddenly hundreds of angry crows descend on them, painting the trees, bushes and rocks an insidious black. The birds form a tight circle around the boys.

"Je-s-us fucking Christ," Jeremy whispers. "Where did they come from?"

"Does it matter?" Jacob asks. "The point is, what the hell are they doing?"

"What do they want?" Jason asks, his voice trembling.

Jeremy turns to his younger brothers. "We have to get out of here."

"How?" Jason scans the surroundings. "There are crows everywhere."

Jacob moves closer to this oldest brother. "Have they come after us because of what we did?"

"I don't know. But I don't think we should stay and find out. We should run."

As they start to sprint for safety—each heading in a different direction—the crows spring into action, swooping and gliding over their heads. Their calls are loud and piercing, as if they are sounding a battle cry.

The brothers can run but they cannot hide. It matters not to the crows who killed their ten comrades. In the eyes of the crows, the Nash brothers are equally culpable.

~

Jacob sprints down the path that leads to the parking lot, hoping the crows will not follow him, but the black birds remain in hot pursuit. They soar high above the trees and swoop down below the underbrush, keeping their target in sight. Their eerie cackles reverberate throughout the dense forest of stately pines.

"Jesus. Jesus. Jesus." He cries out. "Just leave me the fuck alone."

With beak snapping and talons poised to strike, the first crow finds its mark, landing a blow to the back of the Jason's head.

The pain is immediate. The stinging is intense. He stumbles but does not fall.

"Holy fuck," he yelps.

Willing his feet to move faster, Jacob braces for another attack, as one, then two, and three and four crows swoop in and connect, grabbing chunks of skin and hair from his scalp.

His foot turns on a rock. He stumbles and tries to maintain his balance, but the pain coursing through his body has thrown his equilibrium into a tailspin.

"Oh my God," he screams. He falls hard, landing face-first. His teeth cut into his bottom lip and blood pours from the wounds on this head. He's confused, dazed, unsure of what he should do next.

He pulls himself up to his knees, blinking away blood and tears. He screams as two large crows swoop in and strike at his face.

One opens a gash on his left cheek that immediately begins pouring blood. The other makes a direct hit to his right eye, plucking it out as if removing candy from a gumball machine.

The searing pain sends convulsions throughout Jacob's body. Pulling himself to his feet, he does not know what to do. He can barely stand straight, and he can hardly see.

"Jeremy. Jason!" His call is feeble. "Someone help me!"

As the crows land blow after blow, Jacob accepts the inevitable—this is where he dies.

~

Although Jeremy can hear Jacob's cries, he cannot help his brother. He's trying to save his own skin.

"Just leave me the fuck alone," he yells at the of crows.

The birds are relentless. They chase the oldest Nash brother down a path toward a tiny lake that's nestled serenely near the middle of the park. Their guttural cries shatter the usual peace and quiet of this place.

There is no place for Jeremy to hide from the crows. It's clear to him that the black birds want him.

He stops suddenly as he reaches the water's edge, plants his feet and turns to face the enemy. To his left, he sees a mother duck and her ducklings quickly swimming away. He wonders if they can sense his panic.

Jeremy quickly bends and picks up a tree branch. Brandishing the makeshift weapon, he braces for the first strike.

"You motherfuckers want me, come and get me."

He knows there is no escape route for him except through the water, and that will be his last resort.

Seeing several crows move into attack posture, he swings the branch wildly to try to fend them off.

The crows strike quickly. The blows to his chest and head are powerful, and the pain is instant.

"Fuck," he yells, backing up closer to the water.

The full flock has gone into attack formation. He knows this will be it.

As the crows glide toward their mark, Jeremy swings the branch, knowing it is a futile effort.

He screams as the crows deliver blow after blow to any exposed area they can find on his body. The pain is searing. The attack is brutal, causing Jeremy's body to shut down.

He falls backwards into the water, striking his head on a rock. It's the final wound.

As the lake swallows him, Jeremy never regains consciousness.

~

Terrified and feeling isolated, Jason has no idea whether Jeremy and Jacob have made it to safety. He has no idea where he should go. He knows his only recourse is to hide from the rampaging crows, if he can.

He remembers the tiny cave in one of the rock outcrops in the dense woods that surround the lake, where he and his brothers played when they were youngsters. Jason decides that's the place that will offer him refuge.

But he must get there.

With one eye to the sky, he makes a beeline for the cave, hoping that he can still squeeze into its small opening.

Willing himself to run faster than he has ever run before, Jason feels his heart flutter when the rocks suddenly come into view. He believes safety is now within reach.

His elation is short-lived, however, as a group of ten crows suddenly swoops down and land on the rocks between him and the cave.

His breath catches in his throat. "Shit."

It won't be long until they attack. With nowhere to hide and no escape route, Jason knows he's trapped.

Hoping for forgiveness, he drops to his knees. It's his only chance.

"Please," he pleads. "My brothers and me were stupid, hurting the other crows. I'm sorry for what we did."

The ten crows stare at him, unblinking. He can feel their twenty beady eyes moving over his body as if they are examining him or, worse, looking for vulnerable spots.

Tears stream down his cheeks.

"Forgive me," Jason pleads, his voice trembling. "If you let me go, I promise I will never hurt another crow for as long as I live. From now on, I will protect crows at all costs. I will lay down my life for you."

The crows remain still as if considering his plea for mercy.

"Please." He sobs. "I know what we did was wrong. If I could take it back, I would. What can I do to make it right?"

The crows suddenly spring from the rocks, swoop above the trees and then come directly at him. Jason braces for them to strike.

One by one, the ten crows pass over him, narrowly missing his head. They pass so close they ruffle his hair.

Then the black birds spread their massive wings, catching the wind currents, and climb into the air.

"Thank you," he whispers, watching them disappear into the clouds.

He understands the crows. They have chosen to spare his life.

He wipes tears from his eyes. He will live another day to serve his new masters.

~

As the temperature plummets and the sky grows darker, the crows soar off to an unknown destination.

Their revenge has been served and it has been brutal.

That they spared one life does not mean weakness. It means the young man is forever in their debt, a debt that he will have to pay and repay.

45: The eclipse

Night has fallen, but it is only four o'clock in the afternoon.

The eclipse is at its zenith and the darkness has veiled the sun's light, driving living creatures into a frenzy.

The moon has come between the earth and the sun, leaving thousands of people in awe and triggering the crows' mission. They are compelled to carry out the ancient rituals that their ancestors performed hundreds of years earlier, the same rituals that were carried forward through the generations. It is their sacred duty.

The spectacle will end at quarter to six when the sun fully emerges from behind the moon, breaking the dark spell that has gripped this place. That is when the crows will rest, having come together to erase the collective memories of every resident in this town of the horrific events.

The Spirit Crow has joined the murder. Hundreds of crows will unite with the albino crow at the centre. They will meld their minds and combine their energy to carry out their mission.

Only the chosen one will remember what has happened during the past three days. Protected by the Spirit Crow, Alex Goodwin will emerge from the eclipse with his memories intact, fully aware that the crows have once again done what they always do and that is to protect this town and those who reside here. Everyone else will remember the eclipse, but nothing more.

As the crows commune in their roost, Alex is at the hospital with his family and friends, while they await word of Warren Hamilton's condition. The bullet fired from Warren's pistol entered the right side of his head and became lodged in his brain, leaving him in critical condition.

"He's lucky to be alive," Charlie says to Alex and Oliver, who are meeting with him near the room where Warren is in an induced coma. "It was very close. The bullet should have killed him."

"Jesus." Alex suddenly grips Oliver's arm to keep from collapsing.

Oliver takes him by the elbow. "Are you okay?"

"I think so," Alex answers. "I suddenly felt a little dizzy, but it's passed now."

"Maybe you should sit down." Oliver guides him to a chair near the nurses' station.

"You look really flushed, Alex," Charlie says. "Do you feel ill?"

Alex looks at the middle-aged men who are now hovering over him like two worried nursemaids. "I don't know what happened. I just suddenly felt weird. Like a wave of energy washed over me. My heart skipped a beat and for a second, everything went black. It was one of the strangest things I've ever experienced."

"What do you think that means?" Oliver asks.

Alex gathers his thoughts. "It may have something to do with the crows."

"How so?"

"I believe the crows are congregating in numbers we haven't seen in many years." Alex stares blankly at his friend. "They are at the epicentre of the energy surge I feel. They are fulfilling their sacred duty."

Charlie studies his nephew. "What do the crows have to do with any of this? And what do you mean by their *sacred duty*?"

"They have everything to do with this, apparently," Oliver answers.

The two men stand back to give Alex some breathing room.

Charlie says in a low voice, "I know Alex and those crows have some sort of special bond that I don't understand, but right now, he's got me a little worried."

Oliver smiles. "I've been through this sort of thing with Alex many times, and I assure you that he's not in any danger. The crows will never harm him because he's the chosen one."

"There you go again, talking in riddles," Charlie says. "Is there anything I can do to help him?"

Oliver shakes his head. "He's got this."

"Okay then. This is out of my league, apparently, so I'm going to trust you to take care of my nephew," Charlie says. "I have got to go check on my patient."

"You go right ahead," Oliver replies. "I'll stay here with Alex."

"Oliver," Alex whispers once Charlie has gone into Warren's room.

Oliver kneels in front of his friend. "Have you figured out what's going on?"

Alex nods. "I fear the crows have done something drastic."

"What do you mean?"

"Remember those dead crows in the park?"

Oliver nods. "The ten."

"Well, the crows figured who was responsible for that massacre and they've dealt with it."

"They *dealt* with it how?"

"As only they can."

"Does that mean there's been more death?"

"Afraid so," Alex says.

~

In the exam room where Warren is resting, hocked up to of machines that are monitoring his vital organs, Charlie wishes he had some positive news to share with the friends and family who are gathered there, but at this point there is no update on the man's status.

"So," he says to Lisa and her daughters, who are at Warren's bedside, "I have heard from Dr. Vivian Ashcroft. She is the best neurologist east of Montreal and, based upon the scans that I sent her, she believes it's best that we do not move Warren until he is more stable."

Bree speaks up, tears streaming down her face. "Are going to operate on him here to remove the bullet?"

"I can't do that kind of surgery," Charlie says. "The procedure requires a neurologist who knows her way around the brain. Normally we would airflight him to Halifax for the operation, but Dr. Ashcroft is afraid that transporting him, even by air, might be too dangerous as the vibrations may cause the bullet to move. We were lucky that the paramedics didn't do more damage when they brought him here."

Lisa squeezes Warren's hand tighter. Charlie thinks it's as if she won't let go for fear of losing her husband. "You're just going to do nothing?"

Oliver says, "Dr. Ashcroft is on her way, and should be here within an hour. She will decide our next course of action, but either way, that bullet must come out because it's lodged too close to the vagus nerve."

"What is the vagus nerve?" Bree asks while hugging Lauren close to her.

Charlie turns to address the young women directly. "The vagus nerve, also known as the vagal nerve, is the most essential nerve in our brains." He speaks softly, but matter-of-factly. "It is the main component of our nervous system, which oversees things like control of our mood, immune response, digestion, and heart rate. These functions are involuntary, meaning you can't consciously control them, and you can't survive if the vagus nerve is damaged."

"So it controls everything?" Bree cries.

"Yes." Charlie nods. "That's why we need a specialist to handle this."

He turns to address Julie and Cliff Graham—Lisa and Warren's best friends—who Charlie has also allowed in the room at the family's request. "Can you stay with the girls? I have other patients to check on, and I don't want to leave them alone in here."

"Of course," Julie tells him.

"Lisa understands this because of her background in emergency medicine, but you all need to know that it's vitally important that Warren remain very still. We don't want that bullet to move," Charlie says. "That's why we have him sedated."

"We'll watch him," Julie says.

"The monitors will notify us if there are any changes, but please come and get me if you notice anything that you think I should know," Charlie says as he turns to the door.

"Hey, Doc," Cliff says. He follows Charlie out to the corridor. "Got a second?"

"Of course, Cliff. What can I do for you?"

"Is he going to make it? Warren's my best friend."

"We're all doing the best we can here, but I'm going to be up front with you, Cliff. This is a very serious injury. Warren is lucky that the bullet didn't kill him instantly."

"Is there anything we can do?"

"I know you're not a religious man, but this might be a good time to pray."

~

"What do you think the crows did to the Nash boys?" Oliver asks Alex.

"I can't even begin to imagine." Alex regains his footing and rises from the chair. "I assume their revenge was brutal and severe. Those idiots deserved whatever they received."

Oliver nods. His eyes narrowing, as he considers Alex's words.

Alex is about to say more when his parents and Luna burst into the emergency department waiting room. He rushes to meet them and Samantha hugs him tightly. "What's going on?" he asks. I told you I would call when there was anything new to report on Warren."

"It's Jace," Luna answers. She shows no emotion, as if she is detached from reality.

"Jace? What's wrong with him?"

"Alex, honey," Kate says, "Jace is coming. The ambulance is just pulling up now. I'm really not sure how we got here first."

"What the hell happened?"

"He fell." Samantha releases her embrace and steps back.

"Down the stairs," Kate explains. "We don't know what happened, but apparently Luna saw it."

The young woman appears to be dazed. She stares at him but does not respond.

"Luna? What happened to Jace?"

Her face showing no emotion she says, "He fell, Alex."

"How?"

She shakes her head. Her face remains blank.

Alex glares at her. "Come on, Luna. Tell me what happened to Jace."

"I don't know."

Alex studies the young woman he's known for years. "Did you push him?"

"I don't remember."

46: A convergence of realities

Tuesday, April 9

Alex Goodwin carries a heavy burden this morning but, as the chosen one, he knows that is his destiny.

While everyone else in town struggles to deal with the tragedies that have rocked this small community, Alex wonders how he can carry the secret that the crows have entrusted him with—that these deaths were not by natural causes, nor were they accidental, but were, the result of acts of violence.

He understands the crows have carried out their sacred duty, as they have done for centuries. By using a power he does not profess to comprehend, the black birds have erased the collective memories of the local residents—all but his.

Because of his unity with the crows, Alex accepts that he is entitled to know the truth, and that truth can exact a serious toll. Carrying this secret will weigh him down, as most secrets have a way of doing.

The fact that seventeen people died violently over the past four days when humans and animals had lost self-control is a dark secret to keep bottled up within himself. It is clear to him that the crows believe knowing the reality of what transpired during the eclipse would cause irreparable damage to the tapestry of this town as most would seek revenge for the actions against their loved ones.

In their view, Alex believes, there would be hell to pay, total chaos.

He scans the surroundings for any signs of crows—his guardians. He needed this early morning run to clear his head, and he is not alarmed when he spots his feathered companions.

The presence of ten crows perched in two nearby birch trees—six in one tree, four in the other—provides a level of comfort to Alex that only a few other humans could appreciate, especially at a time when he is contemplating his very existence.

"Thank you for always being with me," he says as he approaches the murder of crows.

The ebony birds remain silent. But they observe, their pellet-like eyes fixed on the human they've followed since his birth. They—and the entire murder of crows that roost in this town—remain forever watchful of the chosen one.

Alex knows that he must keep the truth to himself, for he is in union with the crows. For the chosen one to carry out his anointed duty to protect and serve the crows he must be in full concert with them, for his work is far from done. He knows that something more sinister waits for him in the future, and that the crows hold the secret for his survival.

He wants to share the truth with Oliver and Bree, his two most trusted confidants, but giving them this heavy burden would be too much for them to carry. They would not be able to deal with the knowledge that those who committed violence will not be punished for their deeds—at least, not according to human law.

Crow law, however, may be a totally different story, he thinks.

He will accept his responsibility. But he must find some way to put the memory of these heinous deeds in a place where they do not become an albatross around his neck. That's why he has come to Pine Grove Park—his sanctuary—on this foggy grey morning following the eclipse, hoping to find answers. Even though this place feels "heavy" today following the deaths of two of the Nash brothers here yesterday, he still hopes to find solace.

The police have cordoned off a section of the park while they conduct their investigation into the deaths, but Alex is determined to reach a different area.

He's not sure if his Great Uncle Silas Moores or the Spirit Crow will present themselves there today, but he hopes they will answer his calls. He must talk to them.

"Okay, Uncle Silas," he says, when he reaches the small clearing where he first met the mysterious old man and the mystical albino crow. "I don't know if you can hear me, but I really must see you. I have so many questions. I require your guidance."

He stands firm, eyes narrowed into slits, scouring his surroundings. He quiets his breathing and steadies his nerves. He feels the energy around him intensify, becoming electric. The tiny hairs on his arms and back of his neck stand at attention.

The moisture-thick breeze becomes still. The leaves and wildlife fall silent. The birds in nearby trees stop singing. The chipmunks stop chattering.

The world is at a standstill.

"Uncle Silas?" He whispers. "Are you here, Uncle?"

"I am." The gravelly voice sounds strange, as if disconnected from the world.

Alex turns. The old man looks remarkably well for someone who professes to be one hundred and four years old.

"I am so relieved to see you."

"And I, too, am relieved to see you." With the energy of someone much younger, the old man strides to a boulder at the side of the clearing. "Come," he says. "Sit beside me. Tell me what's troubling you."

"I believe you already know what's bothering me." Alex sits.

"Do I?"

Alex nods. "I need to know how the crows can do what they have done. How did they make every person in this town forget the truth about all these tragic events? There were so many of them."

"The crows, Alex, do whatever they must do to protect the people in their charge. This ancient power they possess goes back many centuries. It has been passed down through the generations. They believe anger would become the order the day as humans could not deal with knowing the truth."

"I'm still not sure I understand." Alex shakes his head. "Why do people react this way during the eclipse?"

"There's an age-old legend that may provide a clue. It says that during an eclipse some people may become insane. There was a time when, during an eclipse, people—especially women, children, and the elderly—were sequestered in their shelters for their protection."

"Could it be more than just an old wives' tale?"

The old man stares into Alex's eyes as if he is trying to reach his soul. "During an eclipse, some people resort to their basic instinct, which is to survive. They lose their grip on reality."

"Whatever reality is."

"Yes, whatever reality is."

"So, for them, it becomes kill or be killed."

"Precisely." The old man nods and takes Alex's hand. His touch is gentle even though his skin feels rough, like sandpaper. "But why such a thing happens in this place and not others remains unknown, a dark mystery, shrouded in the passage of time. I believe it has something to do with the supernatural forces—which run strong in this place—colliding with natural forces and releasing a powerful burst of energy. It's a convergence of realities that only happens at the time of the eclipse."

"And why have I never encountered the Spirit Crow before now?"

"Because you didn't need it. The Spirit Crow only presents itself at the time of the eclipse when the threat to the chosen one is the greatest. Normally, the crows can rebuff any threat to the chosen one, as you've seen. Sometimes they require the help of a designated protector—in your case, Oliver Lewis. Together, the crows and Oliver are sworn to protect you, the chosen one. You've experienced this power."

"I have. Many times," Alex says. "There have been some close calls, but thankfully, I've managed to survive."

"With some help."

Alex nods. "So why couldn't the crows and Oliver protect me during the eclipse?"

"Because the dark power is too strong. Not even the protector is immune to the effects of the eclipse, so the Spirit Crow stands watch in case your protector loses his way."

"But, as it turns out, Oliver was fine."

"He was. You were very lucky this time. As you know, I was the chosen one before you, and there was a time when my protector snapped under the immense pressure, and I lost her. I never found a replacement, so I am glad that your protector is still there to watch over you."

Alex considers the old man's explanation. "Will I ever see the Spirit Crow again?"

"You might. It chooses when and where to be seen, and by whom."

"Sounds like I should count my blessings, then."

"You should." Silas studies his great nephew. "I know this is a great deal to take in. How are *you* doing Alex? You are strong, and you have had to face many challenges, but I sense that you are struggling with something beyond keeping the secrets of the crows."

"I'm worried, Uncle Silas," Alex answers, the wobble in his voice betraying his emotions. "Two people who mean a great deal to me are fighting to survive injuries they sustained during the eclipse."

"Tell me about them," the old man says.

"My girlfriend's father was shot yesterday and he's basically just hanging onto life by a thin thread. He needs very serious and delicate surgery to remove the bullet that is lodged in his brain."

Alex looks his great uncle in the eyes. For the first time he realizes just how dark they are—like the black of night.

"Warren is a good man, and he didn't deserve this," he says. "And of course Bree and her family are devastated. They will be lost without him."

"You must have faith, Alex." Silas squeezes his hand with more strength than Alex would have thought possible for someone of his age. "I can feel how much Warren means to you. You must believe that he will fight through this. The forces that embrace us work in mysterious ways. Just believe."

"As if that wasn't bad enough," Alex continues, "there's the issue with my best friend, Jace. He either fell or was pushed down a flight of stairs and we're afraid there is a serious spinal cord injury. It's not clear if he will ever walk again. We have to wait until the swelling goes down, before we know for sure what he's facing."

Alex brushes the tears from his eyes.

"Again, Alex, you must have some faith. Remember, the crows feel your pain and they are always with you."

The old man releases Alex's hand and rises from the rock. "Now, before I depart, I must remind you that while I know you are tempted to discuss this reality with those whom you trust, you must resist the urge. You must keep these secrets close to your heart as others will not understand this power you possess. The crows' greatest strength is the secrets they keep."

"I will try, but it's difficult as some people, especially my mother, are very perceptive. She may pick up on some of my vibes and she can be like a dog with a bone if she thinks something is bothering me."

"You must resist. To keep them safe, you cannot reveal anything of what I have told you." Silas turns to leave. "Lean on your protector. Oliver Lewis has proven himself to be a worthy ally. If you feel compelled to tell someone, share your secrets with him."

"And what about you? Where are you going?"

Looking over his shoulder as he turns a bend in the trail, Silas smiles. "Me? I am not here, Alex."

"What do you mean?"

Alex jumps from the rock and sprints after his great uncle. Rounding the bend, he discovers the old man has vanished.

"Jesus." Alex whispers, feeling as though he's losing his grip on reality. "Was he even here?"

Scanning the trees that line the trail, he's taken aback when he sees the white Spirit Crow perched on a nearby branch.

Approaching the white bird with the mystifying pink eyes, he considers his great uncle's words—"I'm not here."

His knees become weak. "Is that even possible?"

Epilogue

Monday, June 3

Alex studies his Uncle Charlie from across the cluttered desk. The tall, slender man with the greying hair and worry lines etched into his forehead appears to be aging prematurely. Alex can't help but wonder how he'll make it through two months without his uncle by his side, let alone how he'll make it on his own once Charlie retires in a year's time.

The man has been a major influence in his life since he was a child and his mentor through his arduous journey to become a doctor. Now he's about to take over his uncle's practice.

"Are you ready for all of this to be yours?" Charlie asks.

He glances up at his nephew over the tall piles of file folders on his desk. While most of the new files are done electronically, these older files contain information from earlier patients, of whom some have died, and others have been with Charlie for many years. Once he sifts through them, he and Alex will keep anything that's still pertinent and shred the rest.

"The question is," Alex says, "are you sure I'm ready? Because I'm not so sure."

"Oh my God, Alex, if there's one thing that I'm sure of, it's that you are more than ready to step into my shoes."

Alex chuckles nervously. "Those are awfully big shoes."

Charlie winks at his nephew. "Don't be so hard on yourself. If I wasn't sure that you can do this, I wouldn't place the care of my patients into your hands. You are more than ready to step up."

"Okay, Uncle Charlie. You've convinced me. I'm going to be one hell of a bad-assed doctor."

Charlie chuckles. "Yes, you are."

"Any word on when they're discharging Warren?" Alex asks, deciding they've both had enough ego stroking for one day. "Bree and her mom are anxious to have him home."

"As of my conversation with Dr. Ashcroft last evening, the plan is for them to bring Warren back here as early as today, or tomorrow at the latest."

"And he'll be in hospital here for another week?"

"That sounds about right, so we can watch him for a few more days. Dr. Ashcroft says he's made a remarkable recovery. Within a month or two he should be back to his old self. It's a miracle, really, that he's even still alive."

Alex grimaces, recalling the day Warren was shot. "It was touch and go for a while there."

"Has there been any further news from the investigation into who shot him?"

Alex shakes his head. He hates lying to the people he loves and respects, but that's the way it must be, according to the law of the crows. "All the police know is that it appears an unknown assailant jumped Warren from behind, pulled his weapon from its holster and shot him. They have no idea who that person was or why it happened."

"It was pure luck that Dr. Ashcroft was available." Charlie pauses. "If I required brain surgery, I'd want her to do it."

"Thank God she was there when we needed her. I'm glad Warren is on the road to recovery," Alex says. "I only wish Jace was doing as well."

"Still having a tough time coming to grips with the idea that he may never walk again?"

Alex nods. "I tried calling him last night at the rehab centre, but he wouldn't talk to me. If it's okay with you, I'd like to take Wednesday off, to drive into Halifax and visit with him. I'll make him see me."

Charlie smiles. "I'm sure Jace could use his friend right now."

"Yes, especially now that it seems like he and Luna have split up. I'm sure he's hurting a lot."

"Are they breaking up for good?"

"I don't know. Luna told Bree that Jace won't even see her, so she doesn't know where they stand."

"Do you think he blames her for the fall?" Charlie's right eyebrow rises.

"I'm not sure. He says he doesn't remember much about what really happened."

Alex has never been forthcoming with anyone about it, but he believes that Luna did push Jace down the stairs. He believes she was under the influence of the eclipse. He understands she can't remember anything from that time because, like everyone else in town, her memories were erased when the crows carried out their sacred duty.

The all-powerful crows, he thinks, wishing this was one time he could break the rules and tell everyone what really happened. *Hail to the black-feathered gods.*

"It seems to me she suffered a major trauma, so she may never regain her memories about that day," Charlie suggests. "The truth is, Jace may never know if his girlfriend pushed him down the stairs or if he slipped. That's a lot to live with, especially if he can't walk again."

"Speaking of mysteries did you realize that today is the third of June?"

"Ah, yes. That's what the calendar says, Alex." Charlie nods toward the small calendar on the corner of his desk. "What's so important about June third?"

"A rare event known as the Parade of Planets occurred this morning."

"I've never heard of that before."

"All I know is what I heard on the news. The Parade of Planets is when six planets in the solar system—Mercury, Mars, Jupiter, Saturn, Uranus, and Neptune—are aligned in a straight line and are visible just before sunrise for the next two or three days. Apparently, it's quite rare and a spectacular sight."

"Huh." Charlie shrugs. "I didn't know that. It's kind of mysterious, like the eclipse in April. You know, when strange things happened in the sky and all those people died?"

Alex nods. "That was quite the coincidence, don't you think?"

"What are you suggesting, Alex?" Charlie shudders. "That we should expect more weirdness?"

Alex chuckles, nervously. "Come on Uncle Charlie. You know better than to ask that question. Did you forget where you live? We should always expect more weirdness around this town."

Charlie places his elbows on a pile of file folders, clasps his hands together and rests his whisker-covered chin on top of his hands. He stares at his nephew but says nothing.

Alex says, "You know anything can happen in this town."

"I do know that, but it's like that old saying about ten crows. How does that go?"

"It's ten crows for a time of joyous bliss."

"But it's also true what they say—ignorance is bliss."

Alex remembers the words of his Great Uncle Silas Moores, and knows he cannot reveal any of the crows' secrets.

The two men return to their work, reviewing the charts and files. His uncle will reduce his office hours until he leaves for his two-month trip to Europe with Oliver Lewis. After that, Charlie will work toward his retirement in a year's time.

Alex is about to ask about a patient's file that he's studying when his cell phone rings. He sees that it's a "private caller." He then glances at Charlie, who nods.

"Hello. Dr. Alex Goodwin here." The title still sounds weird to him, especially when he says it out loud.

"Hi Dr. Goodwin, it's Constable Nolan Shaw. Do you have few minutes to talk?"

Constable Shaw, the most senior officer at the detachment, is in charge while Corporal Warren Hamilton recovers from his injuries.

"How can I help the police today?"

"I need to pick the brain of a bird expert."

"I'm not sure I can help you with that. I am a lot of things, but a bird expert is not one of them."

"That's not what I've been told. I've got a bunch of dead birds on my hands, and it has been suggested that you might know a thing or two about this stuff."

Alex considers the constable's comments. "Who suggested I could help?"

"Retired corporal Cliff Graham, who just happens to be right here. Says he was in the area this morning and became curious about all the police activity down on the waterfront. He thought of you when I asked him if he knew anything about dead birds."

A sudden chill causes Alex to shiver. "Tell me, Constable Shaw, are there any crows involved?"

"Yes, a few, but there are also dozens of other dead birds around town, every kind you can imagine."

"I don't like the sound of this," Alex mutters as his thoughts drift to dark places he'd rather not go to.

"Can you help us, Dr. Goodwin? I'm really at a loss here."

"Where are you?"

"I'm in the town parking lot, and it's like it's raining dead birds down here. They're falling everywhere. Crows. Blue jays. Seagulls. Sparrows. Doves. Can you come and have a look? It's pretty disgusting and I have no idea what to do."

"I'll be there in a few minutes. Can you do me one favour?"

"Sure. Anything."

"Take a look around the area where the dead birds are being found and tell me if you see any crows lurking around that aren't dead."

"Just give me a minute, please."

As he waits to hear from the officer, Alex whispers to his uncle, "Remember what we were just saying about weirdness and how it always happens around here?"

Charlie grimaces.

"You still there Dr. Goodwin?" Constable Shaw asks.

"I'm still here."

"As a matter of fact, there are a few crows and it's like they are watching us. Freaks me out, if I'm being honest."

"Did you count them, Constable?"

"There are eleven and they seem to be really interested in what we're doing."

Eleven crows for good health, Alex thinks. "Okay, Constable. I will be there shortly."

As Alex ends the call Charlie says, "Is it crows? Do you need me to come with you?"

"I'm not sure what it is." Alex stands. "And yes, for sure you can come with me if you'd like. I might need your help."

"Okay, I could use a break from these files." Charlie heads to the door with his nephew. "And just for the record, Alex, you don't need to ask my permission to answer your phone or leave the office. You are your own person, so you can make your own decisions."

"That's true," Alex says. "But sometimes it's like other forces are compelling me and I have very little control over my life."

Acknowledgements

I want to start by sending a huge shout-out to my loyal and enthusiastic fans. This series would not be possible without you, so thank you for being supportive throughout this extraordinary journey.

As I have said many times, creating a book is a major undertaking, and while the writing often takes years and is usually done in isolation, numerous people play key roles in completing the process. It's appropriate, then, to acknowledge a few of those people who helped along the way.

I must extend my deepest and undying gratitude to my supportive and enthusiastic publisher, Brenda J. Thompson, and my extraordinarily-talented editor, Andrew Wetmore, for their continued belief in me. They are the driving force behind Moose House Publications, and who knows where these books would be without their support. Thank you for your guidance throughout the process.

I also wish to extend my gratitude to graphic artist Rebekah Wetmore for the amazing cover design. Capturing the essence of an entire book in one image is no easy assignment, but she delivered a cover so compelling that it is simply stunning. Thank you, Rebekah. You do amazing work.

Another person I must acknowledge is my very talented photographer friend, Amy Grant. Thank you, Amy, for going above and beyond to make me look good.

A special thank you to my friend and fellow dreamer, Marci Lin Melvin, for her continued support and encouragement throughout the years. Her never-give-up-attitude, positive reinforcement and insightful feedback have helped to carry me through this journey.

A heart-felt thank-you goes to the booksellers and bookstore owners for their unwavering support over the years. Those of us who dare to think we can make it as writers would flounder without the support of such outlets. There are too many to name individually, but I hope you know how deeply I appreciate you.

I've saved my last and most heart-felt thank-you for my most important supporters, my family, especially my wife, Nancy. She has been my rock through the many years I've been chasing this dream of becoming a published author. She is always the first one to give an insightful word of advice and gentle criticism when it is needed, and to pick me up when I'm sad or frustrated. To say I could not have done it without her is an understatement. There are not enough words to say how much I love and appreciate her.

Stay tuned for *Eleven Crows for Good Health,* coming soon!

About the author

Vernon Oickle was born and raised in Liverpool, Nova Scotia, where he continues to reside with his wife, Nancy, and their family. Growing up in a small, rural town, he had always wanted to pursue a career as a newspaper reporter.

After completing high school in 1979, he attended Lethbridge Community College in Alberta. He graduated in 1982 with an honours diploma in Journalism and returned to Liverpool, where he worked at the local weekly newspaper, *The Advance*, for 13 years before becoming the editor of the *Bridgewater Bulletin*. His community newspaper career spanned 33 years.

Vernon is an award-winning journalist and editor, and is the author of 48 books, many of which collect and preserve the heritage and culture of Atlantic Canada. His best-selling books include *Ghost Stories of the Maritimes, Ghost Stories of Nova Scotia, The Nova Scotia Outstanding Outhouse Reader, Strange Nova Scotia, The Bluenosers' Book of Slang, Red Sky at*

Night, Forerunners: Harbingers of Death in Nova Scotia, *Grandma's Home Remedies* and *The View from Here: South Shore essays*.

He also writes fiction in the popular "Crow" series, based on the old Maritime poem 'One Crow Sorrow.' In 2024, the seventh book in the series, *Seven Crows for a Secret Yet to be Told*, won an International Impact Book Award, taking first place in the Historical Mystery/Thriller category.

In addition to his long list of newspaper awards, in 2012 Vernon received the Queen Elizabeth II Diamond Jubilee Medal, recognizing his contributions to his community, province and country; and in 2015 he received a Distinguished Alumni Award (Community Leader) from Lethbridge College. He was inducted into the Atlantic Journalism Awards Hall of Fame in the spring of 2020.

As a testimony to his outstanding career, in 2014 the South Queens Middle School in Liverpool announced the creation of the Vernon Oickle Writer's Award, to be given annually to a student who excels in the art of writing, either fiction or nonfiction.